D0670953

TWO SOULS ENTWINED

"Ye're bleeding." Her soft breath smelled like peppermint candy, and Nicholas knew the strongest urge to take a taste. Gently, she brushed the hair off his face. "In my country, they say when a person saves yer life, ye are part of that person forever. Two souls entwined."

Two souls entwined. Nicholas liked the thought. "Do you know what they say here in mother England?"

Innocent curiosity lurked in those uncanny eyes. "What do they say?"

"They say when a person saves your life, you owe that person a token of gratitude—whatever he or she desires."

She studied him for a moment, her gaze drifting over his hair, his jaw, his throat, and then directly into his eyes. "And what is it ye desire?" she murmured.

A long, curly lock of her hair dangled close to him. His fingers itched to feel it, to know if it was as smooth and soft as he imagined.

Nicholas grasped the silken length and tugged her gently forward. "A kiss is what I desire."

He had expected outrage, perhaps an outright denial followed by a stinging slap that would knock his jaw out of alignment. Yet intrigue lit her eyes as her gaze moved to his mouth.

"Then 'tis a kiss ye shall have."

Other Kensington Books by
MELANIE GEORGE

LIKE NO OTHER

DEVIL MAY CARE

And look for the next
book in the Sinclair series

THE DEVIL'S DUE

Coming in November 2001

HANDSOME DEVIL

Melanie George

ZEBRA BOOKS
KENSINGTON PUBLISHING CORP.

http://www.zebrabooks.com

ZEBRA BOOKS are published by

Kensington Publishing Corp.
850 Third Avenue
New York, NY 10022

Copyright © 2001 by Melanie George

All rights reserved. No part of this book may be reproduced in any form or by any means without the prior written consent of the Publisher, excepting brief quotes used in reviews.

All Kensington titles, imprints and distributed lines are available at special quantity discounts for bulk purchases for sales promotion, premiums, fund-raising, educational or institutional use.

Special book excerpts or customized printings can also be created to fit specific needs. For details, write or phone the office of the Kensington Special Sales Manager: Kensington Publishing Corp., 850 Third Avenue, New York, NY 10022. Attn. Special Sales Department. Phone: 1-800-221-2647.

If you purchased this book without a cover you should be aware that this book is stolen property. It was reported as "unsold and destroyed" to the Publisher and neither the Author nor the Publisher has received any payment for this "stripped book."

Zebra and the Z logo Reg. U.S. Pat. & TM Off.

First Printing: July, 2001
10 9 8 7 6 5 4 3 2 1

Printed in the United States of America

*To my son Andrew ... you're the best.
Don't ever change.*

I'd like to thank three lovely women who patiently listened to me talk shop to the exclusion of all else. My mother, Barbara, my good friend and fellow dog lover, Cara, and my sister-in-law, Dorothy. You all should be canonized for your unparalleled endurance.

Chapter One

Shantytown
Boston, Massachusetts
1880

"Jesus, Mary, and holy Saint Joseph. Naked as the day she was bor-rn! Oh, me head. 'Tis reelin'. Catch me, hoosband. I fear I'm about to swoon."

"Ther-re, ther-re, M'ther," Joseph Delaney soothed in his heavy Irish brogue, wrapping a chunky arm about his wife's sagging shoulders. " 'Tis surely not as bad as ye may be thinkin'." As one, they turned their hopeful gazes to their daughter, expectancy crackling in the thick, oppressively hot afternoon air. "Is it, macushla?"

Sheridan Delaney, immigrant from County Kerry, Ireland, feckless and fickle some would say, but never boring, gave her parents a weak smile. " 'Tis not as bad, Da. I had on me knickers."

Sheridan's mother swayed dramatically. "Faith, and may the Lord see fit to take me in his cradlin' arms as I'm surely about to die."

"There'll be no dyin' around here, Mary Margaret," Aunt Aggie countered, levering her hefty bosom on top of the table, giving it a perch on which to rest. She then proceeded to extract a dirty handkerchief from between her cleavage and dry her moist brow. " 'Tis my time for the dyin', and I'll thank ye to remember that." Turning to her nephew, she said in what Sheridan termed her gasping-for-her-last-breath voice, "Be a good lad and fetch Father Donovan for me. I feel a weak spell comin' on. Me heart is thumpin' like a drum roll musterin' the Queen's dragoons."

Whenever *Her Royal Hyney* was mentioned, Aunt Aggie felt inclined to add, "May the black plague descend upon her withered brow."

Her aunt fanned herself with the handkerchief while her other meaty hand clamped over the pocket of her apron where the little silver flask containing her *medicine* was concealed. " 'Tis the lifeblood of Ireland," she would say reverently before taking a swig that would knock most men on their backside.

Sheridan's father guided his wife to a rickety chair at a small table. "Now, M'ther, don't spell yerself over the lass. 'Tis not as if such behavior is new to her."

The reminder of a lifetime of antics made her mother collapse against the chair. The wood groaned under the pressure of her weight, which was by no means great. The chair had seen better days, as had the rest of their meager possessions.

Sheridan, her parents, her brother, Shane, her sisters, Shannon, Shawna, and little Sara, along with Aunt Aggie and Uncle Finny shared two rooms in an overcrowded boardinghouse, which Sheridan doubted had *ever* seen better days. The walls were thin enough to hear the Danihys bickering next door.

Mrs. Danihy cursed her husband for imbibing too much at the groggery. Mr. Danihy retorted that she was a two-headed harpy and both mouths contained a forked tongue. The inevitable slamming of the door followed, jangling the dull tin plates and bent forks on the scarred, rough-hewn table next to Sheridan's mother.

Out in the street, bawdy music blared from the Wubble Dhiskey saloon, followed by high-pitched drunken laughter. Sheridan had become used to the constant din. At least the noise muted the sounds of the rodents scurrying beneath the floorboards.

"Well, lass?" her father prompted. "What could have possessed ye to do such a thing?"

Sheridan shrugged her shoulders, the material of her blouse clinging to her damp flesh. "I just wanted to cool off. I didn't think anyone was about."

Sheridan knew exactly what her mother would say to her explanation. Mentally, she recited every word.

"May the savin' saints preserve me. I don't know what to do with the child."

Sheridan sighed inwardly. Why did trouble seem to follow her? Wherever she was, catastrophe trailed not far behind.

She tried to behave, but it just wasn't in her to be prim and proper like her sisters. Her family might be *those damned Irish,* as people sneeringly referred to them, but they'd carried tradition with them across the ocean to their new home.

Meaning a devout Catholic girl was to be covered up at all times and never stripped down to her altogethers to cool off in an inviting inlet of the Boston Harbor.

Only her father understood her. He claimed her spirit was possessed of an impish pixie who couldn't keep out of mischief. "What's in the marrow is hard to take out of the bones," he would say.

Sheridan wondered if the same justification would spring from her father's lips if he knew she'd sneaked into the tattoo parlor near the Italian side of town two weeks past and had Big John McGurk give her a wee wicked tattoo in a place only God and her husband—should she ever have one—see.

Did she want to find out?

Perhaps it was best not to rock the boat further.

Her father plunked down in a chair next to his wife and dug his fingers into his thick mane of gray hair—prematurely gray, Sheridan had oft been told.

A small hand gripped Sheridan's fingers, offering a reassuring squeeze. She looked down to find her youngest sister, Sara, staring up at her, a gap-toothed smile on her freckled face, her emerald eyes alight with the winsome charm of the fairies.

As always, Sara lent support to her big sister in her time of woe—which seemed to be every other day.

"What ar-re we goin' to do about the lass, hoosband?" her mother lamented again.

"Ye should give her a whippin', Da," Shannon piped in, casting a glare in Sheridan's direction.

At twenty-three, Shannon was the eldest, and still unmarried, placing the blame squarely on Sheridan's shoulders for that. Shannon wanted a husband and claimed no man would look at her because they were afraid she would be as untamable as Sheridan.

When Sheridan glanced at her other sister, Shawna, she found no quarter there. Shawna, too, wanted a husband, asserting that at twenty-one she was very nearly decrepit.

Her sisters bemoaned their fate at every opportunity,

wearing their father down to a wisp-thin frazzle. It didn't make the situation any better that their irrepressible brother taunted them mercilessly about their unmarried state.

Sheridan's gaze returned to her father, who scratched his stubbled jaw in bewilderment, wishing, she suspected, he could take a slug from the battered flask burning a hole inside his coat pocket. Yet his flask wasn't filled with the lifeblood of Ireland as was Aunt Aggie's, but with straight, undiluted poteen.

Irish Whiskey.

Sheridan had taken a sip once. Her eyes had bulged and she had gagged as if the fires of hell scorched a path down her throat. Never again.

Staring around at the numerous eyes focused expectantly on her face, Sheridan prayed for either the floor to open up and suck her in or for the Archangel Gabriel to ride down from heaven on a bolt of white lightning, a flourish of angels trumpeting his arrival, and sweep her away.

Closing her eyes, she pleaded her case with the Almighty. Opening one eye and seeing the scowling faces of her family still centered squarely on her, Sheridan figured the Lord must have turned a deaf ear. Well, what did she expect?

Shawna said, "Aye, Da. Maybe if ye give her a beatin' she'll learn a lesson. She'll surely ruin us all if she doesn't mend her wild ways."

How Sheridan ached to make a stinging retort. She refrained only because she was in enough trouble already. The taunting gleam in her sister's eyes told her Shawna would take full advantage of that fact.

Her father turned his gaze to Shawna. "And when, may I ask ye, have I ever beatin' any of ye? Well, except for yer brother, that is. But he needs a wee cuff in the head every now and again 'cause he's a lad. 'Tis necessary to keep him from becomin' a spring flower, if ye ken my meanin'. But females, ye see, must be treated like tender buds if they ar-re to grow into the roses they're meant to be."

Shannon sniggered. "Danny's no rose, Da. She's the thorns."

Sheridan clenched her hands into fists. "Aye, and me sting is fierce, make no mistake about it."

"I'll have no such talk from ye girls. Ye hear?" He waited for each of them to nod. "Now, I'm sure the good Lord will bless us with a solution to this problem. If we have faith."

Her father had been saying the same thing for as long as Sheridan could remember and the Lord had yet to see fit to bring deliverance.

Deliverance . . .

She smiled as she lit upon an idea

"There's always Jules, Da."

Jules Sinclair had befriended Sheridan when her family was struggling in the first few months after their escape from British tyranny only to find America just as inhospitable. Signs everywhere read, *No Irish Need Apply*.

Boston swarmed with immigrants just like Sheridan and her family. Work was scarce. They would have starved in their new home as surely as they would have starved in their homeland had it not been for Jules.

She had helped Sheridan's mother and sisters find work in a friend's house as scullery maids, and she had secured Sheridan a position in the kitchen at the Bainbridge Academy for Females, which Jules had attended for two glorious, fun-filled years.

What times they had together, what antics they had pulled. To this day, the headmistress jumped if she heard a frog croak, reminding her of the hundred slimy creatures Sheridan and Jules had let loose in the dining hall.

Sheridan missed her friend now that she was gone. Jules's time at Bainbridge had come to an end and she had returned home to England.

For Sheridan's family, the fact that Jules was English was a permanent strike against her. Worse, Jules was a member of the titled elite, just like the landlords who had owned so much property in Ireland and had worked their tenants to bone—and to bitterness.

The landlords were the reason Sheridan's family had fled Ireland. Her father, brother, and uncle were considered outlaws, having tried to raise a protest against cruel treatment and unfair practices, looking for satisfaction against British hierarchy as thousands had before them. And like those thousands, they had failed. If they had remained in Ireland, they would have been hanged.

"Begorra!" Her mother straightened in her chair. "Ther-re the child goes again, wantin' to sail off to the country of our enemy."

Sheridan frowned. "But Jules is not our enemy, Mum. And I'm not a child. I'm nearly eighteen."

"Nearly eighteen she is, hoosband. Do ye hear that now? The lass is too big for her britches."

"Well, she *is* growin' up, wife."

Her fists on her hips, Mary Margaret's expression said someone would be sleeping on the cold floor if he disagreed with her. "Oh, is she now? And ar-re ye sayin', Joseph Fitzpatrick Erasmus"—muffled snickers flew about the room—"Delaney that I'm a meddlin' mother who doesn't know what's best for her own flesh and blood, the product of her loins, pushed from me tortured womb on a rain-drenched night with nary a midwife in sight?" She liked to forget it was the middle of the afternoon with at least ten female relatives in attendance. "Is that what ye are implyin', *hoosband?*"

Her father swallowed, knowing when his wife called him by his full name, it didn't bode well. "Now, now, my sweet dumplin'. Yer gettin' yerself into a fine fettle over nothin'."

Slowly, her mother rose from her chair, her brows yanked so close together it looked as if she only had one. "Nothin'? Oh, I see." She folded her arms across her chest. "I'm goin' to my unhappy place."

Oh, now her father was really in trouble. Mary Margaret Delaney's unhappy place was so frightening angels feared to tread its dire grounds, let alone one paunchy husband.

"Mum," Sheridan interjected. Her father slumped in relief at having his wife's eyes off him. "Why are ye so opposed to my seein' Jules? Ye yerself know the kind of person she is. Good-hearted and the like."

Her mother harumphed. "For a sassenach," she begrudgingly admitted.

Sheridan notched her chin up. "She's my friend. And she's been very good to us."

"That she has," her father ventured, earning him a quick glare from his wife.

Her mother began tidying the small room, as she often did when she didn't want anyone to read the expression on her face. "I won't deny the English girl has been kind to us, but that doesn't mean I want ye consortin' with a whole passel of the heathens."

Shannon chimed in, "Oh, but, Mum, 'tis just what the English deserve. If ye send Danny into their midst, they'll be sorry they ever set foot on Irish soil."

Shawna's amber eyes lit up at the prospect. "Just imagine the havoc!"

"And just imagine the sanity for the rest of us, God

bless,'' her brother, Shane, added with a devilish smile, winking at Sheridan.

Unlike her older sisters, Sheridan knew her brother was, in his own way, trying to help. He knew she wanted to go to England and see Jules, knew the angry tears she had shed when her parents flatly refused.

Her father had lost five brothers to British tyranny and three to the famine. One had been killed in the freedom fight in Ballengarry, and one enlisted into the sixty-ninth Irish Brigade as soon as he stepped off the boat, forced to defend a country that didn't care about his plight.

Only Uncle Finny remained, and he had never been quite right after a mule kicked him in the head. However, her uncle chose that moment to add his thoughts—which, of course, had nothing to do with the current conversation.

''Sorra, 'twas a bright and cloudless morn when the Battle of the Boyne took place,'' he began to orate, a patch over one eye, its position changing on a daily basis. ''Me and my Jacobites took up position on the south bank of the river. Bloody William's troops wer-re on the nor-rth bank. Come on, gentlemen, sez I, ther-re ar-re yer persecutors! Och!'' He clutched his foot. ''I took a ball to me jackboot.'' He waved a fist in the air. ''Ye scurvy knick-knockers!''

Sheridan and her family had ceased reminding their beloved, slightly askew relative that he would be nearly two hundred years old if he'd served in the Battle of the Boyne. It was too wearisome a chore to keep up with all the wars he claimed to have served in—occasionally fighting for the other side. Once, he'd sworn he was the Pope and stood in the river Shannon baptizing people.

The only trait her uncle showed on a regular basis was his tendency to pinch many an unsuspecting female bottom, making Sheridan wonder if he was more sane than insane.

When her uncle retook his seat and promptly dozed off, a collective sigh of relief rose into the air.

Her father cleared his throat and shifted his gaze from his last remaining brother to Sheridan. "Now, where we? Oh, aye! Yer mother was havin' a fit of the vapors, and Aggie was dyin'—again. Yer sisters were callin' for a beheadin' and yer poor father's noggin' was throbbin' as if struck clean over me tender skull with a mallet." Then he pointed a crooked finger at Sheridan. "And ye, macushla, were paradin' about in yer thinly draped nakedness."

I'm sorry was surely beginning to wear thin, so Sheridan gave her father a weak smile instead.

He stood up and paced the length of the room, which was basically four steps and an about-face. He stopped and peered at her. "England, eh?"

Sheridan raised her hopeful gaze to her father's. "Aye, Da."

Her mother stopped her fussing and stared down her nose at her husband, a rather amazing feat as he stood a good foot taller than she. "Get such foolish notions out of yer head, hoosband."

"Now, Mother."

"Don't ye 'now, Mother' me. I'll not have me wee lass corrupted by those bullies!"

"But I'll be with Jules, Mum," Sheridan pointed out, her mind racing with the possibility of seeing her friend again.

"Just think about it, Mum." Shannon took her mother's hands in hers. "Maybe I can find m'self a man of me own without Danny around to be embarrassin' me."

Shawna's face lit up. "Aye, and me, too, Mum."

"Please let her go," Shannon begged.

Shawna came over and laid her head on their mother's shoulder, gazing up at her with pleading eyes. "Aye, Mum, let her go. Micky O'Flannagan smiled at me the other day. He's ever so handsome, he is. And he's got himself a good job at the chicken factory. I heard he may be moved up from pluckin' the wee beasties to workin' the vat. Oh, I like him altogether. Mayhap he'll look me way if he doesn't have to be reminded Danny is me sister.''

Her mother snorted. ''Don't know when was the last time I saw that boy in church.''

''Church?'' Uncle Finny's head popped up from where it lay against his chest. ''Blessed be the holy tabernacle.'' He gesticulated with a crooked index finger. ''When I was in me Popeship, I did forgive many a sinner, layin' the healin' power of me hands upon their sor-ry shoulders. Yer Popeship, sez they, may the light of yer mercy shine in the kingdom of heaven always. Ah, 'twas luvely, it was.'' Then he promptly dropped his head back to its original position.

The wheedling resumed.

''Oh, Mum, won't ye please reconsider lettin' Danny go?'' As if on cue, a single tear rolled down Shannon's cheek. ''Please? 'Twould mean ever so much to Shawna and me.''

''But what about poor Johnny Sullivan?'' her brother chimed in mischievously. ''He's fairly dyin' with love for Danny girl, the stupid mountainous lout.''

''I wouldn't be callin' him such things to his face, boyo,'' Aunt Aggie put in, now lying prostrate on the single bed in the corner of the room. ''He's liable to send ye to yer Maker.''

''Och now, Auntie, I'm the brother of the woman he loves. Surely he'll treat me as if I were a rare and fragile piece of porcelain so as not to rile Danny.''

Sheridan glared at her brother, who only smiled wider, wagging his brows at her in pure devilry.

John Sullivan, known about town as the Boston Strong

Boy, was well loved, the pride of Ireland for being unbeaten in bare-knuckled brawling. He'd knocked out every one of his opponents so far. Many claimed he would someday be a world champion.

Sheridan couldn't say there wasn't something enthralling about a battle of pure brawn, a certain appeal to seeing two well-muscled males locked in the heat of combat. But never would she marry a man whose wits were addled, who couldn't match her love of life and her thirst for knowledge.

She wanted a man with dreams, a man who could make her laugh . . . and wouldn't mind her occasional fierce temper or her penchant for trouble. Somewhere out there was the man for her.

She hoped.

"I've a feelin' Johnny boy knows he's met his match in our Danny," Shane went on. "Pair the two up, and I bet ye Danny will knock him solid."

Sheridan narrowed her gaze on her brother. "I'll knock *ye* solid, ye overbearin' duffer! I hope Johnny boxes yer ears—and I'll be glad for it!"

Shane chuckled. "Ah, there's that fire he adores. I tried to tell the lad 'twasn't fire but pure meanness in yer blood, sister. Poor bugger wouldn't listen to me."

Sheridan's famed temper began rising to the fore. Obviously her father saw it, stepping deftly between her and her brother. "We'll leave the brawlin' to Johnny, if ye please."

Shawna and Shannon promptly resumed their pleading, telling their mother the whole future of the Delaneys hung by a tenuous thread. How were they to give their parents wee grandbabies to love and adore without husbands? If they sent Sheridan to England, it might change the course of all their futures—for the better, of course.

"I don't want Danny to go!" Little Sara clutched Sheridan tightly about the waist and glared at her older sisters. "Ye two are just terrible to want to break up our family."

Sheridan knelt in front of Sara and smiled. "Ye are a li'l corker, Sara Delaney. Ye know no matter where I go, ye'll always be my family. And the best little sister an older sister could ever want."

Sara threw her arms around Sheridan's neck.

Silence reigned—for three seconds. Then her mother put her foot down. "I've had meself enough of this talk. No one will be goin' to England, and that's final."

Her father cleared his throat and stood up, gazing at his wife in the most steely-eyed way Sheridan had ever seen. "Now, woman, I am the man of this family and I'll be makin' the decisions around her-re."

Her mother cocked an eyebrow. "Oh, ye will, will ye?"

He gave a brusque nod. "Aye, that I will."

Slowly, Sheridan rose from the floor, a spark of hope warming her heart. Yet when she caught her mother's expression, all hope withered and died.

Here it comes, she thought with a mental sigh.

"For nearly eight hoondred years those blighted English have been steppin' on our necks. But we Delaneys survived." Her mother tilted up her chin, fierce pride gleaming in her eyes. "We survived the bitter nights when ther-re was nary enough peat to warm us and scarce enough food to feed a swine. And we survived the exile from our home to live in this benighted promised land."

Sheridan thought her mother's recital was over.

She should have known better.

"And now me own daughter wants to sail into the viper's bosom. I won't have it, do ye hear, hoosband?"

Sheridan expected her father to back down. Surprisingly, he didn't. "Ye've got to let the lass spread her wings, Mother. Jules Sinclair is a sweet girl. And I believe her when she says she'll see no harm comes to our daughter.'' He ambled toward his wife and rested his hands gently upon her shoulders. "And we can send Aggie and Finny as chaperones.''

Sheridan groaned inwardly at the thought of her aunt and uncle coming along. She loved them dearly, but she would end up spending her time keeping them out of trouble instead of the reverse.

"But what about Father Donovan?'' Sheridan asked hopefully. "Aunt Aggie doesn't like bein' far away from him.''

"Aye, the lass has got a point ther-re,'' her aunt stated, her arms folded across the top of her chest as if practicing her death repose. "I cannot be goin' anywhere without the good father. Who would be seein' to me last rites if me time comes?''

Her father frowned, and Sheridan knew exactly what he was thinking. Aunt Aggie was of robust health and would more likely be struck dead by a runaway train than die of an ailment. But, as with Uncle Finny, it was useless to argue.

"Ther-re must be a priest aboard the ship and plenty in England,'' her father rallied.

Her aunt snorted. "Protestants, I wager.'' She shivered in distaste.

"I'm sure Father Donovan can make arrangements for ye, Aggie.''

Desperate, Sheridan rushed out, "I think 'tis best if I go alone, Da. Clearly 'twould be a hardship for Aunt Aggie, and certainly ye need Uncle Finny around here for . . . well . . .''

She bit her lip, knowing her uncle didn't do anything beside drink, recite outlandish stories, and grope women who wouldn't smack him silly because he was touched in the head.

"Ye won't be goin' anywhere alone," her mother said with finality, her expression stern. "So get that idea out of yer head. And I haven't agreed to let ye go now, have I?"

Her father turned his wife to face him. "Let the girl get it out of her system. Mayhap she'll return with less of her impish mischief."

Sheridan doubted anyone would hold their breath for that miracle.

"Ye said yerself we Delaneys are survivors. We shall survive this, I wager."

It seemed as if the whole world went silent waiting for her mother's reply.

She sighed heartily and muttered begrudgingly, "Well . . . all right." Then she quickly added, "But yer aunt and uncle will go, and there'll be no buts about it."

"I'll bring me bayonet!" Uncle Finny piped in. "Skewer the blighters where they stand!"

Sheridan beamed, too happy to be going to protest further. She ran to her mother and hugged her tight. "Oh, thank ye, Mum!"

In her usual brusque yet loving way, her mother hugged her back. "Ye behave yerself, macushla. Ye'll not be a happy lass if ye make yer old mother fetch ye home."

"I'll be good. I promise."

"Look out, England," her brother said, giving her a smile and a wink. "Here comes the wild Irish rose—thorns and all."

Chapter Two

London, England

"*Her Grace, the Duchess of Davenport, is here to see you, sir!*"

The butler's booming announcement snapped Nicholas's head up from its resting place on top of his desk. He shook his head to clear the ringing in his ears and uncrossed his eyes.

Well, that's what he got for hiring a nearly deaf butler who didn't realize his meager windpipes let loose a cannon blast whenever he spoke. Nicholas needed to put chimes on the man's shoes to warn him in advance his butler was coming.

Nicholas's petite, dark-haired cousin whirled into the room, a vision in a pink silk day dress whose décolletage belied the innocence of the maidenly color. She stopped at the threshold, a bemused smile on her lovely face.

Nicholas pushed away from his desk and moved to greet her, wrapping her in a warm bear hug. "Welcome home, minx. I missed you."

She gave a ladylike snort of disbelief. "You probably didn't even notice I was gone."

Pulling back, he gazed at her upturned face, her eyes framed by a thick fringe of black lashes—a Sinclair trait. "Untrue. When you left, it was as if I'd been set adrift upon an endless ocean. Pitched headlong into bottomless Gehenna. I sobbed brokenly into my snifter of Napoleon brandy at every card game I attended."

Green eyes so like his own lit with amusement. "I'm sure you managed to find someone to ease your suffering." The girl knew him too well.

"Whatever you've heard is a twisted skein of lies."

"Oh?" Jules cocked a brow. "I heard you've been a veritable saint these months."

"You did? I mean, of course you did. That might explain the urge I have to walk on water."

She shook her head. "You haven't changed a bit."

"You wound me, puss." Nicholas put a hand to his heart. "I went to church every day and prayed for the strength to carry on."

She laughed. "Oh, please! People made wagers to see if you, Damien, and Gray would even come to the church on my wedding day. They were sure you'd disintegrate into a pile of ashes on the threshold."

Jules gave him an endearing smile. "But there you were, wearing those cocky grins, staring down the guests who gaped in shock, generally intimidating people with your larger-than-life presence—and loving it, I might add." Her expression told him she remembered every nuance of that day quite vividly and would for a long time to come.

"How devilishly handsome all of you looked in your dove gray suits, putting the other men to shame—except my William, of course," she hastily added.

Nicholas chuckled. "Of course."

"Yet, surprisingly, you, Gray, and Damien remained on your best behavior."

He chucked her under the chin. "Only for you would we consider restraining ourselves."

She rose on tiptoe and gave him a sisterly kiss on the cheek, whispering, "Thank you for that."

He whispered back, "You're welcome for that."

Seeing the happiness in his cousin's eyes made an odd yearning rear its ugly head inside Nicholas. Jules had found herself a new champion. He and his brothers used to hold that function exclusively.

They'd never been blessed with a sister, so Jules had assumed that role. They, in turn, took their responsibilities for her welfare very seriously.

Jules liked to tell them they were overprotective just because they had pummeled a few of her more ardent suitors senseless and had threatened their own best friend, now her husband, with a painful neutering should he attempt anything untoward before the wedding day.

She didn't seem to understand that men were carnal in nature and needed to have the ground rules set down— and reinforced on occasion.

Now if that should mean said *reinforcement* was a gut punch and a right hook, well, that was just the way of it.

Although Nicholas would never admit it out loud, he missed being the one Jules turned to in times of need. She alleged he was the most sensitive of the unruly Sinclair clan.

Of course, Nicholas scoffed at the accusation. He was a Sinclair, after all, and that did not equate with sensitivity.

"When did you get back?" he asked.

"William and I returned to Sussex a week ago. I arrived in town last night."

"It's good to have you home. Six months is a long time."

She drew off her gloves. "You know William doesn't do anything in half measure. He promised me the grandest honeymoon a husband could give his wife. My feet can attest to the fact that we toured Italy, France, Scotland, and a few places that have yet to be charted."

Nicholas chuckled, thinking of his friend, William Thornton, eighth duke of Davenport. Nicholas, Damien, Gray, and William had grown up together and gotten into their fair share of mischief.

Jules had adored William from afar for as long as Nicholas could remember. William, however, always treated her like a sister—until the day she returned from the Bainbridge Academy in America, no longer a child but a woman full grown, and a beautiful, alluring woman, at that.

Then the roles had been reversed. William trailed after Jules like a besotted hound, while she led him on a merry chase. Damn if the girl wasn't a true Sinclair!

Jules turned to Emery, who still lurked in the doorway, and graced him with an enchanting smile. "I don't recall meeting you the last time I was here."

Nicholas introduced his butler. "This is Emery, puss. Emery, this is my cousin, Jules Sinclair."

Loudly, she cleared her throat. "Thornton."

Nicholas winked at her. "A mere slip of the tongue, I assure you."

Jules held out her hand to his butler, uncaring that she was a duchess and Emery a servant. She'd always been kindhearted and unconcerned about that invisible line called class distinction. In Jules's eyes, everyone was equal. If only more women could be like his cousin, Nicholas mused.

To Emery, Jules said jokingly, "How unfortunate that you have to work for this irritating lout."

Emery blinked at her like a hoot owl through his thick-lensed spectacles. "Gout? No, your Grace, I don't have gout. But thank you for being concerned."

Confused, Jules gazed at Nicholas.

"Emery doesn't hear very well, I'm afraid," he replied to her unspoken question.

The man was eighty if he was a day. Poor boy had no family. Nicholas had taken him in, but never let his butler think he was there on charity. Emery had a great deal of pride.

Besides, he'd come with a sterling reference from the Tuileries—even if the piece of paper had been yellowed with age since it was nearly thirty years old.

But Nicholas wouldn't complain. Most top-notch butlers didn't want to work for a Sinclair, let alone an untitled one. It was professional suicide.

Nicholas pointed to the item in his butler's hand. "Use your horn." The instrument, shaped like a moose's antler, amplified sound. Nicholas had bought the contraption in an effort to keep his sanity. More often than not, Emery left it somewhere and promptly forgot its location.

More than one of his butler's faculties had deteriorated with age. Nicholas often found himself answering his own door when Emery had fallen asleep in a chair in the hallway.

One time the old boy even took a nap in Nicholas's bed. But did Nicholas rouse Emery from his sweet dreams and send him scuffling back to his own room? No. Instead Nicholas camped out on a chair in case his butler decided to take up sleepwalking and get himself killed. Nicholas woke in the morning with a crick in his neck that lasted for three days.

Emery put the horn to his ear and Jules repeated her comment with a great deal of amusement.

"No, Your Grace. The master is not a lout. He treats me very well indeed."

Nicholas nudged his cousin with an elbow. "See? I'm the very milk of human kindness," he told her, straight-faced, to which she promptly rolled her eyes.

"Will there be anything else, sir?" Emery inquired, attempting to straighten his permanently stooped shoulders. Nicholas swore he heard the man's bones creaking.

"No, thank you, Emery. That will be all."

"Yes, sir." He bowed so low Nicholas could see the bald spot on top of his head. Nicholas was grateful the man had ceased wearing the ridiculous periwig that made him look as if he had stepped out of another century. Gray kept referring to him as Father Time.

Jules chuckled as her gaze moved from Emery's departing figure to Nicholas. "He seems very nice."

"When he is awake, he's quite nice."

She studied him for a long moment as if perhaps a third eyeball had appeared in the middle of his forehead. "I have to admit I'm surprised, though."

"Surprised? At what? That I've grown even more hand-some since you left?"

"That was never in question. You were always too attractive for your own good. I pity the poor women who fall for the Sinclair brothers."

"Well, then, you can go see Damien and ask his wife if she needs some pitying. A *do not disturb* sign would be more apropos. I ate dinner with them one night and they spent the whole time gazing at each other like love-sick geese, yearning oozing from every pore. Frankly, it's sickening. My palms actually get clammy whenever I'm around them.''

Jules gazed at him, unblinking, her look identical to those expressions of stunned shock Nicholas had seen when Damien had returned with a wife in tow—and not just any wife, but a girl who had once intended to become a nun.

The devil had been reformed. And from what Nicholas had witnessed thus far, his brother basked in paradise. All he needed were pretty white wings and a harp to complete the idyllic picture.

Nicholas still reeled. His mentor had gotten leg-shackled—a master of debauchery who had oft been heard to say, ''A man without a wife is like a neck without a pain.''

Nicholas grew up learning there were three essentials to survival and they were not reading, writing, and arithmetic, but rather that he should never try to comprehend the labor of bees, the ebb and flow of the tide, or the mind of a woman. The advice had served him well over the years.

''I can't believe it,'' Jules uttered when she found her voice. ''Damien . . . married.''

''I know, my girl. Damien and married are two words that just don't seem synonymous, do they? It's like heaven and hell. Black and white. Oil and water. Peas and carrots.'' He frowned. ''On second thought, peas and carrots do have a certain harmony, so let's exclude them.''

Jules wasn't listening. Her face still wore a glazed expression, as if Nicholas had just informed her that Jesus was coming for dinner.

Then she blinked and cohesive thought returned. "When? Where? How?" A litany that had oft been repeated in the last month.

"In a convent. About a month ago. And God only knows. Amazing, isn't it? And here scientists claim there are only seven wonders of the world. Bloody skeptics."

She shook her head. "How things have changed in such a short time."

"That's not the only thing that has changed, I see." Smiling, Nicholas glanced down at his cousin's gently rounded stomach. "William has kept you busy."

With all the tenderness of a mother expecting her first child, Jules laid a hand on her swelling womb. Her face glowed with an inner light. "Very busy indeed," she murmured with secret pleasure.

Nicholas beamed. "Now I'll have another generation to teach all about being a Sinclair. The name comes with a certain amount of responsibility, as you well know."

She leveled him with a look that said hell hath no fury like a woman whose baby is tampered with by a roving bachelor. She appeared surprisingly ferocious for a mother-to-be, her rosy glow having nothing to do with impending childbirth but rather with the urge to clout him with the nearest object.

"William will have your heart on a silver platter if you dare corrupt this babe."

William wasn't the only one, it seemed.

"The old boy has become too severe in his dotage," Nicholas scoffed, waving a dismissive hand. "Frankly, I'm surprised he knew how to get you with child."

"Oh, he knew, all right." A slight smile curled a corner of her lip. "And I don't think he will appreciate your comments about his being old, especially since he is only five years your senior."

"Only five? I would have thought at least twenty."

Her hands on her hips, Jules glowered at Nicholas with eyes like thunderbolts prepared to cleave him in two where he stood. "I won't tell him you said that. He might feel it necessary to take issue with you, and I'd prefer not to have my child shrieking in fear when it sees its cockeyed relative."

Nicholas tipped back his head and laughed. "Puss, you've got it backward."

She quirked a brow. "Really? I seem to recall William had the upper hand the last time you two went head to head in another one of those barbaric male tests of strength."

Nicholas frowned. "I let the sod win," he grumbled, disgruntled at the remembrance.

"Male egos are such fragile things." She chuckled and strolled past him, leaving him to scowl at the wall. "So what have you been doing since I left? I hope you haven't gotten into too much trouble."

"Plenty." Turning, he wagged his eyebrows.

"You are hopeless." She tried to ease herself onto the settee, a difficult task with her expanding waistline.

Nicholas moved to help and then settled himself next to her. "Well, now that you are back, you can keep me in line. That is if your slave-driving husband will allow you out of his sight long enough to be my shadow. You don't know how many of the good Lord's commandments I inadvertently bend—or break, rather—without your guiding light to pull me from the black abyss."

Tenderly, Jules brushed a lock of hair off his forehead. "Someday, dear cousin Nicky, you shall get your come-uppance. And I hope I'm here to see it."

"That's not a very benevolent attitude, my girl."

"Pssh! You need a swift kick in the backside."

Nicholas chuckled. "I see marriage has not mellowed you. You still speak your mind at will."

She nodded briskly. "And I shall continue to do so, and you men had best get used to it."

Nicholas gave her a jaunty salute. "Yes, ma'am. Will that be all, ma'am? Should I spit shine your shoes? Polish your pretty buttons? Hold your reticule? Or just cower at your dainty feet?"

"You don't want to . . . *oh!*" Her eyes widened to saucers. One hand gripped the arm of the settee, the other she placed over her stomach.

Nicholas felt like a vise had clamped around his neck when he saw his cousin's pale visage. Quickly, he knelt in front of her. "What is it, Cooch? Are you hurt? Do you want to lie down? Do you need a doctor?"

She took his hand and placed it on top of her stomach. "The baby kicked."

Nicholas swallowed. "It can . . . do that?"

Jules rolled her eyes. "Men!"

Nicholas grinned sheepishly, feeling out of his element. Babies gave him the jitters, as did pregnant women. Something eminently fragile about both made him feel like a clumsy oaf, which was why it was rather strange that he was considering settling down and starting a family of his own—unless he still expected babies to be born the way Gray had claimed they did when Nicholas was a child.

Gray had been a worldly fourteen to Nicholas's ten when his brother had told him that, according to Damien— the oldest sibling, and therefore the wisest—that to get a woman pregnant he had to plant his seed in her.

Wide-eyed, Nicholas had stared down at the sunflower seeds in the palm of his hand, his favorite snack. Panic shot through his system as his mind raced to recall if he had given any seeds to the pretty little blond-haired daughter of one of their tenants.

For weeks afterward, he had dreaded the day that little

girl would tell him she was pregnant. The thought of becoming a husband made sweat trickle down his back— a reaction that still haunted him as an adult.

He had wondered what his parents would say when they found out, wondered if they'd make him leave home, wondered if he could take Martha, their cook, with him because she made pudding the way he liked it, with milk instead of water.

And then came the big wonder: Would his soon-to-be wife have the same bedtime as he? What if she got to stay up later? That possibility had certainly ruffled his ten-year-old feathers. Good thing she wasn't pregnant.

Not surprisingly, he had stopped eating sunflower seeds that day—and he hadn't had one since.

At first Nicholas had blamed his inexplicable desire to end his blissful life of rakehell and rabble-rouser on Damien and the fact his brother had broken a long-standing pact never to be caught in a matrimonial choke-hold. Nicholas had concluded that the urge to hang himself with the same noose had come from a childlike need to do whatever his older brother did, a sort of you-did-it-I'll-do-it thing.

But that wasn't it.

The desire to cleave himself unto a woman he called wife had been in him long before Damien got married. Nicholas had never let himself acknowledge it. But just because he had acknowledged it didn't mean he was ready to jump head over arse into the murky pool of domesticity. Frankly, the whole idea made him shake like a drunk on a three-day dry spell.

The only thing Nicholas knew conclusively was that when he married it would be to a woman of impeachable character; refined, malleable, pure.

Faithful.

Unlike his own mother. The thought of her caused his belly to cramp.

"Are you all right?" Jules asked, laying her hand on top of his.

Nicholas threw off his disturbing thoughts and smiled at his cousin. "I'm fine. Why?"

"You're clenching your teeth."

"I was thinking about the pain in my back."

"What's the matter with your back?"

"Nothing yet, but when I try to heave you off this settee it will be like Muhammad moving the mountain."

"You're a beast!" she huffed, her lip twitching, and then she laughed with him.

When he sobered, he asked in a more serious tone, "Does it hurt?"

She shook her head, her hand smoothing over her stomach. "No. It feels wonderful. Below my heart lies a beautiful little human that William and I created. It moves me in ways I cannot define."

Beneath Nicholas's palm, something stirred, and then he felt what he could only describe as a tiny kick. His heart lurched. "Sweet God," he whispered. Knowing he appeared like a wide-eyed schoolboy, he stared at his cousin with awe. "I'll be damned. It's moving!"

"I should hope so. The cheeky bugger has been quite active of late."

Jules's eyes glowed with love for her unborn child, causing that odd ache Nicholas had experienced on and off since he was a child to wrap around him like a gray, clinging tentacle.

Slowly, he withdrew his hand. "I'm sorry if I upset you."

"Upset me? Don't be a goose."

"Still . . ." Nicholas stood up abruptly, raking a hand through his hair. "Do you . . . need anything?"

Before she could reply, he caught the edge of the cocktail table; legs scraping across the floor as he dragged it over. He put her feet up on it.

"What are you doing?"

"Making you comfortable."

Her shoulders shook with silent laughter. "I'd prefer it if you just sat next to me. I have a favor to ask."

Nicholas vaulted over the table and sat down. "Ask away."

"Do you remember the missive I sent you about a month or so ago?"

Nicholas searched his mind and drew a blank. When it came to his beloved horses, he was known to retain even the most minute details. Everything else got lost in the shuffle.

"I treasure everything you send me," he replied in lieu of an answer.

She cocked an eyebrow, clearly skeptical. "You've forgotten, haven't you?"

He gave her a sheepish grin. "A temporary lapse, I assure you. Refresh my memory."

"Well, I mentioned that a friend of mine was coming to visit."

"For your sake, I hope this friend doesn't have a deep voice and hairy legs, especially if William still has that old blunderbuss hanging from a peg in his office."

"My William is ever the gentleman and not jealous one whit."

Nicholas snorted so loud he was surprised he didn't propel the wing chair across from him to the other side of the room. "Are we speaking of the same William? The one who held the stable master by his ankles over a snake pit because he smiled at you?"

"He did no such thing!" She sounded as authoritative as a little general. "There was no snake pit."

"Does your husband know how roundly you defend him?"

"I should hope so! Although . . ." Her smile slipped.

"Although?"

"He wasn't too happy that I came to town in my condition. I daresay we had a bit of a row before I left."

"Nevertheless, here you are. Something tells me you're still getting your way, terror."

She gave him a hint of a pout—enough to fell any man. "He told me if I was set on coming to town that he would come with me. But he had the estate business to catch up on and parliamentary issues demanding his attention, so I told him to stay. Would you believe the man growled at me? Growled! Goodness, I was only trying to be a considerate wife. Did the big oaf actually think I didn't want him to come?"

Nicholas could just picture it. William standing there, glaring from his six-foot-five height while his tiny wife shook her finger at him and stamped her elfin foot, determined to get her way. And of course, William had eventually caved in like a flan in a cupboard.

How Nicholas would have loved to be there to witness it! Well, at least he knew who would lay down the rules in his house when he finally clamped the ball and chain around his ankle. No bit of fluff was going to dictate to him, by God.

"Something tells me your husband will show up before we know it. Now, what about this friend of yours?"

Jules's spirits perked up at the reminder. "Her name is Sheridan Delaney. She's a friend from Boston."

"Ah, from the hallowed days of the Bainbridge Academy, an institution that was supposed to teach you how to be a proper lady. What happened with that, I wonder?"

Her look told him that pregnant women had less patience than their non-*enceinte* counterparts. "As I mentioned in my missive, Sheridan is coming to visit. She should be arriving any day. You'll love her."

"I will certainly try." He winked.

She swatted him. "Oh, stop it, will you?"

He laid his hand over his heart. "I promise to behave." He put his other hand behind his back and crossed his fingers. "Besides, if the girl is from Boston society, she's probably as stiff as Emery's limbs and has her nose so far up in the air icicles collect on it. We have plenty of that type right here, so I have no doubt I can contain myself."

Nicholas wondered at the expression on his cousin's face. If he didn't know better, he might think she was silently laughing.

"Well," she said in a somewhat strangled voice, "since that's the case, I guess you won't mind if we stay here."

"Stay here? You and she?"

"You won't even notice us—especially since you'll be containing yourself." There was that look again.

"You know I adore you, puss, but why would you want to stay here?" And how could he act the carefree bachelor with two women around? "What about your house?"

She grimaced. "Mother Thornton has commandeered it for the Season."

Nicholas needed no more answer than that. Mother Thornton hadn't been too pleased when her one and only son, whom she adored to the point of smothering, had married one of those wicked Sinclairs. Jules was a force in her own right, but her dour mother-in-law would certainly put a damper on her time with her friend.

"All right, puss. Bring your friend here. I'll try to

behave myself, but you know how trouble seems to follow me around.''

A smile that made a frisson of foreboding slither down his spine tilted up the corners of his cousin's lips. ''You're not the only one.''

Chapter Three

"You shouldn't be walkin' alone at this time of the night, sir . . . and in your condition."

Nicholas's response to his driver's comment was a symbolic gesture of disregard that he hadn't used since childhood, requiring the use of tongue and lips, which often sprinkled an unwitting person standing too close with moisture unrelated to rain.

His driver was that unwitting person.

"Are you tryin' to stay, er, say, that I'm intoxtipated, Nash?"

Odd, Nicholas thought. His jaw moved but his tongue lay like a dead piece of mackerel in his mouth, his words flowing as smoothly as molasses on an ice patch. Even to his own ears it sounded as if he gargled marbles.

"Intoxtipated, sir?"

"I mean inoculated." Something that could have been

a laugh but sounded more like a grunting snort came out of Nicholas's mouth. "Hmm. Incubated?" He stumbled from his coach, trying to get his sea legs beneath him even though he stood on solid ground. "Oh, hell. Looped, soused, three sheets to the wind."

"Yes, sir. That you are."

"I take umbrage, Nash. I'm merely . . . er . . ." He scratched his chin. "What was I saying?"

Nash put his arm beneath Nicholas when he pitched forward. "You were saying it's best if you go home and get some sleep." Nash turned him toward the coach.

"Home?" The impulse to stiffen his spine in indignation shot through Nicholas, but all his body did was sway from side to side. "The night's still young, an' I feel jolly good."

"Jolly, aye, but something tells me the 'good' part will be up for debate come the morn."

"Nonsense . . . er?"

"Nash."

"Ah, yes. Nash!" Nicholas slapped him on the back. "You're a fine fellow and a—what are y' doing down there?"

Nash picked himself up off the ground, eased his shoulders back, and grimaced in pain. "The coach is this way, sir."

Nicholas canted his head over his shoulder. "Indeed it is, and quite a pretty coach, too. Black's always been one of my favorite colors, y' know." In a voice intended to be hushed—but wasn't—he added, "Don't tell anybody, though. It's a secret. Ssh." He pressed a finger to his lips.

"I won't tell." Nash placed a hand beneath Nicholas's elbow and turned him around. "Let's go home now."

"What is it with you and home?" Nicholas plucked his arm from his driver's grip and swung around. Then he breathed deeply. "Ah, there's nothing like the smell of the sea, the salt tang, the hint of earth." He sniffed. "Hmm, what's that other aroma?"

"Dead fish," Nash muttered.

Nicholas quirked a brow, or at least thought he did. His forehead, like the rest of his body, had achieved the physical state of numb. "Y're a gloomy Gus, Nash . . . or is it a gloomy Nash, Gus?" He puzzled for a second and then promptly forgot the question. "Y're as much fun as an impacted tooth, and I must say y're bringing my spirits down. I'm supposed to be happy. I'm getting married, y'know."

Nash's pronounced Adam's apple bobbed, reminding Nicholas of one of his ugly but effective fishing floats. "Married, sir? When?"

"Someday. Probably before y' know it. Definitely in this lifetime." He shrugged. "I think."

"Congratulations." Nash scratched the side of his head. "I think."

"Thank you, my man. I've got the woman all picked up, er, out."

"Oh? And who is the lucky miss, sir?"

"Lady Jessica . . ." Nicholas paused, frowning. "Hell, forgot her last name. Something to do with an ass."

Nash made a choking sound. "An ass, sir?"

"Backside, man. Rear flanks. Ah, that's it!"

"Rear flanks?"

Nicholas snorted, and Nash backed out of spittle range. "No, man! Reardon. Jessica Reardon. I've done all sorts of research on her, an' I think she'll work out just fine as the next Misses. . . ." He frowned.

"Sinclair," Nash graciously filled in. "You researched her, sir?"

" 'Course. Have to make sure I know what I'm getting, don't I?" Weaving unsteadily on his feet, Nicholas leaned forward and added in a man-to-man whisper, "Need a malleable creature who knows her place an'll do as she's told. No surprises for me. No suh." Then he used Nash to steady himself and flung his unruly hair off his forehead. It promptly fell back.

"Well, I'm off. Must find my allistrious, er, elustinous . . ." Hmm. Perhaps he *had* drunk too much. He held up his hand in front of his face, uncurled two fingers but counted four. Interesting. "I've got to find my brother. Must tell him the news."

"Is there nothing I can say to dissuade you from doing this tonight, sir?" Clearly Nash did not embrace the idea.

"Not a thing. I'm a man who knows his mind, in command of my own destiny, a solitary ship sailing into a glorious sunset on a voyage of exploration—and all that rot." With that overblown proclamation, Nicholas headed off.

"You're sailing in the wrong direction, sir," Nash pointed out. "Your brother's ship is at the other end of the dock."

Pivoting on his heel in a splendid display of balance, Nicholas glared at his driver. "Know-it-all," he grumbled and then headed down the dock in search of his brother's ship, *The Lucky Lady,* much to his driver's dismay.

Nearly a week had passed since Nicholas's encounter with Jules and his subsequent discovery that he had relented mentally to allowing her and her friend to stay with him before he'd actually relented verbally. Meaning, that she'd asked his permission merely as a matter of form. Whether he agreed or not, it would be done Jules's way. Thus, in came her luggage, and out went his bachelor's abode.

Worse, there were flowers.

Flowers in a man's house! It defied convention.

The bright-colored, sweet-smelling weeds began popping up in every conceivable location.

As if that wasn't bad enough, his servants promptly forgot who paid their wages, choosing to follow Lady Jules's instructions instead of his, to his teeth-gnashing annoyance. He was an outcast in his own house. Hell, a man's home should be his castle.

"Not if there's a bloody woman in it," he groused.

The last straw had been when Jules slapped his hand as he tried to sample the dinner fare, telling him he was no better than a naughty child. He glared. She glared. And at that point he decided it was time to assert his status as a man.

Ergo, he slunk out of the house like a chastised dog who had left a unwelcome present on a priceless hand-crafted rug.

One would think he'd protest, put his foot down ... or at the very least whine. But had he? No.

"Coward." He stuffed his hands into his pockets, his feet sloughing along the docks, like a child in the throes of a pout.

One would also think he'd change his mind about settling down. But instead of the prospect weighing upon him like a block of granite in fifty feet of water, his spirits were buoyed. His wife wouldn't get away with pulling the same antics as his cousin. His bride would be a different story. He'd be a pampered husband.

"Darn right." He nodded, agreeing with himself, clearly the only one who would. "Any wife of mine will behave. If I wanna pick at dinner, I'll pick, and if I wanna leave a wet towel plopped on top of the bed and dirty clothing strewn around the room, I bloody well will, and if I wanna stalk about in the buff and sing bawdy songs, *so be it.* No female is going to—"

Nicholas stopped in his tracks as the sound of music

registered in the murky depths of his brain, ending his one-sided rambling. A fiddle rang out a jaunty tune and hands clapped in time. He narrowed his eyes, searching for the source. When he found it, his breath caught in his throat at the sight that greeted him.

Illuminated by the golden glow of a single lamplight, a girl danced on the deck of a ship, her waist-length copper hair swinging with her movements, her lithe body mesmerizing him. Her skirt was lifted to her knees as legs that seemed to go on forever moved in perfect time with each note of the jig.

Nicholas blinked, sure his mind played tricks on him. But no. She was real.

God, she was glorious, her rhythm precise and innocently sensual, a banquet for the senses. Every eye on the deck was riveted to her, most of them men, Nicholas noted with some irritation. His vision tunneled, blocking out all else but her.

His need to see his brother became a distant memory as Nicholas watched the girl, his body reacting with an explosive—and heretofore unfelt—lust.

The music ended. A resounding cheer ascended into the air, claps and whistles, voices begging for another dance. Her laughter rang like the sweetest chime, tightening his groin in agony.

Smiling, she shook her head, her hair shimmering like molten fire as she declined their request. Groans of disappointment followed, the men looking downcast as some of them shuffled away.

Nicholas couldn't take his eyes from her. She fanned herself with her hand and tossed that wild mane of hair off her shoulders. Then she wrapped her fingers around the thick strands and lifted it from her nape, stretching the material of her blouse tautly across her full breasts and showing the elegant lines of a neck meant to be nuzzled. His gut clenched.

She shook out her skirt and moved to the edge of the deck, lightly placing her hands on the railing as she gazed out into the night, the wind teasing her hair. There was something vital about her, a love of life that vibrated across the distance.

She glanced over her shoulder. He held his breath, thinking she intended to go belowdecks with the others. Then her gaze shifted to the gangplank and she nibbled her lower lip. She darted another quick glimpse around and then headed swiftly for the ramp. Nicholas watched her as if he dwelt within a dream, damned only to observe instead of participate.

She hesitated at the bottom of the footway, perhaps realizing it was late and the docks were dark.

Then she turned in his direction. She gasped as their gazes locked, a flash of fear registering on her face. Yet the moment of fright came and went as something far more elemental took its place.

Here was a girl who didn't mask her emotions, who did everything as boldly as she danced and would demand nothing less in return.

From the corner of his eye, Nicholas sensed a movement, a dark shadow at the top of the gangplank. Then a burly figure started down the ramp, his footsteps muted by the surf pounding against the hull of the ship. The girl did not hear him coming. Her gaze was intent on Nicholas.

His brain hazy, Nicholas tried to call out a warning, but he was too late. The crewman grabbed her from behind. She tried to scream, but his hand clamped over her mouth.

Nicholas didn't know when he moved, but in the next moment, he closed the distance between them and slammed into the hulking crewman.

Alcohol slowed Nicholas's fists. Iron knuckles said hello to his face. A booted foot gave the same greeting to his ribs. Pain backpedaled against the liquor. The dim recesses of his mind registered the girl's outraged cry, followed by a stream of creative epithets strung together in the lilt of an angel.

Glass splintered, a heavy grunt followed, and finally a whoosh of air as a body collapsed at his feet.

Then the girl knelt beside him. "Are ye all right?"

She had an accent he couldn't place because not all the cogs functioned in his brain and his ribs protested as if Nash had parked the coach on top of him.

Nicholas attempted to sit up. A tiny hand at his shoulder held him down. "Lie still. Ye're hurt."

He peered up at her and felt an unseen foot give him another kick in the gut. Here was a work of art.

He searched for something urbane to say. What came out was, "Did I save you?"

She laughed, a sound so sweet four nightingales promptly vowed never to sing again. "Oh, aye. Ye saved me, all right. How kind of ye to let the man beat on ye so I could clout him over the head with an empty wine bottle. Ye are a clever one indeed."

Nicholas eyed her impish face and smiled. "That was my plan all along."

Lord, she was even more stunning up close. Her features looked crafted from a sculptor's hands: a delicate, gently tipped nose, high cheekbones, a stubborn jaw, full lips, and eyes of a most unusual shade, lavender blue, the color of the wisteria growing in abundance around his family's estate, Silver Hills.

Fascinated, he watched her unbutton the top of her white blouse and reach a hand inside. His mouth dried quicker than a puddle in the sun and his tongue rasped like sandpaper over scorched lips. She produced a small, square piece of linen. Leaning forward, she dabbed the corner of his mouth.

"Ye're bleeding." Her soft breath smelled like peppermint candy, and Nicholas knew the strongest urge to take a taste. Gently, she brushed the hair from his face. "In my country, they say when a person saves yer life, ye are part of that person forever. Two souls entwined."

Two souls entwined. Nicholas liked the thought. "Do you know what they say here in mother England?"

Innocent curiosity lurked in those uncanny eyes. "What do they say?"

"They say when a person saves your life, you owe that person a token of gratitude—whatever he or she desires."

She studied him for a moment, her gaze drifting over his hair, his jaw, his throat, and then directly into his eyes. "And what is it ye desire?" she murmured.

A long, curly lock of her hair dangled close to him. His fingers itched to feel it, to know if it was as smooth and soft as he imagined.

Nicholas grasped the silken length and tugged her gently forward. "A kiss is what I desire."

He had expected outrage, perhaps an outright denial followed by a stinging slap that would knock his jaw out of alignment. Yet intrigue lit her eyes as her gaze moved to his mouth.

"Then 'tis a kiss ye shall have."

Before he had a moment to be amazed at his good fortune, her eyelids fluttered down and she pressed petal soft lips against his, her breasts teasing his chest, making him want to crush her to him.

He groaned as her mouth moved to the corner of his lip, gently touching the cut, soothing it, taking away the sting. Still her kiss was chaste, her lips barely parted, as if she greeted a relative—an old, ugly one. Unacceptable.

He turned, bringing her lips firmly in contact with his.

He cupped the back of her head, allowing no escape as his tongue slipped smoothly between her lips to invade the soft inside of her mouth. A jolt went through her and promptly through him.

She broke away, but he didn't let her go far. "Nay," she whispered, but her protest was weak.

Nicholas lifted slightly, wanting to explore the fullness of her lower lip. He heard the slight intake of her breath. Inwardly, he smiled. Yet he wondered about the surprise reflected in her eyes.

Certainly she'd been kissed before. The way she danced had been sensual, beckoning, and she had kissed him without any maidenly airs or hesitation. Her show of innocence was intoxicating, and when her tongue tentatively touched his, sweat broke out on his forehead.

At his feet, the crewman groaned. The man was going to be in pain when he awoke so Nicholas lulled him back to sleep with a booted heel to the side of his head, accomplished without losing contact with his nightingale.

His arm encircled her waist, hauling her closer as his mouth plundered hers, inviting her tongue to join the age-old mating dance.

Her silken hair fell about them, wrapping them in a world of their own and drugging him far more effectively than any alcohol ever could.

She pulled away, and all he wanted was to pull her back. Her lavender eyes were glazed, her mouth swollen from his kiss. Time seemed suspended as she stared into his eyes. His fingers toyed with her hair, a bountiful mass of curls as wild and unfettered as the woman.

She took a breath and moved away. "Y-ye're h-hurt," she stammered, clearly as affected by the kiss as he was.

Nicholas wouldn't relinquish the length of her hair still wrapped about his hand. "So come back and ease my suffering."

For a moment, it looked as if she contemplated the idea. The tip of her tongue slowly glided over her supple bottom lip. A fond memory of his tongue doing the same thing, perhaps? He wondered if she recognized what she did—or what it did to him.

She stopped abruptly and shook her head. "Ye promised to behave," she said under her breath.

"Excuse me?"

She blinked those long, thick lashes. "What?"

"You said something about behaving." He hoped to God she wasn't talking about him. At that moment, behaving seemed as possible as swallowing his own tongue.

" 'Twas myself I was talking to. Terrible habit, me mum says."

"I disagree."

She gave him a lopsided grin that could cock up the toes of a saint. "And why is that no surprise to me now?"

"Well, how can it be wrong when you say such thought-provoking things?"

Her expression conveyed that she saw through his blatant attempt at flattery. "Ye speak such pretty words. I imagine ye could sweet talk yer way into heaven."

"Who says I don't have an engraved invitation?"

"Anyone can see the mischief in ye. 'Tis the glint in yer eye and the wee hint of a dimple in yer cheek."

The wee hint of a dimple in his cheek? Silent laughter shook Nicholas. His ribs, still throbbing two beats faster than his heart, were unappreciative of the action. "I have a glint in my eye, huh?"

"Indeed. They're very expressive eyes. A thousand shades of green, they are." She bit her lip. "Och, I've got to learn to curb me tongue."

"Do you think you could curb it later? Right now, I think I'm in need of another kiss—for the pain, you know."

"Ye are a wicked one."

"Me?" He shook his head, the small motion causing a shaft of pain to spiral down his spine. "I'm an angel. You as much as said so yourself."

She chuckled. "Aye, and I must have been delirious to have said such a fool thing." She gently tugged her hair from his reluctant grip. "Do ye need any help getting up?"

Nicholas never thought to say no. That would defeat the purpose of remaining close to her. Instead he nodded, gazing at her with eyes he hoped looked sufficiently helpless. "I feel as weak as a newborn foal."

She cocked a brow. "Tch, and have ye never seen how quickly they rise on their shaky limbs?"

She placed a hand behind his head and helped him to a sitting position. Her mouth was so close it took supreme effort to keep from tasting her lips once more.

"Do you know a lot about horses?" he asked to combat the need.

Her gaze flicked to his. There was no artifice reflected within their depths, no hooded intentions or coyness. Just curiosity and honesty.

"Enough."

Nicholas found himself wondering what else she knew. His alcohol-sodden mind was processing the incidentals rather slowly, trying to place her accent and wondering if she would be staying in England or returning on the ship to wherever she'd come from. He hoped to God it was the former and not the latter. This was one woman he wanted to get to know better—much better.

From her dress, which was simple and serviceable, he imagined she was a servant. Did she work on the ship, perhaps cooking or serving the men?

The last thought caused a stab of irritation that—if Nicholas hadn't known better—he might have labeled jealousy, which was patently ridiculous. He barely knew this girl. Besides, the Sinclair men had obliterated that trait in themselves, and therefore, he couldn't possibly be jealous. Possessive would be more in line. Their souls were entwined, after all.

Nicholas was roused from his musings when she slid her arms beneath his and tried to help him up. He pretended great suffering as he gradually rose, never letting on that she wouldn't have been able to budge him if he were truly hurt. The less said, the better.

Now standing, Nicholas noticed something he hadn't before. The girl was tiny. Petite. Her head barely reached the middle of his chest. Obviously he had elevated her to the status of amazon when she stood on the deck of the ship. Had it not been for her God-given endowments, he might think her a child.

"How old are you?"

She canted her head back, looking quite formidable from her diminutive height. "How old are ye?" she returned.

"I asked first."

"An' I'm thinkin' ye shouldn't have."

He shrugged—another move his ribs didn't like. "Ah, but you forget, I saved you. Two souls, remember? Well, my soul wants to know how old your soul is."

"Souls are ageless."

"Are you evading the question?"

"Ye are a brash one."

"It is indeed a cross I bear. Now how old did you say you were?"

She hesitated and then replied, " 'Tis twenty-four I am." Her eyes gave her away, as did the twitch of her lips.

"Really? I'm twenty-four as well."

She scoffed.

"What, you don't believe me?"

"Not a wee bit."

"Oh? And how old do I look?"

Like the elf she was, she danced away from him. "Old enough to be me Da."

"Your—" Nicholas reached out to grab the imp. Chuckling, she deftly skirted his hands. When she pranced by him again, he struck, coiling his arm around her and hauling her close, leaving no body part untouched. "Old, am I?"

She gasped. Nicholas captured the sound in his mouth as he molded his lips to hers, knowing he had been looking for any excuse to kiss her again, to feel her soft contours, to brand her as his own.

Grinning like a satyr, he released her. She stumbled back, staring at him with wide, luminous eyes, her cheeks flushed. God, she was glorious.

"Still think I'm old?"

Instead of replying, she raised a shaky arm, a finger gently touching the cut on the corner of his lip.

Then she slapped him—fingers, palm, and all.

"Damn it, woman! What the hell was that for?"

She stared him down like a warrior, her tiny fists perched on a tiny waist. "The first kiss ye asked for. The second ye took. 'Tis not a tart I am to be treated so." Her indignation could not thoroughly cover the fact that he had affected her. For that, the slap was well worth it.

Notching her chin upward and throwing her shoulders back, she stormed past him. He couldn't let her leave.

Lightly grasping her arm, he said, "Please ... don't go." When it looked as if she might wallop the other side of his face with the olive branch he'd extended, he added, "I'm hurt." Pathetic but effective.

Her icy demeanor melted a bit. "Aye, an' ye'll be

hurtin' a lot worse if ye don't watch where ye put those lips.''

Trying to look contrite and pained, he inched closer to her, until at last they stood toe to toe, big foot to little foot. ''Forgive me.''

''Ye've got the devil's own charm, ye do.'' Her voice was a husky whisper that knifed through him like a white-hot blade. She took a deep breath and a step back. ''There's an inn over there. I'll take ye to it an' make sure ye're made comfortable. But don't be thinkin' to try anything, do ye hear?''

Nicholas wondered if he should tell the lovely sprite that 'anything' was a rather broad term and he was the type who liked to test the boundaries. But why ruin the moment with details? Since she had so nicely offered to see to his needs, who was he to complain? Certainly it would be rude to tell her his coachman waited only a short distance down the docks. Besides, he was drunk. Therefore, he wasn't expected to think logically.

His ribs pleading for mercy, he bowed and waved her ahead of him. With a look of suspicion, she hesitated and then started forward, leaving him to trail behind her and groan as he watched the sensuous sway of her backside.

Chapter Four

The inn wasn't so much an inn as it was a dirty heap of a saloon that seemed to cater to every undesirable within its far-reaching sphere.

Sheridan's second thought was that she had best not let Uncle Finny catch sight of the place or she'd never get him out. If holy water were whiskey, her uncle would go to church every day.

Carefully, she crossed the splintered threshold. She imagined many of the inn's patrons tripped over it and, being too drunk to rise, slept right there in front of the door, ready to start fresh come the morning.

Bawdy catcalls rang out as Sheridan entered. She stopped in her tracks and glared at each and every man who leered or belched a comment that would have her mother washing out their mouths with lye soap and a cat-o-nine.

Most of the men shuffled their feet uneasily beneath the scarred tables at which they sat, returning their gazes to their dirty mugs. A few eyes lingered, but when she didn't back down, they did.

Sheridan felt a presence beside her and looked up at the profile of the dark-haired stranger who had unwittingly become her savior. He was dirty and disheveled, but completely disarming.

Even in his present state, he outshone every man in the room. And from the cut of his clothes, he obviously had money. Every article fit him to perfection, from his snug black trousers to his once pristine white shirt.

Most of the buttons had been ripped away during his struggle with her attacker, leaving his shirt gaping, exposing the width and breadth of a muscular chest unlike any Sheridan had ever seen.

Taut planes, clearly delineated, made her want to reach out and trace their contours. She caught a glimpse of darkly alluring brown nipples and a hint of a rippling stomach.

Just looking at him did strange things to her insides. Perhaps that explained her extreme reaction to him when she'd spotted him poised across the length of the dock. She had been transfixed.

And when he had kissed her, her heart had clanged like the bells of Saint Mary's.

In all her living life, she had never been kissed like that! Truth be told, she had never been kissed at all. She had dreamed of it often enough, though, but always the face of the man who touched her so intimately remained shadowed, a mystery.

"See anything you like?"

Startled, Sheridan's gaze collided with the forest green eyes of her dark angel, and she realized she had conjured the man of her dreams to life.

Notching her chin upward, she replied, "I was merely checkin' to see if ye had any more scrapes I didn't notice before."

He graced her with a devastatingly handsome half grin. "Perhaps I should do the same and look for scrapes on you."

"Still the rascal, I see."

"The very one."

The proprietor, having obviously spotted a patron who could pay his tab, waddled over to them, his belly reaching them before the rest of him did, his body odor quickly following. "Welcome to Puddlebys, sir. Care for a table? A cozy spot by the fireplace just opened up."

Sheridan spotted a plump woman, probably the proprietor's wife, tugging at the arm of a man slumped over the top of a table, a plateful of something dark and congealed lying next to his head.

Unceremoniously, the man fell to the floor and didn't even twitch an eyebrow as he was dragged to a corner where he curled up like a babe in his mother's lap. He promptly resumed snoring at a pitch that shook the rotting timbers.

"A room is all we'll be needin', thank ye," Sheridan told the proprietor.

Muddy brown eyes, small in the man's corpulent face, snapped in her direction. "You're . . . *Irish.*" The words reverberated through the noisy room, drawing the men's gazes back to her, but for an entirely different reason this time.

"Aye, that I am. And what of it?"

A snarl curled the man's lip. "We don't serve Irish here."

Though she was used to such remarks, Sheridan wondered if ever a time would come when they didn't sting.

"What did you say?" her dark angel growled.

Sheridan glanced at him and found his gaze focused on the pudgy proprietor, anger emanating from him in waves.

With foolish bravado, the man returned, "I said I don't serve Irish here."

Her dark angel stalked forward, towering over the man, a tic working in his jaw. "Be forewarned, I have a healthy dislike for dimwits. Now do as the lady requested and get us a room. Quickly."

The man visibly swallowed. "Yessir." Fear made him wheeze like a squeeze box in the hands of a monkey. "Right away, sir." He turned to go.

"Apologize to the lady first."

The innkeeper flashed an annoyed glance Sheridan's way, clearly not wanting to apologize to a lowly Irish girl. "I'm sorry," he muttered, through clenched teeth.

Beautiful blue-black hair tumbled forward as her savior shook his head, unimpressed. "Not good enough, pudgy."

The proprietor's jowls jiggled with indignation, which promptly changed to immediate concern for his welfare at the menacing look sent his way, one that said an apple would be stuffed in his mouth and he would be roasted over a spit until his carcass was sufficiently tenderized.

"Say, 'I'm sorry I spoke to you like that, miss. I'm a fat lout and a mental pygmy. I've led a miserable existence. My mother beat me as a child and it's made me an intolerant little cur.' "

The proprietor's face turned beet red. "I won't!"

Her dark angel leaned forward, causing the man's head to tilt back. Only the innkeeper's immense frontal bulk kept him from tipping over. "You will if you want to see the sun rise over this rat heap tomorrow. Now say it."

Elongating his neck until it appeared he had only two

chins instead of four, the proprietor bit out, "I'm sorry I spoke to ya like that, miss. I'm a . . ."

"Fat lout," her savior supplied.

The proprietor's lips all but disappeared. "I'm a fat lout and a"—his voice dropped to a barely audible level—"mental pygmy." Chuckles rippled around the dimly lit room.

"Good, pudgy. Go on."

It took all Sheridan's strength to keep from doubling over with laughter.

Purple blotches speckled the man's cheeks. "I've led a miserable existence." He wheezed angrily. "My mother beat me as a lad, and it's made me an intolerant little cur." Glaring at the man beside her, he spat, "Satisfied?"

"For the moment. Now show me the room."

Disgruntled, the proprietor shifted his weight from foot to foot as he turned around and toddled toward stairs. The treads groaned like the tormented souls of the damned as he climbed. He showed them to a door at the end of a short hallway. Opening the portal, he ushered them into a tiny room.

"This here's the best we got."

Threadbare curtains hung from the windows and a bed-cover that might have once had a flower pattern on it but now looked like a garden of indescribable weeds graced a bed that sloped toward the wall as if its legs were shorter on one side.

Sheridan had seen worse. "We'll take it."

"That'll be two pounds." He held out a grimy hand shaped like an oven mitt.

Sheridan's innate disgust with shysters boiled up inside her. "Two pounds! Why, this room isn't worth twopence, ye puffed up—"

Her green-eyed guardian slapped the money down in the man's hands. The proprietor smirked, showing two blackened teeth in the side of his mouth. He turned to depart, and her savior helped him along with a boot to his behind, promptly slamming the door after him.

"Jackass," he muttered. Then he turned to survey her, ever the rogue.

Casually, he leaned a shoulder against the portal, and Sheridan wondered if his intentions were dishonorable now that he had her alone. But worse, why was she not sufficiently concerned they might be?

Perhaps because he called to her in some way. It was more than his unearthly beauty, although there was no denying the allure of those emerald eyes, the same pure green that covered the hills and dales of her homeland. And it was more than the rugged jaw begging for feathered kisses, or shoulder-length hair like a skein of ebony silk longing for fingers to ruffle through its thick texture.

No, it was that those green eyes held the same challenging light so often reflected in her own eyes, and that rugged jaw had the same fierce determination as hers, and that shoulder-length hair clearly proclaimed he defied convention, as she did time and again.

They were opposite sides of the same coin.

He watched her with hawk-like intensity, waiting for her to speak.

"Seems ye've come to me rescue twice now," she said instead of demanding he remove his body from in front of the door.

"Hmm. It seems I have. Makes me wonder if another reward shall be forthcoming."

Sheridan's ever present temper rode to the fore. "If ye're thinkin' in that schemin' bonny head of yers that I've brought ye here for a tumble, ye'd best think again. Now step aside."

He didn't budge. "Bossy boots. Just as I thought."

Sheridan's fingers curled into tight fists at her side. She

was not afraid of this good-looking piece of work. She'd box his ears, and then some! "I said stand aside! Or ye'll get the sole of me shoe to yer backside. I've kept me part of the bargain. I owe ye no more."

"If I remember correctly, you said you would see to my comfort. Well"—he smiled the devil's own smile—"I'm not comfortable yet."

Violet eyes sparked with fire, and Nicholas thought the girl was even more beautiful when riled. He wondered how much time he had left before her tiny fist took a swing that would clip him in his aching side since she was too elfin to reach his chin.

Certainly he could oblige her and bend down, but why make it easy? Although something told him she was the type who dealt a blow with one hand and administered aid with the other. He just might test that theory.

" 'Tis not yer nanny I am."

"Would you like to be?"

Her eyes narrowed and she swung. Her left hook missed him. Her well-aimed right undercut, however, walloped him in the one body part that had ached since he had clapped eyes on the spitfire.

Nicholas doubled over, his eyes crossing. "No children . . . in my . . . future," he groaned.

" 'Tis just what ye deserve for such talk."

He expected her to storm out, yet she didn't. A long moment passed with only the sound of his pitiful moaning and the muted jocularity of the unwashed masses coming from the saloon. The pitiful moaning seemed to be working. He could feel her regret.

"Are ye hurt very much?"

Weakly, he nodded.

"Me mum always told me to keep me temper about m'self. 'Tis not right for a female to be beatin' on the men, she says."

From Nicholas's current position, which gave him a lovely view of her hem, he said haltingly, "Wise woman, your mother."

She sighed rather forlornly. "Aye. 'Tis just that me temper is fierce."

She sounded so disgusted it was all he could do to keep from chuckling. "Probably that red hair you have. Ah, do you mind helping me"—to the chair or to the bed?—"to the bed?" Hurt he might be. Dead he wasn't.

She hesitated, then gently wrapped an arm about his waist and helped him straighten. Feigning weakness, he propped an arm around her shoulder and let her lead him to the lopsided bed. As if he were a newborn kitten, she laid him down. Images of being licked clean tumbled through his head.

She stood back and studied him. " 'Tis not much of a fightin' man ye are."

That should have pricked his masculine pride, especially since he was not at his best at that moment. Nevertheless, he liked to consider himself a lover, not a fighter.

"I've been told I excel at other things."

She raised one perfectly shaped brow, disbelief written on her gamine face. "Oh? And what might these things be, ye preenin' rooster?"

The girl was an article. "Don't hold back your true feelings on my account."

" 'Tis not something I've ever been accused of."

He shook his head and muttered, "Preening rooster indeed."

"Aye, ye are. 'Tis so very sure ye are of ye're pretty face and bulgin' muscles that ye tote yerself about like the Queen's cock at dawn."

He pushed aside the cock at dawn remark and went straight to the heart of the matter. "To which bulging muscles are you referring?"

He longed to roll to his side and flex something, but his bloody aching ribs would certainly ruin that plan. He contemplated another pose that might seduce the darling girl, for Nicholas realized quite clearly that was what he intended. His groin was heavy and painfully aroused. His rooster wasn't particularly interested in waiting until the sunrise to cock-a-doodle-do.

She frowned. It seemed his pretty face and bulging muscles were not winning the day. Had he imagined the sweet lips pressed to his as he lay supine on the dock? Or the burgeoning desire reflected in her eyes? Did he look that bad? He took a quick, assessing glance. A little dirty, but otherwise very virile. Sweat and grime were a badge of honor for a man anyway.

"I've got to get back to me family before they notice I'm missin'."

So much for sweat and grime. "What about me?"

"What about ye?" she asked over her shoulder.

"What if I succumb to my injuries?" If only he could spit up blood on cue. "Won't you please stay? Just a little while longer?"

Sheridan paused, warning herself it was a mistake to look at the man again. If she were smart, she'd leave on winged feet.

So much for common sense.

Turning, she almost laughed. His kicked puppy expression was more than she could take. Lord help her, the man was far too dangerous for her peace of mind with his shirt flung wide exposing a V of sun-darkened skin, his hair tousled, his green eyes beckoning, and his big body encompassing much of the bed.

"All right. Just a few moments, mind ye." She already had to go to confession in the morning.

A hint of victory curled the corner of his sensuous lips. He patted the spot beside him on the bed. She pulled up the chair. The disappointment in his eyes made the corner of *her* lip curl with victory. That would teach the wretch!

He groaned as he attempted to roll to his side. "Damn, I could use a drink to ease my soreness. If I didn't think old pudgy would poison me, I'd get us something, perhaps a vintage bottle of yesterday's mashed grapes."

His comment reminded Sheridan of the flask she had tucked in her skirt pocket. She had slipped it out of her uncle's death grip when he had passed out reciting his stratagems for the United Irish uprising of 1798.

He must have had another flask or bottle hidden away somewhere to have gotten so inebriated, because that afternoon, while the ship waited in the harbor to be given quay space, she had surreptitiously exchanged his potent whiskey with watered-down wine.

Even though Jules would think nothing of it, Sheridan wanted to make a good impression, and that didn't include her uncle bowling her friend over with a whiff of his one-hundred-proof cologne.

Sheridan looked forward to surprising Jules. Their ship had arrived two days ahead of schedule. The captain, she had overheard a few crewmen saying, had discovered his mistress was having a tryst behind his back, so he had made record time in the return crossing.

Sheridan slipped her hand into her skirt pocket and removed the silver flask. Perhaps a wee slug would help ease his pain. Certainly it couldn't hurt. It was only wine anyway.

"Is that what I think it is?" he asked, pointing to the flask.

" 'Tis indeed. Would ye like some?"

"Like a babe wants its mother's milk." She handed him the flask. He gazed at it as if God had just told him he was getting a second chance. He saluted her. "Cheers."

The first mouthful hit Nicholas like a gale wind off a

polar ice cap. Had he been standing, it would have laid him flat on his back. As the liquor coursed down his throat, it sucked him along, spun him around, and spit him out. Beneath his closed eyelids, his orbs rotated in their sockets. The stuff was bottled lightning.

"Better?" she asked.

He pried open an eyelid and choked out, "Much." And oddly enough, his pain was receding. He took another swallow, coaxing the liquid down his still-burning gullet. His nerve endings sang a happy song.

Sighing, he rolled onto his side, his early discomfort becoming an amusing tickle. "So you're Irish," he said offhandedly.

She stiffened, clearly telling him the liquor had not bestowed upon him a golden tongue

"There's no need for bristling, my girl. I was merely making conversation."

Her chin notched upward, showcasing that stubborn jaw. "I'm not bristlin'."

He pretended to pluck something from his backside and hold it out to her. "Here, this belongs to you. It's one of your bristles. My hide is covered with them."

She folded her arms across her chest and leveled him with a look. " 'Tis conversation ye're wantin', then? Well, let me point out to ye that ye're English."

"No, I'm not," he replied, beginning to slur his words as the liquor in his mouth lassoed his tongue. "I was stolen by gypsies and sold to the English. Certainly you can't hold that against me?"

She riveted him with a glare worthy of any schoolmarm attending to an unruly student. She was a tough nut to crack, this one.

He sighed. "All right. So I'm English. What does that mean?" He took another healthy dose of the firewater in the flask. "Other than the fact that I crave scones heaped with clotted cream and tea instead of that despicable coffee Americans are so found of.'' He made a face. ''Tastes like boiled dirt.''

''Some say it means we should be enemies,'' she replied coolly, her defiant gaze never wavering.

Thought-provoking rebuttal, Nicholas mused, yet war was clearly impossible. His white flag was already raised. ''Well, we can't be enemies. We are two souls entwined, remember?'' He winked and took another belt. ''Why are you looking at me like that?'' And why was she suddenly so far away . . . and a bit hazy?

''Because I'm thinkin' the liquor is goin' to yer head. 'Tis clear ye're not a drinkin' man to be affected by such a weak liquid as that.''

Weak? What did they drink in her country? Lava?

He shrugged, too languid to argue. ''I'm not a fighter or a drinker.'' Although, in truth, he was both. ''Do you like men who fight and drink?''

''I never gave it much thought, although it seems that all the men I know fight and drink. 'Tis part of who they are.''

Nicholas didn't hear her last few words. Instead he concentrated on the first part. ''So you know a lot of men, do you?''

''Aye.'' No hesitation. A bitter pill settled in his stomach.

He put the flask to his lips and sucked down the remaining contents. The liquor possessed his body and stirred his brain into soup, his last cohesive thought being that his elf was a jade.

''You're very pretty.''

Sheridan shifted in her chair at the drowsy-lidded look he gave her. No matter what his state, drunk or sober, he made her heart beat to an odd rhythm that left her breathless.

"Surely, and ye have kissed the Blarney stone to have been gifted with such a glib tongue."

Like a dangerously beckoning snake, his tongue slid out of his mouth, poised between strong, white teeth—taunting, tempting her as the serpent had tempted Eve. Sheridan knew an unspeakable need to wrap her lips around it.

With intoxicating slowness, he drew the serpent back into its lair. "I speak only the truth. Your beauty beggars my ability to describe it. Do you have a name, my druid maiden?"

For a moment, Sheridan forgot what it was. His mere presence sucked away logical thought. "Danny," she finally managed.

A reckless half grin brought a dimple to his cheek. "Danny," he tested the name. "Unusual. Like you."

A jolt of realization rocked Sheridan, a startling truth she had consciously denied: She was no match for this man, and she had always believed no man was a match for her.

She always knew what to do when it came to males with lustful intentions. Either a few well-phrased words put them promptly back in their place or a knee in the groin did the trick for the more hardheaded ones.

Yet something told her no amount of words would deter this handsome devil, and a knee in the groin, should she even get that far, would backfire. The man defined irresistible.

She had to get out.

Rising abruptly, she stammered, "I—I must go."

He reached out and grabbed her hand. "Don't . . . please."

She trembled as his thumb swept back and forth over the top of her hand. "I have to," she replied, cursing her lack of insistence.

He frowned, looking as if he searched for words. "That crewman who accosted you might still be out there. Stay here. I'll protect you." He scooted over, his eyes moving from her to the space beside him on the bed.

Sheridan could imagine the kind of protection he offered. Worse, he was drunk. The man certainly didn't possess a cast-iron stomach to have been affected so significantly.

Curiously, she plucked the flask from his loose grip and held it to her nose. She took a sniff and groaned inwardly. Sweet lord in heaven, it wasn't wine in the flask but her uncle's special blend of whiskey, strong enough to revive a corpse—or turn the unsuspecting into one. Her uncle must have discovered her duplicity, tossed the wine, and replaced it with whiskey without her being the wiser.

And her dark angel, a man unused to its potent effects, had finished off the remaining contents.

Oh, what had she done? She couldn't leave him like this. He would be defenseless in his condition. But certainly he wouldn't get into any trouble, would he? No, he would sleep. Yet when Sheridan searched his face one thought came to mind: This man loved trouble.

He tugged on her hand, making her decision for her.

She went to sit down in the chair, but he pulled her toward the bed. "I don't feel so good," he murmured.

Heaven help her, he looked good, she thought, promptly berating herself for doing so.

"Lie beside me," he sweetly begged, his hair mussed, a lost little boy in a big boy's body.

Alarm bells clanged in Sheridan's head. Only peril could come from lying next to him. But as was the case with her, whenever something forbidden presented itself, she felt compelled to reach out and take it with both hands. Her mother often told her she was three-fourths daring and one-fourth regret.

Silently praying for forgiveness to both the Lord and her mother, Sheridan eased down onto the bed, telling herself she merely did so to lull her dark angel into sleep, that her actions had absolutely nothing to do with wanting to know what it was like to lie close to a man, to feel the heat from his body, to breathe in the scent of him.

But not every man. Just this one.

"Comfy?" he murmured in her ear, his warm breath fanning across her cheek, causing goose bumps to prickle her flesh and a large knot to form in her stomach. "You're trembling." He took her hand. "Are you cold?"

Hot and cold, she almost replied, but he rolled to his side, wedging his body against hers. Words lodged in her throat. His blue-black hair tumbled across his brow as he levered himself up on his elbow, his smoldering green eyes memorizing her face. Her gaze strayed to his lips, wanting to feel them pressed against hers once more.

"I—I'm fine," she lied.

"But I'm not," he said in a husky rasp. "I think I'm dying."

" 'Tis only the poteen in yer blood. 'Twill go away. I promise."

He took her hand and pressed it against his chest. His flesh was warm and smooth and oh-so-solid. His heart beat fiercely against her palm as she slowly elevated her gaze to his. What she saw pierced her all the way to her soul.

"Save me, Irish," he murmured as his head bent toward her. "Only you can."

Blood raced through Sheridan's veins as his lips feathered across hers, every nerve ending alive and on fire. The part of her that had knelt countless times before the cross, hearing the sharp bark of the priest warning of the evils of the flesh, the shame and guilt any good Catholic girl should feel thinking such thoughts as she was just then—and had been thinking from the first moment she had laid eyes on her green-eyed sassenach—began to float away on the wings of a dove.

"I'm a good girl," she whispered against his mouth, tasting him, honey and sensual heat, learning his texture, needing no alcohol to be intoxicated by his raw physical presence.

"I know," he whispered back, his tongue outlining her lips before dipping inside to duel with hers, his big body pressing her down, encompassing all her senses . . . surpassing all her dreams.

The mysterious man in her dreams now had a face.

And in her heart, Sheridan knew this was the man she was destined to marry.

Chapter Five

Her name on his lips became the sweetest benediction against her cheek, an erotic exhalation in her ear, a building tempest along the contour of her jaw, and divinity as his mouth claimed hers with seamless ease—dissolving thought, annihilating will.

Destiny.

"One look and ye'll know, child," her grandmother had told her long ago. "The soul 'tis a wondrous thing to recognize what the eyes cannot."

Certainly her dark angel had to be her other half, for never had Sheridan experienced such a need to become one with a man. To be touched. To be loved.

He lifted his head and gazed down at her. Something in him called to her in a deep, indefinable way. Those emerald eyes, the exact color of the lush grass that covered the hills around her family's cottage in Tralee, seemed to be a sign from above.

His desire surrounded her, raising her temperature to match his own as his arm coiled about her waist and he rolled her on top of him. He sank his hand deep into her hair as his tongue traced a path down her throat, where his mouth resumed its magic, gently drawing in the flesh at the base of her neck. Hazy pleasure thickened her blood and made her squirm, aching to touch, to taste, to explore as he did.

He groaned and sat her up. His shirt had worked its way free, laying him bare before her eyes. His hard, sun-bronzed skin begged for her touch. She inhaled deeply and placed her palms against the muscled expanse of his chest, her fingers testing his flesh, smoothing over the contours that made male and female bodies so very different. She wanted to taste him.

Instinct guided her as she leaned over and tasted the intriguing dark nipple that fascinated her, using her tongue as he had used his, trailing, circling, sucking. A rumbling of pleasure emanated from deep within his chest.

"Too damned good," he murmured in a raspy voice. He grasped her upper arms and sat her up again. "My turn."

He lifted shaky hands to the top button of her blouse, fumbling with endearing nervousness. Sheridan took his hands in hers and placed them at his sides, fear and excitement warring inside her. She wasn't so naive she didn't know what he wanted.

Her thirst for new experiences and knowledge had made her interested in the lure of the male physique and the relationship between men and women. She hadn't learned much, but she knew more than most virgins, mainly because she had befriended a girl who danced in the burlesque show at Cohan's saloon.

Many a night, Sheridan had surreptitiously watched the goings on between Paddy's girl and his patrons through the balusters on the second floor, an odd stirring settling in the pit of her belly. But nothing had ever come close to setting off the maelstrom of sensations her dark angel made her feel.

Her fingers trembled like leaves in a high wind, hesitating on the last button of her blouse, a small voice of reason warning her to stop before it was too late, that she should be ashamed of her actions. But this was meant to be.

He placed his hands over hers and together they undid the last button. The material of her blouse, though soft, felt like the coarsest linen as it gently slipped from her shoulders. Only her thin chemise covered her torso, but the way his gaze devoured her scorched a hot path down Sheridan's neck and over her chest.

Slowly, her hands rose to the white ribbon at the top of her chemise. She tugged one end, then the other. The material parted, her straps falling off her shoulders.

His throat worked, his green eyes appearing almost black as she let the material shimmy down her skin, halting at the distended peaks of her breasts.

Sheridan shook slightly and the material fell away, puddling at her waist, baring herself to him as she had to no other man.

She peeked at him to gauge his reaction. He was staring. Her breasts grew heavy and full, her nipples hardening painfully under his intense scrutiny.

Feeling as if she'd been too bold or that perhaps he was disappointed to find she did not have small, perky breasts like other women, Sheridan instinctively folded her arms across her chest.

"Don't." He took her wrists and placed her arms at her sides. Reverently, he cupped her breast. "Exquisite," he murmured, dragging her forward, her breasts dangling in front of his face.

A jolt pierced her when the tip of his tongue flicked her nipple. When he took the nub into his mouth and gently suckled while his hand toyed with her other aching peak, Sheridan thought she would die.

He lifted his hips. She felt the thickened ridge of his manhood through the material of her skirt. He rocked gently at the juncture of her thighs, causing hot, damp heat and burning need to center there. She heard a moan and realized it came from her own throat.

Sheridan moved off him and scooted to the side of the bed. He reached for her, the need in his eyes sluicing through her. Sheridan warred with her inner demon, the voice that told her it was not too late. She could still leave.

She slipped off the bed and stood up, standing half naked before his devouring gaze. Her heart thumped wildly, the ache that his mouth and hands had created not abating but growing stronger the more he watched her.

Closing her eyes, Sheridan took a deep breath and undid the buttons at the back of her skirt. The material slipped soundlessly to the floor. Her chemise and pantalets followed.

Slowly, she opened her eyes. Never had she been naked before a man. Never had she wanted to be. Until now.

"Beautiful," he murmured, leaning up on his elbow and reaching his other arm out for her.

Trembling, Sheridan placed her hand within his warm grasp. He pulled her forward, startling her when he leaned toward her and kissed her hipbone, his tongue tracing her tattoo. The gesture was so reverent, so sweet, that it shook Sheridan to the core.

Then he began to feather kisses downward and Sheridan

nearly jumped out of her skin when his mouth drew closer to the nest of curls at the apex of her thighs.

"Nay," she protested, covering herself with her hands.

"Ssh," her dark angel murmured, nudging her hands away. "Let me love you."

Had her knees not been braced against the edge of the bed, Sheridan would have melted to the floor at the first touch of his tongue on her sex.

He cupped her buttocks, holding her firm as his tongue flicked over the heated pearl inside, teasing, moving slowly and then quicker, circling and then drawing the nub between his lips. She cried out at the erotic torture, the new and amazing sensations rocking her.

He wrapped his arms around her waist, his muscles bunching as he drew her down onto the bed. Sheridan felt liquid and on fire.

His mouth plundered hers as he rolled her onto her back. Sheridan's breath locked in her throat as he rose above her, his shoulder-length hair tumbling about his face in sensual disarray. She memorized every detail, storing it away to cherish for the rest of her life.

He moved on top of her, chest to chest, hip to hip, the weight of him a joy to savor.

"You make me wild," he murmured before taking her earlobe between his lips, settling himself firmly between her legs.

Fright and anticipation sluiced through Sheridan as she wondered what was to come. She'd never seen what went on between Paddy's girl and the customers after they climbed the stairs and found a room.

But certainly there could be nothing more wonderful than this, than the feel of his muscled chest rubbing over her sensitive nipples, the intense heat of his body, the delicious strength in his upper arms as she wrapped her hands around the steel bands of muscle, clinging to him, searching for something only he could give her.

His lips drowned her in a sensual haze, the pleasure swirling together. His hand smoothed over her stomach, cupping her and then gently parting her slick folds, his finger resuming where his tongue had left off.

Sheridan arched upward as bliss spiraled through her. Her breasts thrust before him. He took the offering, drawing one straining peak between his lips.

The excitement built to a fever pitch as she squirmed beneath him, heat culminating as his finger moved faster and faster.

He whispered against her breasts, telling her how beautiful she was, how much he wanted her, needed her. Then he gently bit her nipple and color burst behind Sheridan's closed eyes.

She cried out as pulse after pulse of release crashed through her, bringing liquid warmth to the core of her, drowning her in a rush of sensations radiating from her toes to her fingertips.

"Yes," her dark angel murmured against her mouth. "So sweet."

Sheridan wrapped her arms around his neck, her fingers playing with his silky hair as his burning kiss scorched the breath from her lungs.

"I love you," she whispered in Gaelic, knowing she truly did, that this man was her fate, her destiny, come what may.

He shifted his weight, nudging himself upward until the hot, hard length of him probed the place where his fingers had just been. Fear spilled through Sheridan's veins as she realized he sought entrance.

She shook her head. Too late. He plunged into her to the hilt. A half scream died on her lips, tears blurring her vision at the pain.

"Nay," she pleaded, but the alcohol had eclipsed his rational thought. She bit her lip to keep from crying out, but the pain ebbed within a minute and the realization that he'd made them one soared through her. Two souls entwined.

Sheridan clung to him as he slipped in and out of her, lifting her legs, rocking her, filling her, taking her once more to that bright, spiraling place. He tipped his head back and roared as they reached the summit together, his throbbing heat satiating her, completing her.

He nestled his head between her breasts. "Virgin," he murmured groggily as she stroked her fingers through his hair. "Thank you," he softly added, filling her with contentment, banishing the niggling doubts that she had done the wrong thing by giving him her body. God had brought her to this man. For better or worse, their lives were now interwoven.

His long lashes fluttered against her skin as he struggled to keep his eyes open under the drugging sedation of the alcohol he'd consumed.

Tenderly, he pressed a kiss against the curve of her breast. "Shamrock," he murmured in a barely audible voice, referring to the tattoo on her hip, as his breathing lapsed into the measured rhythm of sleep.

"Aye," Sheridan whispered. " 'Tis meant to bring good fortune . . . and here ye are."

Chapter Six

A commotion woke Sheridan from her slumber. She discovered her arms and limbs entangled with those of a man whose name she didn't know. Yet that fact seemed inconsequential in the scheme of things. They had made love, and she had given him her heart.

How unpredictable love was. She'd expected its arrival to be announced by herald angels singing on high, not by the sound of a breaking wine bottle on a deserted dock. And never in her wildest dreams had she imagined it would happen so suddenly, so completely.

And with an Englishman, no less.

Sheridan tried not to think about how her mother would react to such news. Certainly her family would understand that emotions of the heart could not be turned on or off at a whim. And for the moment, Sheridan allowed herself to believe they would eventually accept the fate God had dealt her.

In sleep, her dark angel looked like an engaging young boy with his tousled locks, but the hint of whiskers on his chin and the large, muscular arms holding her close clearly proclaimed he was a man . . .

As did the magic he'd cast over her body in the deepest part of the night when time held suspended and no other world existed beside their own.

Sheridan shivered in remembrance and tenderly swept the hair off his forehead. He murmured something and tugged her closer to him, his body stirring to life, as did her own.

The loud noise sounded again as he began to nuzzle her neck. Then Sheridan heard a distinct voice that caused every limb in her body to go stock-still.

Uncle Finny had found the saloon.

Oh, heavenly Father!

Gingerly, Sheridan peeled her dark angel's arms from her waist and tried to slide out of bed. Her breasts caressed his cheek as she moved. Like a hungry babe, he latched on to a nipple. A searing rush of moist heat pooled at the juncture of her thighs.

She moaned low in her throat as he suckled her, her body remembering the ecstasy he could so easily bring. How she longed to stay within the warmth of his embrace, to taste and touch and marvel once again. But as it had been since her ship had departed Boston Harbor, Sheridan had to chaperone her chaperones.

He groaned sleepily as she reluctantly climbed out of bed and hurriedly donned her clothing. She padded to the doorway. Knob in hand, she hesitated, glancing back at the man who had walked out of her dreams and into her arms.

Dawn had not yet fully pinkened the horizon, but one slim beam peeked through the crack in the drapes, glisten-ing off his dark, sleek back. His arms were thrown wide, and the sheet barely covered his incredible backside.

Knowing she should go, Sheridan still traveled back to the bed. She tucked the sheet around him and kissed his forehead. "Sleep well, m'love."

"Danny," he murmured.

Sheridan's heart clenched at the sweet sound of her name on his lips. She forced herself to leave his side and hurried down the stairs. Alarm rifled through her as she came to a halt at the bottom step. Two burly, uniformed men glanced up at her.

The law.

In between them was her uncle, his head flopped forward onto his chest, their meaty hands clamped around his upper arms.

A snap of cold dread washed over Sheridan. The police had never been a friend to the Delaneys or to the Irish in general. Even the paddies back in Boston, who, ironically, were mostly Irish, looked at their countrymen like second-class citizens.

The lace-curtain crowd had embraced their new home and now were Americans of Irish extraction, drawing another line only a privileged few could step over. The unfairness of their treatment angered Sheridan, as it always did.

"What are ye doing? Get yer hands off him!"

Her voice must have registered with her uncle because his head slowly rose. She gasped. He sported a black eye and a swollen lip.

"Oh, uncle, what has happened to ye?"

He gave her a gap-toothed smile. "Ther-re's a good lass comin' to her puir uncle's rescue."

Glaring at the men, Sheridan demanded, "What have ye done to him?"

"Nothin' he didn't deserve," one of the surly blocks

of granite said, shaking her uncle. "Put your feet down, Mick."

In his usual rebellious fashion, her uncle had his feet lifted off the floor and tucked back, leaving the men to hold his full weight.

"The back of me hand to ye, ye dirty blatherskites!" her uncle spat, followed by a long stream of Gaelic curses, everything from a pox on the men's family to a painful bout of dropsy, impotency, and their manhood falling off and being eaten by a pack of vicious wolfhounds.

"What are ye doing with him? Ye have no right to be treatin' him so!"

The larger of the two men bent forward, his expression menacing, his face round like a boulder, his complexion far whiter than the teeth he bared when he snarled, "If you don't want to follow him to the hole, sweet piece, I'd watch what you're sayin'." His gaze raked her body, mentally stripping her naked, trying to cheapen her. She wouldn't allow it.

Sheridan tilted up her chin and gave him her haughtiest glare. "Ye'll keep yer looks to yerself," she told him, firm on the outside but quivering on the inside. Then she nodded to her uncle. "What has he done?"

For a moment it appeared as if the man might take exception to her remark. Instead he answered her question. "He laid a hand on his betters."

"Bloody no-good Irish," an angry voice called out.

"Go back where ya belong," another added.

Sheridan's gaze rolled over the scruffy group of men and women. "We belong here just as much as any of ye!"

"We don't want your type here!"

Sheridan would not allow her despair to show. Why did she continue to hold out hope that people could put aside their prejudice and hatred and learn to live together?

Turning back to the constables, she said, "Ye can't throw a man in jail just because he touched someone."

"He pinched me bum!" a female voice cried out indignantly.

Sheridan scrutinized the young barmaid, a peasant blouse hanging off her shoulders and barely covering her ample bosom. Sheridan highly doubted this was the first time the girl's bottom had been sampled by roving male hands. The patrons of Puddlebys were not cut from the finest cloth.

"He meant no harm," Sheridan appealed, hoping for some understanding, but getting none.

"Let's go," the constable ordered. The men headed toward the door, her uncle dangling between.

"Wait!" Sheridan jumped in front of them. "Where are ye taking him?"

"To the stockade they ar-re," her uncle answered, wriggling his body to annoy the men. Obviously the alcohol had worked its way out of his system—and without the soul-persuading powers of twelve tumblers of strong drink, her uncle was at his worst. Pure cussedness, her mum liked to say.

"I sez to them, I'm a humble man. I've merely come to see to me flock. Bah! sez they. 'Tis a drunken old sot ye are. A drunken old sot! sez I with me gall all puffed up and me fists feelin' powerful mean at me sides. Oh? sez they in that snortin', bullyin', spalpeen way of theirs, who ar-re ye then if not a drunken old sot? I gave them the eye." He pointed to his left one, since his right sported his ever shifting patch.

"Spewin' the wrath of God I was. 'Tis sorry ye'll be when ye find Saint Peter barrin' yer entrance to heaven, for I'll have nary a kind word to say about ye, sez I. They guffawed in their blustery way. And why should we care

what ye have to say, sez them. Why? sez I, indignant and
the like. Because I'm—"

"Father Pius Divine," Sheridan finished for him, heaving an exasperated sigh.

Father Pius Divine was one of her uncle's favorite cast
of characters and generally only presented himself in her
uncle's more lucid moments. He preached the word of
the Lord on one hand and got into all sorts of mischief
with the other hand.

"This guy is a loon. He should be locked up for good."

Sheridan ignored the hateful giant and instead quietly
asked her uncle, "What are ye doing here? I thought ye
were sleeping."

"Aye, I was. But ther-re come upon me this ter-rible
thirst. A wee cup o' warm milk 'tis all I intended, mind
ye." He shook his head sadly. "Never did get the milk."

Sheridan looked up at the two men, trying to gauge
which one might feel for her plight. Her heart sank. They
wore identical expressions of steely determination.

She tried the direct approach. "I'll take him with me.
He won't be bothering ye anymore tonight."

"Oh no, you don't," a beefy voice rang out.

Sheridan turned to see the proprietor waddling toward
her. Dread shot through her at the look in his mud-puddle
eyes. Clearly, he intended to make her pay for the embar-
rassment heaped upon him earlier.

"I want the Mick in jail."

"Where d'ya think I'm takin' him?" the constable
snapped.

Something calculated and glimmered behind the innkeeper's eyes as he shot a glare in Sheridan's direction.
"Make sure you add thievery to his charges."

"Thievery!" she fulminated. "He's never stolen anything in his life!" Which wasn't entirely true. Her uncle's
favorite battered flask, for example, had been plucked

right out of a beggar's hands as the man slept off the evening's revelry. Nevertheless, her protest went unheard.

"What did he steal?" the constable inquired with renewed interest.

The owner scratched his armpit. "He stole, er . . . money from my wife. That's right. Straight out of her hand and everyone here will attest to it."

"Ye're lying!"

The proprietor's face mottled. "Don't you dare call me a liar, ye filthy Irish whore!"

The cutting words sent Sheridan reeling as if he'd dealt her a physical blow.

An earsplitting shriek like that of a stuck pig pierced the air. "Call my colleen a tart, will ye? I'll kill ye, ye blubbery amadan!" Her uncle twisted in the men's arms, his legs flying wildly to try to get at the proprietor, who had scooted back, a satisfied smirk on his fleshy face.

"Nay, uncle! Don't!"

But it was too late for reasoning. One of the men had his arm clamped around her uncle's neck and the other attempted to grab his flailing limbs. The man didn't realize her uncle's legs were quite spry for his age. He needed to be quick to outrun the barkeep seeking payment.

The constable almost had him, but her uncle got in one last kick, which, as luck would have it, struck the inn-keeper in the groin.

"Ha-ha!" her uncle chortled with glee. "That'll teach ye, ye bloated cod!"

The constables finally captured him and dragged him away, his feet scraping behind him as he continued to cackle, while the proprietor ranted that he'd see her uncle hanged. Sheridan had no choice but to follow and pray she could resolve the problem.

With one last glance toward the stairs, she hurried after her uncle's rapidly departing figure.

* * *

In the daylight, all the ships berthed at the wharf looked identical. Not a single one stood out to Nicholas's eyes. The girl could be on any one of them or she could already be out to sea, gone forever from his life.

Damn it to hell.

Why it bothered him so much that she might be gone was a mystery. It must be because he felt cheated. He wanted to see her in the daylight, if for no other reason than to discern if she truly was as glorious as he remembered or if his mind had been playing tricks on him and his passion had been alcohol induced. Many a man had sunk to his doom at the bottom of a bottle. If only he hadn't passed out!

What was in that flask she'd given him? A liquid mallet? Nicholas had awakened with a mouth that tasted like mud and tribal drums playing in his head, a hundred little feet doing a jig behind his eyes.

The entire night was a blur that no amount of coaxing on his part could completely piece together—although from the sated feel of his body, the girl had made love to him with the expertise of a French courtesan. The thought made Nicholas's "preening rooster" jump to attention.

Smiling at the remembrance, he had reached for her only to be greeted by emptiness . . . and speckles of blood dotting the sheets. A hazy memory of a pummeling—his own—came to mind, so Nicholas dismissed the blood.

Yet something nagged at him, a brief image of her crying out, as if she were in pain. Could he have been rough with the girl in his inebriated state? He didn't like the possibility.

He prided himself on pleasuring women. The more they enjoyed it, the more he enjoyed it. Had he done something to her that made her run away?

He needed to find her.

Nicholas sought out Pudgy the Proprietor, who, in a gloating manner, told Nicholas the girl had left hours earlier—with another man.

Anger roiled inside Nicholas as he wondered if, for the first time in his life, the tables had been turned and he had been the seducee and not the seducer.

Worse was the realization that he wanted to find the girl's lover, rip out the man's heart, and stuff it down his throat.

Why did the thought of her as a common trollop grate on him so? Nicholas had had his share of flings of the married and unmarried variety, but this was different. This girl was different. Or so he had believed. When he'd looked into her eyes, he'd seen something there, a connection, a gut feeling that made him think she could be . . .

"Don't be an ass," he cut himself off. The girl was no better than his mother. Sex was a game to be played. And damn it, he'd played it all his life! But he hadn't wanted to play it with this one tart-tongued, pixie-faced Irish lass.

Nicholas consoled himself with the reminder that he didn't have time for a tryst with a new female, let alone a wildcat with a mean right hook, not when he had to woo Jessica Reardon.

Lady Jessica would give him the respectability he desired and would be faithful. He had it from good sources that she was chaste and would not consider playing bedroom roulette, as he suspected his Celtic goddess often did.

Jessica's main ambition in life was to be a devoted wife and mother. That's exactly the type of woman Nicholas wanted, not a lavender-eyed hellion with an adorable lilt whose tongue could flay the flesh from a man's hide and just as quickly soothe it . . . and whose body could make him vow he'd swallow nails if he could have her.

He didn't need any distractions.

And if he kept telling himself that, he might just forget her.

Chapter Seven

"This is the end, I tell ye," Aunt Aggie claimed in a gasping voice. "M' final sunrise. I'm goin' fast to meet me Maker."

Sighing inwardly, Sheridan clasped her aunt's hand—the one that wasn't clutched to her heart—and prayed for strength.

For two long weeks, Sheridan and her aunt had waited to discover Uncle Finny's fate. During that time, Aunt Aggie had been on the verge of passing on to the great beyond more times than Sheridan could ever recall.

Now, as they stood in the bleak courtroom awaiting the verdict, her aunt's histrionics were finally beginning to wear Sheridan down.

Yet she knew her aunt's endless love affair with death was not the only reason she felt out of sorts. Night after night, she had tossed fitfully and dreamed of her dark angel.

She had returned to the inn only once since she'd left in the predawn hours, and that singular visit had been horrible.

Fearful of being tossed bodily out the door, yet refusing to show that fear, she had pressed her shoulders back, held her head high, and breezed into the inn as if she owned the place.

"You!" the proprietor spat, heaving his bulk around the edge of the bar, a rolling pin clutched in his meaty grasp. He thumped toward her, his eyes narrowed to black dots.

"Don't ye dare touch me!"

"Get out!"

Sheridan took two steps back so that she stood outside the front door. "I'm out—and I didn't want to come inside in the first place. I only wanted to ..." *Inquire about the sweet stranger who stole my heart as soon as I looked into his green eyes.*

"I know what you came for, you dockside tart!" he snarled. "Did your lover leave without paying you?"

For a moment, his words didn't register. When they did, shame flushed Sheridan's cheeks. "Ye're a vile creature."

He snorted. "As if I care what you think, trash. Now get out of here. If I see you again, you'll be sharing a dank cell with your rummy uncle."

Heavyhearted, Sheridan left without learning anything about the man with whom she'd shared such passion-filled hours. She ached, knowing she might never see him again.

"Och now, here they come." Her aunt's tremulous voice brought Sheridan back to the present. "Oh, the cup of Ireland's misery is surely overflowin' today."

" 'Twill be all right, Aunt. Certainly they'll let Uncle Finny go." But Sheridan didn't feel as hopeful as she sounded. Her uncle had a number of strikes against him.

He was Irish, unrepentant, and meaner than a prodded bag of snakes without the mellowing aspects of alcohol. As well, since his incarceration, he had not been a model prisoner.

The two dour-faced brutes who had hauled her uncle to the gaol stood at the bench with the judge, speaking in low tones. Sheridan strained to hear what they were saying, catching only a few words.

Shanty bastard.

Guilty.

Beating.

The first word made her temper soar. The next two lanced her heart.

There would be no fair trial for Finnegan Delaney.

In came the prisoner, shackled like a murderer. Tears formed in Sheridan's eyes at her uncle's haggard appearance. His cheeks were hollow, his eyes sunken, his usually ruddy complexion ashen. Sweet Saint Catherine, what had they done to him?

"Finnegan Delaney," the judge intoned, the tenor of those two words already boding ill for her uncle, "you have been charged with the crime of molestation and thievery. What say you about these charges?"

Please, Uncle, Sheridan silently beseeched, *behave just this once.*

Yet she knew her prayers were futile before her uncle spoke. Drunk or sober, sane or insane, her uncle bowed to neither man nor beast.

Leveling an insolent gaze at the judge, he replied, "May all the birds flock together an' leave their callin' cards upon yer blighted head."

Bang! The gavel cracked like a bolt of lightning signaling the end of mankind.

"Oh, Uncle," Sheridan murmured in despair while her

aunt babbled about seeing a white light and her dead mother at the end of a tunnel.

The judge, his face a mask of rage, pointed the gavel at her uncle. "One year in the gaol or five hundred pounds. This is my verdict."

Bang!

"I simply don't know where she could be."

Nicholas glanced at his cousin's worried visage as he stood at his mirror trying to tie his cravat. Loop, over, under, around, he repeated like a litany, yet the bloody piece of material continued to best him. His sour mood had been escalating for two long weeks.

Ever since that night.

Two souls entwined. Like hell.

Whose soul was the girl entwined with tonight? Nicholas wondered, and then asked himself for the nine hundredth time why it mattered. It wasn't as if she were the only beautiful, vibrant, exciting, captivating woman around—even if she might be the only one with an emasculating uppercut.

Nevertheless, London abounded with women and, he thought with a satyr's grin, he had always enjoyed a certain degree of popularity among the fairer sex. He was a Sinclair, after all. Besides, it wasn't as if he was a wart-nosed old man and couldn't have his pick.

Right?

Nicholas peered closer at his image. Was that a gray hair? Certainly he was too young to be graying. He studied the offending strand and discovered it was just a spot of that ridiculous powder Emery liked to sprinkle on his balding pate, claiming it had thickening properties.

Every time the man sneezed, white particles like fairy dust sprayed through the air, clinging like tenacious little bastards wherever they landed—normally on Nicholas's pristine black jacket or his newly shined shoes.

Really. What was the matter with him? He wasn't losing his sex appeal. It was a ridiculous notion, just like thinking that little crease around his left eye was a wrinkle. It wasn't, of course.

Certain something itched his stomach, Nicholas pulled his shirt from his waistband and scrutinized his torso. Nope. No itch. No redness. No flab. Still taut. Well-muscled. He turned to his side to check that angle.

"What are you doing?"

Nicholas's gaze snapped back to the mirror to see Jules staring at him, her eyebrow raised questioningly. Hell and damnation, caught in the act of stupidity. "Huh? Oh. Something was scratching me."

Hurriedly, he tucked his shirt in and resumed trying to tie his blasted cravat, avoiding his cousin's curious regard. A dim recollection streaked through his brain that she had been telling him something. Since he hadn't the foggiest notion what it was, he decided a nod and a smile were the best course of action.

However, his thoughts quickly filtered back to their original path, beginning with his plans for that evening. He would escort Lady Jessica to the theatre. He'd seen her three times this week, and things were progressing quite well. He had worked hard to get her father to see him as an acceptable suitor, considering the fact that Nicholas was untitled.

And a Sinclair.

To Nicholas, being a Sinclair was a great gift. He had two older brothers who were his best friends. They had sheltered him from an uncaring mother and a father who fell further into despair with each passing year, eventually dying a broken man.

Damien and Gray were the reasons Nicholas had a

happy childhood—although to their faces he would declare them blighted pains in the posterior, to which they would reply that they had wanted a dog instead of a baby brother. Translated, it meant they loved one another without the gushy sentiment.

However, to other people, being a Sinclair meant husbands should hide their wives, fathers guard their daughters, and people remove themselves from the vicinity if a brawl broke out—they wouldn't be responsible for injuries sustained by innocent bystanders.

Nevertheless, Nicholas had managed to work his way around his reputation with Lord Harrington, Jessica's father. Their mutual love of horses had eventually built a bridge, allowing Nicholas to court Jessica.

Nicholas suspected the viscount had designs on not only a possible union between Nicholas and his daughter, of which the man had four, but a union between one of the viscount's mares and one of Nicholas's pure-blooded studs, which suited him well enough. Once they were family, such a union would benefit him.

"Are you listening to me?"

Nicholas discovered his cousin frowning at him. Good Christ, he had stepped into it again. What had she been saying? He searched his mind for the thread of conversation, then took in concerned visage and figured he could probably make a fairly accurate guess.

"Of course, I am. You were telling me about your missing friend." What was her name? Something Gilhooly. All he needed were more females hovering about to grate on a man's nerves.

"I'm worried. She should have been here by now."

Saved from female pique, Nicholas resumed fussing with his cravat. "You know these ships are rarely on time, puss, what with the usual congestion and jockeying for quay space." He finally managed to get his cravat in some semblance of order. Turning, he asked, "How do I look?"

Jules spared him a brief glance. "The same."

Nothing like a female to prick a man's pride. "Well, that's saying a lot," he muttered, reaching past her to swipe up his jacket.

With a push, she hauled herself to her feet. "I'm sorry. It's just that I'm worried about Sheridan. She's never been to England before, and my mind has grown fertile with pictures of various catastrophes."

"Fertility is clearly something you excel at." Nicholas smiled and patted her swollen stomach.

"Cad." She stuck her tongue out at him.

He chuckled softly. "Save that expression for William. I'm sure his response will differ greatly from mine."

The reminder of her husband made her smile turn wistful. "If he ever forgives me for coming to London without him."

Nicholas struggled to keep from informing his hard-headed cousin that in his office at that very moment were at least twenty missives from her equally hardheaded husband.

Nicholas had received one every day since Jules arrived—all of them asking, in different ways, how his wife was faring. Did she miss him? Was she eating well? Sleeping enough? And, inevitably, wrapping up the letter by asking yet again if she missed him.

Nicholas had been so busy replying to William's correspondence that he was barely getting any work done, and this was foaling season. As well, his colt, Grayfriar, would be put to stud for the first time in less than a month.

Ah, what a fine animal—clean lines, regal bearing—just like his sire, Narcissus, aptly named because the black loved to prance and gaze at his reflection in puddles.

Gently, Nicholas clasped his cousin's hands. "William

adores you, my girl. Who wouldn't, after all? Give it another week and he'll be pounding down my door, ready to sweep you off your feet—or attempting to sweep you off your feet, at least." He glanced pointedly at her stomach, which earned him a gentle slap and a smile. "Now, about your friend, Suzanne—"

Jules poked him in the chest. "It's Sheridan."

"Yes. Well, I'm sure everything is all right with Sharon and she'll arrive before you can say John the Baptist. You know these Yanks get easily confused, don't know a bum from a backside. As we speak, she's probably driving some poor, hapless man crazy."

A sweet peal of laughter poured from his cousin's lips. She gave him a look that said she had a secret she was dying to tell—but not to him. "That, dear hapless cousin, was never in question."

"Five hundred pounds!" Aunt Aggie wailed, pulling her flask from her skirt pocket. "We barely have *five* pounds to our name!"

Sheridan grabbed her aunt's wrist before she tipped the bottle to her lips. "If ye're not wantin' to be sittin' next to Uncle Finny," she said in a hushed voice, "then I would put that away. As ye can plainly see, we're surrounded by the law." And Sheridan didn't doubt for a moment the constables were looking for a reason to toss all of them in the gaol and rid themselves of the Irish menace.

Taking her aunt in a gentle but unyielding grip, Sheridan left the small, dank building. Out on the bustling street, she looked about and wondered why trouble dogged her like an unwanted shadow.

"Give yer old auntie back her medicine, lass."

Sheridan glanced down to find she still held her aunt's

flask. How tempted she was to pour out the contents, toss the container in the gutter, and jump up and down on it.

She contemplated doing that very thing when a sharp tug on her arm swung her around. She gasped, coming face to face with a grimy lad trying to rip her small pouch off her wrist. The pouch contained the few pounds they had left, and she would not relinquish it without a fight.

"Leave it be, ye spineless little squint!" She smashed her boot down on his foot. He yowled and cursed foully but did not release his grip on her purse.

Sheridan nearly wrested her purse from the thief's mean little grip when the cord securing it around her wrist snapped. She stumbled back, her fingers loosening for only a moment, but that was all it took. Her attacker sprinted off, rapidly disappearing into the crowd.

"Our money!" her aunt cried. "He's gettin' away!"

Sheridan didn't think twice. Hoisting her skirts, she took off after the bandit. No one stole from a Delaney and lived to breathe another day!

She could barely see the lad's dark head as he wove deftly through the throng of people tending to their marketing.

Bedevil her skirts for hampering her! The material kept wrapping around her legs, slowing her up. Had it not been for her small size, she would have lost the boy by now.

She ran on. He was only five feet ahead of her! Four feet! Two feet! She lunged for him.

And crashed right into a fruit stand.

Chapter Eight

Three . . . four . . . five . . .

"Oh, for the love of God!" Nicholas muttered when the doorbell went unanswered. Bloody Emery must be asleep again. Bellowing down the hallway would do no good. Unless his butler had his horn to his ear, it would be like shouting for help in the eye of a storm.

Nicholas tossed his cravat to the side. He had just arrived home from a night at the theatre with Jessica, still surprised by the maidenly kiss she'd given him. A first, and definitely a step forward.

Yet . . . there was something missing. Nothing had sparked to life inside him at the press of her lips against his, not a glimmer of a possibility or a tickle of one. He'd felt nothing.

But certainly that would change over time. When Jessica came to him on their wedding night, her innocence would incite his senses and test the boundaries of his control.

He'd want to possess her, wholly, passionately, to ease between her thighs and know he was the only one, to stare into those violet eyes and see the love shining clearly.

Violet eyes?

The realization of what he'd thought, of whom he had pictured beneath him, brought Nicholas up short. He shook off the image, concluding fatigue had him in its grip. The Irish lass was a distant, albeit pleasant, memory.

Really? So why have you been going to the docks every day?

To see Damien, of course.

Oh? Then why haven't you seen him yet? If you haven't figured it out by now, he is not the type to consort with the patrons of Puddlebys. Certainly that's been the reason you've gone into that particular establishment at least a half dozen times now, isn't it?

I think I lost something in there, smart ass.

You did. Your mind.

The bell chimed again, rasping against Nicholas's already frayed nerves.

"I'm coming, God damn it!"

Passing the open door of his cousin's bedroom, he paused. Jules lay curled on her side, sleeping. She napped quite a bit, the babe making it harder for her to keep the active lifestyle she enjoyed.

As much as he might silently grouse, Nicholas felt a sense of contentment having her around. For a short while, he could be her protector again.

Or she could be his.

Smiling, Nicholas continued on, taking every other stair on his way down to the foyer. He quirked a brow as he passed a snoring Emery asleep in his favorite chair. "Having a nice nap, are we?"

Emery gave a half snort, half wheeze and smacked his lips as if dreaming fondly about the pheasant they'd eaten for dinner.

With more force than he intended, Nicholas swung open the front door and stared at the woman framed on the threshold eyeing him as if he were a fresh cut of meat from a prime corn-fed bovine.

"Yes?" he drawled in a less than friendly manner. "May I help you?"

"My, but ar-ren't ye the comely one."

The accent, although far harsher, rang familiar, considering he had been hearing it in his head for over a fortnight, making him a perfect candidate for Bedlam.

"Excuse me?"

"I said ye ar-re a bonny lad. Ye fair take me breath away." She shrugged. "Or it could be all those hidious steps I had to climb. 'Tis not a young woman I am, if ye hadn't noticed."

He'd noticed.

Nicholas glanced outside. He counted four *hidious* steps. Quite a climb.

The woman held a scrap of paper in front of her face and squinted. "Is this . . ." She rattled off the address written down.

"You have the right place, but—"

"Thank the merciful heavens!" She swiveled her stout hips over the doorsill and into his house uninvited, something swishing in the pocket of her skirt as she breezed past him.

"Now look here," Nicholas began, but she paid him no mind. Instead she eyed the floor, the walls, the furniture—the *valuables*—before deigning to cast him a look over her shoulder.

"I'll be speakin' to the master of this house, if ye don't mind, thank ye. Now if ye'll scoot off to get him. An' while ye're at it, me brawny boy, ye can get me a wee drop of somethin' to warm the cockles of me heart. 'Tis cold out tonight, and I've walked a long way.''

His hand poised on the knob, Nicholas leaned against the edge of the door. "And may I tell the master who is calling for him at such a late hour?''

She narrowed her eyes at him. "Bein' sassy, are we? Well, 'tis to be expected. Can't get good help these days. Although''—her gaze once again raked his form—"good or not, I'd keep ye. Ye are as rugged a piece o' work as ever I saw.'' She sidled up next to him, her massive bosom coming within two inches of his chest.

Visions of being smothered assailed him. Nicholas shivered.

"Troth, but I think ye could warm the cockles of me heart much better than a drink, and 'tis a fact I'd be likin' it more.'' She smiled, showing him a lovely gap where a tooth should be while the rest of her teeth looked as if they'd been jammed into her gums.

The woman was something else. Blunt and brassy . . . just like another female Nicholas knew, one who'd left a permanent imprint of her hand on his face.

And her image in his mind.

Reluctantly, Nicholas smiled. "Thank you for asking, but I don't think it would warm the cockles of *my* heart.''

She heaved a hearty sigh, her bosom expanding to dangerous proportions. " 'Tis a sad lot for a woman of me lusty nature to be left alone.'' She extracted something from her skirt and Nicholas discovered what had been swishing. A flask.

Seeing it reminded him of a woman with a similar flask. Reminded him of her hair, her eyes, those lips. Reminded him of the feel of her pressed against him.

Reminded him he'd awakened in an empty bed.

Damn.

The woman thrust the flask in his face. "For the likes of ye, I would share me special medicine."

Her *medicine* smelled one hundred and fifty proof, and a single whiff nearly knocked Nicholas out—just like another liquor had done to him.

Double damn.

He put a hand in front of his face to ward the woman off. "How gracious of you to offer, but I'll have to decline. I have my own medicine, and something tells me yours and mine won't mix. Now or ever."

"Suit yerself." She slapped the metal container to her lips and took a swig that would lay a horse out on its back. Screwing the cap back on, she returned her medicine into the black gulch whence it came. "Well?"

"Well?"

She rolled her eyes. "Bonny ye are, but not much rummagin' around between the ears now, is there?"

Nicholas was too amused to take offense.

"There's no time to be prattlin'. I need to see the master of the house—and I need a chair. Pull that fancy one over for me weary bones to rest upon." She pointed to a chair only five feet from her.

Nicholas wasn't sure why he didn't put an end to the lunacy instead of pulling the chair over.

She plunked down and flapped eyelashes that looked like bat wings at him. His stomach heaved and dipped.

"May I relay a message to the master?" he asked in his most subservient tone. This should be interesting.

"Aye. Tell him the puir girl is sittin' in the gaol. 'Tis not a place for a female to be—not when the men have that look in their beady eyes, if ye ken my meanin'."

A creeping suspicion settled in the pit of Nicholas's stomach. "What girl? And what look?"

The woman sighed heartily, as if what she spoke of should be patently obvious. "Sheridan Delaney's the name, and the look is the kind a man gets when his mouth is sayin' 'good-bye' but his trousers is sayin' 'hello.' ''

Nicholas blinked. ''Are you trying to tell me Sheridan Delaney . . . is in jail?''

'' 'Tis a long time ye have in the uptake, me boy. Now, ye must wake yer master and save the lass from the likes of them spalpeens.''

Nicholas pressed his thumb and forefinger to the bridge of his nose to stave off the headache he knew was coming. It was going to be a long night.

The bloody girl was behind bars. Not an auspicious way to begin her visit. Nicholas was starting to understand his cousin's looks and giggles in reference to the elusive Sheridan Delaney.

He glanced up the stairs, thinking about Jules, knowing she'd want to hear about the fix her friend found herself in. He didn't have the heart to wake her, nor did he want her worrying. He could run to the jail and secure the girl's release before his cousin was the wiser.

Nicholas sighed, resigned to his fate. ''Where is she?''

''Southwark.''

Good Lord, what was the chit doing in Southwark? The place was overrun with criminals. Even the law was on the take. A person could get shivved in the back, drop dead in the middle of the street, and people would step over the body.

Nicholas moved to the chair Emery slept in and shook him awake. It took a few moments for his butler to focus and blink up at Nicholas with eyes magnified fifteen times through the thick rims of his spectacles.

''Yes, sir?'' he croaked, and then cleared an abundance of phlegm from his throat.

''I have to go to Southwark, Emery.''

''You're going to the park, sir?'' A puzzled frown

pulled his woolly gray eyebrows together. "Isn't it too late?"

"I'm going to Southwark, not the park."

"You won't be back before dark?"

"Southwark, man!" Nicholas scanned the area for Emery's horn. As usual, the blasted contraption was nowhere to be found. Taking a deep breath, he leaned close to Emery's ear and enunciated every word. "I will return shortly. Please take . . ." He glanced at the woman he assumed was Sheridan Delaney's maid. The girl must have poor eyesight to have picked this one. "What's your name?"

"Aggie. But ye can call me sweet lips if ye like." She winked.

Not if his life depended on it. "Emery, please show *Aggie* to the servants' quarters."

"Here now!" she huffed. "I ain't no servant. 'Tis a guest I am."

Nicholas was not in the mood to argue. "Beg pardon." Then he said to Emery, "Take Miss Aggie to the guest quarters. And do not say anything to Lady Thornton should she awaken. I don't want her knowing her friend is in trouble."

"On the double? Yes, sir!"

"No, I didn't . . . Oh, the hell with it."

Nicholas arrived at the building meant to pass as the lockup for the Borough of Southwark, with its dank walls, dank air, and dank people. He could imagine the fear rattling through Jules's friend, Sally . . . or was it Sydney? Whatever. It really didn't matter. It wasn't as if he'd be using it. A generic "miss" would suffice.

He chuckled as he thought of the prim and proper graduate of the Bainbridge Academy, accustomed to tea parties and shopping for fripperies, caged like a common thug.

He pictured her adorned in some frou-frou outfit on a hard cot fearing the moment someone would speak to her, a giggling blond with fluff for brains. How else could she have gotten into such a predicament?

Nicholas stalked to a wide desk sitting atop a tall base, requiring the person standing in front of it—him—to cock his head back to glare at the person sitting behind it—currently, a myopic moron with a bulbous nose.

Clearly, the lofty pedestal was another tactic meant to intimidate the general public and extend the long arm of the law.

The man behind the desk didn't even glance up, which annoyed Nicholas. Therefore, the first order of business was to irk the man in return.

Mimicking his butler, Nicholas cleared his throat loud enough to wake the dead, rattling mucus the way Damien had taught him long ago when they had contests to see who could spit the furthest.

That did the trick.

"May I help you?" the man inquired in a tone that clearly communicated, *May I hit you?*

"I'm here to retrieve a Miss Sheridan Delaney from your gracious establishment."

"Take a seat," he mumbled, returning his attention to something on his desk. "I'll be with you when I'm finished."

Nicholas sniffed the air. "Ah, yes, you must get back to that all-important ham sandwich." He made a face. "Domestic ham at that, topped off with a wedge of overly ripened cheese." He shook his head. "Pyrosis in the making." A rather frightening term for an ailment physicians referred to as heartburn.

The man squinted one eye skeptically at him, probably

wondering if he should be concerned. Then he har-rumphed, obviously concluding pyrosis, whatever it might be, was the last thing he need worry about dying from with so many felons looking for an opportunity to slip some ground glass between two slices of bread and serve it with an arsenic cocktail.

Once more, Nicholas found himself ignored, which only increased his desire to irritate the clod.

He gestured to his surroundings. "What do you call the shade of gray on the walls? Kiss of death?"

Focusing that same skeptical look on Nicholas, the man muttered, "A comedian, I see," and continued to shuffle through his papers even though he wasn't looking at them. "As if we don't get enough of *those* in here."

In that moment, Nicholas made a startling observation. Awash in the dim light that cast a pall over everything it touched, the man could pass for a bald Pontius Pilate. If he washed his hands, he'd be a dead ringer.

At last, Pontius quit shuffling, held up one of his papers, and peered at Nicholas with obvious dislike. "Yeah, we got a Sheridan Delaney. Who are you?"

"Is that really pertinent, or just your insatiable curiosity asking?"

The constable shook his head in slow lawman fashion. "And here I thought the girl was a pip. You two deserve one another."

Nicholas sincerely doubted it. "What has she done?"

"Destroyed a fruit stand."

"And how does one destroy a fruit stand? Take a machete to it?"

"One runs into it, is what one does."

Nicholas would have been amused by the man's first, albeit meager, attempt at drollery if the information he imparted hadn't been so intriguing.

The girl ran into a fruit stand? How the hell did she do that? Trip over her kid slippers?

This only confirmed his early suspicion that Jules's friend was a nit. Someone should write a letter to the Bainbridge Academy and inquire if the curriculum included destruction instead of deportment.

"How much to get her out?"

"One hundred pounds."

"What? You're insane. All the fruit in London wouldn't cost that much."

Pontius shrugged. "I don't make the rules. I just enforce 'em."

"I shiver to think what might happen if you did make the rules," Nicholas grumbled in disgust. "What else?"

"Well, there's also a fine for disturbing the peace."

This was really too much. "To what peace are you referring?" His sarcasm garnered him no reply. "How much?"

"Fifteen pounds."

Muttering, Nicholas drove a hand into his pocket and retrieved his money clip. Peeling off the required amount, he slapped it down on top of the desk.

"That ain't the whole of it." A bucktoothed grin split Pontius's face and Nicholas wondered how the man's head would look on top of a pike. "Twenty-five pounds for resisting arrest."

"Resisting—" Four-letter words choked in his throat. "Anything else?" he ground out.

"Just a ten-pound processing fee."

Insane laughter welled up inside of Nicholas, but went unvented. "And what, pray tell, does the processing fee consist of?"

"It consists of me telling you all the fines."

Nicholas's hand shook with the desire to yank the man's spine out through his throat, but he was in no mood to find himself sequestered in the same jail cell with Jules's fruit-destroying friend. He might just wring her scrawny Boston neck.

With complete ill grace, Nicholas handed over the remaining money.

"Nice doin' business with you."

"Go peddle your cheese," Nicholas grumbled, walking toward the front door to cool his ire before confronting the chit.

The man called to his counterpart, "Bring out the wild-cat, Jake."

Nicholas frowned. Wildcat? What did the man mean by that?

He had little time to ponder that question before a female voice raised in anger echoed down the corridor, spewing words he couldn't understand, but were amusing in their ferocity.

"Here you go, and good riddance."

"I'll give ye good riddance, ye fatheaded louse!"

Nicholas froze in place. That voice. That accent. It couldn't be.

With leaden feet, he rotated on his heels. Stunning violet eyes clashed with his, sending his heart racing, only to harden a moment later as he remembered the craving this girl had filled him with and the empty bed he'd found come morning.

"Hello, Danny."

Chapter Nine

Sheridan's heart lodged in her throat as she came face to face with her dark angel. She had begun to believe she had conjured him up, creating an image in her mind spun together with the threads of her hopes and dreams. But here he was, tall, handsome, and marvelously real.

While marking time in the gloomy confines of her cell, refusing to allow the menacing guard outside her door or the scurrying rodents inside to scare her, this man's face had sustained her strength. She had prayed he would save her.

And he had.

Sheridan didn't stop to wonder how he had found her. Their destinies were interwoven. How she knew it to be so, she couldn't say.

Perhaps the awareness stemmed from the powers of the druid blood running through her veins, the ancient lure and legend of the special breed of people from whom she descended, the belief that once every lifetime forces merged, drawing soul mates together, creating a bond so pure, so completely blessed that nothing could tear it asunder.

Smiling, Sheridan stepped toward him. Unsmiling, he stepped away. The action rocked her back on her heels. She gazed into those eyes that had haunted her dreams, and the look reflected in them cut her like razor-edged glass.

He was angry. No, furious. Why?

Could it have something to do with the fines he'd had to pay and the lateness of the hour? Certainly that could test any man's patience. Yet his anger seemed directed at her alone.

"It seems ye've come to me rescue again."

Self-mockery shone in his eyes. "And here they say no good deed goes unpunished."

The barb struck her cleanly and deeply. She wanted to ask him what was wrong, but not here, not with all eyes upon them.

Swallowing the pain, she moved toward him. A flicker of something warm flashed in his eyes, but ice quickly replaced it, making his gaze as cold as a bog hole on a frosty night. Sheridan trembled, but did not stop walking until she stood directly in front of him.

He studied her face, his gaze sweeping over her hair, her eyes, her nose, and stopping at her mouth. Unconsciously, she licked her lips.

"Ever the seductress, I see." A muscle worked in his jaw. "When I'm finished with my business here, I'd be more than willing to oblige you." He leaned forward, his voice dropping to a husky grumble. "You left me hungry for more, my dear. It seems I have an ache only you can assuage."

His callous words fell like a lash across her back even as his nearness made her weak with need.

Sheridan lifted her hand to slap him. Like a viper, his fingers coiled about her wrist. "You got away with that once," he growled. "It's an experience I don't wish to repeat."

He pushed past her then, his angry stride carrying him to the officer at the desk. "This is not the girl I came for."

His words rang in her ears.

This is not the girl I came for.

What did he mean? He had not come to save her, to take her out of this wretched place and into the light? His presence and hers were merely . . . coincidence? The coldness in his eyes told its own story.

With sudden, painful clarity, the grim truth struck Sheridan. Her dark angel was sober, and she had been nothing more than a night of pleasure. What an utter fool she had been to believe her fanciful daydream.

Did your lover leave without paying you?

Tart.

Whore.

"Whaddya mean that's not the girl?" the officer snapped. "You asked for Sheridan Delaney, didn't you?"

"I did."

The man pointed. "Well, that's her."

A thousand thoughts tumbled through Nicholas's head, the least of which was the fact that, if the smug bastard was correct, he had made love to his cousin's best friend.

And heaven help him, he wanted to do so again.

Danny. Short for Sheridan.

He swung around on his heel to face her.

She was gone.

* * *

Sheridan ran down the dark street, heedless of where she was going. She only knew she had to escape, flee from the memories. Flee from the truth.

Tears streamed down her face, and she cursed herself for the weakness that made her shed even one tear for the emerald-eyed sassenach—for believing he was *the one*.

Her breath rasped through her lungs, her limbs weak from lack of sustenance, her heart heavy with foolish dreams. She ached for her mother and longed for forgetfulness.

A vision of poor Uncle Finny still locked away made Sheridan stop her aimless flight. She couldn't leave him, couldn't allow the pain throbbing inside her to make her forget about her loved ones. Her family. People who needed her.

Who cared for her.

She had to find her way to Jules's home. Her friend would know what to do. That's why Sheridan had sent Aunt Aggie to fetch her.

Sheridan realized how stupid she'd been to believe she could fix the problem on her own, but she hadn't wanted to show up on her friend's doorstep with burdens. In the end, she had failed—in so many ways.

Now she had no other choice.

One candle, burned down almost to the nub, glowed in the foyer as Nicholas ranged the parquet floor. Only the sound of his booted feet clicking restlessly back and forth disturbed the dismal silence.

Damn, he'd had the girl in his grasp, but like an Irish mist, she had eluded him again.

The knowledge burned his gut.

The mysterious Sheridan Delaney. What were the chances they would meet in such an improbable fashion not once, but twice?

Two souls entwined.

How he was growing to hate those three words.

He kicked a chair and sent it spinning on its side across the recently waxed floor.

Damn, he'd been duped. Why hadn't Jules fessed up that her friend was Irish? Why had she let him believe he dealt with some Boston socialite?

It wasn't that he cared if the chit was Irish and not a socialite. Those things didn't matter to him. What galled him was that he'd been taken off guard, hoisted with his own petard, so to speak, and he hated the feeling.

Now Nicholas truly understood his cousin's cloaked remarks and sly smiles. Married or not, Jules was still a minx.

What was he going to tell her when she awoke? That her friend was now amongst the missing because he had lost control of his emotions? And without a doubt, he had some very strong emotions regarding Sheridan Delaney.

Perhaps that explained his anger when he'd seen her. Innocent, angelic, disheveled. Magnificent. His joy at having found her eclipsed rational thought.

Yet the joy twisted into rage when Nicholas remembered she'd run off with another man before her spot on the bed had grown cold.

Could he have given her reason to run away? He remembered the drops of blood on the sheet. Perhaps he had hurt her, been rough. That would explain her flight. He'd been drunk, after all, and couldn't remember anything after she had lain down next to him on the bed. He could have lost control.

Rape.

No, damn it! He couldn't believe himself capable of forcing himself on a woman. People might think him a first-class reprobate, and he hadn't done anything to dissuade them, but he was a deuced phony, attempting to keep up with his brothers' scandals, yet doing so in word more often than in deed.

After all, hadn't Damien always said the three of them put the "sin" in "Sinclair"? The only solid thing in Nicholas's life were his brothers; his only comfort was knowing he was part of a whole.

Nevertheless, he had acted rash with the girl, his behavior uncharacteristic and disturbing. He hadn't allotted her a chance to speak. His irrational anger had overwhelmed him.

Now calmer, he recalled how she'd greeted him with a happy smile. Then again, he imagined anyone who had spent more than five minutes in a putrid cell in Southwark would be happy as hell to be released.

A noise outside halted Nicholas's pacing.

Extinguishing the candle, he eased behind the door and listened. He heard a low, muffled voice and the sound of someone shuffling about. A burglar was exactly what he needed at that moment. A good brawl might relieve his tension.

His hand poised on the doorknob just as he felt it wiggle, confirming the fact that whoever stood outside was up to no good.

Quietly, Nicholas slid the lock back, then wrenched the door open so fast the pictures on the walls rattled. He heard a startled gasp before a body tumbled into the foyer and fell rather ignobly onto the floor.

In the darkness, Nicholas lunged after the squirming

figure. He managed to snatch a handful of material and yanked. Buttons flew and the material ripped in his hands, followed by a female cry of alarm.

He immediately let go. Mistake. A small fist slugged him in the jaw and an equally small but powerfully determined foot slammed down on his toes. Then she made a dash for the door.

He grabbed the edge of her skirt, but she fought him like a wildcat, a knee driving into his gut, sharp nails scoring his chest.

A white beam from the hunter's moon overhead slanted through the door, and Nicholas saw the intruder intent on changing him from a stallion to a gelding.

Sheridan.

"You!" she gasped as if this was her house and he the trespasser.

Clearly she was not happy to see him; the elbow she rammed into his bruised ribs brought that point home conclusively.

Reflexively, Nicholas released her. She bolted across the threshold, but his arm whipped about her waist, hauling her back against his chest.

"Let me go!"

"Ssh," he breathed in her ear. "Stop fighting me. I'm not going to hurt you."

"Liar!"

She tried to get him in the knees, stomp on his toes again, aimed another elbow at his ribs. Quite amazingly, he remained unscathed.

"I promise I won't hurt you. Cross my heart and hope to . . ." Hmm. Perhaps in this instance it would not be wise to hope to die. The she-cat might willingly oblige.

She wriggled impotently within his embrace. "I'll not believe a spalpeen like ye! Ye're tongue could fertilize thirty acres!" Then she regaled him with words he didn't understand but which he imagined condemned him to a slow, painful death in the pits of Hades. "Let me go, I say!"

"Not until you relax."

God, it felt good to hold her again, even if she had sunk her sharp talons into his hide and apparently would give anything to pluck out his eyeballs and serve them with his heart.

"You always want to beat on me." He pulled her a little closer. The scent of hyacinths tickled his nostrils. "That's not nice, you know."

" 'Tis exactly what ye deserve, ye arrogant, no-good—"

"Preening rooster?" he supplied, smiling at the remembrance.

Those must have been magic words, because some of the fight left her. "Aye," she returned with her usual defiance. "The king cock."

Ah, the images such a remark produced. Nicholas pressed his cheek against the soft mass of her hair and desire swirled to life inside him. As much as he wanted to deny the passion he felt for the girl, his body would not allow him to forget.

"Let me go," she said again, but with less ferocity.

"In a moment." He should release her, but she fit so perfectly against him that it seemed criminal to yield to her demand—although he imagined she'd like nothing better than to see him slathered in honey and buried in an anthill. "Why did you run away?"

Mutiny lifted her delicate chin.

"Not speaking, are we?"

No response.

"I looked for you."

She snorted.

"For at least an hour."

Louder snort.

"Where did you go? And how did you find me?"

That got her. "As if I was lookin' for ye, ye arrogant, no-good—"

He held up his hand. "Let me guess. Preening rooster? We traveled down that road already."

She shot him a glare that could have frozen a hot spring. "Nay . . . *bastard!*"

Ouch. "Why do you persist in hurting my pride? It is so fragile, after all." Apparently, she was not in a humorous mood. He sighed and muttered, "Laugh and the whole world laughs with you. Cry and you cry alone."

"Ye make no sense."

"Excuse me if my wits are addled. I've been sorely abused tonight."

She muttered something about his wits being permanently scrambled and not to fool himself to the contrary. Clearly he was making headway.

Nicholas searched for the ire that had sustained him when he'd seen her at the jail and wondered why it deserted him now. The girl had a way of casting a spell over him unless he kept her at arm's length, and sometimes not even then.

Perhaps her fragrance bewitched him. Flowers battled to smell like her, to achieve that special blend of hyacinth and something else unique and elusive, a druid potion with the power to make him forget his name and turn him to stone—or certain parts of him, at least.

Chemistry appeared to have worked on her as well, because she no longer insisted he release her. For a moment, he couldn't help but wonder why fate kept throwing them together. This time, however, he realized it had not been fate, but his cousin.

"You came looking for Jules."

She deigned to glance his way, her tough veneer cracking for the briefest moment. She appeared utterly vulnerable and heartbreakingly beautiful. "Aye. Is she here?"

"She is."

Her relief was audible. "I must see her."

"You will. In the morning. Now you must deal with me."

He waited for a stinging retort, something to the effect that she'd rather pitch him headfirst into the Thames. Instead, she stared at him mutinously and folded her arms beneath her breasts, which, unfortunately, brought his gaze to the soft flesh revealed by her torn shirt. Obviously, she didn't know she was in such a lovely state of dishabille.

A gentleman would tell her.

Who said I'm a gentleman?

Don't be an ass.

Hell.

Without releasing his hold about her waist, Nicholas slid around to face her. Ever the mule, she refused to meet his gaze.

"You're trembling." Was she chilled, or was he affecting her? Certainly she had affected him.

Leisurely, his hands moved from her waist to capture the front of her shirt and pull it together.

"What are ye . . ." she began, and then noticed the condition of her attire. With lightning speed, she clutched her hands around the material and dragged it closed. "How dare ye!" she fumed, her eyes branding him a lecher.

"I was just—"

"Aye, ye were just tryin' to put yer rovin' fingers on me, and I'll not have it."

Silent laughter shook Nicholas. "Can you blame my roving fingers? When they see something they like, they have a mind of their own."

"Sure, and 'tis not their mind that should be worryin' ye. It should be pickin' the stumps off the ground when I'm through with ye."

The girl was a pistol.

"I'm sorry," he said. Sorry for himself. The lure of her beautiful body was a temptation Nicholas doubted even the most pious could resist. He checked his lip to make sure he wasn't drooling.

"Tch! Sorry. And I'm Saint Patrick."

"I don't believe Saint Patrick had—"

"Don't ye dare say it!"

"Red hair," he finished, suppressing a chuckle. "What did you think I was going to say?"

Nicholas was glad Sheridan wasn't partial to carrying weapons. Bleeding to death on one's doorstep was such an ignoble way to die.

His conscience prodded: *Give her your jacket.*

I'm not wearing one.

Well, then, give her your shirt.

Hmm. My shirt.

Every now and again his conscience came up with a good idea.

"What are ye doin'?"

"Giving you my shirt."

"I don't want it."

And Sheridan really didn't, not if it meant looking at him naked to the waist. She might hate him for his callous treatment, for taking the special gift of her virginity, but her traitorous body still responded to him.

She remembered the subtleties of his flesh, hard where she was soft, straight where she was rounded, the cool texture of his hair running through her fingertips, the heat of his body scorching her lips as she tasted his neck, his chest, those silky brown nipples that now peeked at her, taunting her, making her want to reach out and trace their velvety smoothness with a finger.

"Here," he said, his voice deep and alluring as the night. "Slip your arms in."

Sheridan hesitated, battling the need to throw the shirt in his face and the desire to wrap herself in it like a cocoon.

He came up behind her and she relented. The large shirt slipped easily over her shredded one, the soft material caressing her throat. A scent she remembered vividly coiled about her, triggering memories best forgotten.

With shaky fingers, she buttoned the shirt. Nicholas shifted in front of her, laying his hands over hers, sending sparks along her nerve endings.

His hands mesmerized her. They were so large compared to her baby-sized hands, so dark to her light coloring, so filled with strength . . . yet so eminently gentle.

Tension curled around her. Visions of his hands skimming her body, exploring, evocative, expert in pressure, featherlight when sweeping over a nipple, bolder when cupping her breast.

What was the matter with her? This man didn't care for her. She was nothing more than an object to warm his bed. How many countless others had come before her? How many had he enchanted with hungry gazes and sweet, whispered words? Why did she never learn from her mistakes?

And why did she still want him with a yearning that could not be dispelled?

The soul 'tis a wondrous thing to recognize what the eyes cannot.

Nay, this man was not her destiny. But he would be her downfall.

Sheridan turned away. "Tell Jules I'll come back in the mornin'."

He took hold of her arm. "Where are you going?"

She flicked a glance at the hand wrapped around her upper arm and then at his face. " 'Tis none of yer business, so I'll thank ye to let go of me."

He released her and slid his hands into his pockets. Yet he didn't need his hands to hold her captive. His gaze ensnared her, and her feet refused to move. Sheridan shook her head to defuse the strange spell he cast over her.

Taking a deep breath, she pivoted on her heel.

"Why don't you stay here?" His words halted her more effectively than his hand.

Stay here? With him? A tiny thrill shot through Sheridan, only to be squelched by reality. Was he asking because he hoped she would lay with him again? That she would let those drowsy green eyes seduce her, that silky smile entice her?

Never! She had pride, more than her fair share—with an excess of temper to match. Unfortunately she had a dearth of common sense. A volatile mix.

She also had a long memory, and the man standing in front of her, moonlight washing over his features, making him appear hewn from stone, had done things and said things she would not soon forget. He'd expressed his feelings for her quite clearly at the jail when he'd made his crude proposition.

She'd made a mistake. It was not her first, and although it was by far her worst, Sheridan doubted it would be her last. It was, however, one life lesson she wouldn't repeat.

As her mother always said, 'We Delaneys are survivors.' And Sheridan would survive, even if her heart was breaking.

She'd never let him know he'd hurt her.

"I can't stay."

"Why not?"

"Because I have other sleepin' arrangements."

His jaw hardened. "I'm sure you do," he said tightly. "But this is where you were meant to be."

Only a few short hours ago, Sheridan would have thought such a statement prophetic. Now the words were meaningless.

He added, "You came to see Jules, remember? Well, she is staying with me."

Sheridan's stomach twisted into a knot of foreboding. Until that moment, she hadn't connected the pieces, hadn't wondered how their paths had crossed twice in the same night, hadn't thought about the fact he had told her Jules was sleeping in his house. She hadn't even wondered about his identity. The last thought brought a cold clamminess to her palms.

Swallowing the lump in her throat, she asked, "And who are ye to Jules?"

"Ah, that's right. I know who you are, but you don't know who I am. We were rather busy, after all."

His meaning was reflected in his eyes, heating Sheridan's cheeks even as she tried to combat the dart of longing his words evoked.

"Allow me to correct that oversight," he murmured. Without warning, he took her hand in his and raised it to his lips. "Nicholas Sinclair, cousin to Jules, brother to Damien and Gray, and reckless fool to one Irish lass, at your service."

Chapter Ten

Of all the men in all the world, why oh why did it have to be this man who came to her rescue, this man whose smile had charmed her, this man who had asked for a kiss as his reward and had stolen her heart instead?

Nicholas Sinclair, her best friend's cousin, and her own dark angel.

His lingering, warm lips sent hot and cold chills skittering over Sheridan's flesh as he kissed the back of her hand. As she yanked her fingers from his grasp, he quirked an eyebrow at her telling action.

"There must be a mistake," Sheridan said in a shaky voice, wanting to refute the truth.

Her lapse in judgment had suddenly, irrevocably, been compounded. How could she look Jules in the eyes? Jules had always been perceptive. Sheridan could rarely hide anything from her friend. What would Jules think of her should she find out about Sheridan's actions with her cousin?

Oh, but she must never find out! Ever! Jules would surely hate her if she discovered the truth.

"What mistake?" he asked. "That I'm Nicholas Sinclair? Or that Jules is staying with me? I assure you, I speak the truth in both matters."

Sheridan turned away. "It can't be," she murmured, voicing her thought.

"What can't be?" He came up behind her. "Are you talking to yourself again?"

Sheridan closed her eyes. Why did he continue to prick her with memories of that night? And why did he have to stand so close? His nearness suffocated her, boxed her in, eroded her ability to reason.

She edged around him, careful not to make contact. "I can't stay here."

He folded his arms across his chest, looking incongruous standing next to one of a set of large topiaries flanking the door. "Running away again?"

"I'm not runnin' away," Sheridan denied, hating the small voice that said she was doing exactly that.

"No?" He paused, his lips thinning into a grim line. "Is there another stallion in the paddock awaiting your return, perhaps?"

Sheridan frowned, not understanding his meaning.

"Oh, come now, my dear. I've had enough of this mongoose and cobra act. Certainly you're not going to play the innocent with me. We both know the truth."

Nicholas wasn't sure what demon possessed him to want to dent the girl's armor, but his barb hit its target. She reeled as if he'd slapped her.

Damn if he didn't feel a twinge of regret. He'd never spoken so coarsely to a woman, but that sweet look of innocence on her face wore on his nerves, and the spirit reflected in those beautiful eyes and her ever defiant stance inflamed his senses.

He realized he wanted to hurt her—almost as much as he wanted to kiss her. And that cursed need grated on him like saltpeter in a wound.

Understanding sparked in her eyes, the temper she had once called fierce leaping to life like twin flames, her slim frame vibrating like a harnessed thunderstorm.

A smile suddenly lit her face, which should have given him fair warning. She dashed forward and plucked an object off the ground. Nicholas almost lost an ear when she hurled a weighty rock at his head.

And then another.

And another.

Each rock progressively larger than the last.

"Damn it, Danny!" he swore as a spiky plant whistled past his nose.

Clearly, it was time to take cover.

Nicholas ducked behind the topiary as a hunk of grass, dirt and all, smacked him in the back.

Peering at her from between the leaves, he said, "Why all the anger, my girl? If you're upset because I fell asleep on you at the inn, I promise it won't happen again."

Wrong thing to say.

If her eyes could have flung daggers, his body would have been covered with them.

"Why ye rotten, arrogant, bloated, *English* cod-monger!" She scrambled for something else to toss.

Well, what could he expect? He had thrown down the gauntlet, and she had picked it up and walloped him with it.

Seeing an opportunity for a rear attack with her back to him, Nicholas lunged for her, but she sidestepped at the last moment. He landed in a prickly green shrub, the branches scraping his naked chest.

His attacker muffled a snicker, but it quickly turned into gales of laughter at his bloody expense. Damn, but it was a beautiful sound.

Rolling over, he groaned. "You think this is funny, do you?"

She nodded, her smile infectious. "As I said before, 'tis not much of a fightin' man ye are."

Nicholas gritted his teeth. "When I put you over my knee and redden your luscious backside, we will see who's laughing then."

"You'd never catch me."

Like a whip, he reached out and snagged the hem of her skirt. "Oh no?"

That wiped the smile from her face. "Ye wouldn't dare."

"I would dare," he returned, his words leaving no doubt as to his sincerity.

The clearing of a throat interrupted their mutual glaring.

Sheridan swung around to see a reed-thin Chinese man standing in the open doorway, staring at her curiously. His hair was black as polished onyx, but slivers of moonlight painted it with streaks of silver.

He had his mane pulled back and plaited. When he shook his head, clearly amused by the goings-on, Sheridan could see a hint of a red ribbon securing the end of his long braid. Intelligence shone from his piercing, almond-shaped ebony eyes.

The jacket of his black silk outfit had a curved front flap fastening to the right with loop and toggle closures; wide sleeves ended with turned-back white inner facing His pants were loose and gathered at the bottom. On his feet, he wore brocade slippers of black with a hint of red shaped in the design of a dragon.

"Ah, Ho-Sing," Nicholas said. "As usual, you have arrived in time to witness my humiliation."

Ho-Sing nodded. "True, true. Very funny."

"Not if you're on the receiving end."

"What you do on ground, Boss-man?"

"I'm practicing the manly art of self-collapse."

Her antagonist's endearingly disgruntled tone brought Sheridan's gaze back to him. Nicholas wiped dirt from his arms and chest, making her wish she hadn't looked. He glanced up and caught her gaping. A slow half grin curved his full lips.

"Ah, to be in England now that war has broken out," he murmured, holding her gaze, clearly telling Sheridan that battle lines had been drawn and he intended to be the victor.

"Missy throw rock like she mean to kill you, Boss-man."

"That's because she did mean to kill me, Ho-Sing." Laughter danced in the hint of a dimple. "Missy have fierce temper."

Sheridan narrowed her eyes. How dare he make light of her anger! "Missy won't be missin' ye next time," she vowed.

Nicholas heaved an exaggerated sigh. "See what I mean, Ho-Sing? All I did was offer the girl a warm bed, and she clobbers me."

The little man chuckled. "Ho-Sing want to know which warm bed."

That changed her tormentor's tune. "If Ho-Sing doesn't want to eat only rice cakes for the rest of his life, Ho-Sing will refrain from comment."

"Ho-Sing filled with remorse." He bowed his head, but not before winking mischievously at Sheridan. She bit her lip to keep from smiling.

Nicholas looked skeptical. "Hmm. Somehow Boss-man doesn't think so, but I'm too beat up to argue."

Ho-Sing's head snapped up. "All fine and dandy now? Ho-Sing take Missy to room?"

Sheridan schooled her features and straightened her shoulders as her nemesis regarded her. She tried to dredge up the hate she should feel for him. But one thing she had refused to acknowledge earlier kept nagging at her, unwilling to be relegated to the back of her mind.

He had not been the sole cause of her hurt.

Sheridan knew she could not blame him entirely for her downfall. She had been a willing participant.

Nicholas gave her a hesitant smile. "I promise your room won't even be on the same side of the hallway as mine. I'll put you in the room next to Jules. Will that make you happy?"

No, Sheridan thought. She wouldn't be happy unless he stayed somewhere else. How could she possibly put him from her mind if she was forced to see him all the time? It wouldn't work. But what excuse would she give Jules for not staying?

Ho-Sing said, "I place patch-eyed man at end of hallway." He lowered his voice. "I think he smoke the loco root."

Ho-Sing's words captured Sheridan's attention. "Patch-eyed man?" It couldn't be.

Nicholas strolled toward her, his green eyes piercing and dark. Sheridan ordered her feet to stand firm. "Had you not clobbered me, I would have told you that your uncle is upstairs sound asleep."

"My uncle . . . is here?"

"Indeed he is. And let me say the man's quite a character. He reminds me of the west wind; he can't be kept out or kept quiet. On the ride, he regaled me with a story about the Cattle Raid of Cooley. He claimed he was—"

"Maeve, Queen of Connaught?"

Nicholas smiled. "Yes. He mentioned something about capturing a famous bull and someone named Cuchulain."

"That's Uncle Finny, all right."

"Interesting family you have," he murmured, a hint of amusement in his tone that Sheridan didn't appreciate.

"I don't understand. How did ye know me uncle was in the gaol?"

His eyes skimmed over her hair. Tenderly, he brushed wisps away from her face, pausing briefly to capture a few strands. Sheridan tried to ignore the warmth swirling in her stomach, and the jolt that sluiced through her when his gaze moved to her lips and then her eyes.

"After your hasty departure, I tried to find you." His voice rippled over her like warm honey.

Sheridan blinked, surprised to hear such a confession. "Ye did?"

He nodded. "When my search bore no fruit—no pun intended—I returned to the lockup to question the officer about you."

"Me?"

"Mmm-hmm." The sound vibrated along her nerves. "After some arm-twisting and thumbscrews, I found out about your uncle."

"But his fine—"

"Was quite hefty, and suspicion tells me it was also unwarranted. But I'll deal with that issue at a later date."

Sheridan shook her head. "I don't understand."

"What is there to understand?"

"Why would ye do such a thing?"

Nicholas opened his mouth to reply, but Ho-Sing answered for him. "Boss-man like Missy, that why."

Nicholas clenched his jaw and glared at his manservant, as Ho-Sing preferred to be called. Ho-Sing gave Nicholas one of his practiced *I-good-Oriental-man* smiles.

Ho-Sing, like Emery, had been an outcast. He'd worked

as a slop boy on a merchant ship and had been cruelly treated by the crew. Injustice had always rankled Nicholas, perhaps because he had been judged on his family's reputation and not his own, making him an outcast of sorts, as well.

Nicholas noticed Sheridan's flushed cheeks and the way she averted her gaze. If he didn't know better, he might think his nearness flustered her, and if bloody Ho-Sing would do him the favor of dropping off the face of the earth, Nicholas would have proceeded to test his theory.

Since that wasn't likely to happen, he held out his arm for her as if he weren't naked to the waist, dirty, scratched, and his pride bruised.

"Jules is anxious to see you, and it appears the rest of your entourage is safely tucked away in bed. So you see, you have no reason to leave—unless there is something else holding you back."

Nicholas studied her face, wondering if her reluctance had to do with a man. Maybe she had another rendezvous with the chap she'd deserted him for.

Or perhaps someone else waited for her. Many a man would sacrifice an organ to hold this girl in his arms, gaze down at that guileless face, and stare into those deceptively innocent eyes.

"I—I need me things."

Inwardly, Nicholas heaved a relieved sigh. Although Sheridan hadn't verbally relented, he knew he'd won, and the small victory was sweet.

"We can get them in the morning." Once more, he offered her his arm.

Once more, she ignored it.

She looked to Ho-Sing, as if asking him what she should do.

"Ho-Sing see to Missy personally. I let no harm come to you."

By the glint in his manservant's eyes, Nicholas knew exactly to what 'harm' Ho-Sing referred, the one that walked upright and paid his wages—and the one who was greatly tempted to put the man's little bamboo suitcase out on the curb.

Ho-Sing, reading Nicholas's mind, as the bloody man often did, snickered behind his hand and then held out his arm to Sheridan, who, to Nicholas's growing annoyance, took it without hesitation, leaving him standing at the bottom of the steps like a disgraced court jester.

He sighed, wondering about the explosion to come while he marveled at the sensual way Danny walked. She put her whole body into each step, creating a harmony of form that had a hypnotic effect. Nicholas felt like a dim-witted canine with his tongue dragging on the ground waiting for another kick as he followed on her heels.

"Here Missy room," Ho-Sing said, opening the door.

Nicholas stood back and watched. Sheridan hesitated on the threshold, gazing into the room. He could see only her profile, but it was an expressive one, a hint of a smile, a trace of color in her cheeks, her gaze touching here and there on the furnishings.

"This is . . . my room?" Disbelief echoed in her tone.

Nicholas stepped behind her. He sensed that underneath her tough-as-nails veneer was five kinds of passion just waiting for a trigger to set it off. He wanted to be that trigger.

"Is it all right?" he murmured.

She glanced at him over her shoulder, and for a moment, the anger dissipated from her eyes. " 'Tis lovely altogether. Thank ye."

"You're welcome."

Such little things made her happy. Nicholas's mind ruminated on other things she might enjoy—an odd concept, considering she had a tendency to assault him and had caused him a considerable amount of trouble. Yet something about her warmed him, soothed him. Eased the restless ache in him.

He gazed at her lips, so soft, so full. Lips meant to be kissed, often and vigorously. He wanted to explore their contour, savor their shape, renew their acquaintance, to know if her mouth tasted as sweet as it looked.

He bent toward her . . .

And bloody Ho-Sing cleared his throat.

"Very late, Boss-man. Missy need sleep so she can pummel you again tomorrow."

With a muted growl, Nicholas glared at the man, having to restrain himself from hammering Ho-Sing into the floor.

When Nicholas returned his gaze to Sheridan, the look in her eyes told him to step back or lose a limb. He wondered if perhaps she found him more charming when he was embalmed in bourbon, a thought that required further exploration at a later date.

Sighing inwardly, he trudged across the hallway. "If you need me, I'll be in here hiding from insanity." He opened the door to his bedroom.

"Ye said yer room was away from mine."

"No, I said your room wasn't on the same side of the hallway as mine. And as you can plainly see, it is not." Nicholas pointed to the closed door further down the corridor. "I also said I'd put you in the room next to Jules. Another promise kept."

Behind those glorious eyes, Nicholas could see she was planning his demise. He imagined only Ho-Sing's presence kept her claws retracted.

With a muffled screech, she spun on her heel, her hair flying out like a long red whip as she stormed into the room. The last thing he saw was her gloriously angry face promising retribution as her door closed with a contained click instead of feisty slam.

Shaking his head, Nicholas headed into his bedroom, knowing only one thing conclusively.

His time with Sheridan Delaney, of the fighting Delaneys, would not be a holiday on the sea of tranquility.

Chapter Eleven

"Eight a.m. and all is hell," Nicholas muttered as the shrill voice of his housekeeper raised in a cry of alarm pierced the early morning stillness and twanged a nerve in his spine. He jerked involuntarily, sending his papers shooting off his desk in all directions.

The most important document, the one that dealt with the transfer of an estate from his brother, Damien, the current earl of Blackstone, to him, floated in the air out of reach, and headed straight for the fireplace and certain destruction.

Nicholas lunged for it, his hand swiping through the flames as a corner of the paper started to sizzle—and his flesh along with it. He tossed the parchment to the floor and stomped on it while shaking away the pain in his hand.

"God bloody damn it!" he swore through clenched

teeth, wondering why he was not surprised that mayhem had already broken out even though the sun had barely crested the horizon.

Grimacing, Nicholas reached for the charred paper that now bore dirt from his Hessians. He imagined he should be thankful he had his boots on, otherwise the sole of his foot, along with his hand, would currently be throbbing.

Whatever the fracas outside his door, somehow it had the name Delaney written all over it. Ever since Danny had barreled into his life, Nicholas had been one big bruise.

He had begun to hope the shriek that had shot him from his chair like a cannonball had merely been a hallucination when the distinctive voice of his housekeeper rang out, *"We've been robbed!"*

"Ah, an ill wind that blows no good," Nicholas grumbled, pinching the bridge of his nose.

Tossing the scorched document onto his desk, he strode to the door, swung it open, and nearly collided with his housekeeper—Mrs. Dora Dimshingle, the terminally righteous.

She was a little sparrow of a woman who always clutched the top of her blouse as if expecting him to ravish her at any moment—which just might happen should he some day develop a craving for pigeon-chested females who had been swaddled in ashes and sackcloth.

It wouldn't have been so bad if he could call her Dora, but she had piously informed him when he hired her that she wished to keep their relationship on a strictly professional level.

Therefore, she preferred to be addressed as Mrs. Dimshingle. She had proven quite good at her job, so Nicholas couldn't complain, but that didn't mean he couldn't grimace.

"What's the matter Mrs. Dimshingle?"

"Oh, sir," she squawked like a hen who'd lost her eggs, "we've been the victims of a heinous act of thievery."

"Thievery?" Who would be foolish enough to break into his home? "What's been stolen?"

She fidgeted with the button at the top of her blouse. "Well, there is the candelabra from the dining room table and what was left of last night's roast duck."

Last night's roast duck? Nicholas frowned. Who the hell would want a half-eaten fowl? And what kind of thief would take an old pewter candelabra when there were other, more valuable items to filch?

Mrs. Dimshingle added, "And that portrait of your mother that she gave you last year that you stowed behind the sideboard and only took out when she came to visit is missing."

Now Nicholas was worried. Clearly the thief was demented to want the picture of his mother.

"Oh, and one of those old crossed swords in the study is gone, too." Another unlikely item of booty, but one whose disappearance hurt far worse than the other pilfered goods.

Nicholas noticed the distaste on his housekeeper's face at the mention of the sword. He knew she didn't like the various pieces of armament he had collected over the years. She said they reminded her of things better left dead and buried.

For Nicholas, the hauberk, battle shield, lances, and chain mail—claimed to have been worn during the time of King Arthur—brought back days of myth and legend, days when a lady gave her favorite knight a token to take into battle.

Days, he thought, glancing up the stairs and catching sight of Sheridan, *when a lady looked as this one did.*

He forgot about the half-eaten roast duck and candelabra. He even forgot his name as he watched Sheridan descend with regal aplomb.

Attired in a simple navy blue skirt and white blouse, Sheridan's understated beauty set her apart from other women who needed maids and hours of primping to look their best.

Her hair crackled with life. She left it loose and flowing, cascading over her shoulders and down her back like a river of fire.

Nicholas found his voice when she reached the bottom step. "Good morning," he murmured.

"Good mornin'," she returned, her head high, pride and defiance gleaming in her eyes.

She bore not a trace of fatigue from her incarceration. Another woman would have stayed abed for the remainder of the day, servants running ragged to do her bidding, smelling salts at the ready as she swooned at each and every remembrance of the horrid affair—if one could believe another woman could get herself into such a predicament, that is.

But Sheridan appeared as bright as a pence in water and as full of life as when she'd danced on the deck of the ship and riveted his attention, a memory that had yet to ebb.

She greeted his housekeeper. "Hello," she said courteously, introducing herself, since Nicholas had lost his tongue.

Mrs. Dimshingle sniffed. "How do you do."

Nicholas caught a hint of something he didn't like in his housekeeper's regard, a glimmer of disdain quickly hooded. He cast a sideways glance at Sheridan, whose face gave nothing away, but whose eyes gave everything away.

Ignoring their guest, Mrs. Dimshingle queried, "Should I call the constable about the *incident*, sir?"

"No," Nicholas replied more curtly than he intended. "That will be all."

Clearly affronted by his brusque manner, she nodded stiffly, twirled on her little bird feet, and marched away.

"She doesn't like me."

Nicholas's gaze swiveled to Sheridan, who stared straight ahead. He felt a twinge of hurt for her even as he recognized such cutting behavior could not be new to her. Yet, clearly, she wasn't immune to it. But how could anyone who possessed as much heart and soul as this girl did ever be immune to human suffering?

He had never paid much attention to the plight of the Irish, wrapped up as he was in his horses and problems closer to home, but he knew the cruelty his fellow man was capable of inflicting. Perhaps his innate sense of outrage over injustice had failed him on this account.

Yet on the other hand, he wondered if his feelings for Sheridan weren't born out of that same sense of injustice, a need to help the underdog, as he had with Emery and Nash and Ho-Sing, and, to some degree, even Mrs. Dimshingle.

No. This was different.

The answer came from somewhere, and he did not dispute it.

"Does it matter if she likes you?" he quietly asked.

He had thought to challenge Sheridan's assessment, tell her she imagined his housekeeper's scorn, yet he would be lying, and he knew she would see through him. He wanted her trust, and dishonesty was not the way to get it.

But why did he care if she trusted him or not? Why did he care about anything regarding this wild Irish lass? She'd run out on him, not the other way around. If anyone should be angry, it was he. Which made him curious. Why was she angry, anyway?

She peered at him with clear, sad eyes that allowed him a moment to glimpse inside her. Then she blinked. "What?"

Nicholas figured she hadn't meant him to hear her remark. She had been speaking to herself again. "I asked if it matters if the housekeeper likes you."

Her eyes shuttered. "It would make things easier, I suppose."

"Have things been that difficult?"

A slight frown marred her brow, as if she'd given away too much. " 'Tis nothing I can't handle on me own."

Nicholas studied her for a moment, wanting answers to the questions plaguing him, like why she had run off. A particularly ugly thought reared its head again.

Could he have hurt her when they'd made love?

Snippets came to him, glimpses of them together in unbridled passion. Dream or reality?

Either way, the desire he felt was entirely real.

He opened his mouth, but an excited shriek from the top of the stairs halted him.

"Sheridan!"

Sheridan's eyes widened, a jubilant gleam making them sparkle. "Jules?" She whipped around. "Jules!"

Hoisting her skirt above her ankles, Sheridan flew up the stairs and wrapped her arms around her friend, hugging her close, allowing the joy she'd put on hold for more than two weeks to pour forth.

Jules stepped back, her face glowing with the same happiness reflected on Sheridan's face. "Oh, Danny! It's so good to see you. How I've missed you!" Jules gave her another quick hug.

"I've missed ye as well."

"Where have you been? I've been worried sick!"

Sheridan nibbled the inside of her lip, wondering how much to reveal to her friend. Telling Jules the details of her delay meant inevitably imparting something about Nicholas's rescuing her, and that might lead to other things—things Sheridan was not prepared to discuss.

An odd way to think, considering she and Jules had shared everything at one time. Seeing her friend reminded Sheridan of the conversations they'd had about their families. Sheridan suddenly recalled a few tidbits Jules had imparted about Cousin Nicky, as she called him.

Jules had said he was a handsome devil—sensitive, sweet, and charming. To Sheridan's ears, he had sounded too good to be true, a character straight out of a fairy tale or a white knight from the days of yore.

But what stood out the most in Sheridan's mind was Jules's claim that her cousin had changeable eyes that shifted from jade to emerald and all shades in between.

Sheridan had assumed her friend waxed fanciful. Yet Jules hadn't exaggerated. Nicholas Sinclair did have shade-shifting green eyes, and an unequalled perfection of face and form—and his smile could charm the bark off trees.

Sweet and sensitive, however, was clearly Jules's love for her family speaking.

Sheridan cast a quick glance at Nicholas, trying to ignore how devastatingly handsome he was, the way the morning sun shining through the rectangular window in the vestibule streaked his hair with gold. His eyes glistened like gems, and the look he gave her made her heart skip a beat no matter how hard she tried to harden herself to its effect.

Returning her gaze to Jules, Sheridan smiled. "I'm sorry I worried ye. 'Tis a long story, and I want to hear about this first." She patted her friend's stomach, wondering if ever the day would come when she, too, would be a mother. "Ye never told me ye were expectin'."

Jules's eyes held secret delight. "So many times I

wanted to tell you, but I kept hoping you'd be able to visit so I could surprise you.''

'' 'Tis a joyous surprise.''

Enraptured, Nicholas watched a wistful smile cross Sheridan's face, making him wonder how she felt about children. Did she want to have any? If so, would she prefer a boy with whom she could climb trees or a little girl to dress up? Did she fancy two children or ten?

He pictured her with two little cherub-cheeked urchins hanging on her skirts, gazing up at her with love and adoration. The thought never crossed his mind that she might not want children. She was too full of life not to share such a gift.

For himself, he wanted a brood, strong sons and sweet-faced daughters. He wanted to be the kind of parent his parents never were.

A beautiful, awe-filled expression spread across Sheridan's face. ''The wee lassie is kickin' her knickers up like she's tappin' an Irish jig.''

Jules's belly jiggled like old Saint Nick's. ''And how do you know it's an Irish jig? Why not a nice English two-step or a Scottish reel?''

''Bite yer tongue!'' Sheridan scolded. ''Scottish reel, indeed. 'Tis too strong a kick this babe has to be doin' anythin' other than a lively jig.''

Nicholas sat down on the step and wondered how this woodland sprite made whatever emotion he experienced ten times stronger—anger, joy. Desire.

''And how do you know it's a wee lassie?'' he asked.

Her smile turned saucy. '' 'Tis easy. This babe has too much spirit to be a man.''

Nicholas quirked a brow. ''Too much spirit?''

''Aye.''

''And men don't possess spirit?''

Sheridan's expression became contemplative, her eyes

probing, as if the answer to her question resided inside of him. "Some do, but 'tis a rare few that possess the soul of a lion and the heart of a saint."

The soul of a lion. Nicholas turned the words over in his mind and wondered about her remarks regarding the soul—a part of him he'd never given much consideration.

"Besides," Sheridan added "me mum says I have the gift."

"The gift?" Jules inquired.

Nicholas noticed how content and calm his cousin looked. Something about Sheridan Delaney soothed the troubled spirit, his included.

"Aye. She says when I lay my hands on people I see things."

"See things? Like what?"

"Oh, I don't know. 'Tis different for each person, but mostly 'tis a feelin' inside me. Then there are times when I feel nothin' a'tall. Can be a vexin' and fickle thing." She sighed. " 'Tis just a shame I can't see my own life. Perhaps 'twould be less trouble I'd be findin' m'self in." She appeared so disgruntled, Nicholas was hard-pressed not to laugh.

The deep, abiding friendship between the two women was clearly evident. No matter her other faults, Sheridan was a true and loyal friend to Jules, and Nicholas suspected she behaved similarly with everyone she cared about.

It struck him then that he wanted to be her friend as well, something he'd never considered in relation to a woman.

To him, women were for enjoyment, keeping a man's home, and bearing his children. He gave them the respect due, placed them on a pedestal for the most part, but never shared himself with them.

But Sheridan was different. Nicholas sensed he couldn't

reach that elusive place inside her without knowing her. She wouldn't give herself up easily. Yet the twinge of hurt he'd glimpsed in her eyes when she looked at him made him wonder if he hadn't already lost his chance.

Fascinated, he watched Sheridan sink to her knees in front of Jules and place both her hands on the swell of Jules's stomach.

Jules's bemused gaze swung to Nicholas and then down at Sheridan's head. "What are you doing, Danny?"

"I must tell the wee one a story."

"A story?"

"Aye." She nodded. "Me mum started her storytellin' when me brothers and sisters were still inside her belly." Her face took on a faraway expression. "Every night as the sun was setting, she'd sit in her rockin' chair, me Da in his, in front of our cottage and gaze across the water.

"There, out in the middle of the briny blue, in a spot she called the glass lake because of its utter calmness, rose an island out of mist and magic. Legend says only the true of heart can see Tier na Nog."

"Tier na Nog?" Nicholas asked, in thrall to a pixie lass with the face of an angel and the heart of a warrior.

" 'Tis the land of eternal youth, a special place where all dreams, no matter how fanciful, can come true."

"How lovely," Jules murmured.

"Aye, 'tis." Sheridan's voice held a wistful note. "But for me, Tier na Nog exists wherever belief exists." She paused. "Do ye believe, Jules Thornton?"

"I do."

Sheridan turned those incredible eyes Nicholas's way. "And ye, Nicholas Sinclair? Do ye believe?"

Nicholas stopped himself from climbing the rest of the stairs and taking this enchantress in his arms. "I do, Danny Delaney."

Sheridan gifted him with a smile that lit her whole face

and sapped Nicholas's breath. Then she bestowed that smile upon her friend. " 'Tis a Delaney tradition to tell the story and pass it on through the family."

"But I'm not a Delaney."

Sheridan clasped Jules's hand in hers. "Ye are the sister of my heart. Ye possess the true spirit of a Delaney, and I want to share this with ye."

Jules smiled gently and squeezed Sheridan's hand. "Then go on," she murmured, emotions filling her voice. "Tell us the story."

Nicholas had climbed six more steps before he realized what he was doing and stopped. The words that flowed from Sheridan's mouth entranced him.

"Once upon a time, ever so long ago," she began in a melodious voice, "before the days of Saint Patrick and King Boru, lived two opposin' factions, the leprechauns of the south of Ireland and the pookas of the north.

"The pookas, ye see, were given to makin' mischief. The leprechauns were no angels either, mind ye. They loved to play practical jokes and enjoyed a certain advantage over the pookas. In the twinklin' of an Irish eye, they could wish themselves anywhere, any time.

"Well, one day, Paeder Og, king of the pookas, weary of the constant warrin' between the spirit forces, challenged Rory, king of the leprechauns, to a battle. The winner would be the king of both the leprechauns *and* the pookas. 'Twas quite a nice deal, ye see, and who could resist?"

Resistance was the last thing on Nicholas's mind. What about this girl made him forget his plans for the future and believe a place such as her mystical Tier na Nog existed?

"Oh, but Paeder Og was a sly one," Sheridan continued, with the skill of a true bard, "and made Rory promise not to do his disappearin' tricks. King Rory was quick

to accept the challenge, confident he'd beat the livin'
bejabbers out of his foe . . ." She paused, and the breath
held suspended in Nicholas's throat.

Well? he wanted to shout. *What happened between
Paeder Og and King Rory?*

Moreover, could he convince Sheridan to tell him a
bedtime story?

With her mouth close to Jules's stomach, Sheridan said,
"Tonight, me wee lassie, I'll tell ye the rest of the tale.
And 'tis quite a tale indeed, full of daring-do and fair
maidens in distress."

Nicholas figured her story bypassed the poor males
who were bedeviled by gamine-faced females and the
length of hemp with which said males hung themselves.

Jules bent forward and placed her hands beneath Sheridan's elbows, raising her from her knees. "You haven't
changed a bit, Danny. Still an original piece of work."
In a conspiratorial whisper that carried, she added,
"Although you have filled out quite nicely. Someday
soon you'll be telling stories to your own child."

That remark brought heat to Sheridan's cheeks that was
beyond charming to Nicholas. She darted a glance at him.
He raised a questioning eyebrow, his expression saying,
I would be honored. Could we get started now?

Her expression said, *Not if your life depended on it*—
the abbreviated version, excluding the epithets of both
American and Irish extraction her eyes flung at him.

He sighed. Where were those magical sunflower seeds
when he needed them?

Jules chuckled. "Oh, don't mind him, Danny. Just treat
him like another one of the girls."

Nicholas scowled at his cousin. "Now wait a blasted
minute!"

Jules's face had minx written all over it. "Don't forget,
dear cousin, you told me you'd be containing yourself,"

she said with a chuckle, reminding him of the words he'd *innocently* spoken to her weeks earlier—before he'd known what he was getting into.

Or with whom.

Nicholas was about to take issue with his cousin when a hackneyed voice that cracked in varying degrees and sounded like the warbling of a bilious turkey rang out in song.

> *When St. Patrick this order established,*
> *He called us the "Monks of the Screw,"*
> *Good rules he revealed to our abbot*
> *To guide us in what we should do.*
> *But first he replenished our fountain*
> *With liquor, the best from on high;*
> *An' he said, on the wor-rd of a saint,*
> *That the fountain should never run dry.*

With a sinking sense that the day was going to be a long one, Nicholas climbed the rest of the stairs. Coming down the hallway was Uncle Finny—otherwise known as Maeve, Queen of Connaught.

In one hand, he held a pewter candelabra.

In the other, Nicholas's favorite sword.

Chapter Twelve

"Halt!" the old man bellowed, thrusting the sword in front of him. "Who goes there?"

An embarrassed blush stained Sheridan's cheeks. "Uncle! What are ye doing? Put that sword down right now!"

"Come to me, child. I'll save ye."

"Oh, uncle. I don't need to be saved." She moved toward him. "Now, please, give me that sword before ye injure yerself."

Nicholas placed a hand on Sheridan's arm, stopping her. "Let me do it. I don't want you to get hurt."

Chivalry was not dead, he thought, but clearly she wished him that unhappy fate if the scowl on her face was any indication.

She sunk her hands onto her hips. "Faith, and yer thinkin' me own uncle would do me harm now?"

"I was just trying to—"

"I know what ye were tryin' to do." She jutted that stubborn jaw forward. "You were tryin' to act like a preenin' rooster and save the lassie from hurtin' her bumblin' self. Well, I need no help from ye and I'll thank ye to remember that," she finished in a huff.

He returned her scowl, conflicted between wringing her supple white neck or paddling her luscious behind. "Christ, woman. You are the most hardheaded, irritating . . ." He gritted his teeth. "You're as—"

"Stiff as Emery's limbs and has her nose so far up in the air icicles collect on it?" Jules interjected, barely contained amusement in her voice as she prodded him with his own words.

Nicholas was too focused on Sheridan to reply to his cousin or realize what Jules might think about such an exchange between him and her friend.

"If you want to get yourself killed, by all means, go ahead."

Sheridan poked him in the chest. "Ye're more likely to get yerself killed by jumpin' into the fray unprepared." Her expression clearly reminded him of another time he'd jumped into the fray unprepared and been pummeled to within an inch of his life.

He growled.

She gloated.

"Fine," he ground out. "I'm just a man anyway."

"A *hapless* man," Jules chimed in, apparently enjoying his discomfit by bringing up everything he'd once unwittingly said about her friend.

From the sudden wide-eyed look on Sheridan's face, it appeared she'd just remembered Jules's presence. He could almost hear her saying she had to learn to curb her tongue.

The quibbling ended and the three of them faced Uncle Finny, who looked like *Don Quixote* in his getup.

"So ye've sided with the enemy, niece? Oh, how ye've broken an old man's heart."

Sheridan heaved a pent-up sigh. "I've sided with no one, uncle. Do ye not recall who helped ye with yer armor when ye went to fight against King Henry II?" She walked toward him, unconcerned about the sword faltering in his unsteady grasp. "Or when I hid you in the larder to save ye from the wrath of Cromwell?"

Her uncle grimaced, making his face appear like a particularly withered prune. "Bloody puritan," he spat.

"And who plied ye with tea so ye could stay up and write yer poetry about sorrowin' maidens, vanished glories, and divine salvation?"

Eyeing her skeptically, her uncle withdrew an item from the pocket of his worn brown jacket with the patched elbows. It appeared to be a leg from the missing duck carcass. Sticking the limb in his mouth, he tore off a piece of meat and said while chewing, " 'Twas ye that did, me girl."

"Aye. 'Twas me."

Reaching him, Sheridan carefully pried the sword from his hand. He relinquished it with nary a sound, absorbed as he was in his food. She balanced the sword in her hand quite expertly, her eyes lifting to Nicholas's, a hint of a smile playing about her lips, telling him clearly that she pictured him carved in small pieces.

With a careful tread, he moved forward and stopped in front of her, the sword inches from his stomach. He held out his hand—and the bloody wench hesitated!

He narrowed his eyes and she cocked a sleek, copper brow. Then, with a soft lilting chuckle, she relinquished her weapon.

Nicholas shot her one last glare before shifting his gaze

to her uncle. "You wouldn't, perchance, have a painting stashed away of an older woman who resembles me, albeit remotely, would you?"

His question stopped dear disturbed Uncle Finny in mid chew. He proceeded to squint one murky eye at Nicholas. "Ye mean the woman with the wiry yellow hair an' her lips pursin' like she'd taken a bite of an unripe persimmon?"

A more accurate description Nicholas himself couldn't have given. "That's her."

The man patted Nicholas's shoulder in a sympathetic gesture. "I kilt her. She were evil, lad. 'Tis a better world without her."

A soft imprecation came from Sheridan. "What did ye mean ye killed her?"

Uncle Finny shook his head. "Skewered her, I did."

"Oh, uncle, what did ye do?" A sinking feel settled in the pit of Sheridan's stomach.

"I ran me sword through her treacherous heart."

"Are you trying to say that you ran a sword through the portrait of my mother?" Nicholas asked, disbelief ringing clearly in his tone.

Sheridan squeezed her eyes shut and wondered when the nightmare would end. Her first day with Jules and already her family had begun to wreak havoc on Nicholas's home and possessions. And that was *after* the man had bailed her and her uncle out of jail.

She looked askance and noted the incredulous expression on his face. Surprisingly, he didn't appear upset, but mildly amused. His composure made her wonder if she had judged him too harshly when he'd come to the jail.

He had been summoned from the comfort of his home late in the evening, after having been accosted by Aunt Aggie—and Sheridan didn't doubt for a moment that her aunt had put on quite a show.

Add to that the very real possibility he might have been asleep when her aunt arrived—or perhaps otherwise occupied—which inevitably made Sheridan wonder what he might have been occupied doing.

'Tis none of yer business.

But that didn't mean the thought disappeared. It was altogether possible he had . . . a lady friend. Several, in fact. Yet that thought hadn't crossed her mind when he'd patted the spot beside him on the bed at the inn.

"Come, uncle." Sheridan plucked the candelabra from his grip and shoved it toward Nicholas without looking at him, her mind focused on how she would repair the damage to his mother's picture.

"Where ar-re we goin', lass?"

"We have to pick up our things from the hotel." Hovel would have been a better term for the establishment.

"Oh, aye. Puir Scally will be missin' ye. Ye know how much he looves ye, lass."

"Scally?"

The irritated rasp of their host brought Sheridan's head up. A slight tic worked in Nicholas's jaw, his gaze direct and penetrating.

"Who's Scally?"

Sheridan would have told him had his tone not been so demanding and belligerent. "I guess ye'll have to wait and see now, won't ye?"

He didn't appear to appreciate that answer, if the glower directed her way was any indication. "I'm not a particularly patient man, my girl. And"—he leaned forward— "whatever patience I may have possessed was wrung dry recently. Now," he said with steely determination, "your uncle will have some breakfast and you and I will retrieve your belongings." Glancing over his shoulder, he said to Jules, "Will you see to our guest, puss?"

"I will."

"Now wait one—" Sheridan's words were stillborn as Nicholas gripped her upper arm and tugged her away.

"There's no need to thank me."

"Thank ye!" she fumed. "Why I'll—"

Hauling her closer to his side, he whispered in her ear, "I'd watch your tongue, my girl. We have an audience."

She glared.

He shook his head. "Don't you think it's time to bury the hatchet?" he asked as they descended the stairs.

"Oh, aye. I'll bury it all right. In yer head!"

How had he known she'd say that?

"Emery, please have the coach brought around," Nicholas instructed.

Emery, dozing off in the chair, snorted a few times, blinked, and then rattled his head like a person in the throes of a seizure. Nicholas swore he heard the man's small fossilized brain clanging as he attempted to clear the hundred-year-old cobwebs in the large hollow that was his skull.

Slapping a skeletal hand to his back, Emery cracked every vertebrae descending his decrepit spine.

"What was that, sir?" he croaked. "You found a roach on the ground? I'll have it cleaned up in a lick."

Rising like an ancient piece of licorice, Emery began to scuttle off at a rate of speed that would take him two days and nights to reach the housekeeper's quarters.

Nicholas sighed. "Never mind. I'll take Kdansk."

"You're going to a dance?" Emery's querulous, watery eyes fixed on Nicholas. "Isn't it too early?" Before Nicholas could throw an internal bout of histrionics, Emery dismissed him, turning his gaze to Sheridan. "You look very pretty, miss. The master's a lucky man to have you at his side."

Nicholas gazed down at Sheridan, expecting to see the daggers of feminine wrath she liked to throw his way directed at poor, witless Emery. But damn him if the woman wasn't smiling at his butler. Smiling!

She must have felt his stunned regard because when she looked up at him, the fulminating glare returned to her eyes. She flicked a glance at his hand wrapped around her arm. "Ye'll stop yer manhandlin' or I'll scream the house down."

God, she was something when she was riled. "Go ahead. Something tells me the house isn't going to remain standing long with its current occupants anyway."

As soon as the words were out of his mouth, Nicholas regretted them. He cursed himself roundly when he saw the touch of hurt flash briefly in her eyes before being cloaked.

"That can be fixed," she said tightly, trying to yank her arm out of his grip.

"I'm sorry. I didn't mean that."

"Ye did."

"I didn't."

"Ye did."

"Damn it! I didn't!" Nicholas fired back, his ire beginning to rise once more.

Seeing an audience gathering, he marched her out the door and toward his waiting stallion. The woman was the most exasperating hundred pounds of female he knew, but she was also the most exciting.

His stallion, posted in front of the house after an early morning ride through Hyde Park, whickered when he saw Nicholas coming.

Sheridan pivoted on her heel, brandishing a mulish expression. "And just how do ye think ye're goin' to get all my family's things on this horse, may I ask? Carry them on yer head, perhaps?"

"I'm sure you'd like to see that. But such a feat won't

be necessary. I'll hire a hackney when we get to your hotel and we can load your belongings into it. Satisfied?''

She harrumphed and presented him with her back—and quite a lovely back it was, slender, delicate, shapely.

And so rigid her spine would slap him in the face should she bend over.

He cupped his hands together to give her a leg up. She ignored him and hoisted herself into the saddle of a horse a good seventeen hands high with a fluidness of motion that communicated skill and long familiarity.

She arranged her skirt and then stared down at him with a triumphant, how-do-you-like-that expression. ''And where is yer horse?''

''You're sitting your pretty fanny on him.''

''So ye intend to walk then, do ye?'' she asked, ever belligerent.

''No. I intend to ride.'' Nicholas grasped the pommel, swinging himself up behind her. ''With you.''

Anger sizzled up her spine and would have launched him from the saddle had his chin been over her head. She tried to turn around, most likely either to take a swing at him or to incinerate him with one of her fire-spewing glares.

He wrapped an arm tightly about her waist and pulled her close, telling himself he did so only with the intention of remaining unscathed.

She bristled like a porcupine, a hint of a memory sliding through his brain as he pictured that same pique directed at him while they were ensconced in a room above Puddlebys. But the image was fleeting and frustrating.

He expected her to demand he remove his arm from her person. To his amazement, she didn't utter a sound. The girl was a stunning contradiction in terms, and he couldn't help being intrigued.

He gave Kdansk a nudge behind the girth and they

started down the street. Nicholas contemplated picking up the pace, but was in no hurry to end the sweet torment of having Danny's body tucked closely to his, to smell the hint of hyacinth that seemed to belong to her alone waft from her hair.

He had to resist the urge to bury his face in her thick, silky locks. A few strands swept over his face like an elusive reprieve to a man facing execution.

A companionable silence descended, and he tested the boundaries of his good fortune, his free hand tentatively exploring her waist.

He found the indentation of her belly button, an outie. No surprise. The girl was too contrary to have anything contained. Gently, he probed the small mound without trying to appear he was doing so.

He thought her barriers were crumbling and the old Sinclair charm was working its magic when she said, "If ye don't want to find yerself called Lefty, I'd remove yer fingers from me belly button."

Silently, he chuckled. "Oh? Is that your belly button? I thought it was an odd-shaped, bloodsucking bug."

"If yer lookin' for blood," she said tightly, "I'd be happy to oblige ye." The girl was a pip to the steel marrow of her bones.

"Can't we call a truce? As the Good Book says, vengeance is best left to the Lord."

Where he came up with that statement, Nicholas wasn't sure, considering he and the Lord knew each other only in passing and the Good Book was not on his preferred reading list.

Where, exactly, would he put such a thing anyway? His tomes were arranged alphabetically, which would place the Bible between his dog-eared childhood pictorial on female anatomy and *Craps: Do Loaded Dice Count?*

He imagined the quote stemmed from a latent recollection from one of the religious zealots who used to follow his brother Damien around, warning him to repent from his life of degradation and sin.

Clearly unimpressed by Nicholas's magnanimous, and frankly charming, offer Sheridan retorted in her usual bold and brassy way, "As I told ye before, I'd rather bury the hatchet in yer head—"

"Don't you mean in my *bonny* head?" he interposed.

"—than to make nice with ye."

"Hmm. Make nice. I like the sound of that. Could we explore the definition?"

The scathing look she sent his way made him feel like a long-tailed cat in a room full of rocking chairs. Yet danger had a certain intoxicating power he couldn't deny.

"If memory serves, you said I had a wee hint of a dimple and a glint in my eyes. Do I still?"

"I also said I'd make ye sorry if ye persisted in proddin' me."

"And let me say you've accomplished that feat quite admirably. Never have I been sorrier."

She stiffened.

Damn. He'd put his foot in his mouth again. Obviously, she had taken his remark the wrong way. Where the hell had his finesse flown off to?

"I was kidding," he said, thinking himself insane to prefer her verbal abuse to her silent censure.

"I need no apologies from ye, and I want none, thank ye."

"Who said I was apologizing?"

That stumped her—for all of a second. " 'Tis regrettin' yer words, ye were."

"And don't you have any words you regret saying to me?" He could recite them, if she had trouble recalling them all.

He bestowed upon her his most winning smile, certain to soothe any ruffled feathers.

Yet no apology was forthcoming.

"Well?" he prompted.

"Well, what?"

"Have you nothing to say for yourself? Or nothing to say to me, rather?"

"And what could I possibly have to say to ye? Other than ye are a boorish, pigheaded, irritatin'—"

Nicholas drew Kdansk to an abrupt halt in a quiet side alley. A perfect spot to commit mayhem.

And if the girl didn't retract her words, mayhem was what she'd be getting.

"What are ye doin'?" she demanded.

A muscle worked in Nicholas's jaw. "You owe me an apology, and I'm not moving another inch until I get it."

"An apology!" she shouted, attempting to shift around enough to glare at him. Finally, she tilted her head back, her hair puddling in his lap. "I owe ye no such thing!"

He ground his teeth together. "Yes . . . you do."

"I don't!" She tried to lift her head. His hand around her hair held her immobile. "Let me go!" she screeched.

He dropped his head forward, eye to eye with his irate pixie, and growled, "Not until you apologize."

For once, he had the upper hand. He had her trapped in a precarious position, and beneath the layers of his anger, beyond his ever present desire, and betwixt his general confusion and the remaining shreds of his pride, he chortled with glee—and he was not a man known to chortle.

Dainty nostrils flared. "I wouldn't apologize to ye if

ye were the last man on the face of the planet and sayin' those two words meant the difference between dyin' of thirst 'cause ye owned all the water or lettin' the elements dry me into dust.''

Nicholas's touted control began to slip in light of the girl's continual nudging, tweaking, goading defiance. He had rescued her not once, not twice, but bloody thrice.

And three times was a charm.

''Is that your final answer?'' he asked, praying she'd say yes so he could act, knowing what he wanted from her was driven more by desire than anger.

''Aye! 'Tis my final answer, ye arrogant pain in the arse.''

A slow grin spread across his face. ''Then this is my response.''

Before she could draw a breath, he gripped her waist, lifted, shifted—and settled her across his lap.

Facedown.

''What are ye—oh, ye wouldn't dare!'' He was not going to paddle her backside!

''Oh, but I would.''

She flailed in protest and fury. A weighty arm settled across her shoulder blades. ''The last man who dared lay a finger on me was nursing his wounds for three months!''

''So you went easy on him, hmm?''

She screeched and the horse sidled. ''Ye touch me and I'll carve ye into little pieces and toss yer mangy carcass to the four winds!''

He was unmoved by her threat, but never more determined. ''You've been asking for this since the moment I laid eyes on you. You've pushed me.'' *Swat.* ''You've prodded me.'' *Swat.* ''You've beaten on me when your mother warned you not to abuse men.'' *Swat.* ''You gave me swill that rearranged my vital organs.'' *Swat.* ''And caused me to blot out what should have been a memorable evening.'' *Swat.* ''You left me alone in bed and made me miss you.'' *Swat.* ''You had me searching the docks day and night to find you.''

''Stop! No more!'' A sob welled in her throat, more from humiliation then any pain his hand caused.

''Not until you apologize.'' But his words lacked heat, and she detected a hint of regret. Another swat to her behind was not forthcoming.

''I won't! I won't!'' A tear slipped down her cheek.

''Damn,'' Nicholas muttered and quickly turned her over. Sitting her across his lap, he pulled her to his chest. ''God, I'm sorry.'' He sounded agonized. ''I don't know what came over me. It's just . . .'' He shook his head, his arms holding her close, his face pressed against the top of her head. ''Please forgive me.''

Sheridan's heart crumbled. She suspected her resistance would always waver when it came to this man. She sniffled, and hated herself for acting like a weepy female. She couldn't abide such women and vowed never to be one. But she couldn't help herself. The tears flowed and they wouldn't stop.

Nicholas tightened his arms around her. ''Did I hurt you, Danny? Please don't cry. Hit me. Slap me. Do something. You're tearing me up.''

She wiped her moist face on his nice clean shirt and hiccuped. '' 'Tis just what ye deserve''—her bottom lip quivered—''ye brute.''

''I know. I'm the worst sort of monster.'' He placed a finger beneath her chin and tilted her face up.

Sheridan's breath locked in her throat as remorseful green eyes stared down at her. She knew then as clearly as she had known that fateful night at Puddlebys that she would never be a match for this man. He was part of her heart and soul, no matter how much she fought it.

Gently, he stroked away a lone tear that escaped her lashes. "Tell me what I need to do to make it up to you. I'll do anything."

Angry impulse made her want to tell him to jump in the Thames and pull London in over his head. Desire and longing, however, had a different idea.

"Ye ... ye can kiss me, I suppose," she murmured, anticipation and excitement flooding her senses, making her realize that all the angry, prodding words she'd flung at Nicholas had been done with the hopes of inciting him to action. She wanted his touch. She wanted emotion. She wanted him. Only him. "Please," she breathed, " 'Twill soothe the hurt."

A heart-melting boyish grin edged up one corner of his lips, entrancing her as completely as it had the first time he'd bestowed it upon her.

"I remember another kiss that soothed my hurt. One I'll never forget. Let's see how adequately I can return the favor."

Unconsciously, Sheridan moistened her lips, watching the slow descent of his head, uncaring of their surroundings. At that moment, no one existed but them. Her eyelids fluttered closed at the first press of his mouth against hers.

Bliss. Pure, aching, consuming, heavenly bliss.

He molded, shaped, plundered, and drew every ounce of need from her. She wrapped her arms around his neck and held on for dear life, her body tingling in all her secret places, remembering how finely he had played each part of her, drawing her on passion's rack until shattering ecstasy exploded inside her.

"Danny," he murmured against her jaw. "Danny." Her name was a sweet caress as his mouth found her ear and he whispered words that made the blood thicken in her veins.

She wanted him. Oh, how she wanted him, to feel the weight of him, the heat of him, the slick satin and steel of him slipping inside her, making them one.

She tasted his flesh, exploring his textures, his heat burning her. His words flowed back to her, telling her she had judged him too harshly.

You left me alone in bed and made me miss you.

You had me searching the docks day and night to find you.

He had looked for her. Missed her. The knowledge thrilled her and began to heal the aching place in her heart that had screamed she'd been callously used.

His hands slid over her body, caressing her as she wanted to caress him, communicating more clearly than words that he desired her, wanted her. Needed her. As she needed him.

"M'love," she whispered against the smoothness of his jaw, her tongue swirling in the dent in his chin before gliding across his lower lip.

He captured her tongue between his lips, drew it in again and again as his large hands cupped her buttocks and lifted her, straddling her legs across his lap, her skirt bunching up to her thighs.

Without removing his mouth from hers, he guided Kdansk into a darkened alcove in the alley, cloaking them in shadows and sensual heat.

His mouth trailed down her throat. She threw her head back, allowing him better access. His hands cupped her breasts, teasing her nipples through the material of her blouse. She moaned.

Cool air touched her skin as he undid the buttons, his

tongue trailing a path down the exposed flesh until it reached her chemise. He took the ribbon holding her chemise together between his strong, white teeth and pulled. The laces separated as if no more than moonlight held them together.

"I thought I had only dreamed how beautiful you were," he murmured in a husky tone, his mouth drawing a taut nub into his mouth, teasing and soothing, flicking, nibbling, driving her to the brink.

He leaned her back over his arm, increasing the aching sensation in her nipples as he suckled them. His hand swept up her thigh. She throbbed in anticipation, knowing where his fingers were going.

The first touch against her wet, swollen pearl sent lightning soaring through her. "Nicholas," she groaned.

"Yes, sweet. Hold nothing back. I want everything. Everything."

He stroked, faster, bolder, slipping a finger into her just when she felt on the threshold of that bright, spiraling place, prolonging the tension, the agony until she could bear no more.

"Please," she begged in a ragged moan, her hips rocking against his hands. He obliged her need with rampant grace.

His tongue flicked her nipple as his finger flicked her engorged nub. Heat culminated, pulling her inside herself, drowning her, coiling about her muscles until a flood of liquid warmth cascaded through her, making her thankful for the strong arms that held her as pulse after pulse of her release washed through her.

"Danny," he murmured against her throat, his hands gliding through her hair with sweet reverence. "You make me crazy. I forget everything and everyone when you're near. What are you doing to me?"

Sheridan felt languid, sated, drugged by passion, the world existing inside a hazy, pleasure-filled bubble.

She dug her fingers into Nicholas's hair, reveling in its cool texture, jubilation soaring through her at knowing this handsome, charming, virile man was hers. She kissed him with all the love inside her.

A ragged sound escaped his lips. "Please . . . no more. Otherwise I'll take you here and now."

Brazen, hot blood danced through Sheridan's veins, her skin on fire, her desire for Nicholas a living, breathing entity, consuming her. She wanted his possession, his bold demand. Her hands slipped inside his shirt, her fingernails scoring his silky pebbles.

"Stop, Danny," he said in a hoarse voice, his head bowing forward. "I don't want to take you like a rutting animal."

Sheridan didn't heed the warning. Her fingers skimmed his ribs and her mouth feathered kisses along his collarbone. "I've dreamed of ye." Her tongue tasted his earlobe. "I've missed ye, angel of mine."

Nicholas's fists clenched at his side. Sheridan could feel his tenuous control slipping. She longed to break his restraint, make him weak, imprint her memory on his brain.

Wicked delight consumed her as she tried to make him touch her. She squirmed in his lap and his jaw clenched, his face a mask of agony.

Sheridan leaned forward, her breasts caressing his chest as she whispered in his ear, "Touch me." He squeezed his eyes shut. "I need you." Air hissed between his teeth. "Love me."

Nicholas grasped her arms, holding her away from him. He had to end this madness. He wanted Sheridan with a desperation he'd never felt before and doubted he ever would again. But she was his cousin's best friend, and that changed everything.

He should have let it go, left her alone, forgotten about her. But, damn it, she tormented him. Those beautiful eyes haunted him mercilessly; whispered words and fragmented memories wreaked havoc on him.

With one fateful encounter, she had become a potent drug he couldn't relinquish. And if he took her now and she slid further into his system, his heart, his soul, he might never be able to walk away, and he had to walk away.

The thought of making her his mistress filtered through his mind, but Jules's angry face flashed before his eyes. His cousin would never understand or condone such an arrangement. With another woman, she might, though somehow he doubted that.

Jules was liberated, opinionated, and strong-willed, a dangerous mix that had earned him an earful about how to treat women on many occasions.

Therefore, any relationship with Sheridan would be out of the question. Jules would demand he make Sheridan his wife, and if things were different, if *he* were different, Nicholas might have considered it.

He could not risk a lifetime on a woman who might not be faithful to him. Passion was an integral part of Sheridan's nature. It consumed her when she was angry, when she was happy, and whenever she touched him.

He couldn't bear to lose that passion, to have another man sample it, want it . . . need it as he was coming to need it. He couldn't risk his heart.

Her luminous violet eyes gazed at him, confusion, desire, vulnerability all clashing within their depths. "Nicholas . . ."

His name on Sheridan's lips nearly undid him, his consuming lust barely bridled.

Averting his gaze, he tugged her blouse together, trying not to notice the rosy flush on her skin from her woman's pleasure, or the flawless beauty of her flesh, a golden-tinted paradise—a banked fire lit from within, and he could never possess her.

"Let's go get your things. Jules will be worried about us."

Chapter Thirteen

"Leave off, y' smarmy bastard, or I'll gut y'!"

"What in God's name was that?"

Halting in the process of packing her meager belongings, Sheridan glanced over her shoulder at Nicholas, who gaped at a covered object on the floor. When his gaze slid her way, he wore a bewildered expression.

"Have I lost my mind, or did something under that sheet just call me a smarmy bastard?"

Sheridan was greatly tempted to let him find out on his own what lay beneath the worn cotton. It would serve him right. His defection still stung, his withdrawal tangible and bittersweet. Yet she refused to let her hurt show.

Coming to stand next to him, Sheridan bent over and pulled the cover off. "Nicholas Sinclair, meet Scally. Say hello, Scally."

Scally slanted a tiny black eyeball at Nicholas and said in his usual cordial fashion, *"Suck on rat poison."*

Nicholas's eyebrows inched toward his hairline. "Scally's . . . a myna bird?"

"Aye, that he is. What did ye think Scally was?"

"I'm not sure, but I know what I didn't expect, and this bird is it."

"Cough bricks, y' brainless Bedouin."

Nicholas sank to his haunches and shook his head. "This is really too much. What's next, I wonder?"

Scally regaled them with a four-letter serenade that would have burned the ears of society's most jaded.

"I've never heard a bird speak so . . . colorfully," Nicholas remarked, amusement tingeing his voice.

Sheridan hesitated, then knelt beside him. She picked up a small crust of bread lying on the floor outside the cage and fed it to Scally through the wire bars. "Scally is short for scalawag."

"Apropos."

"Aye. Scally belonged to a salty old sea captain who died during the ship's crossing. The man's brother hated the bird and bet him away in a card game. 'Twas the only time Uncle Finny won a hand of cards. He's smart, though—the bird, that is—and has quite a vocabulary and learns very quickly."

"Hmm. Interesting. May I?" Nicholas held out his hand for a small piece of bread. Uncomfortable with his nearness, Sheridan plunked the bread in his hand and stood up, wondering if she should warn him.

"Damn it!"

Too late. "Tch, I forgot to mention that Scally doesn't like strangers and has a penchant for biting."

Nicholas swiveled his head and gazed up at her, his look clearly asking her why she hadn't told him *before* he stuck his finger into Scally's cage.

He rose slowly, purposefully. And when at last he stood at his full towering height, she had to tip her head back to return his intense regard. No man intimidated Sheridan Delaney. No matter how much she quivered inside at that moment, he'd never know.

"I think you did that on purpose," he said.

"Did what?"

"Don't play innocent with me."

"I don't know what ye're talking about."

He gritted his teeth. "That bird could have taken off my finger."

She waved a dismissive hand. "And wouldn't ye have had four left?"

"That isn't funny," he said, as if his expression didn't convey clearly enough he was not amused.

She shrugged. "I don't know. I thought—"

His growl cut off the rest of her intended gibe. "You're acting like a spoiled child."

Anger began to bubble inside Sheridan. "Actin' like a child!"

"You're angry because of what happened before."

She didn't need further clarification to know what *before* meant. And he was right. She was angry—angry enough to pound his bones into mulch.

But she was also sad, disheartened, and in love with the big lout. Nevertheless, she'd take that information to her grave.

She cocked a brow and met his glare. "Oh? And what happened before?"

He leaned forward, giving her a look that proclaimed he was a man and ruler, and therefore the world should drop to its knees before him.

And her look reiterated Scally's words: *Cough bricks.*

"I'd be happy to remind you," he said in a low, rumbling voice, "in detail, if so desired."

Heat coursed over Sheridan, visions of his hands running along her body, building her to fever pitch.

Shucking off the turbulent memory, she folded her arms across her chest and raised an eyebrow. "And what of it?"

"What do you mean, 'what of it?' Don't try to tell me what happened between the two of us didn't mean anything to you. And don't," he emphasized, "tell me you didn't want me."

It meant everything to her. And she did want him, even at that moment. Probably forever. "It didn't. And I don't."

"Liar."

She narrowed her eyes on his handsome, arrogant face and itched to slap it.

His expression gentled, a look of regret in his eyes. "I didn't mean to hurt you, Danny, but it's better this way. A relationship between the two of us wouldn't work."

Emotions threatened to choke Sheridan. She turned away. "Ye're actin' as if I care. I don't."

He moved in front of her. "But I do."

She vowed not to speak to him, but her mouth opened anyway and vulnerability spilled out. "Is it because . . . I'm Irish?"

"No." He cupped her cheek, soothing her when she didn't want to be soothed. "You should know better than to think I'd care about that." He tilted her chin up. "Does it bother you that I'm English?"

For her mother's sake, Sheridan wanted to say yes. For her family who had struggled, fought, and lost to British tyranny, she wanted to say yes. For every Irish woman who had watched a son or daughter die from starvation, she wanted to say yes. For every kindred soul of Erin who had slaved and sweated and given their very life to the land, she wanted to say yes.

But for Sheridan Delaney, it would be a lie.

"Nay. It never has. If ye were a hated landlord, then I'd have issue with ye."

"I don't own any property in Ireland." But even as he said the words, an elusive memory tickled the back of Nicholas's mind. He quickly dismissed it, knowing his brain had not been reliable of late. "It must have been a difficult thing for you to leave your home."

" 'Twas the worst thing ever. Even though life was hard, everyone was family, and ye were always welcome no matter where ye went. 'Tis a part of me I can't let go."

"And you shouldn't. Your heritage is what makes you who you are."

"Aye. 'Tis just that I wish I could do somethin' to help. The landlords care nothing about the people who work the land, wearin' them down to the bone, the ache in their backs constant from tryin' to till lifeless soil. We were driven out of Erin like the children of Israel." She sighed. "My heart still aches with homesickness. Ireland 'tis a rare and special place." She glanced at the floor and murmured, "I thought to raise my children there, but now . . ."

Her children.

Nicholas remembered her words to Jules. Sheridan wanted a family of her own. He couldn't help but wonder what kind of man would capture her heart, and why it bothered him so much to think of her with someone else.

But if he knew only one thing conclusively in that moment, it was that Sheridan would be a wonderful mother—caring, attentive, loving. A mother any child would be blessed to have. The kind of mother Nicholas wished he had been blessed with.

"Do you think you'll ever go back?" he asked.

"Not unless the bounty is taken off my family's head." She shrugged. "And probably not even then. We have no money to return, and our home was seized by the landlord anyway. So what's left for us?''

Nicholas felt for her plight, imagining the fear and uncertainty of living a rootless existence.

"You can start over again. It's not everyone who can do that." Certainly he couldn't. In many ways, his life was set in stone. Even at that moment he felt like a rock rolling along to its destiny, unable to go back ... but suddenly not wanting to go forward either, at least not in the direction he'd so recently chosen. If only he'd met Sheridan before.

Before what? Before Jessica? Would that have made a difference? Sheridan would still have come from an opposite world. Funny thing was, that opposite world wasn't keeping them apart. He was.

Nicholas acknowledged the truth, but could do nothing to change it. And he owed his mother for that. If only he could erase the memory of the pain her faithlessness had caused their family, the children taunting Nicholas about her, his rage at seeing his father humiliated.

If only.

"Start over?" Sheridan scoffed. "Doing what? And where? If ye haven't noticed, we Irish aren't exactly wanted." She moved away from him and stared out a grimy windowpane, wiping away some of the dirt.

She looked so small and defenseless that Nicholas's heart ached for her. He wanted to do something for her, but what? What would make a difference? And why would he be doing it?

To assuage his guilty conscience for hurting her.

Regardless of what she said, he knew he had hurt her. He had treated her no better than a dockside tramp. But his need to touch her had overwhelmed him. He still wanted to touch her, and had fought a battle within himself the entire ride to the hotel—and did so even now.

He told himself to get her belongings and get out fast. Yet she looked defeated standing by the window, and he knew a need to comfort her. She would resist, perhaps even fight him. This was not a girl who bowed to weakness. He admired that about her. She had a strength many men didn't possess.

He stepped up behind her. She flinched, but did not acknowledge him. "It will be all right, Danny. I'll do whatever I can to help."

She swung around, her back pressed against the window. "I don't want anything from ye! Ye hear? I'll not be yer charity case." She shoved her hands against his chest. He didn't budge. "And I'll not have ye thinkin' ye owe somethin' to the poor little Irish girl who threw herself at ye! I want nothing from ye! Nothing!"

She pushed at him again. He grabbed her wrists. "Stop it, Danny!"

"Leave me alone! I hate ye!"

"No, you don't."

"I do!"

Nicholas pressed closer to her, trying to still her squirming. "I'm sorry."

"I don't want yer apologies! Just go away and leave me alone! Just"—her voice broke—"go away." She bowed her head.

A knife twisted in Nicholas's heart.

Two souls entwined.

One soul damned.

He leaned down. He wanted to see her face but she averted her gaze. "I'm not going away, Danny. You're Jules's friend. And now you're mine."

Nicholas wasn't sure what he was offering. How could he possibly ever be just Sheridan's friend? But he knew he had to be something to her. He had to.

"I don't want to be yer friend," she said, refusing to look at him.

Hearing the choked sound of her voice, Nicholas released her wrists and put a finger beneath her chin. She pushed his hand away, but he wouldn't be deterred.

Finally, she looked up at him. Tears that she tried to blink away welled in her eyes, making them appear a luminous lavender blue—making him wish once more things were different.

"Don't shut me out, Danny."

"Why do ye do this to me?"

"Do what?"

She bit her lower lip as if she didn't want any more words to escape. She tried to look away again. He wouldn't let her.

"Do what, Danny?"

"Make me want ye," she whispered, "when ye don't want me."

"Not want you? Are you crazy?" He crouched down until they were eye to eye. "How can you stand here and not feel the desire you build in me? I can't stop touching you, as much as I tell myself to leave you be."

"But . . . ye said . . ."

"I said a relationship between the two of us wouldn't work, but I never said I didn't want you. If I can't give you something of myself, then I don't want to prolong this for either of us."

She shook her head. "I don't understand."

Nicholas would never hurt her by telling her he didn't feel he could trust her, that he was afraid her deep-rooted passion would lead her to other men. One man could never satisfy her. And he had to be the only one.

"Can't you see what Jules would think should I trifle with her best friend? I don't want to ruin your friendship."

"Jules wouldn't . . ."

"She would, Danny." Seeing a chair, Nicholas took her hand. Sitting down, he pulled her reluctant form onto his lap. "Jules is a wonderful person, but she can also be fierce in her beliefs. Like you. That's probably why you two are so aptly suited. But there are some things she would never accept. Our relationship is one of them. Her understanding goes only so far."

Sheridan wanted to refute Nicholas's words. She couldn't believe Jules would end their friendship if she and Nicholas married. She had thought her friend would be happy about it.

There are some things she would never accept.

Like an Irish peasant as her cousin's wife?

Her understanding goes only so far.

And it seemed the line was drawn at Sheridan.

The pain of discovery hurt worse than any other discrimination Sheridan had ever felt. Her heart screamed for her to deny Nicholas's words. Her brain demanded she accept it.

It was a silly girl's dream to believe Jules's friendship automatically meant nothing stood between them. The fact remained that Jules was English and titled, Sheridan poor and Irish. They had overcome the barrier that would make them natural enemies, if enemies could ever be considered natural.

But becoming family in the true sense of the word was a high wall that could not be scaled.

She could not blame Jules. Sheridan knew she expected too much of her friend. Jules had already given far more than any other person Sheridan knew.

"I understand," she said, holding her head high, forcing the tears back.

We are survivors, we Delaneys, she could hear her mother say.

But when will we ever be saved? a small voice asked.

Sheridan summoned her strength. "We better finish packing." She tried to rise from Nicholas's lap, but his arm snaked about her waist, tugging her back. "What are ye doing?" she demanded, her anger rallying forth to help her. She drew her outrage about her like a cloak.

"I wasn't kidding when I said I wanted us to be friends."

Sheridan knew she was being petty, but she couldn't be his friend. She couldn't. She wanted to be more than that, but that was an admission wild horses couldn't drag from her.

Praying her hand would not tremble, she held it out to him. "Friends."

He stared at her proffered hand and then took it between both of his large hands. "Friends."

Chapter Fourteen

Friendship would be the death of Nicholas.

What insanity had made him think he could possibly be Sheridan's friend and nothing more? That he could smile and make nice and smell the hint of hyacinth in the air whenever she flitted past him and continue to look at the world with rose-colored eyes?

For two weeks, her nearness had vexed him and her family's antics had begun to color his hair prematurely gray.

The first few days had been the worst. Sheridan had been politely distant. They tap danced around each other, saying all the right things, deftly skirting each other's perimeter and making sure their shadows didn't even touch.

Torture.

Her laughter drew him to her time and again, even if she clammed up once she caught sight of him.

One day he stood outside Sheridan's bedroom door listening to her and Jules giggling and carrying on, the conversation muted. He'd pressed his ear to the portal. They were trying on clothes.

When Nicholas heard Jules say, "Oh my, any man who saw you in that clinging sheath would die," he almost did, the vision enough to accelerate his heartbeat.

He'd shut his eyes to block out the image. When he opened them, Ho-Sing stood beside him, arms clasped behind his back, an eyebrow raised, which clearly said, *Boss-man very bad.* Translated further, it said, *Moral degenerate.*

After that, Nicholas had done his best to stay away, either sequestering himself in his office or going to the steam room at his club and losing himself in the fog.

And while he'd been losing himself in the fog, Sheridan had become acquainted with his groundskeeper, namely a strapping Scottish lad named Ian McDonough.

Something jabbed Nicholas in his palm. He glanced down to find he'd broken his pencil in half. He threw it across his desk and abruptly rose from his chair. He needed to concentrate on more important things, like his upcoming evening with Jessica.

Things had been progressing quite nicely with the girl—better than he had expected, in fact. If she was a bit chilly, that was only natural. And if his blood didn't run hot every time he saw her that, too, was not out of the ordinary. He should feel proud a girl of her caliber and moral fiber would even be seen with him. Proud, if not bored.

A ruckus outside his door brought Nicholas back to the present, one voice in particular capturing his attention.

Sheridan.

Nicholas heaved a sigh. "Ah, another day in Bedlam. I might as well go crazy so I can be less conspicuous."

He swung the door open and came face to face with the grinning maw of a wildly flapping myna bird.

"Hello, jerk-face," the benighted thing squawked. It flew past Nicholas and into the office, but not before leaving a gooey-white gift on his newly polished boots.

In the space of three seconds, Nicholas had gone from quietly brooding to a steaming cauldron of rage. "I'll throttle your scrawny feathered neck and serve you for dinner, you bloody gutterworm!"

Scally cackled and landed on top of the papers on Nicholas's desk, scraping his claws against the sheets and causing little tears.

"Damn it!" Nicholas swore. The charred paper from his brother was on the top and he still hadn't read it.

The bird was history. His little blue-black carcass would be roasting over the cook's hot coals that very evening.

Nicholas pivoted on his heel, glee in his face as he began to stalk the bird. He'd barely taken two steps when something—*someone,* rather—slammed into his back, sending him flying headlong to the floor.

"Oh, my!" an all-too-familiar voice exclaimed.

With several muffled curses, Nicholas rolled to his back and glared at the perpetrator. Sheridan's eyes were wide, her hand over her mouth.

"I didn't see ye there," she said instead of apologizing, which inevitably raised Nicholas's ire to a new high, his insides churning like a cat who had swallowed a sour mouse.

"Of course not," he muttered, dusting himself off and rising to his feet. "That would require keeping your eyes open."

Once straightened to his full irritated height, Nicholas was about to let her have it, looking for any outlet to relieve the tension that had been coiling inside him, when another body came skittering around the door, hitting Sheridan, which sent her tumbling forward . . . right into Nicholas's arms.

"Oh, I didna see ye there, Danny lass," came the booming voice of one Ian McDonough. "Are ye all right?"

Sheridan didn't hear the question. Instead she concentrated on Nicholas's strong arms wrapped about her and the feel of having him so close. Her traitorous body wanted to melt into his.

It had been fourteen days, six hours, and twenty-three minutes since he'd last held her. But it wasn't as if she had been counting the seconds or anything.

She had moped for the first few days after his offer of friendship, but with Delaney blood running through her veins, moping was not a state she could stay in long.

She had come from a noble line of fighting Irish, and she wasn't about to change a glorious history. She would fight, but she hadn't made up her mind if she'd fight against him—or for him.

The only thing she knew for sure was that he'd be sorry he'd ever toyed with her emotions, even if he hadn't done it purposefully.

His polite, congenial attitude grated on her nerves, making her want to drub him but good. Since she couldn't, not without reason, she had settled for seeking out trouble to get his attention.

Trouble was her middle name, after all.

"May I ask what the bloody hell that bird is doing flying around the house?"

The sound of tightly leashed anger in Nicholas's voice caused Sheridan to glance up at him—always a mistake. She couldn't think straight when she delved into those green eyes.

Ian saved her from explaining. " 'Tis my fault, sir. I wanted tae see the talkin' bird, so I opened the cage."

An unholy half grin lifted the corner of Nicholas's mouth. "And you were bitten by the feathered Lord of Hades, right?"

Ian shook his head, confusion etched on his brow. "Nay, sir. Scally was quite well behaved."

Nicholas's grin evaporated into a frown. "Behaved? Compared to what? The Marquis de Sade?"

The bird tittered and shook his back tail feathers as it sauntered all over Nicholas's lovely burled wood desk, wreaking havoc with impunity.

"Stop that, you benighted shuttlecock!"

"Shove off, swab," Scally retorted, dancing along toward a lit cigar in an ashtray. Sheridan watched in wide-eyed shock as Scally put his beak down and knocked the ashtray off the desk.

"Oh, that's it!" Nicholas bellowed. "You're d-e-a-d!" He lunged after the bird, grasping air as he sprawled over the top of his desk.

"Nicholas! Don't!" Sheridan pleaded, but he didn't hear her. He trailed after Scally, almost getting the bird once but coming away with only a feather. He climbed on top of his desk and she panicked. He would surely break his neck. "Don't be a hardheaded duffer! Come down from there!"

Scally, unappreciative of her attempt to save his life, swooped right past Nicholas's nose. Nicholas thrust a hand out, leaning a little too far forward. He teetered on the edge of the desk, trying to right himself.

Sheridan's breath locked in her throat. She thought Nicholas had caught his balance, but he placed his foot on top of round glass paperweight and toppled off the desk, hitting the floor with a resounding crash.

"Oh, sweet Lord!" she gasped, rushing to his side.

His eyes were closed, a pained expression on his face. She leaned over him, her hair pooling on his chest as she cupped his cheeks. "Nicholas? Nicholas, are ye all right?" She lightly slapped his cheek.

He growled low and cracked open an eyelid. "Stuffed and mounted. By all that's holy, I swear I'll see that blighted animal on a plaque in my trophy room."

Sheridan had to fight the urge to smile. "Ye don't have a trophy room."

"Oh, but I will after this. Mark my words." A grimace of pain crossed his features as he rose to his elbows. "Where is the little Philistine? There's a pot with his name on it. And I have no doubt the bird from hell will be the best brisket I've ever had. Twenty pounds—no, *fifty* pounds—to whoever catches the bloody thing."

"I've got him, sir," Ian said.

A fierce scowl marred Nicholas's face. "Got him?"

Sheridan glanced over her shoulder and nearly choked. Scally perched quite peaceably on Ian's shoulders. She couldn't let Nicholas see that. His reaction would be more explosive than fireworks on the Fourth of July.

He went to sit up. Sheridan practically threw herself against him.

"What in God's name?"

"Ye're hurt. Lie still." Sheridan pressed her hands firmly against his shoulders and tossed over her shoulder, "Ian, can ye find Ho-Sing and send him to me?"

"But—"

"We'll take that walk later."

"That's not—"

"Ho-Sing, please."

She breathed a sigh of relief when Ian tromped away, praying Scally's beak would remain shut and that he would return to his cage without further incident.

She should have known better.

"In your eye, blue-nose!" Scally's words filtered down the hallway.

Leave it to Scally to get in one last jibe.

"What the hell was that about?" Nicholas demanded.

A bittersweet memory seared Sheridan with longing as she stared down at him. He had looked just this way that night on the docks, all glorious green eyes, wildly tangled ebony hair—and in pain. How could a man be so battered and still look so incredibly wonderful?

" 'Twas only a joke."

"I'm not talking about the feathered Satan."

Sheridan realized with a start that she held him down. Her palms against his shoulders suddenly burned with heat. She drew back, but he captured her wrists.

"Not so fast." He laid her hands against his chest and imprisoned them there. "You didn't answer my question. Why the rush to remove McDonough? Afraid of what I might do to your new friend with my current state of mind teetering on the edge?"

Sheridan narrowed her gaze on his smug, glorious face. "And what might ye have done to Ian? The man outweighs ye by a good three stones. In Scotland, he beat every comer, and that's sayin' a lot, mind ye. Highlanders are known for being fierce fighters."

His eyes glinted with anger. Another woman might have been deterred by such a sign. Sheridan wasn't.

"So we're back to that again, eh?" he asked in a tight voice.

"Back to what?"

"Back to you and all your female glee over buff and brawny men—or should I say *brawling* men?"

"Female glee? And what do ye mean by that?"

"You practically swoon over men who fight."

"Swoon! I've never done such a thing in me life!"

He ignored her. "Is it something about blood that

excites you? Or is it that brains and ambition don't mean anything to you?''

In less than a minute, Sheridan's concern for the wretch reverted to boiling anger. ''How dare ye say such a thing! Ye don't know me.''

''You're right. I don't. You won't let me know you. I thought we were . . . friends.'' A slight frown creased his brow.

''And who could be a friend to ye? Ye are an inconsiderate, ill-mannered . . . ooh!'' She tried to wrench free from the viselike grip he had around her wrists. ''Let go!''

''No.''

Sheridan refused to acknowledge the leap in her heart at his refusal. She denied this physical contact was what she wanted all along, something besides a gracious smile and gentlemanly courtesy.

''I swear by all that's holy I'll pummel ye if ye don't let me go. I don't care how hurt ye may be!''

''And do you know how hurt I am?'' he asked, his tone having changed to a husky rumble, taking Sheridan completely off guard. She could deal with an arrogant Nicholas, but she had no defense against a charming Nicholas. ''Do you even care?''

No formed on Sheridan's tongue, but the word would not come out. ''Ye're too hardheaded to be hurt.''

''If you prick me, do I not bleed?''

''Aye. Like a geyser,'' she returned, sucking in her cheeks to keep from laughing at his injured expression.

''Oh? And what about your precious Ian? I imagine he's too good to bleed.''

His disgruntled tone endeared him to her even as Sheridan told herself not to make more out of his words than was there. ''I wouldn't know if he bleeds.''

''You mean you haven't hit him? You reserve that for me? Should I be honored?''

"Ye're the only one deservin' a cuff."

He made no reply. Instead, he glanced at Sheridan's hair, still pooled in the middle of his chest, and took a length between his fingers. Time held suspended. Sheridan's breathing quickened, her bodice suddenly feeling tight against her breasts.

Nicholas's gaze elevated and locked with hers. He stroked her hair over his cheek and then across his lips. "You have beautiful hair," he murmured. "Like molten fire." His hand began working its way upward until his fingers dug into the hair at the side of her head.

Sheridan closed her eyes, leaning her cheek into his hand, savoring the magic of his touch, squelching the small voice warning her to resist.

Her head rolled back as he caressed her scalp. "Nicholas," she whispered, not realizing she had done so aloud.

"Danny," he murmured back, his other hand rifling through her hair, cupping the back of her head, pulling her down. Sheridan's blood sang through her veins, her lips tingling with the expectancy of his kiss.

A voice chuckled. "Ah, Ho-Sing see things progress with Missy and Boss-man."

Nicholas cursed.

Sheridan gasped, her eyes flying open as she tried to dislodge herself from Nicholas's intimate embrace. He released her, but slowly, a glimmer of something resembling disappointment in his eyes, coupled with a brewing tempest of other emotions.

"If you're desirous of seeing the dawning of another day," Nicholas growled at Ho-Sing, "I wouldn't say another word."

"Oh, but Ho-Sing must speak. Have something very important to tell Boss-man."

"Stow it."

"But—"

"What did I just say?"

Sheridan wondered at the slight grin tugging at Ho-Sing's lips. "Suit self, Boss-man. Don't say Ho-Sing not warn you."

Sheridan frowned at that cryptic remark and turned to gauge Nicholas's reaction. A moment later, an uneasy feeling prickled the hair on the back of her neck.

"Nicholas?" a new voice called out in a dulcet, caressing tone.

Beside her, Nicholas tensed. "Jessica?"

Sheridan swiveled her head to see an exquisite tall blond standing in the doorway, her hair coifed to perfection, her complexion flawless, her seafoam gown hugging a slender figure, and her eyes a stunning shade of blue-green. Yet when those eyes traveled to Sheridan, female ire hardened them to chips of ice. Sheridan returned the woman's bold regard, glare for glare.

So this was Lady Jessica Reardon, the woman Nicholas had been seeing almost every night. Sheridan had allowed herself to believe the woman was wart-nosed and fat. She had always been possessed of a good imagination. Unfortunately, wishing didn't make the dream reality.

Nicholas released Sheridan's wrists and roused himself to a sitting position. Sheridan resisted the urge to sit on top of him.

"What are you doing here?" he asked Jessica, no longer brusque but the epitome of civility, which made Sheridan itch to slap him.

"What are *you* doing here?" the lady returned, her tone clearly miffed.

Nicholas propelled himself to his feet. Sheridan glared up at his chin, waiting for him to offer her his hand. He didn't. She had been forgotten, an odd occurrence for a girl whose antics normally made her the center of attention. Well, she'd fix that unintentional oversight.

She slammed the heel of her hand down on Nicholas's toes.

"God—" The rest of his curse was muffled. Obviously, he was attempting to contain himself in front of his guest. Well, at least she'd gotten his attention.

He glowered down at her.

She smiled up at him.

"Are ye all right?" she asked sweetly, knowing her eyes said *I hope it hurts.* "Me hand must have slipped as I was tryin' to get up—unaided."

He reached a hand down, his eyes promising repercussions if she didn't cease and desist. Rising, she innocently brushed against him. His gaze whipped to hers.

"Thank ye," she murmured, resisting the urge to stick her tongue out at him.

"Well, Nicholas?" Lady Jessica demanded, making her the focal point once again, a fact that ruffled Sheridan. "What is going on here?"

"Nothing is going on here." Nicholas smiled at Jessica, not the polite smile he had bestowed upon Sheridan for two long weeks, but the charming devil smile, the one that put a beautiful dimple in his cheek and never failed to melt her into a puddle. And as she glanced at Lady Jessica, Sheridan could see his grin begin to work its magic.

"I took a bad spill," he went on. "And Miss Delaney came to my aid." His last word sounded a bit choked.

"How fortuitous," the woman replied tersely, her eyes raking over Sheridan. "Delaney. That wouldn't be *Irish* now, would it?"

Sheridan suspected she wouldn't like the woman. The feeling had now been confirmed. Her chin and defenses went up. "Aye. It is."

"Hmm." The woman flicked one last haughty glance at her and then returned her regard to Nicholas. Before

Sheridan's astonished gaze, the woman's features softened, her big blue eyes forlorn and innocent, her lip
quivering slightly. "I guess I've picked an inappropriate
time to visit." She sniffled delicately. "I just wanted to
bring you some flowers from my garden."

Flowers, Sheridan silently scoffed. What man wanted
flowers?

"I love flowers," Nicholas said, refuting Sheridan's
thought.

"You do?" Lady Jessica asked in a squeaky voice.

"I do."

"Well, if that's the case . . ." The woman stepped aside,
and Sheridan got her first glimpse of another body behind
Lady Jessica.

The person's face was completely hidden behind a
mammoth bouquet of vibrant flowers, bursting with color
and arranged to perfection, and definitely not done by the
lily-white hands of Lady Jessica Reardon.

Brushing past Sheridan, Nicholas moved toward Jessica. "They're lovely." He pressed a tender kiss on the
woman's hand.

A strange and unwelcome emotion corkscrewed inside
Sheridan. She had an overwhelming desire to dump the
flowers over Nicholas's thick skull and yank every blond
hair from the head of Lady *That-Wouldn't-Be-Irish-Now-
Would-It?*

Jessica's lashes swept down, showcasing their long
length, before she gifted Nicholas with a practiced expression of the coy maiden. "I made this bouquet especially
for you." Her voice dropped a notch as she added, "To
thank you for another wonderful evening."

Jessica snapped her fingers. The body framed in the
threshold waddled forward and presented the flowers to
Nicholas, who took them as if the crown jewels had just
been bestowed upon him.

"I hope you like them," the blasted woman simpered.

"Without question. I'll put them on the round table out in the foyer so everyone can see them."

A small voice told Sheridan to leave well enough alone, but that small voice had never held sway over her in all her eighteen years.

Coming to stand next to Nicholas, she pointed to a white, trumpet-shaped blossom. "What's that one called?"

Jessica's gaze flicked her way, sending Sheridan a warning look that Nicholas didn't see. "That one? Why that's a . . . a . . ."

"A lily, m'lady," the body next to Jessica answered with an accent Sheridan immediately recognized.

A smug smiled filtered across Jessica's face. "Ah, yes, a lily. I was just about to say that."

Sheridan momentarily ignored Jessica. Tilting her head to the side, a plump-faced, rosy-cheeked young girl in a mobcap greeted her with a wink and a smile.

"That will be all, Maggie." Jessica waved a dismissive hand over her shoulder. "Wait for me in the carriage."

Maggie bobbed her head. "Yes, mum."

"Ho-Sing," Nicholas said, "can you see Jessica's maid out?"

Ho-Sing bowed crisply, something Sheridan doubted he did often. "Right away, Boss-man."

Maggie shot one last quick grin at Sheridan before disappearing out the door.

Jessica's tut-tutting brought Sheridan's gaze back to her. A look of distaste marred the woman's cameo-shaped face. "I don't know how you can stand these foreigners in your house, Nicholas." She darted a glance at Sheridan, clearly conveying she was lumped into that category. "I'd fear being murdered in my bed."

Sheridan waited for Nicholas to speak in Ho-Sing's defense—in loud, angry tones, hopefully. Instead he said mildly, "That is the last thing I worry about. Ho-Sing is extremely competent. I don't know what I'd do without him."

Jessica gave a sharp twist of the white gloves in her hands, obviously not appreciating her remarks being dashed to bits instead of heeded with all due haste. "You have all these odd characters roaming about."

"I happen to like odd characters."

Even though Nicholas wasn't looking at her, Sheridan felt his remark was directed at her.

"Do you know what that senile butler said to me when I told him to take my wrap?"

"No, what did he say?" Humor tinged Nicholas's voice.

"He told me it was too early for him to take a nap."

Nicholas chuckled and Jessica bristled. "It's not funny. My father would never employ such a slipshod character."

That wiped the smile from Nicholas's face. "I'm not your father."

Sheridan could see that Jessica realized she was not getting anywhere and changed tactics.

She leaned forward, probably with the intention of mesmerizing Nicholas with her cleavage, but her overly ostentatious flower arrangement lay squarely between them, little fronds vexing the woman as she tried to move closer to him. Sheridan hid a grin.

"I'm sorry, my darling," she purred. "I don't know what came over me. It is just that I worry about you. These people aren't like us."

These people aren't like us.

The words resounded in Sheridan's ears, seeping into a part of her she believed too toughened for any more hurt. Perhaps the realization that Jessica's words were true made them sting all the more. Sheridan wasn't from Nicholas's world.

Jessica was.

English and Irish. Enemies for nearly eight hundred years. Sheridan had heard that statement often enough from her mother.

She doubted there'd ever come a time when Nicholas could be her enemy, though. Still, she wondered, as she had far too many times since that day at the hotel, if Nicholas's reasons for wanting to be friends had more to do with his feelings about who Sheridan was than with how Jules would react.

"Well," Jessica sighed. "I have to leave, darling, but I will be anticipating tonight."

Sheridan tamped down the shame that made her want to slink out of the room and hide. She'd always faced down any threat. She didn't intend to back down now.

Folding down a handful of blooms, she smiled at her nemesis. "Och now, what's happening tonight?"

Jessica turned her way, her eyes shooting blue daggers. "Do you mind?"

"Mind what?"

"Leaving." Returning her gaze to Nicholas, Jessica pouted, "Are your servants always so belligerent?"

That did it! Sheridan wasn't taking any guff from Miss High and Mighty. She had seen plenty of Lady Jessica's type in Ireland, daughters of the wealthy landlords, galloping about in the fields all day while their Irish servants toiled.

Well, they weren't in Ireland now.

And Sheridan Delaney was nobody's servant.

Nicholas stepped deftly in front of Sheridan, blocking her as she reached for Jessica. "Miss Delaney is my cousin's friend," he explained.

"Jules?" Jessica's tone clearly implied that it figured

Jules would have a friend such as Sheridan. The woman quickly returned to form and gave Nicholas a doe-eyed look. "I know my being here isn't proper, but I wanted to speak to you for a moment—*alone.*"

The request, Sheridan noticed, took Nicholas by surprise. He hesitated, then pivoted on his heel and pressed the blighted bouquet into Sheridan's hands. "Do you mind getting a vase for these, Danny?"

Did she mind? Did he mind walking with a limp?

She pasted a smile on her face. "And why should I mind? They are just lovely flowers now, aren't they?" And she knew a lovely spot for them.

Her step light, she whisked past the lovebirds, her prize clutched tightly to her.

Standing outside the door, Sheridan listened to the low-voiced conversation, making out only a word here and there, her nerves jangling when her highness giggled at something Nicholas said.

Her teeth gritted, Sheridan hastened to the kitchen, filled a lovely vase to hold the lovely bouquet, and with a purposeful stride, she returned to the foyer. She glanced at the round mahogany table in the center of the hallway and then down at Nicholas's sweet-smelling blossoms.

Another giggle echoed through the house.

Sheridan held the flower-filled vase out in front of her, smiled, and recalled another Delaney trait.

Tit for tat.

The vase crashed to the floor.

Chapter Fifteen

He who cannot risk cannot win.

Those words reverberated through Nicholas's head as he stared vacantly out his office window the next morning.

What would make him think of the American naval leader John Paul Jones at a time like this?

The answer came to him in the form of a mental picture of an Irish hellion standing beside a shattered vase, lilies and other flowers strewn around her, water running in a rivulet on his recently polished parquet floor.

Her expression was not the least contrite, not with that slight smile playing about her lips.

Her challenge clearly said: *I have not yet begun to fight.*

Famous last words.

Nicholas dragged a hand through his hair, surprised to find he had any left. What could he have been thinking to give Jessica's flowers to Sheridan? Had he actually thought they'd make it to the foyer without mishap, intentional or not?

He shook his head. Living with Sheridan was like having one foot in a grease slick at all times. Unstable.

He had seen the tumult brewing between Sheridan and Jessica, like two hissing alley cats sharpening their claws on each other's hide. Yet if Nicholas were honest with himself, he'd admit he had enjoyed getting a rise out of Sheridan. The girl was chockful of strong emotions. *Passionate.* And whether that passion was expressed in anger or desire, she was a sight to behold.

Perhaps, if he wanted to take his honesty a step further, he might confess he'd had an inkling of what Sheridan might do with Jessica's bouquet. When he'd seen the destruction she'd wrought, he had scowled on the outside, but crowed on the inside.

He hadn't crowed long, though. The entire household had assembled to enjoy the comic opera while Nicholas sought to work his way through Jessica's tirade.

He had just managed to calm her when dear, demented Uncle Finny slipped out of a crack in the woodwork and pinched her behind.

Nicholas struggled to resist the urge to level the man and erect a normal human being in his remains. Better yet, Nicholas could end the entire demented masquerade by flinging himself into the black hole of Calcutta and pulling the hole in with him. Problem solved.

His soon-to-be intended bolted from the house screaming as if being pursued by the hounds of hell, toppling the entourage to their knees in a gale of laughter.

Before Nicholas could seek out the initial cause of his troubles—a petite lass with a capacity for great destruction—Jules whisked Sheridan away, sequestering them in Jules's bedroom.

Of course, his agony hadn't ended there. What Nicholas

had thought would be a better-than-average evening with Jessica turned into a disaster.

He had discovered the girl had quite a temper, which surprised him. He had always believed she possessed a certain ethereal serenity, an unflappability.

Not so. She could pitch a fit with the best of them. Her eruption had made Nicholas wonder what else he didn't know about her.

Nicholas jumped as a brisk knock sounded at his door. Consequently, he banged his head against the window-pane. "Damn it," he muttered. "Bloody Armageddon has arrived." He rubbed his head and winced. "Never expected the grim reaper would knock."

Lord, he'd become conditioned to the pandemonium already, waiting for someone to come winging through the door, like one of those crazy pookas from whom Sheridan's uncle claimed they were descended.

Whoever dared to bother him would not be taking a trip to the moon on gossamer wings.

With a resigned sigh, Nicholas flung over his shoulder, "Come in."

"I'm already in."

Nicholas reeled around to find his brother, Damien, slung against the door frame, appearing vastly amused and every inch a man at peace with the world, even after choosing to forever shackle himself to that madness called woman.

Damien cocked a brow, his gaze trailing over Nicholas's less than pristine appearance. "A rough night, brother?"

"Don't ask," he grumbled, wondering when he had lost his sense of humor.

Damien chuckled. "That good?"

"You don't want to know."

The throbbing in Nicholas's head had just abated when

a shriek that sounded like the ill wailing of a calliope under a coach wheel rattled the pictures on the walls.

Damien leaned back, peering into the hallway. "Someone is writhing on your floor, brother. You'd better come quick."

Why, Nicholas wondered, had he thought for even a moment that today would remotely resemble those halcyon days he had once known? A case of rising gorge was fast developing, and that didn't generally happen until after he'd eaten breakfast. This was an all-time record.

Striding past his brother, whose amused expression grated on Nicholas's nerves, he proceeded into the hallway to see what new method of torture was being inflicted on him in this conspiracy to drive him insane.

"Oh, lud, this is it," Aggie moaned, her corpulent body prone on the floor, a hand clutched around her cross. "Everything's goin' dim. The wor-rld is fadin'. There's me sister, Minnie, waitin' for me at the pearly gates." She frowned. "She looks heavier than I remember her."

Nicholas contemplated cutting notches into a piece of wood so he could tick off the number of times Sheridan's aunt swooned, gasped, gurgled, saw the white light, and claimed to have spoken to every relative who had passed on to the final reward—a fate Nicholas wished for himself in that moment. Aggie had no intention of going quietly into that good night.

Aggie spotted him then. "Oh, me brawny boy, come keep me company in me final hour." Nicholas sighed and headed toward her, wondering why death had chosen to take a holiday in his home. "Not ye, lad." She pointed a crooked finger at Damien and used it to beckon him forward. "I want *ye.*"

Damien's eyebrows rose and he pointed a finger at himself. "Me?" It was the first time Nicholas could recall his brother looking truly afraid. Nicholas knew the feeling.

"Seems your presence has caused today's bout of death for Aggie," Nicholas said, his humor restored. "Yesterday it was the milkman. The day before it was a young chap who accidentally knocked upon the wrong door." Nicholas shook his head. "Poor sod will never be the same." He clapped Damien on the back. "Well, cheer up, brother. There's only one baptism of fire, and today you're the lucky recipient."

"Come, come, now, me muscled marauder." Aggie's finger wiggled like a fat worm too long in the apple orchard.

"You heard the lady, brother. She wants you. And this is one time I won't toss a coin to see who wins the wench. She's all yours."

"I knew I should have stayed in bed this morning," Damien muttered beneath his breath.

"And let me enjoy all this alone? Perish the thought! We are kin, after all." Nicholas winked. "Share and share alike."

Damien glared. "If you'll notice, I'm not laughing."

"I noticed. I, on the other hand, am laughing to beat all hell."

"Laugh out loud and my fist will give you a one way ticket straight down." Grim-faced, Damien quietly asked, "What does she want from me?"

"My guess is a rousing tumble. You wouldn't mind obliging her, would you? Perhaps I can avoid having Father Sheehan here again. The man always takes the best slices of meat at dinner. And here I thought gluttony was a sin."

Another death gasp rose into the air. "Quickly, lads. Me time is at hand."

Damien hitched a thumb over his shoulder. "What would happen if we ran the other way?"

"It will just prolong the agony." Nicholas gestured his brother ahead of him. "Lead on, MacDuff."

Nicholas and Damien cautiously approached Aggie, kneeling down on opposite sides of her. She took one of their hands in each of hers, her grip as strong as a blacksmith's. "Ye ar-re good lads to be seein' to me in me time of need."

Emery shuffled up to them, his stoop more pronounced than usual. "Shall I fetch Father Sheehan?" he boomed, his meager chest collapsing like a windbag.

Nicholas sighed and nodded. "Yes. And tell him to be bloody quick about it."

"You want me to give him a kick? Yes, sir." Emery ambled away.

Damien shook his head. "Jules told me things were interesting around here since Sheridan Delaney and her family arrived."

Nicholas scoffed. "I see she gave you the sugar-coated version. Now let me tell you the truth. My sweet dreams have been postponed by a nightmare with an Irish accent.

"No bleating sheep are bounding over fences when my eyes drift shut for the night. No fluffy clouds with silver linings are floating in azure skies. No rolling green hills with tall grass blowing gently in the wind reach toward the horizon."

Damien chuckled. "Not even a buxom barmaid named Belinda to bounce on your knee, brother?"

"Nay, and nay again, brother. Rather I see priests, leprechauns, Henry VIII eating a chicken leg, crossed swords hanging over my head, Richard the Lionhearted and the knights of the Round Table—that one is somewhat baffling—and there are midgets juggling fruit, and"— he frowned slightly—"one enchanting shamrock."

"That beats any dream I've ever had hands down."

Speaking of hands, Nicholas tried to surreptitiously

extract his from Aggie's punishing grip. She only squeezed harder.

Grimacing in pain, he inquired, "So what brings you here today? I'm surprised you would leave your wife's side with such a rampant case of mutual fascination."

"Wife!" Aggie groaned and yanked them closer.

Ignoring the pain radiating up his arm, Nicholas added, "I thought you and Eden were still post-nuptualizing on a cloud of euphoria."

Damien held his face away from Aggie, who extolled the glory of his pale blue eyes, and grimaced at Nicholas. "Trust me, your ugly face is the last thing I wanted to see today."

"If you think that's ugly, you should read my thoughts right now." Nicholas expelled a long-suffering sigh. "Since I've discerned that you haven't come here merely to exchange gibes with me, then what, pray tell, has torn you away from home?"

"I've come to retrieve the transfer of ownership papers I had my solicitor send you a month ago. One would think you'd hasten them back as a gesture of goodwill, perhaps even penning a brief reply, such as 'Thank you for your generous gift, dear brother, now drop dead,' sort of thing."

A slight frown puckered Nicholas's brow. "Transfer of ownership papers?"

Damien returned his frown. "Yes, didn't you get them?"

Nicholas recalled the document singed in the fireplace, stomped on by his boot, and clawed by one feathered piranha.

Between wooing Lady Jessica and the three-ring circus that had become his life, the papers had been pushed to the side and forgotten among his other correspondence.

He gave his brother a sheepish grin. "I haven't read them yet."

"Haven't read them? Well, that's gratitude."

"Aye, 'tis a bad thing ye've done, me lad, to ignore yer brethren," Aggie felt inclined to add before resuming her pitiful moaning.

"You're giving me one of your properties?" Nicholas asked.

Damien nodded.

"As a gift?"

"I believe I clarified that as well. You do know what a gift is, don't you? It's something that is bestowed upon another voluntarily and without—"

"Ha-ha. What I want to know is why."

"Why?" Damien held up a fist. "You do know what happens when a solid force meets a fixed object, don't you? Something's going to give. In this case, it will be your jaw."

"You know what I mean, damn it. You're the earl of Blackstone. Those lands belong to you."

"And as such, I can do with them as I so please. Well, it pleases me to give one to you—and one to Gray, of course."

Damien's generosity overwhelmed Nicholas. "Why?" he persisted.

"Because I bloody well wanted to, that's why! And if you ask me again, you won't like the outcome."

Nicholas smiled and raised a hand in supplication. "A wise head keeps a shut mouth."

"Dead men tell no tales," Damien countered.

"I recognize a threat when I hear one." In a more serious tone, Nicholas said, "Thank you."

"You're welcome," his brother returned gruffly.

"Oh, how lovely that was!" Aggie wept, releasing their hands only to wrap her arms around both their necks and yank them down so that their cheeks were smashed against her abundant bosom.

"Father Sheehan is here, sir!" Emery blasted.

There was a god. Amen!

Nicholas extracted his neck from Aggie's chokehold. His brother, he noted with some amusement, had a more difficult time.

Only when Damien agreed to give Aggie a kiss on the cheek did she finally release him. He tumbled back. And then Damien Sinclair, feared by many, a bruiser at two-hundred-twenty-five pounds and six-four at last measurement, scrambled away, his back pressed up against the wall. A rather ignoble position for an earl, not to say extremely amusing. As a recent recipient of property sans payment, Nicholas decided to keep his observations behind his teeth.

Rising, he held out his hand to his brother. "Shall we retire to my office and discuss this matter further?"

"Does your office still have a well-stocked liquor cabinet?"

"It does. Filled with the nectar of the gods."

Damien slapped his palm into Nicholas's and jumped to his feet as if propelled. "Then what the hell are we waiting for? I'd sell you for a drink right now."

Nicholas chuckled. "And I know how much you treasure me, after all."

"May I ask why you're doing that?"

Sheridan paused in her appraisal of her masterpiece to glance up at Jules, perched quite serenely on an atrocious stone bench whose legs resembled an elephant's—clearly the taste of a man, one with green eyes, coal black hair, and a charming little dent . . .

Enough of that, Sheridan Delaney! The man was a

beast. He'd had the audacity to accuse her of dropping Miss High and Mighty's bouquet on purpose.

Sheridan had, of course. But how dare he say so!

"Hello?" Jules prompted.

"What?"

"Am I boring you?"

"Of course not! Lord, ye are a ninny sometimes. Borin' me indeed."

Jules had apologized frequently about her condition, which made it difficult for her to do as much as she'd like. Therefore, the two of them spent a lot of time reminiscing and giggling like schoolgirls.

"Well, it just seems your mind is elsewhere today. In fact, you haven't been quite yourself since you arrived."

"Faith, and what makes ye say such things? Not meself. I'm more meself than I've ever been, I'll thank ye to know."

"If you say so."

"I say so."

"All right."

"All right."

Sheridan narrowed her gaze on her friend's face, wondering about the slight smile that played on Jules's lips. Something whirred behind those innocent eyes.

Why had Jules capitulated so easily? Her friend could be more tenacious than a bear with a thorn in its paw when trying to extract information.

Sheridan's gaze dropped to Jules's lap where a blanket lay, colored in shades of soft pink, blues, and yellows. The blanket was not yet completed. Jules had been working on it for a week. The week before she had knitted gloves for Sheridan and a somewhat misshapen sweater for her husband, even though it was the middle of summer. Booties piled up as if Jules were expecting eight babies instead of one.

Sheridan remembered the day she discovered her friend weeping over William's one-sleeve-longer-than-the-other sweater. When Sheridan demanded to know what had upset Jules, her friend confided to her that her husband loved her.

Sheridan frowned, not understanding why such a thing would make Jules cry. To hear a man say *I love you* seemed the most wonderful thing in the world. Sometimes Sheridan wondered if a man would ever say those three words to her.

Jules informed her that pregnancy caused her emotions to run amuck; laughing when tears would be more appropriate and crying when joy should be the response.

Sheridan could relate to such a thing. Her emotions had been out of line ever since she'd stepped into Nicholas's home, and the tension between them had, on a few occasions, made her nauseous—and she was as stout as an oak, no less.

A few moments passed with only the click-click of Jules's knitting needles and the chop-chop of Sheridan's pruning shears.

They relaxed in a small but lovely walled-in garden, the gorgeous flowers the result of Jules's handiwork during her courtship with William.

Jules had hied off to Nicholas's house often so William would think she spent her time with prospective suitors, refusing to let William know he'd won her heart the first time he'd smiled at her when they were children.

The man, she huffed, had barely looked her way when they were growing up. She certainly didn't intend to ruin a perfect opportunity to nudge the wretch.

"Sometimes a woman needs to use a little trickery— not the kind that wounds, mind you, but the kind that gets her point across," Jules said.

The kind that gets her point across. At last, a concept Sheridan understood.

Without looking up from her knitting, Jules remarked, "Your arrangement is shaping up quite nicely."

It should be, Sheridan thought. She'd been rearranging the blasted flowers for over an hour. She'd never imagined it would be so difficult to get a simple bouquet in order.

The blossoms vexed her at every turn. Too many reds on one side. The yellow and the blue looked bilious together. The sprigs of greenery needed to bend like tender reeds, not point skyward like flagpoles.

"Why all the interest in flowers today?" Jules inquired, her tone all too innocent for Sheridan's comfort.

"Ye know how much I love flowers."

Jules laid her knitting needles down in her lap. "You love flowers, do you? Since when, may I ask?"

"Oh . . . for a long time." Sheridan reached for a tall spiky plant in a stunning blue-purple color that, she hoped, would remind Nicholas of the exact shade of her eyes.

"I wouldn't touch that if I were you."

Sheridan halted and peered over her shoulder at her friend. "Why not? 'Tis lovely."

"Lovely, but poisonous."

"Poisonous?"

Jules nodded. "That's monkshood, often called wolfsbane."

"Wolfsbane? What a terrible thing to be callin' such a winsome plant."

"It was given that name a long time ago when meat was poisoned with its juice to kill off wolves."

"Well, I don't intend to drink it, mind ye, just add a sprinkle here and there for a wee hint of color."

"Some people get rashes from even touching it. Cousin Nicky, for example. His hand barely brushed the plant one day and his entire arm reddened and itched. He was miserable.''

Sheridan slowly pulled her hand back. ''Well why don't ye get rid of it, then?''

''I'm the one who tended the garden. When I got married, the plant flourished. My cousin won't get near it, and I'd prefer not to take my chances with it. I'm uncomfortable enough as it is.'' She rubbed a hand over her stomach, a slight grimace marring her smooth brow.

''Well, 'tis a fine thing to be poisoned in yer own home.''

Jules chuckled. ''If Nicky would hire a gardener, he wouldn't have to worry about it, but he won't. He often threatens to level my beautiful garden and erect a nice billiard room in its place. He claims flowers don't belong in a man's home, even though his own brother, Damien, has a rose garden that could make a horticulturist weep.

''Nevertheless, I gently informed him that if he so much as touches a petal, he will have to contend with me.'' Jules winked at Sheridan. ''That always seems to work.''

Flowers didn't belong in a man's home? Sheridan gritted her teeth, remembering Nicholas's words to Jessica the day before.

I love flowers.

Liar.

A fresh stab of pain struck Sheridan's heart as she concluded the reason Nicholas would have made such a false claim.

He liked Jessica Reardon—perhaps even . . . loved her.

Love could make one do or say things they wouldn't normally. Sheridan should know.

''This project of yours wouldn't have anything to do with that little mishap in the foyer yesterday, would it?'' Jules queried. ''An apology of sorts?''

"An apology?" Sheridan snorted. "I dropped the vase by accident, need I remind ye?"

"Hmm."

"And what does *hmm* mean?

"Nothing."

" 'Tis a bad liar ye are, Jules Thornton."

"I merely wondered what prompted you to take up flower arrangement when we've sat here in the garden nearly every day since you arrived and you barely did more than sniff a blossom."

Sheridan stiffened in umbrage. "I thought you'd like a nice bunch for your room. Are ye satisfied now?"

"Oh, so those flowers are for me? Hmm."

"Not another *hmm,* do ye hear?" Sheridan jammed a denuded stem in the vase, having plucked away every petal in her pique.

"I'm sorry. I guess I thought . . ."

"Thought?"

Jules shrugged. "That they were for dear Cousin Nicky."

"For dear—for him? Never! I wouldn't give that irritating, obnoxious, pigheaded *louse* . . . ooh!"

Jules's brow escalated with every disparaging remark. "So you like him that much?"

"Like him! *Like him!*"

"Methinks she doth protest too much."

"Don't ye start with yer clever English prattle!"

"More like clever English observation. Did you think I haven't noticed how you two look at each other? Even your glares are heated with passion."

"Oh, aye. I feel passionate all right—passionate enough to clobber the duffer!"

Jules laughed. "I'm pregnant, Danny. Not blind. I don't know why you and he fight so strenuously to cover up your feelings. I think it's wonderful."

Sheridan blinked. "Ye . . . do?" she whispered, as if saying the words too loud might make Jules retract them.

"Yes. I couldn't be happier. You and Nicky are perfect for each other."

"We are?"

Jules smiled tenderly. "You are."

Sheridan's chest constricted with sisterly love for Jules. Her friend had given her blessing, though Sheridan had never asked. Jules had seen the truth and embraced it with open arms.

Deep in her heart, Sheridan hadn't been able to accept the fact that Jules would scorn any relationship between her and Nicholas. But if Jules endorsed Sheridan's relationship with her cousin . . . then Nicholas had lied to her.

There are some things Jules would never accept. Our relationship is one of them. Her understanding only goes so far.

Another stab of pain jabbed at Sheridan's already bruised heart. Nicholas had used Jules as an excuse to extract himself from an awkward situation.

She'd asked him once if it mattered that she was Irish and he English. He'd scoffed, telling her it made no difference. Had that been the truth or another lie? What other falsehoods had he told her?

An Irish peasant and an English aristocrat. A long black line that had never been crossed. What made her think she could bridge the gap?

Two souls entwined. The worst of lies.

"Oh!" Jules gasped, drawing Sheridan from the darkness of her heart.

Sheridan's gaze snapped up to see Jules's face pale, her hands clutching her belly.

Tossing her pruning shears aside, Sheridan scrambled

over to her friend. "What's the matter? Is it the babe again?"

Mutely, Jules nodded, clamping her bottom lip between her teeth as the pain crested and then subsided. Closing her eyes, she took a deep breath.

Sheridan squeezed her friend's hands reassuringly. "What has the doctor said about yer difficulties?"

Jules's eyes didn't meet hers. "He reprimanded me for not telling my husband . . . that early labor is prevalent in my family." She added the last few words in a nearly inaudible voice.

Sheridan sat back on her heels and stared.

"Say something, Danny," Jules begged, the worry she'd been carrying around, alone and unvoiced, showing clearly in her green eyes.

"How could ye not confide such a thing to yer best friend?"

Jules's expression beseeched forgiveness. "I'm sorry. I . . . I didn't want anyone to worry."

"So ye just kept it all to yerself, addin' more burden onto yer meager shoulders? Oh, 'tis a perfect way to make sure yer havin' this babe early."

"I know I should have told someone."

"Yer husband, at the very least."

"Oh, I couldn't tell him. He worries so much about me as it is. He wouldn't have let me come to town had I told him. He'd force me to stay in bed until the babe was born, driving himself and me crazy, and I wanted so desperately to see you."

Jules dropped her head. "My motives were not entirely pure, though. In fact, they were utterly selfish. You see, I needed you here, needed your comfort. I'm . . . afraid. This is my first child. My mother's dead and I . . . I don't have many female friends . . . and all around me are strapping men who faint at the sight of a pregnant woman.

I—I didn't want to be alone." She peeked up at Sheridan with woebegone eyes. "Am I terrible?"

Sheridan gripped her friend's hands and squeezed comfortingly. "Nay, not so terrible." She smiled. "And I wouldn't want to be anywhere but with ye. Ye are my best friend."

Sheridan's smile did not reach inside her. Memory plagued her—the strange and frightening sensation she had experienced when first laying hands on Jules' stomach the day she had told the story of the leprechauns and the pookas.

Sheridan had managed to squelch her concern, telling herself her visions could be fickle, like her. Sometimes she had them. Sometimes she didn't.

But deep down, she knew. This vision was strong.

And all too real.

Rain, hard and battering, pelted down, thundering on the roof like a thousand pebbles. Jules lay in a bed Sheridan had never seen before, her face fearful, knowing her time was at hand.

Sheridan could not see herself in the picture.

Jules was alone—the very thing her friend feared.

"Will you finish the story, Danny?" Jules softly pleaded. "The one about the leprechauns."

Sheridan nodded. She needed to ease her friend's fears. Perhaps she needed to ease her own as well.

Sheridan's melodious voice lured Nicholas down the hall as surely as the call of the sirens led many a sailor to his doom. Those men, he imagined, had met their Maker in peace, however.

Nicholas doubted the same fate would be granted him.

Yet as he stood unnoticed in the doorway leading to the garden, admiring Sheridan's animated profile and the joy she brought to Jules, Nicholas wondered if perhaps such a fate wasn't a bad thing.

"Ah, but 'twas a grand fight while it lasted, kippeen and shillelagh bangin' and clashin'. And with that much yellin' from all the pookas and the leprechauns, the din could be heard from Dunqueen in the west to Cashel in the east.

"Oh, but all that fightin' and bangin' and yellin' was most displeasing to Him"—Sheridan pointed upward—"who was at that very time tryin' to take a wee nap. 'I'll put a stop to those ructions,' " he said. And he did.

"The Creator sprinkled the stardust of forgetfulness on both pookas and leprechauns so their bad habits would be banished." Sheridan smiled. "Well, some of them, at least.

"So 'twas with that stardust He bestowed upon all Irish men—and women, mind ye—the gift of imagination to compensate them for what they are not, and a sense of humor to console them for what they are."

"Bravo."

Sheridan tensed, hearing Nicholas's voice. Slowly, she turned her head, her gaze locking with the emerald green eyes of the man who had become her downfall.

He leaned against the doorjamb, the epitome of the casual gentleman in fawn-colored trousers that delineated the strength of his thighs, and a brilliant white shirt, sleeves rolled back and open slightly at the neck, emphasizing his dark skin.

Sheridan berated herself for the slight leap in her heart that always occurred when she saw Nicholas. Pride quickly came to her rescue, reminding her of his lies, and his convenient excuse they'd be hurting Jules if their relationship continued.

"You're looking revived this morning, Nicky," Jules

remarked. "Did you have a good evening with Lady Jessica?"

"Well enough—after its rocky start." He gave Sheridan a pointed look, placing the blame squarely at her doorstep for his problems with Jessica.

"That's nice," Jules remarked. "I had a bit of a headache myself."

Headache? Sheridan frowned. She'd been with Jules all night and she had been as animated as a summer lark.

Concern etched Nicholas's face. "Are you all right, puss?"

"Oh, yes. I'm fine." Mischief twinkled in the slight tilt of Jules's lips. "Seems my pregnancy has lessened my ability to tolerate shrill voices, and Lady Jessica's tone was particularly piercing yesterday. Her anger surprised me. She always struck me as rather mild-mannered and soft-spoken."

Nicholas's jaw clenched. "Her anger was justified. And I certainly know some other females who possess a healthy temper."

"Oh, don't get me wrong, Nicky darling. I'm sure Jessica has some wonderful qualities."

"She does."

"Clearly, she is a nice, stable girl."

"She is."

"Any man who marries her will know that every day will be exactly like the one before."

Nicholas frowned. "What does that mean?"

"Nothing bad, of course. I just mean that life with Jessica will be predictable. No surprises. But that's good for a man who wants a staid home life."

"Some men don't like surprises. Some men prefer not to wake up every morning wondering if they are taking their lives in their hands by leaving their bed. Some men might enjoy staid—"

"Boring," Jules murmured loud enough for all ears.

"*Staid* to unpredictable. A man wants to know his wife will be home where she belongs."

Wife? The word reverberated through Sheridan's head. Had Nicholas been speaking hypothetically? Or was he thinking of marrying Lady Jessica?

Jules said, "Then Jessica Reardon is a perfect catch. "Yet . . ." She stopped.

"Yet?" Nicholas prompted, his lips pressed in a grim line.

Jules shrugged delicately. "Well, her outburst yesterday does give one pause. She behaved a tad, shall we say, irrationally? Makes a body wonder what other small things might push her over the edge. Oh, but what do I know?" Before Nicholas could reply, she said, "Danny, will you help me up? I'm feeling rather tired. I think I'll take a nap."

Sheridan blinked, rousing herself from her stupor at the thought of Nicholas and Jessica as husband and wife.

Jules winked at her, and Sheridan knew her friend's remarks had been for her benefit. Another sweet gesture, but unnecessary. Sheridan wanted nothing from Nicholas.

Nothing but a pound of flesh.

And she would extract it one small bit at a time.

Sheridan wrapped her arm around Jules and helped her up. "I'll walk with ye to yer room."

Jules waved a dismissive hand. "Don't be silly. I'm pregnant, not aged. You stay here and keep my cousin company. I'll see you later."

Before Sheridan could protest, Jules was gone. Sheridan faced Nicholas, whose body suddenly seemed to encompass the entire doorway, blocking her escape, a slight smile playing about his lips.

Sheridan had no intention of allowing him to intimidate her, which is exactly what he was trying to do. She set back her shoulders, tilted up her chin and attempted to breeze past him.

His outstretched arm barricaded her grand exit. "Not so fast."

"Get out of the way."

He shook his head. "You heard Jules. She said to keep me company."

"I'd rather keep company with the devil."

He eyed her. "Rather nervy of you to be angry with me, when I have every right to be angry with you. You nearly ruined my evening with Jessica."

"And wouldn't that have been a shame now?" Sheridan cursed her unruly tongue for giving away how she felt.

He cocked a brow. "If I didn't know better, I might think you were jealous, Danny."

"Jealous? Ha! 'Tis no concern of mine what ye do with yer precious Jessica. Ye deserve each other."

"Please retract your claws from my lower extremities. God made me a man, and I'd like to stay that way. Now, could we skip the gristle and get down to the bone? What, exactly, is eating you? You have not been all that is sweetness and light lately."

Sheridan's eyes looked like sapphire peaks of ice, treacherous and beckoning, and Nicholas had not donned his spiked shoes.

She smiled. "Go to blazes."

"Don't sugar coat it now. Give it to me straight."

"Fine. I'd rather be thrown headlong into a snake pit than to spend another moment with a big ape like ye! Now step aside! I've other things to do with me time."

Nicholas's smile evaporated. "Like spending it with Ian McDonough?"

" 'Tis none of yer concern what I do or who I'm doing it with!"

"Anything that goes on in my house is my concern. I'll not have you dallying with the servants."

"Dallying!" Sheridan choked, and then reacted, smacking him across the cheek, the sound of flesh against flesh ringing loudly in the still afternoon.

Nicholas grabbed her wrists, his hold unyielding as he yanked her forward into his chest. Eyes blazing fire, he growled low, "You're pushing me, Danny. I'm not a nice man when I'm pushed."

"Yer not a nice man ever! So don't be foolin' yerself." She tried to wrench free. His grip only tightened.

"In that case, you'll understand this."

His mouth slammed down upon hers, robbing the breath from her lungs and sealing off any protest. He took what she didn't want to give, his kiss meant to punish, to humiliate, to show her who was master. He meant to dominate her.

The more she struggled, the more demanding his kiss became and the harder Sheridan fought not to respond. Yet her heart, body, and soul conspired against her. The feel of his hard frame crushed against hers, the scent of him, the heat of him drew her in, annihilating her will, obliterating thought.

His hands slid down her back and cupped her buttocks, pressing her firmly against his arousal. Her fists uncurled, her palms testing the flesh of his chest, reveling in the bunching muscles in his shoulders, before sinking into his thick, silky mane.

"Danny," he murmured as his lips slanted over hers. "God, how I've missed you."

He took her hand and led her away from the door and into a small embrasure. He dragged her forward, hard against the broad expanse of his chest, his mouth swooping down and capturing her lips once more.

She returned his kiss with all the pent-up passion inside

her, the yearning, the endless weeks with only memories of their lovemaking to sustain her, building the hunger until it fairly consumed her.

"I want you, Danny. I'm tired of trying to deny it."

Sheridan's heart soared, even as a voice warned her not to trust his husky words. Yet she, too, was tired of denying what she felt for Nicholas, of fighting the feelings he roused in her.

Perhaps he had finally realized, as she had from the start, that they were meant to be together. Or perhaps he'd sensed Jules's acceptance. Or perhaps her temper and stubbornness had pushed him away.

Weren't her sisters forever reminding her no man would tolerate her bold opinions, wild ways, and penchant for doing the opposite of whatever someone told her to?

"There's no reason we can't be friends *and* lovers, is there, Danny?" Nicholas murmured against her ear, sending rivulets of fire through her veins.

"Aye," she breathed. "Friends . . ."

"And lovers."

She smiled against his throat. "That, too."

He cupped her chin. "Very much of *that*." He kissed her lightly, sweetly, adding, "At least until I marry Jessica."

Sheridan's body froze faster than water in the North Sea. "What?"

Nicholas continued to sprinkle kisses over her face, heedless of the change in her. "I'm one of those men who wants to be faithful to his wife. Odd, I know. But how can I expect the same fidelity in return if I don't act the part? Until then, however, we can have a good time."

Sheridan felt as if a hand squeezed the air from her lungs. "A . . . good time?"

"A very good time," he murmured, his gaze promising delight. "Will you come to my bedroom?"

Sheridan stifled the pain ripping its way through her in favor of anger. She would weep no more tears for this man.

He wanted no surprises? She'd barrage him with more than he could handle.

He'd prefer not to wake up every morning wondering if he took his life into his hands by leaving his bed? She'd make him sorry he woke up at all.

He wanted staid rather than unpredictable? She'd give him a heaping pile of unpredictable.

"Aye. I'll come to yer room."

His beautiful smile bespoke his ignorance of what life held in store for him from that moment on.

"Meet me in ten minutes."

She halted him as he turned to leave. "I have something for ye."

Sheridan hurried over to her flower arrangement, making sure Nicholas couldn't see her hands as she quickly slipped on her gardening gloves, swiped up the pruning shears and cut a nice batch of monkshead for his bouquet. Then she removed all the flowers from the vase and presented him with the arrangement, made especially for him and *only* him.

"These are for ye."

A slight frown marred his brow, as if a warning bell clanged. "That's very sweet of you."

" 'Tis the very least I could do, what with droppin' yer sweetheart's lovely arrangement."

"You know, I truly think you're sorry."

Sheridan smiled. "Ye'll never know how sorry." But he would soon enough. "Smell them. 'Tis a special scent they carry."

Tentatively, Nicholas held the bouquet to his nose and

Sheridan bit the inside of her mouth to keep from laughing with glee.

"Beautiful," he murmured. "Like you."

Ignoring his empty flattery, she stood on tiptoe and whispered in his ear, "I hope every time ye look at these flowers, ye'll think of me and remember this moment."

Chapter Sixteen

He would kill her.

The minute Sheridan walked through the front door, Nicholas planned to wrap his long, strong fingers around her silky, oh-so-easily-snapped neck and spin her head so fast it would travel back in time.

Damn, he itched!

Bloody wolfsbane.

The lesser of the two banes in his life at that moment. Nicholas also had to contend with the deadly Irish-Lass-Seeking-My-Imminent-Demise-and-Won't-Give-Up-Until-I'm-Dead bane, contracted when one came in contact with the slender, violet-eyed Sheridan flower, whose poisonous, prickly thorns were cleverly hidden beneath magnificent petals.

Ever since she had plowed into his life, he'd been walking a tightrope in the middle of a hurricane. He could have sworn just that morning he saw someone hanging a sign on his front door: *Asylum for the Insane.* Anyone who walked into his house was instantly corrupted.

Nicholas himself was a prime example. He was beginning to relate to Uncle Finny, glimpsing occasional lucidity in the man's eyes and a hint of pity, making Nicholas wonder if Sheridan's uncle was not so much mad as a March hare, but rather clever, his lunacy a ruse to protect himself from the females in his family.

A particularly vivid memory came to mind from a week earlier.

Birds chirping gaily. Sun shining brightly.

Female glaring menacingly. Shoe flying wildly. Reflexes reacting slowly.

Uncle Finny speaking rationally.

"Now there be a spoon ye'll sup sorrow with yet, boyo," he had remarked to Nicholas, nodding his head at Sheridan's retreating form, her back ramrod straight as she marched unevenly down the hallway, one foot minus the shoe she had winged at Nicholas's head after he innocently suggested she wear her hair up instead of letting it dangle down her back like a wild woman.

His request had nothing to do with the fact that Sheridan's lush tresses swung enticingly over an equally lush derriere, thereby distracting him to the point of physical pain and drying his mouth to a pasty substance. Nothing at all.

Propriety dictated certain rules for women. Ever the gracious host, Nicholas felt it only right he should inform Sheridan of said rules.

"Oh, ye want me to put me hair up, now, do ye? Like the way Lady Jessica wears hers, perhaps?"

"Well, now that you mention it . . ."

Next thing Nicholas knew, Sheridan's not-so-dainty

shoe whistled past his ear and hit his bedroom window with such force it cracked one of the panes.

Uncle Finny patted him on the shoulder. " 'Tis a good thing ye're quick, lad. I've seen the girl take off an ear. Keep low, 'tis my advice," he said, shuffling away.

Nicholas grimaced at the memory and scratched his itchy chest like a dog with fleas.

"I hope every time ye look at these flowers, ye'll think of me and remember this moment," he mimicked Sheridan's last buckshot-filled words to him before she had conveniently disappeared for the rest of the day.

When he had prodded Jules for information on Sheridan's whereabouts, his cousin merely eyed the red, blotchy spots marring his skin and laughed hysterically. He stalked off.

At first, and foolishly, Nicholas believed Sheridan had put the wolfsbane in the bouquet accidentally. She had seemed rather amorous with him in the garden after all, her kiss telling him she wanted him. And he had wanted her, by God, to the point he would have overlooked just about anything.

Even after the itching started and an hour had passed with no sign of Sheridan, Nicholas continued to tell himself she was innocent, that she didn't realize the harm the plant could cause.

Two things clarified his delusion.

Nothing Sheridan Delaney did was accidental.

Nothing Sheridan Delaney did was innocent.

Combine that with her conspicuous absence from his bed and from the house, and his conclusion was airtight.

Nicholas prowled his office, a room from which a thousand indecisions had been launched, but where he made one very definite decision that day.

Retreat and regroup.

He had met the enemy. And he was hers.

* * *

Holding her shoes in her hands, Sheridan tiptoed down the dimly lit hallway, one sconce showing her the way. The night cloaked her in shadows—and the shadows were a friend to a lass endeavoring to be clandestine.

She'd sneaked in the servant's entrance with Ian, who, having fallen on good times as the recipient of fifty pounds of Nicholas's money for capturing Scally, had shown her a most enjoyable evening.

Ian attempted to teach her a Scottish reel. She, in turn, demonstrated an Irish jig. They talked about their homes, their families, and their dreams.

Yet no matter how much fun they had, Nicholas's face overshadowed the evening, the way he had looked at her in the garden, the desire burning in his eyes, his mouth upon hers, branding her as he had from the start. Her body's response had been immediate.

Sheridan realized with despair that the only way she might be able to put Nicholas Sinclair from her mind— and heart—was to return to Boston. A hollow sensation settled in the pit of her stomach at the thought.

And what about Jules? How could she think about leaving when Jules needed her? Sheridan couldn't desert her friend. That left her with only one choice.

Retreat and regroup.

She had met the enemy. And she was his.

Sheridan started as the ormolu clock chimed midnight.

Clutching the newel post at the bottom of the steps, she took a deep breath to settle her suddenly jangling nerves and headed up the stairs to her bedroom.

"Welcome home," a silky voice murmured, sounding none too welcoming.

Sheridan froze in mid step.

Dislodging her heart from her throat, she quickly

counted the remaining stairs to the second floor landing, wondering if she could outrun him.

Twenty-four steps. Why did the English have to live in houses with more than one floor?

Glancing down at her skirt, Sheridan scowled, knowing the blasted thing would hamper her escape. Tomorrow she would start wearing breeches.

Still, a Delaney never gave up without a fight. So Sheridan tested the boundaries of the anger she heard in Nicholas's voice and placed her foot on the next tread.

"I can make it to the top of the stairs in less than four seconds," he warned. "I was a sprinter at Oxford."

Figures.

Sheridan eased her other foot onto the step.

"I also enjoyed wrestling."

That stopped her cold. Nicholas was the last person with whom she wanted to wrestle. She'd capitulate at the first touch of his hands upon her body.

Chin up, shoulders back, feet leaden, she turned to face the music—a mournful tune eerily similar to a funeral dirge, and she could well imagine whose funeral it was.

"I could take ye in a heartbeat," she challenged instead of retreating.

Then her eyes settled on his face—his handsome, blotchy face. She prayed for the strength not to laugh, pressing her twitching lips together tightly.

"So you think I look funny, do you?"

Sheridan shook her head because to open her mouth would inevitably mean mirth would pour forth.

He grimaced and scratched behind his ear.

That was all Sheridan needed to see. She doubled over with laughter.

"I'm . . . ye're . . ." She couldn't get any words out between breaths. Every time she made the mistake of glancing up at Nicholas, whose scowl deepened with every guffaw, she broke out in a fresh gale.

She sobered immediately when he grasped her wrist and began dragging her toward his office. "W-what . . . what are ye doing?" she panicked, wishing she hadn't removed her shoes. In her stocking feet, she slid like a skater across the floor.

Would he spank her again?

Or would he throttle her outright this time?

He yanked her in front of him as soon as they stepped over the threshold of his office. Sheridan twirled toward a leather settee and landed in a rather ignoble heap.

Nicholas slammed the door shut with a booted heel.

She was trapped.

"Join me in a drink, will you?" Before Sheridan could reply, Nicholas strode toward the sideboard, his entire body rigid with anger. "Nothing like a good vendetta to give one a thirst."

He poured two glasses of straight whiskey and turned, a determined gleam in his eyes as he stalked toward her. Sheridan had to fight the urge to dash behind the settee to keep a barrier between them.

Then he was in front of her, pressing the glass into her hand. "Take it."

"I—I don't want it."

His look warned her further protest would be futile, as well as potentially dangerous. She took the glass, a fine tremor shaking her hands.

Piercing eyes studied her as she raised the drink to her lips. Sheridan couldn't take her gaze from Nicholas, regarding him over the rim of her glass as she took a sip of the fiery liquid. If he had been expecting her to choke on the potent brew, he would have a long wait. Her uncle's undiluted poteen made regular whiskey taste as mild as water.

"Satisfied?" she prodded defiantly.

"Satisfaction is one word I doubt I'll ever utter in relation to you, my dear."

His words were double edged, reminding her of the pleasure they could have found in one another's arms that afternoon and for who knows how many afternoons to come. But she wouldn't be his plaything. His mistress.

How foolish to think he had a noble bone in his body, that he might have ever thought of her as a woman he could make his wife. How wrong she had been.

She rose on shaky limbs from the settee—bringing her chest to chest with Nicholas. His white shirt clung to his broad shoulders, and the V of bronzed skin it exposed made her want to run her fingers over his warm flesh.

He did not step back or move to the side to allow her to pass. He didn't do anything but stare at her, yet his presence wrapped around her like invisible arms.

"I'll be goin' now," she told him with as much authority as her constricted lungs would allow.

"I think not." He put his large hand on her shoulder and shoved her back down onto the settee.

She gasped in outrage. "Ye'll be keepin' yer manhandlin' to yerself or I'll—"

He bent forward, bringing them face to face, his heat blasting her, his eyes glinting emerald gems. "Or you'll what?"

Sheridan swallowed. Words would not come. Why couldn't she hate him? Why, when she most wanted to slap him, rake her nails over his skin, did she also want to touch him, soothe him . . . become one with him? What magic spell had he cast over her?

"Just leave me alone," she whispered.

"No," he whispered back, settling his big body on the settee close to her, overwhelming her as he always did. "I waited up for you."

Sheridan tried to ease away from him, but her back was already jammed into the corner of the settee. As well, Nicholas's booted foot was ever so conveniently placed on the hem of her skirt. Why he thought such a tactic necessary, she didn't know. He would swoop down upon her like a big, sleek bird of prey before she could move an inch.

"Where did you go?" he demanded.

She raised her chin, matching him glare for glare. "Out." She knew she sounded like a petulant child, but how dare he act so autocratic, as if he was the master of her? She didn't owe him any explanations.

His slight smile had the gleam of a dagger's blade. "You're taxing my patience, and I'm not feeling particularly benevolent, if you haven't noticed." Then he growled as a fit of scratching came over him.

A twang of something Sheridan might have labeled regret stole off her. He was in a great deal of discomfort, that much was evident.

Her momentary bout of compassion fled when he said, "I had to cancel my evening with Jessica because of you."

Sheridan twisted her fingers into her skirt. " 'Tis sure I am that she'll get over it. Not every woman will die for want of yer company."

The leather creaked and groaned as he shifted his body, sliding toward her, boxing her in even further. "And what about you, Danny? Will you die for want of my company?"

Her heart said *yes*. Her mouth said, "I don't even want to breath the same air as ye, ye big-headed buffoon."

His smile never lapsed as he edged ever nearer, his arm rolling along the top of the settee. Sheridan nearly leaped out of her skin when he took a long length of her hair in his hand. "Perhaps a mouth-to-mouth sedative will unruffle your feathers and loosen your tongue,'' he murmured, closing the distance.

Before Sheridan's hazy brain could comprehend his meaning, Nicholas's lips were against hers, hot, demanding, and thought destroying. Outrage died without having ever been voiced as his tongue plunged between her lips, his body pressing her down.

The weight of him was a heady delight, his warmth banishing her chill. His mouth molded her, plundered, sought every last ounce of resistance and annihilated it.

His silky hair skimmed her neck as his lips trailed a path down her throat. There was no tenderness in his touch, just a primal urge that matched hers. No amount of anger could make her deny the hunger Nicholas caused in her.

She tore at his shirt like a wild being, needing to feel the strength of him, the solid expanse of his chest, to cling to the bunched muscles of his shoulders.

Like magic, his fingers worked her buttons free. He took the top of her chemise and tore it down the center, the sound of ripping material blasting through the high-ceilinged room and eliciting a gasp from her, which he smothered with his mouth.

Her nipples tightened painfully. He soothed the ache with his mouth, suckling her, drawing her on passion's rack. She tossed her head and groaned as each taste, each touch drew darts of ecstasy through her body.

She arched her back. He slid his arm beneath her and pulled her closer as he settled firmly between her legs, his manhood hard and throbbing against her.

He grasped her ankle, his hand kneading her flesh, moving upward over her knee, skimming her outer thigh, and then cupping her buttocks. He rocked against her. She matched him thrust for thrust.

He groaned, his warm breath against her nipple tightening all her muscles, a tempest building inside her that only Nicholas could shelter her from.

She gasped as he pulled her upright, her legs straddling his lap, her chemise hanging in tatters about her, her skirt bunched up to her thighs, her nipples thrusting forward, swollen and aching for him to resume his sweet torture.

The touch of his tongue flicking out to tease her nipple almost caused her to buck right off his lap. He held her firm, his free hand slipping between their bodies, his fingers easily separating the slit in her pantalets and finding her engorged nub, rubbing it fast and then slow, massaging, flicking, teasing until Sheridan felt the storm culminating inside of her. When he stopped abruptly, she thought she would die.

Nicholas undid his trousers, his long, hard length springing free. Before Sheridan understood what was happening, he lifted her, impaling her on his engorged shaft, touching her all the way to her womb. She cried out.

He grabbed the back of her head, taking her lips in a searing kiss. "God, you're beautiful," he murmured, the words touching Sheridan's soul.

He settled his large hands on her waist and showed her the motion. Up, down. Up, down. Oh, God.

She clutched the top of the settee as she moved over him, the feel of him sliding in and out of her pure, blessed torture. She was in control. She decided the when, where, and how.

His face was frozen in a mask of pleasure/pain as he closed his eyes and tossed his head back against the settee. Sheridan watched his face, reveling in the responses she could bring with different movements. A demon inside her wanted him to writhe, wanted him to suffer, wanted to prolong the intense, beautiful agony.

His eyes popped open, impaling her as completely as

his manhood. His arms coiled around her waist and he stood up. "Wrap your legs around my waist."

Erotic ecstasy ripped through Sheridan, having him so deeply inside her, feeling the strength of his body as he moved toward the wall. He pressed her back against it and plunged into her, rocking her as he took control, holding her as if she weighed no more than a feather.

The pictures on the wall rattled with every thrust, but he didn't care. The house could have fallen about their ears. Nothing mattered besides the moment.

The friction drove her wild, the heat building once more to a fevered pitch until her breath locked in her throat and warm pulses rained down over him while his fury stroked inside her. His brow glistened with sweat and his shirt clung to him as he thrust one last time, groaning his release, his warmth mingling with hers.

Sheridan collapsed against his shoulder. Had he not been holding her, she would have melted into a puddle at his feet. Tenderly, he brushed a kiss against her forehead. She allowed herself a moment to enjoy the sweet gesture before reality stole in to haunt her.

How could she have given in so easily? Allowed a smile and a kiss to tame her anger?

Why did she ask why?

She knew the answer. She loved Nicholas, and only time and distance might ever change that fact. She couldn't mistake passion for love, pleasure for concern.

Gently, he slid out of her and then slowly lowered her feet to the floor. He didn't let her go, though, or move away. Instead he stared down at her, an emotion reflected in his eyes that Sheridan dared not study too closely. Softly, almost reverently, he brushed her hair back.

"I'm sorry," he murmured. "I don't know what came over me. I've never been so out of control. So . . . unlike myself."

Sheridan didn't want to hear apologies or acknowledge the confusion and compassion etched on his face or understand the sadness in his eyes—a sadness that mirrored her own.

She slid away from him, her back pressed tightly against the wall, her gaze accusing, condemning . . . begging for surcease from the torment he put her through.

He reached out for her, and she cringed. "Sheridan . . ." Her name was a plea on his lips.

Her stomach tightened. No! Not the queasiness. Not here. Not now.

Not in front of this man!

She shoved away from the wall, clutching her shirt to her chest with one hand and flinging the door open with the other. She ran into the dimly lit hallway and prayed no one would see her, know where she was coming from, or recognize what she had done. Mock her shame. Scorn the weakness inside her that had become part of her since setting eyes on Nicholas.

She fled from him.

Fled from herself.

Nicholas started after her, but stopped at the bottom of the staircase, watching her disappear from sight like an illusion that existed only in his mind, leaving a lingering hint of flowers and the memory of crimson and lavender blue.

He realized she ran from him, that he had pushed her away again when all he wanted was to hold her close and keep her within his embrace forever.

Why couldn't he let her go? Leave her alone? End this torment for both of them? Nothing could come from this madness but heartache.

He had never thought much about the whims of fate that had made him the man he was, that soul-deep need to find a woman who completed him, fulfilled him, who would be his mate for life. If ever he wanted to toss away his fear of what a faithless woman could do to a man, break the shackles that bound his soul, he should do so now.

But, dear God, Sheridan frightened him.

What he felt for her was too strong, holding him in thrall, looming, threatening to destroy him should he be foolish enough to give his heart to her—and that's what he wanted to do.

He wouldn't deny it. He'd denied his feelings from the moment he'd opened his eyes on the dock and seen her gamine face hovering above him, and that refusal had taken its toll on him, tearing at him bit by agonizing bit.

Time away. That's what he needed. Time to think. Time to forget.

Time to work Sheridan out of his system.

In the morning he would leave for Silver Hills.

But as Nicholas mounted the stairs to seek his bed and toss fitfully for yet another night, a small voice he recognized as his own told him Sheridan was already a part of his system, and neither time nor distance would erase that truth.

Chapter Seventeen

"*Going with me?* What do you mean you're going with me?"

Nicholas gaped at his cousin, who stood in the middle of the foyer, trunks to the left and right of her, a feathered hat perched on her coifed head, and a matching pelisse draped over her shoulders. Her stomach appeared to have ripened even further overnight.

Jules's eyes were clear and focused steadily on him, demanding—in typical Jules fashion—that he refute the fact that he had been about to slink away into the early morning mist with nothing more than a hastily written note to let her know he had departed. But Ho-Sing, his soon-to-be-*ex*-manservant, had snitched on him.

"You didn't expect us to stay here, did you?"

At the mention of the word "us," Nicholas glanced up the stairs. Sheridan stood at the top of the landing, her face pale, dark smudges beneath her eyes as if she hadn't slept, which would make two of them. Still, she looked utterly lovely and completely beyond his reach.

"I haven't been to Silver Hills in ages," Jules went on. "I want to show Danny where I spent some of the most wonderful days of my life."

"But I—"

"I imagine you felt it unnecessary to extend a formal invitation, as we are kin.

"Well, I—"

Jules held up her hand. "There's no need to explain. As you can see, we are packed and ready to go."

Nicholas raked a hand through his hair. Clearly his cousin didn't intend to loan him a cup of air with which to argue. If she wasn't so, well, pregnant, he might have had more leverage, but whenever he looked at her, fragile, helpless—*round*—he liquefied into two hundred pounds of aspic.

"Do you think you should be traveling in your condition?" he asked, genuinely concerned about her welfare. William would bend him into a horseshoe if Nicholas should let anything happen to Jules.

"I'm fine," she declared, a little too quickly. "Besides, we are only going to Kent. Hardly a long trip."

"What about William? His last missive to me said he was coming to London, intent on being your shadow until the baby was born."

"I've already taken care of that. I wrote William this morning and told him to come to Silver Hills instead." Jules waddled up to him, looping her arm through his and smiling. "It will be like old times."

Nicholas grimaced. If memory served, he had been the brunt of much grief in the *old times*.

And nothing had changed in the present day.

Nicholas heaved a sigh, envisioning Silver Hills, the

oasis, Shangri-la, and sovereign new state where he reigned supreme, fading into the distance, Uncle Finny's words ringing in his ears.

Keep low, lad . . . keep low.

As she watched the scenery roll by her window, Sheridan began to revive, to pull herself from the dark despair that had dogged her through the night and well into the morning, her mind replaying each moment in Nicholas's arms.

She shivered and hugged herself tight as the memories pervaded. A cool touch of air against her skin felt like the whisper of his lips. The rays of the sun slanting through the coach window enveloped her like Nicholas's warmth. She could feel his hands upon her as if the two of them were still entwined in each other's arms.

How she had wanted to protest when Jules told her they would be leaving for Silver Hills that morning with Nicholas. How Sheridan longed to confide in her friend, to tell Jules she couldn't go, couldn't be near Nicholas. She had wanted to bare her heart and soul to Jules.

But she didn't. She couldn't burden her friend, not in Jules's condition, not when Sheridan had to be the strong one.

Not when she would soon be a mother herself.

Sheridan closed her eyes, a wave of fresh nausea stealing over her. All the symptoms fit. She was pregnant. Perhaps she had known the truth all along, her mind refusing to acknowledge what her heart already knew.

Nicholas's baby.

The very idea of having his child thrilled her even as it frightened her. If she couldn't have Nicholas, she could at least have a small, wonderful part of him.

But how was she to raise this child alone? Protect it

in a world that scorned her kind and would revile her plight? Her decision would leave her child fatherless. A bastard.

For she could not tell Nicholas of her condition. He would believe it his duty to marry her, and as much as she dreamed of being his wife, she wanted him to propose out of love, and love alone. Not because he felt honor bound.

Yet the other part of her, the part that said to deny Nicholas his child would be to deny her child a father, protested, clawed at the very fiber of her beliefs.

Didn't every child have the right to be loved by both parents? To have a piece of his mother and father? To know their heritage? What would she tell her son or daughter when they asked about their father?

Sheridan knew Nicholas loved children. How would he feel should he ever discover he had missed out on his child's life? Would he condemn Sheridan? Hate her forever? He might not be able to give her his love, but she couldn't bear his scorn.

"Here we are."

Jules's soft voice broke through Sheridan's thoughts, pulling her back to the present.

Sheridan focused on the view in the distance. It seemed as if a whole new world had opened up before her eyes, a world of stunning beauty and surreal charm.

The landscape, a green, lush extravaganza, swept in all directions. In the distance rose a fairy-tale castle, round towers and turrets peeping through the trees, making her think of days long ago when a fair maiden might have stood on the parapets waiting for her knight to return. Medieval splendor and timeless craftsmanship. She dared not blink for fear it would all disappear.

The coach rumbled along, ascending a gradual steep, and found a passage through a rocky gorge between the abrupt termination of a range of hills to the left and a rocky ledge that rose dark and sudden at the right.

They rolled past a park wall built of loose stone and mantled here and there with ivy, crossed a shallow ford, and moved down a grass-grown road with many turns and windings leading up to the castle, which was nestled under the shadow of the woods.

As they approached the house, the road skirted the edge of a precipitous glen clothed with hazel, dwarf oak, and thorn, and the silent house stood with its wide-open hall door facing a moat. A towering forest and great trees framed the castle, courtyard and stable.

Through the air wafted an abundance of fragrances: roses, boxwood, azaleas, wisteria, water lilies, and specimen shrubs.

Jules's glowing face appeared next to Sheridan's as she pointed out the window. "There, beyond that profusion of plants, are hidden pathways to explore. As a child, when I walked down the flagstones and disappeared into the thicket, I felt as if I'd stepped into another world. There is no place quite like Silver Hills."

Sheridan silently agreed.

The coach rolled to a stop in front of the drawbridge. Sheridan felt rooted to the seat. Her mouth dropped open, her gaze roving over stone and mortar crafted into singular splendor.

A warm chuckle shook her from her staring. Nicholas held open the coach door, his hand outstretched.

"Welcome to my home, Danny Delaney."

His home. A home she would deny their son or daughter when she returned to Boston. A wonderful home full of lore and undoubtedly legend.

Her child's birthright.

Jules's chuckle mingled with Nicholas's as she nudged Sheridan in the back to get her moving. Sheridan stared at Nicholas's proffered hand, afraid to touch him, knowing what one touch could do, how it could break her resolve.

Tentatively, she laid her palm within his. Warm, welcoming fingers wrapped about hers, encompassing, protecting. Safe. She stepped down, standing toe to toe with him. He smiled, and it touched her like the last ray of an autumn sun.

It was as if Sheridan had been cast under a spell. And the spell wove further about her as Nicholas took her arm and tucked it in the crook of his. For that one beautiful moment in time, she felt as if she belonged to this castle.

That she was Nicholas's fairy princess.

The ornate, intricately carved double doors opened, and Emery poised on the threshold in all his stooped glory, awaiting his employer. The man bent at the waist and beckoned them forward. Like reigning dignitaries, she and Nicholas swept into a circular, high-ceilinged room.

Sheridan absorbed the grandeur in wide-eyed awe. " 'Tis the most wondrous sight I've ever seen."

Nicholas squeezed her hand, bringing Sheridan's gaze to him. Pride and love for his home reflected on his face.

"I say the same thing every time I see the old dame. When I'm here, nothing else exists besides this small slice of heaven. Come." Like an excited boy, he led her toward the drawing room. "We call this room Paradise."

Sheridan could well understand the reason. The room's vaulted ceiling thronged with painted birds of all colors and sizes, its walls decorated with Aesop's fables, making her feel she had just stepped into the Garden of Eden. A feast for the senses.

While pointing out all the intricate details, Nicholas told her about other rooms with similar themes: astrological symbols, nature's creatures, the pleasures of the seasons, biblical characters dressed in gilt robes, Moorish designs, and heraldic features. Decadent splendor, he called it.

He then showed her a library with row upon row of books, stacked all the way to the ceiling. Carved into the center of one wall was a huge marble fireplace. Beyond the mullioned French doors, two flowing fountains gurgled and rich greenery spread out as far as the eye could see.

Jules had excused herself from the tour, claiming she wanted to unpack. But Sheridan could see the ride had taken much out of her friend. A sensation like bottled lightning had churned in Sheridan's stomach when Jules clasped her hand briefly, a vision of her friend's face twisted in the throes of childbirth. Her time was close at hand.

As Sheridan watched Jules depart, she knew the strongest urge to confide Jules's secret to Nicholas, to forewarn him of what was to come. He needed to be prepared, just in case.

Yet she refrained, keeping the truth locked inside for yet another day. Jules had begged her not to worry her cousin with something that might very well not happen.

Yet Sheridan read the concern in Jules's eyes, belying her words. Nevertheless, Sheridan didn't want to compound Jules's fear by telling her friend of the things she had seen only within her mind's eye.

Besides, Sheridan intended to be there for Jules when her time came, and Jules had assured her the doctor lived close by. Sheridan could handle anything that arose until the doctor arrived. She had delivered a few babies.

One stillborn.

She shook the disturbing thought from her mind. Jules and her baby would be just fine. Sheridan would see to it.

Out of the corner of her eye, Sheridan spotted an item on a half-moon table by the far wall that she hadn't expected to find in Nicholas's house.

"A Celtic cross."

Nicholas followed Sheridan's gaze, enjoying the pleasure on her expressive face. Enjoying her. The urge to stomp about and rail at the fates that had saddled him with two women had left him.

" 'Tis lovely," she murmured, studying the cross.

Nicholas's father had brought the cross back with him from Ireland when he had gone to check on their property right before he died.

Property now in Nicholas's possession.

In an ironic twist of fate, Damien had deeded to Nicholas a house and lands in Ireland—a holding Nicholas had forgotten all about.

Damien was, in his own way, being amusing. He had thought it apropos to relinquish that particular estate, having heard about Nicholas's unique houseguests of the Irish persuasion. Hence, Gray got the property in Wales, and Nicholas received Mulholland Manor, making him the last thing he wanted to be.

A landlord.

Since the day he'd signed the papers, Sheridan's words had haunted him.

If ye were a hated landlord, then I'd have issue with ye.

Nicholas stood next to Sheridan, trying to ignore her loveliness and the way he felt when she was near. How would he ever tell her about his latest acquisition? He could almost picture her expression, the shock paling her face, dulling her eyes. Anger would follow.

Then the look of betrayal, accusation changing whatever she felt for him into hate. Regardless of what he told her, he would still be the one thing she despised the most.

Sheridan traced her fingers over the cherub faces decorating the four corners of the cross. ''Where did ye get this?''

Nicholas realized her question gave him the opening he needed to tell her about Mulholland Manor, to explain how the estate had come to be in his possession.

But why did he have to explain? He could own property wherever he damn well pleased. It wasn't as if he had planned to deceive her.

It occurred to him that perhaps this turn of events was exactly what he needed to sever whatever was building between he and Sheridan, to break the bond he'd never felt with any other woman.

So why, then, did he want to tell Sheridan gently about his new property, to make sure she understood? Perhaps it was best not to look too closely at his reasoning.

''The cross has been here a long time,'' he returned evasively.

A twinge of pain touched him as he studied her profile, serene and lovely. His arm lifted, the desire to stroke back the wisps of hair caressing her cheek nearly overwhelming. Instead, he balled his hand into a fist and dropped it to his side.

He had to get out before he did something foolish, as he had done more than once with Sheridan. A ride on Narcissus was the remedy he sought—to gallop far afield, over hills and along ledges at breakneck speed, hoping to outdistance the hounds of desire.

He felt Sheridan's eyes upon him. Too late for retreat. His gaze slid upward from the perfection of her cheek and locked with violet gems. The sadness reflected in their depths rocked him. Had he caused her pain? Lord knows he had done things, said things, he wished he could take back.

Her vulnerability chipped away at his resolve, making

him question the decisions he had made that dictated his life, his future.

Why couldn't he try to make things work with her? Maybe if he held tight and gave her all he could offer, she'd love him, stay with him. Not betray his heart.

Something undeniable lay between them. If only he could let go of the pain and open his heart to possibilities, forget the vindictiveness of his mother and the slow destruction of his father.

Sheridan wasn't his mother and he wasn't his father. Nicholas wouldn't let the same thing happen to him and Danny that had happened to his parents. He'd keep control of the situation.

Control. Of Sheridan Delaney, the uncontrollable. The fruit-destroying, shoe-flinging, fiery-tempered, Nicholas-abusing Sheridan Delaney.

Try.

A voice, loud, coarse and woefully familiar, echoed down the long corridor, breaking the moment.

Uncle Finny and Aunt Aggie had arrived, the death and destruction twins.

Nicholas heaved a sigh, wondering why people who knew the least knew it the loudest.

He backed away from Sheridan, thinking about what he had almost done, what he had wanted to do. He had to clear his head, be alone, and he knew exactly where to go. He pivoted on his heel and strode from the room.

Chapter Eighteen

"Sweet Jesus, what's happened?" Nicholas demanded when he saw his prize stud, Narcissus, drop to his rump and try lying down on his side. Only the tight hold the stable master had on Narcissus's reins kept him upright. Nicholas ran over to help, maneuvering the horse back on to its feet.

"Thank goodness you have arrived, sir," his stable master, Jeremiah, said. Lines creased the young man's forehead, worry marked his eyes. "Narcissus was fine until a short while ago. I exercised him in the paddock and returned him to his stall. I left for only a short while to exercise Grayfriar. When I returned, I saw Narcissus nipping at his flanks."

That one symptom was all Nicholas had to hear. It foretold an ailment that made horse owners shudder because of its unpredictable nature.

Colic.

The disease lacked a singular explanation and could afflict a horse at any time with little or no warning.

Narcissus had to be kept on his feet and moving. If he laid down he would roll, and if he rolled, that could cause twisting or tangling of the intestines, which could result in a kink or knot that blocked the passage of blood or food. The result could be fatal.

"Has there been any change in his diet or usual activities?" Nicholas asked, his hands running over Narcissus's belly, finding it hard and distended.

"No, sir. He was prancing around all morning, as if he knew you were on your way."

"What about his stabling conditions?"

Jeremiah shook his head. "Everything is exactly the way it has always been, sir."

Nicholas stared down into the large, frightened eyes of his horse, stroking the Arabian's neck. "Have you sent for Timmons?"

"Yes, sir, but . . ."

"But what?"

"Well, he's on another emergency and doesn't know when he can get here."

Nicholas gritted his teeth. He shouldn't be surprised the man was otherwise occupied, being the only veterinarian in a fifty-mile radius.

Nevertheless, Timmons's absence would not cause a great hardship. Nicholas knew as much or more about horses than most people, having bred and raised them for a good portion of his life. Narcissus had colic one time before and Nicholas had pulled him through just fine. He could do so again.

He shrugged out of his jacket and rolled up the sleeves of his shirt. "Well, I guess it is just the two of us, then." When Jeremiah remained silent, Nicholas's gaze snapped to him. He didn't like what he saw reflected in his stable master's eyes. "What is it?"

"Narcissus isn't the only one afflicted." Jeremiah nodded toward another stall. "Eclipse is as well."

Nicholas raked a hand through his hair. Two of his best horses down. Damn it! Narcissus and Eclipse were the central part of his breeding business. Horse lovers flocked from all destinations to buy a fleet-footed foal sired by one of these two horses.

If Nicholas lost them, not only would he be losing two splendid animals that had become an integral part of his life, that knew him as well as he knew them, but he would also lose an essential part of his business.

The look in Jeremiah's eyes told Nicholas more bad news loomed on the horizon.

"What else?"

"It's Wind Dancer."

Nicholas's body tensed. Wind Dancer was his pregnant mare, carrying Narcissus's next foal. "What about her?"

"She's gone into labor."

"Are you finished, miss?"

Sheridan jumped at the sound of the footman's voice. He stood poised beside her chair, neatly attired in emerald and gold livery, his buttons gleaming, one white-gloved hand held out.

It took a moment for Sheridan to realize what he wanted. Her gaze dropped to the gold-rimmed plate of cold, congealing food placed smartly in front of her, the utensils unmoved, her wine glass still full. She'd been staring into the liquid's crimson depths, seeing things swirling within the wine that disturbed her.

"Aye, I'm finished."

With crisp efficiency, the footman whisked the plate

from the table and vanished behind a cleverly hidden door that Sheridan imagined led to the kitchen.

She dined alone, uneasiness weighing heavily upon her. Yet her tension did not stem from the fact that she sat in solitary grandeur at a table spacious enough for twenty-five people; Jules having not even made an appearance, as she had retired early. No, something else gnawed at Sheridan.

Whether her disquiet came from some impending sense of doom, her ever present nausea, or worry over her friend, she did not know. Yet her unease remained unabated.

She rose from the table, wondering if perhaps the immense house had swallowed up her dinner partners. Certainly there were intriguing hidden doors that led to other places besides the kitchen. Ho-Sing had awed her with sconces that moved, revealing dark, beckoning pathways, daring someone to discover where they ended.

Ho-Sing had also hinted at improprieties related to the secret corridors, midnight rendezvous previous owners had had with women who were not their wives.

Sheridan wondered if perhaps Nicholas would seek her out through one of these tunnels, appearing at the base of her bed, towering, dark, and seductive. A shiver coursed through her at the thought.

What would she do should her fantasy become reality? Would she relent as she had every time he'd touched her? Or would she finally find the strength to push him away? She decided it best not to probe the question too deeply.

Sheridan roamed the hallway, not eager to return to her cavernous room, where unhappy contemplation seemed to be her only friend, angel and devil riding her shoulders, confusing her at every turn.

Her gaze was drawn to the portraits running the length of the long staircase. Sheridan drifted over to them, trying to see a bit of Nicholas in each image and finding characteristics in a hint of a dimple or a glint in an eye or a wicked smile.

Each portrait bore the name of the person whose likeness dwelled within the gilded frame. Nicholas and his brothers, Damien and Gray, were in a row, Nicholas at the end as the youngest. They wore identical smiles that promised trouble, the charm of their youthful faces foretelling the handsome men they would become.

Sheridan paused at the picture of their mother and father. Odd, but she felt an immediate kinship with Niles Sinclair. Not an attractive man, but one whose expression whispered of laughter and love. Yet a trace of sadness marred familiar green eyes, sadness locked inside . . . a sadness Sheridan had glimpsed once or twice in Nicholas's eyes—his father's eyes.

Now Beatrice Sinclair . . . Sheridan shivered and took a step back. Nicholas's mother had eyes that seemed alive, cutting Sheridan to the quick.

No smile rode her lips, no laugh lines creased her eyes, no love emanated from her dour face. What must it have been like to grow up with such a woman? Did she ever bend down to give her children a hug? Tell them how wonderful they were? How much she loved them?

Somehow Sheridan doubted it. How could a man like Niles Sinclair, who looked so full of life and had gifts to share, have married such a woman?

Perhaps Sheridan judged Lady Beatrice too harshly. Really, what could a picture tell her?

Yet as she turned away from the portrait, Sheridan felt the woman's eyes drilling into her back as if warning her she was not welcome.

Worse, those eyes hinted at a secret . . . a dark secret, the kind that left wounds.

"Ah, there, Missy!"

Sheridan's gaze snapped to the speaker. Ho-Sing stood at the top of the landing wearing a kung fu suit in red, his shiny ebony hair reflecting the golden hue of the candles glowing down the length of the hallway. His eyes danced with intelligence, humor, and mischief.

Ho-Sing came down the steps and stopped next to her. "Missy look forlorn."

"I'm fine," Sheridan lied, a lingering remembrance of Lady Beatrice's eyes upon her.

"You miss Boss-man."

"Of course I don't!" she replied a bit too vehemently.

Ho-Sing nodded, but his expression told her he didn't believe her. "Boss-man in stable."

Sheridan folded her arms across her chest. "So?"

"So you go see him."

"Ye go see him," she countered, silently cursing the petulant note in her voice.

"He need you."

Nicholas needed her? If only she could believe Ho-Sing. "Did he . . . ask for me?"

Ho-Sing shook his head, and Sheridan's spirits deflated. "Ho-Sing know he need you. I feel it. Here." He pointed to his heart.

Sheridan had felt such conviction once. She wanted to believe she had obliterated any fanciful thoughts, but she knew she hadn't. "Why is he in the stable?"

"Horses very sick. May die."

During the ride to Silver Hills, Nicholas had spoken freely on many subjects, becoming more animated the closer they got to their destination. He and Jules exchanged tales of a bygone youth spent cavorting with wild abandon, days when they would lock Jules in the loft of the barn and stage mock duels to rescue her from her evil captor.

His demeanor changed when he spoke of his horses,

the love he had for his animals coming through with every word. And it seemed whenever Sheridan had convinced herself she could harden her heart to him, he said something or did something that made her love him all the more. He had so many admirable qualities. If only he had a little love to spare for her.

Sheridan shook off her wishful thinking and bid Ho-Sing a quick good-bye. She hastened out of the house and toward the stables.

Barely visible clouds blotted out the moon as she flew across the grass toward the stable. She had grown up on horses. Most days they had been her best friends. To hear of a sick horse, one so ill it might die, made her heart ache.

The moment Sheridan opened the stable doors, she knew the situation was dire. Nicholas was trying to coax a beautiful black stud onto its feet. It sat dog-like in a pile of hay. Further down, a man Sheridan didn't know walked a blood bay stallion.

"What are you doing here?" Nicholas barked when she stepped into the stall, barely sparing her a glance.

Gone was the pristinely attired gentleman who had escorted her about his house earlier. In his place was a man with hair tousled as if raked by a thousand fingers, a lock slanting across his brow in reckless abandon.

His white shirt bore stains and a film no amount of cleaning would remove. His once highly polished jockey boots were scuffed and muddy, and his black trousers were dusty, a jagged tear at one knee.

"Stand back!" he ordered. "You're liable to be kicked, and I don't need any more problems right now." Taut lines of worry radiated around his eyes, and his lips were set in a grim line. Sheridan couldn't help respecting a man who cared so deeply about another living being.

He was a man who would love his child more than life itself.

Sheridan shook off the thought. Now was not the time to question her decision.

She squared her shoulder and said, "I've come to help."

She thought he would snap at her again. Instead, his features softened, and Sheridan caught a hint of sadness in his green eyes—that sadness he shared with his father, a hurt that made her want to pull him close and soothe whatever troubled him.

"Do you know anything about horses?"

Sheridan recalled him asking her that same question the night their paths had intersected, a night she'd never forget no matter what courses their lives might take, and she gave him the same reassurance she had then. "Enough."

A glimmer of a smile touched his lips. The way his gaze captured and held hers caused a hot rivulet of desire to ripple through her veins.

"All right, then. I could use the help." His next words startled her. "Do you know anything about birthing?"

Birthing. Why did it seem an omen that he should ask her such a thing?

Sheridan swallowed. "Ye mean foaling?"

He nodded. "My mare, Wind Dancer, has gone into labor. She wasn't due for another month. I think the smell of sickness has frightened her into early labor."

Early labor. Sheridan briefly closed her eyes, willing back the ghosts sliding out to haunt her, picturing Jules. Her friend had not surfaced from her bedroom for most of the day.

When Sheridan had checked on her earlier, Jules's complexion had been somewhat pale, her lips pinched. Jules claimed she was fine. Sheridan prayed that was true.

"Can you handle the mare?" Nicholas asked, pulling Sheridan back to the present. "I'll be right here to help."

She cocked an eyebrow. "Foalin' 'tis second nature for we Irish. I'll have the wee stilt-legged thing out of his mother's belly before Uncle Finny can finish a pint."

Nicholas looked as if he would say something. Instead he nodded and then bellowed, "Jeremiah!"

Hay rustled as feet pounded toward them. "Yes, sir?"

"Miss Delaney is going to help us with the horses."

Jeremiah blinked at her as if the prospect of having a woman getting her hands dirty in the stable was too unbelievable to comprehend. "She is, sir?"

"She is." Nicholas turned to her. "Jeremiah will get you anything you need."

Sheridan took a deep breath and stood up. "Well, then, I'll be needin' a spare lantern, small and large towels, tail wraps, somethin' to cover me hands, a sharp knife, a bucket with warm water, needle and thread, rolled cotton, and a pocket watch. Oh, and please make sure there is fresh hay down for the dam. No shavings."

Jeremiah nodded and dashed off to get her requested items, leaving Sheridan alone and very conscious of Nicholas. He rubbed his horse's side, staring at her. "You know what you're doing. I'm impressed."

"And did ye think I didn't?"

He shrugged. "I wasn't sure." He studied her, his expression contemplative. "I'm beginning to realize that there are a lot of things I don't know about you."

Sheridan ached to tell him that if only he'd asked, she would have willingly imparted whatever he wanted to know.

"It's not too late," he said, his voice soft.

"Not too late for what?"

"To know you."

Sheridan warned herself not to read too much into his words. "What is there to know?"

"Quite a bit, I imagine. A girl like you probably has

a thousand tales to tell, each more interesting than the last."

Sheridan's back went up. "What do ye mean *a girl like me?*"

"Spirited, vibrant, brave. A survivor."

That was not the description Sheridan expected. His sweet words took the wind from her sails. " 'Tis not so very brave I am."

"You are to me."

Sheridan knew a desperate moment when she wanted to confide in Nicholas, tell him about the life growing inside her. Tell him he was going to be a father. But this was not the right place, the right time.

Yet where was the right place? And when was the right time? There seemed to be no clear answer. Perhaps after the horses had been restored to health she could find a quiet moment with Nicholas. She would tell him she didn't expect marriage, nor would she accept any proposal he might feel obligated to make. She would marry for love . . . and love alone.

Nicholas might desire her, but he did not love her.

"So tell me about yourself," he said. "What did you dream of when you were a little girl?"

Dreams. Sheridan had more than her share. The strength of those dreams had kept her going, the belief that some day she'd reach the heights she aspired to. Yet her dreams were not particularly grand in scale.

She didn't require wealth to be happy. She didn't want material possessions. She wasn't one for parties and ball gowns and jewelry.

She desired simple things. A cottage nestled in the hills of Ireland, perhaps a wee gurgling stream nearby, cool and inviting for her bairns to frolic in—and she wanted lots of bairns, freckled-faced boys and rosy-cheeked girls who called her Mum.

She would gather them close in front of the fire, like her mum had done with Sheridan and her siblings, and tell them tales about the land of eternal youth, where no one grows old and all wishes are granted.

She would tuck her children snug in bed, kiss each on the forehead, and sigh as she closed their bedroom door, happy to have made it through another day with the little rapscallions.

Then the night would belong to her and her husband.

Tall, his gaze penetrating, his body silhouetted by the firelight, turning him into a golden god, her husband would open his arms wide, beckoning her. Sheridan would lift her skirts and fly into his loving embrace, knowing that home existed wherever he was.

Together, they would move to the window, watching the last pink rays of the sun melt behind the horizon, an array of beautiful, sleek-coated horses dotting the landscape . . . their horses, their land. Their home.

"Sheridan?"

Sheridan shook her head, stunned to find she had drifted off to another place. She glanced up to find Nicholas regarding her with concerned eyes.

"Are you all right?" he asked.

She nodded because words would not come. He looked as if he wanted to question her further, but Jeremiah returned with her supplies, saving her from having to delve into dreams whose misty corners she feared to tread.

Huge brown eyes blinked at Sheridan when she entered Wind Dancer's stall. The mare's sleek mahogany coat glimmered in the light of a single lantern, her belly extended, her udders full, telling Sheridan the mare's time was near.

Sheridan propped the supplies in a corner. Whenever possible, it was best to let the horse foal on her own.

Still, Sheridan was concerned about the amount of time the birth was taking.

" 'Tis all right, girl," Sheridan murmured, kneeling at the mare's head, moving carefully, not wanting to frighten Wind Dancer. "Ye are a sweet lass now, aren't ye?" She stroked the mare's neck. "And ye are about to become a mother. Oh 'tis a wondrous thing."

The horse's abdomen constricted. Sheridan shifted, laying her hands against Wind Dancer's taut belly. "All right now, girl. Ye must keep yer strength up to push yer babe into the world."

The birthing started slowly, the mare's placental sac breaking, fluid saturating the hay. Sheridan cleaned it away and put down fresh hay.

The sac appeared next. Wind Dancer's contractions became more fierce as she tried to push a seventy- to ninety-pound foal through a small birth canal.

Several times Sheridan prepared herself to assist, concerned about the difficulty the young mare was having. Each time, Wind Dancer showed her strength and rallied forth.

The process seemed to take hours, but finally two tiny hooves appeared, then the nose, the birthing membranes clinging to the foal's wet skin. Sheridan cut some of the membranes away from its nose to allow it some air.

A sudden loud whinny from Narcissus startled Wind Dancer. Her head flailed and a back leg jutted out, clipping Sheridan in the side and heaving her against the wall.

Sheridan groaned and clutched her side, her mind racing with thoughts of her baby and what such a blow might do to the small life growing inside her. She squeezed her eyes closed and forced the negative thought from her mind. She was strong and healthy. She would be fine.

She waited for the pain to subside, knowing the mare hadn't meant to hurt her. Wind Dancer was nervous. Her foal was large, making it a difficult birth. As well, Sheridan doubted her presence helped much. She was a stranger to the mare.

Wincing, Sheridan resumed her post and pulled the foal out a little to help the straining mother until, at last, the foal had been completely expelled.

Sheridan blinked back tears at the precious bundle before her. "Ye have a lovely little filly, Wind Dancer."

The mare whickered softly as if understanding her job was complete and she had succeeded in bringing a new life into the world.

Sheridan grabbed a towel and began vigorously wiping down the foal. She knew she had to acclimate mother and baby quickly if she didn't want the mare rejecting her offspring.

Sheridan lifted the foal, a difficult task as the foal weighed a substantial amount. She laid mother and daughter nose to nose, allowing them to breathe in each other's scent. Now Sheridan hoped Wind Dancer wouldn't balk when the foal suckled. That was always a chance. But if Sheridan knew Nicholas, he had prepared the mare well in advance.

"Magnificent."

Startled, Sheridan glanced over her shoulder to see Nicholas framed in the stall doorway, Narcissus behind him. Some of the dull film had lifted from the horse's eyes, but Sheridan knew a long road still lay ahead of them.

Narcissus and the other downed horse would have to be walked until they were out of danger, and there were oil dosings and perhaps a water treatment that might be necessary to clear the stallions' congested intestines. But at least they had one bright spot to lift their spirits.

Sheridan smiled down at the foal and stroked her sleek neck. "Aye, she is a fey little thing."

"That she is, but I wasn't talking about the foal."

Sheridan's hand stilled. "Ye weren't?"

"No."

"Then who . . ."

"You." Before she had a moment to savor his compliment, he said, "I thought I should bring the proud father by to see what his manly prowess has wrought."

A startling image of what Nicholas's manly prowess had wrought caused heat to scorch Sheridan's cheeks in a startling rush, her hand settling on her stomach in a subconscious gesture.

Nicholas chuckled, mistaking her blush. "You do know how Wind Dancer got in such a condition, don't you? If not, I'd be happy to explain."

His remark made her whole body warm, to her mortification, and she averted her gaze. "I'll thank ye to keep a civil tongue in yer head."

"I've been sufficiently chastised." The amusement in his voice relieved some of the tension that had been making Sheridan's heart beat in slow, painful strokes.

"Do you want to name her?"

Sheridan's stunned gaze lifted to his. "Me?"

He nodded, an endearing smile curving up the corners of his lips. "Anything you'd like."

She glanced down at the foal, not wanting Nicholas to see the vulnerability his offer had opened inside her.

The foal made its first attempt to rise on shaky limbs, wobbled, and then plunked down into the hay.

Sheridan remembered the beautiful little buckskin mare she had owned back in Ireland—before she had been forced to leave the horse behind when her family fled for their lives. The pain had never quite healed. Emotion choked her.

Even after all this time, she still felt the dagger of

anguish tear through her when she'd relinquished the mare's reins to a local farmer and had to walk away.

"Hannah," she murmured, a single tear running down her cheek. "I'd like to call her Hannah."

"Then Hannah it is."

Chapter Nineteen

Damien had always told Nicholas that there were three things a man couldn't see coming: the blade's edge, the wind . . . and love.

Nicholas wondered when, exactly, he had fallen in love with Sheridan.

Could it have been when she'd been sitting Indian style on the stall floor hours before, stroking a foal named Hannah, her shirt stained, her skirt rumpled, her hair in a halo of disarray, and a smudge of dirt slanted across one porcelain cheek?

Or perhaps it had been the moment he'd glimpsed her on the deck of the ship, dancing like a sea nymph, her fiery copper hair flying out, her face lit from within, a smile of delight riding her sweet lips.

Or had he known in that first glance their souls were entwined before she had uttered the words?

Nicholas had learned not to doubt anything after Damien, a man supposedly untamable, unrepentant, and surely consigned to hell by his peers, had married. If Nicholas had taken away even one lesson from that, it was to expect the unexpected.

And Sheridan was about as unexpected as they came.

Whether asleep or awake, Sheridan's face haunted him. When she hurt, he hurt. When she was happy, he was happy. When she was angry . . . he ducked.

Nicholas hated to admit the truth, even to himself, but Sheridan scared the hell out of him—the pain she could inflict upon him should he get entangled, losing himself in her eyes, baring his soul a little more every day, relinquishing his heart.

His feelings for her were so strong. She could destroy him, just as his mother's betrayal had destroyed his father.

"Ye're lookin' awfully serious. What are ye thinkin' about?"

Sheridan's soft voice washed over Nicholas like a warm summer rain. His gaze lifted. She stood opposite him, holding Eclipse's reins. They had been walking the horses for hours. Soon the sun would crest the horizon and time would tell if the horses would survive.

Perhaps time would also tell him what to do next. He had accused Sheridan once of running away, but all this time he had been the one running. Now it was time to stop. No matter his fear, he had to talk things out with her. He had to know how she felt.

"If ye're worried about yer horses, I think they'll be fine. Ye've done everything ye could." Sheridan smiled and nodded toward Hannah. " 'Tis a wonderful new addition ye have there. The wee lassie is strong and healthy. She'll make a fine mother herself some day."

"As will you."

Nicholas's compliment caught Sheridan off guard, not

merely because it was unexpected, but because it hit too close to home. If she didn't know better, she might think he knew about her condition.

Perhaps now was the time to tell him about their baby, in these quiet predawn hours when the world lay dormant and something warm and strong settled between them.

Sheridan knew she couldn't live a lie. Maybe she had known all along she would tell Nicholas the truth. Her upbringing demanded she do no less.

Yet the image of Lady Beatrice's cold face gnawed at Sheridan. She wanted to know Nicholas, to understand what things had formed him, made him the man he was.

Perhaps she needed to know what kind of father he'd be. That meant finding out how he had been raised, about his parents, his life. His childhood. Things he'd always been reticent to discuss.

"Nicholas?"

"Yes?" His gaze was clearer than Sheridan had ever seen it, as if the clouds had lifted and she could finally see all the way to heaven.

"I'd like to know about yer mother."

A slow frown pulled his eyebrows together. "What about her?" His tone was slightly brusque and Sheridan hesitated, not wanting to destroy the moment with a subject he clearly didn't want to discuss. But she had to know.

"What was she like?"

"Why?"

"I saw her portrait and I'm curious about her."

His jaw tightened almost imperceptibly, and he started forward with Narcissus, resuming the walking he had stopped to smile sweetly at her.

Sheridan watched him over her shoulder, bidding herself to leave well enough alone. Yet the change in him worried her. For the sake of their baby, she had to understand his reluctance to speak of his mother. For as long as Sheridan had known Nicholas, he had avoided the topic.

"Do ye like yer mother?"

"Does it matter?"

"Aye," Sheridan said, not backing down. "It does." He turned suddenly, his look hard. "Why?"

"Because . . . I think she hurt ye in some way, in a place deep down that ye don't want to acknowledge or examine."

"You know nothing about my mother or my life."

"Aye, ye're right."

Nicholas stood at the opposite end of the stable, still as death and more impenetrable than stone. "Look, my mother is not like yours, all right? She didn't sing me lullabies or tell me tales about mystical places or tuck me in at night. Is that what you want to hear?"

"I don't want to hear what yer mother isn't. I want to know what yer mother is."

"A bitch." The quietly hissed words had the force of thunder. "There? Are you satisfied?" He turned his back on her and stroked Narcissus's neck.

"I didn't mean to bring up a hurtful topic."

"Then why did you bring it up?"

"Because I want to understand ye."

He pivoted on his heel. "Why now?" The intensity reflected in his eyes blasted through Sheridan. "If you will recall, you've treated me like a leper. Actually, lepers were treated better."

Sheridan forced her chin up. "And I told ye me temper was fierce."

"You weren't lying."

Sheridan bit back a retort, realizing he was purposely baiting her. "I'll not allow ye to take yer anger out on me."

"I'm not angry."

"Ye are. Ye're puttin' up yer defenses, treatin' me like I'm the enemy, as ye have since the first."

"I'm sorry if you were expecting a skinny dip in paradise and got me instead."

Sheridan's temper bottlenecked in her throat, then burst forth like a steam kettle. "Oh, but ye are a jackass! What makes ye so righteous? So high and mighty that ye can walk over people at yer whim? Who made ye God? 'Tis a spoiled lad ye are. No more. No less."

Sheridan saw a muscle work in his jaw. He started toward her, stalking her with the same determination and frightening mien as Hamlet's ghost. Involuntarily, Sheridan moved back. She swallowed when he came to stand before her, but she would not be cowed.

She waited, her breath suspended, watching his jaw clench and unclench. He looked like he wanted to shake her, yell, rant, curse. But he did none of those things. Yet when he spoke, his words rocked her.

"Do you care for me, Danny?"

Did she care for him? Did she care if the sun rose and set? Or if she lived to breathe another day? Or that the babe growing in her womb be healthy and happy?

Aye, she cared. Too much.

But she would no longer plummet to the valley and soar to the peaks on the basis of Nicholas's whims, more of this and less of that, to seek out that magical balance that would make her into exactly what Nicholas wanted.

No, she had found a way back to her true self. And he could love her for who she was or not love her at all. Either way, she had won. Because she had rediscovered what she had lost.

Her soul.

"Well, Danny?"

He wanted an answer, and she had several to give. Her

mind clamored that this was her chance, her opportunity to level him with cruel words, fling his vulnerability back in his face and pick up the scattered pieces of her pride.

But she couldn't.

Nicholas wrapped her hands gently around her upper arms. "Do you love me even a bit?"

A bit? What was a bit? More than the moon, the sun, or the stars? More than she loved Ireland? Her family? Herself?

Aye, then she loved him more than a bit.

"Does it matter?" she asked.

"More than anything."

She glanced down at the hay-strewn floor. "Ye know how I feel."

He pressed a finger beneath her chin and tilted her head up. "Do I?"

Sheridan didn't want any more games, any more gentle gliding around the subject. She wanted to scream at the top of her lungs that she loved him—had loved him from the first. But she could take no more rejection. No more hurt. He had to say it first.

He had to heal her heart.

"Ye cannot demand answers of me that ye barricade yerself from, lettin' no one in—allowin' no one to know ye."

Slowly, he withdrew his hands and sank them in his pockets. "You don't know what you're talking about."

Sheridan scoffed. "How convenient that excuse is." She wheeled away from him and led Eclipse to his stall.

She hadn't heard Nicholas move, but when she turned, he stood directly behind her.

"My mother hated me."

My mother hated me. Each word exposed him, laid him bare, pricking Sheridan's heart. He stood before her not as a life-hardened man shielded by an invisible wall, but as a young boy, pained and bewildered.

Sheridan could no longer resist the urge to touch him. She brushed aside the lock of tangled ebony hair falling across his brow and cupped his cheek.

"Who could hate ye?" she whispered.

He took hold of her wrist but didn't move her away. Instead he closed his eyes and leaned into her hand. "For too many years I waited for the day when my mother would lay a tender hand on my face or tousle my hair or simply tell me she cared. She never did." His eyes opened, his gaze a forest-green well of anguish, showing her his true depths, revealing the feelings he kept so carefully contained.

"I told myself I'd never let anyone hurt me like that again, to ache for a smile or a kind word or some form of acknowledgement. And I swore no woman would destroy me like my mother destroyed my father. He gave everything to a woman who never possessed the capacity to care about anyone but herself."

Sheridan believed she was finally starting to understand what caused Nicholas to distance himself, to be emotionally aloof. She had known he was complex. She had never known how much.

"So now ye don't want to care about anyone?"

He shook his head. "It's not that."

Sheridan thought about the emotional scar left by his mother's cold and callous behavior and how it might have affected him. The answer seemed clear. "Ye don't trust women, do ye?"

Nicholas shifted uneasily, averting his gaze to Narcissus. "Some, perhaps." He shrugged. "It's not important."

" 'Tis important to me."

He closed himself off to her then, shutting down as he

always did when the hurt skimmed too near the surface. "I have to put Narcissus back in his stall."

Sheridan faltered, knowing she had gleaned more insight in the past few minutes than she had since meeting Nicholas. She should let it rest. But she couldn't.

"What did ye mean by 'some' women?"

Nicholas wouldn't look at her. He took the halter off Narcissus, checked the hay and water, and turned to leave the stall.

Sheridan blocked his path. She knew he could bowl her over like a reed of grass, yet she held firm.

He sighed heavily. "Let it go, Danny. You don't want to hear the truth."

She sidestepped as he tried to move around her. "Don't ye tell me what I do or don't want to hear. 'Tis a grown woman I am, with a mind of me own."

"You're too damned stubborn is what you are. You need to learn when to let a matter drop."

"And what ye need is a solid kick in the backside!"

A hint of a smile tugged at his lips. "And I imagine you are the one who will administer said kick?"

"Aye, if I must."

He folded his arms across his chest. "I believe you very well might do it."

Sheridan matched him, folding her arms across her chest. "Just try me and ye'll find out."

He studied her for a long moment, the look in his eyes warming her from her toes up. Before she could savor the feeling, his gaze hooded and he moved around her. "It's almost dawn. Why don't you get some sleep?"

He walked away, dismissing her, shutting her out again. The anger she'd held at bay flooded her veins, a culmination of pain, frustration and love.

"For once, stand and fight! Ye can't be a coward all

yer life!'' As soon as the words left her mouth, Sheridan regretted them.

Nicholas stopped abruptly. Seconds that seemed like hours ticked past before he pivoted on his heel, facing her across the distance like two duelers at dawn.

His gaze narrowed, his jaw clenching. Sheridan cringed, sensing an explosion, perhaps wanting one. But it was his softly spoken words that always pierced her heart the most.

''I'm sorry I don't fit your image of what a man should be.''

''I didn't mean—''

A glance cut her off. ''I guess there are things that can't be changed about either of us.''

''Then we should learn to accept the things we can't change.'' Slowly, Sheridan moved toward him.

''Perhaps we're too different.''

''Perhaps we're not different at all.'' She came to a stop in front of him. Hands shaking with a fine tremor, she reached for the top button of his shirt. He took hold of her wrists. ''What are you doing?''

''Let me love you. Let me heal yer pain.''

Those few words shattered Nicholas. No woman had ever offered such a thing or cared about the wounds he carried deep inside. Sheridan's submission moved him in ways he couldn't define, bringing a bright ray of sunshine to a place long since devoid of light.

Nicholas knew Jessica would never have done all this for him. She wouldn't have dirtied her hands for his horses. Until Sheridan careened into his life like a whirlwind, Nicholas hadn't realized how it could be between a man and a woman.

Now he saw with stunning clarity that although Jessica would have been a wife and a mother, she wouldn't have been either in the true sense of the word. Not like Sheridan.

Tea parties and fripperies would come before him, and he imagined they would take precedence over any children he and Jessica might have had.

How had he been so blind not to see the truth? Not to recognize that what Jessica lacked was heart and soul? Passion.

He had told Jules once he preferred a staid wife and a life devoid of surprises. He'd been a fool.

"Nicholas . . ." Sheridan sweetly beseeched, rising on tiptoe, the press of her lips bringing a searing rush of heat to his groin. He ached to make this woman his, only his. Now and forever.

She moved her hips against his arousal and he groaned, nearly coming undone. The uninterrupted hours in her presence, smelling her, watching her, wanting her had been a slow burning fire. Their argument had further ignited the flame. Now only urgent desire remained.

He snaked his arm around her back, locking them close together, his mouth slanting over hers, his body quickening, her soft moans driving him to the brink.

He told himself to take it slow, not be a rutting animal. But he had to have her. Here. Now.

He grasped her wrist and hastened toward a small room in the back of the stable where the tack was kept along with a cot for the stable boy. Nicholas thanked God he didn't have a stable boy at that moment. Jeremiah slept in the lower part of the house with the rest of the servants. He had Sheridan to himself.

As soon as he was through the door, he hauled Sheridan hard against his chest, cupping her buttocks and lifting her feet from the floor. Instinctively, she wrapped her legs around his waist. He rocked her against his arousal while his tongue dueled with hers.

His breath rasped through his lungs as he tore his mouth from hers. "Undo your blouse."

Her chest rose and fell enticingly, making him impatient. He very nearly grabbed the material with his teeth and yanked.

At last, her breasts lay bare before him, the rosy-tipped nipples stiff and thrusting upward, begging for his touch.

Like a man denied sustenance, he took the tight peak between his lips, drawing it in time and again as the friction built between their bodies.

Finally, he could take no more. He walked them toward the cot but stopped, spotting a saddle draped across a low rack. He knew what he wanted to do.

Sheridan gasped as he turned her around, jerked up her skirt and her thin lawn chemise, pressing her forward, over the saddle, exposing her legs and buttocks.

Nicholas ran his hand over one smooth globe. Perfection. He skimmed his fingers down her outer thigh, enjoying the supple, firm flesh.

"Spread your legs for me, love," he murmured, his voice a husky rumble.

Sheridan shivered in anticipation as she did what Nicholas bid. She needed him inside her, bringing them together in the one way that was always right, where no harsh words or angry regret existed. The one pure bond between them.

Sheridan whimpered as his finger slid between her moist, swollen folds and found the pearl of her womanhood, stroking her.

"So wet. You're ready for me."

Her head dropped forward, her hair wrapping her in a cocoon of darkness, the world swept away.

Nicholas's finger slid inside her. His groan mingled with hers. The buttons on his riding breeches popped open one by one, the small noise inflaming her, setting her blood to racing.

Pleasure arced through her, her stomach tightening, the

fever his fingers created climbing higher and higher until pressure escalated inside her. Words tumbled from her mouth, incoherent and passion-induced, as a shattering climax ripped through her. Sweet fire coursed through her in mind-numbing waves.

"Good sweet God," Nicholas rasped. "I have to have you." His warm, large hands gripped her waist as his manhood surged into her, his heavy, throbbing shaft filling her, his groin pressing hard against her bottom. He plunged into her again and slowly withdrew, but not all the way, teasing her, making her want to scream for surcease.

He must have sensed the desperation in her because he drove into her hard, his tempo increasing until he rode her fast and fierce, pumping away.

Sheridan arched her hips upward, pulling him further inside, his scorching heat sluicing through her, the ecstasy cresting again until he plunged into her one last time, his muscles going rigid with his release, mingling with her soul-shattering climax.

With care, he adjusted her skirts and turned her to face him. Gently, he brushed her hair to the side and bent forward to press the sweetest of kisses to her lips. Sheridan's knees felt weak, and the strength-draining expense of her release made her body languid—but oh, how she wanted him again and again, to put aside their differences, the strain.

"You look tired," he murmured. "Why don't you lie down on the cot for a few minutes?"

The idea sounded delicious. Her pregnancy had sapped some of her usual hearty strength. "Only if ye'll lie with me."

His boyish smile made her insides quiver. "I thought you'd never ask."

He led her toward the cot and laid down, his back pressed against the wall. He patted the spot next to him.

A poignant rush of emotions washed over Sheridan, the memory of the first time she'd lain with this man, the spell his fingers had woven over her, the pure magic of his touch, entwining their bodies as surely as their souls.

Sheridan lay down, her back pressed snugly to Nicholas's chest, one thought filling her head as her eyes slowly drifted shut.

Her baby. His baby. He had to know.

"Wake up, Danny," a soft, deep voice murmured, a hand lightly shaking her shoulder.

Sheridan swatted the hand away, not wanting her beautiful dream to be interrupted.

She lay naked on a huge four-poster bed. Sheer panels of white enveloped her. A white satin coverlet caressed her heated skin. The panels separated at the end of the bed and there stood a bronzed god. Muscles chiseled his lean torso and bulged in his huge arms. Her gaze drifted down to the long silky length of him, telling her what he'd come for.

Sheridan writhed on the coverlet as he knelt between her thighs, his handsome face coming closer, his big body encompassing her.

Nicholas, she breathed.

He opened his mouth to speak, to utter something that reflected the emotion in his eyes, but his image slowly began to fade. Sheridan reached for him, but her fingers groped the air. He was gone.

No!

"Wake up, Danny," the voice came again, this time more insistent. "We overslept. People will be looking for us."

Finally, the words registered in her brain. She lay in

the cot in the stables, where anyone could have seen them together.

Sheridan sat bolt upright and collided with Nicholas's solid frame. "Och, I'm sorry."

He smiled that tender smile. "I'm not." Then he kissed her, softly, reverently, and all too quickly. "Come on, let's go." He stood up and held out his hand for her.

Sheridan smiled in return, but the smile slipped from her face as the nausea boiled up inside her. Oh, how could she have forgotten the sickness she experienced every morning, the weak limbs and dizzy head?

Please God, she begged, not now! *I know I should have told Nicholas about our baby, but I don't want him finding out like this!*

"Danny?" She could hear the concern in Nicholas's voice, penetrating the fog enshrouding her brain. She shot from the bed, praying she could make it to the house even as she knew she wouldn't.

As soon as she stood upright, her head began to swim and the world faded to black.

Sheridan awoke to strong arms cradling her, her cheek pressed against the soft cotton of Nicholas's shirt, a hint of his musky cologne tickling her nostrils.

"Are you all right?"

She glanced up to find troubled green eyes intent on her face. "Fine," she murmured.

"God, you had me worried."

The truth of his words rang clearly, and Sheridan's heart constricted. Every time she thought she couldn't love Nicholas more, she did.

"As soon as we get back to the house, I'm sending for the doctor."

"No! Ah, I mean, that's not necessary. I'm all right."

"No, you're not. You still look pale." His knuckles

swept across her cheek, a slight frown tugging his brows together. Then he scooped her up in his arms.

"I can walk," Sheridan protested.

Nicholas ignored her and headed out of the tack room. Narcissus whickered, his sleek head bobbing as they passed. Sheridan smiled, warmth settling inside her at seeing the two horses restored to health. She and Nicholas had worked together to save them. They had made a wonderful team.

"I want to see Hannah."

"Later."

"Now," Sheridan countered.

Nicholas scowled down at her. "Stubborn."

He stopped at Wind Dancer's stall, lifting Sheridan enough to see over the top of the stall door. Both mother and daughter stood on their feet, Hannah's stilt legs sturdy for a one day old as she suckled her mother's teat. The bond between mare and foal had been forged. Everything was going to be just fine.

Sheridan sighed in contentment. Closing her eyes, she dropped her head back against Nicholas's chest. All felt right with the world as he carted her up the wide expanse of lawn toward the house.

But her euphoria was short lived as Nicholas entered the front door.

And came face to face with Lady Jessica Reardon.

Chapter Twenty

Sheridan stood in the shadowed embrace of the hallway listening to the loud, muffled voices coming from Nicholas's office. She longed to creep down the stairs and put her ear to the door.

Was Nicholas telling Jessica that what she'd witnessed had been nothing? That her rage was unfounded, a terrible misunderstanding? For certainly he and Jessica spoke of something. They had been holed up behind his closed office doors for nearly an hour.

Sheridan didn't know why Jessica had come to Silver Hills, but she couldn't help wondering if Nicholas had invited the woman. It was not outside the realm of possibility—not if he intended to marry her.

Did he still plan to do so? Sheridan wondered. The prospect wrapped a chill around her, despair settling on her shoulders like a sodden cloak. She had been so close to reaching that elusive part of Nicholas, the part she doubted he'd shared with anyone, not even Jessica.

Sheridan had begun to believe Nicholas might not be upset to hear she was pregnant, that might even be happy about it. Now she was not so sure.

Either way, today she would tell him she carried his child.

"Was that Lady Jessica who just stormed out of here?"

Nicholas didn't turn around at the sound of Jules's voice. Instead he continued to stare unseeingly out his office window, wondering about what he'd just done, yet knowing he'd made the right decision.

"In the flesh," he murmured, his gaze drifting to the stables in the distance.

A slight smile lifted his lips as he thought about Sheridan and how, together, they had made magic. Whatever the future held for them, he would face it squarely. She'd said she wanted to heal him, and in so many ways she had.

She hadn't told him she loved him, but she had conveyed what she felt with her eyes . . . and with her body. He knew he could trust her with his heart.

"May I presume you've finally come to your senses, dear cousin?"

Nicholas turned to face Jules. The girl had always been far too perceptive for his peace of mind.

He leaned a shoulder against the wall. "Come to my senses? About what, *dear cousin?*"

Nicholas noted the dark smudges beneath Jules's eyes and worried about how she was sleeping, if the babe was causing her trouble. Jules's petite frame carried William's child—and William was a huge man.

Nicholas wondered if William would arrive in time to

return his wife to their home in Sussex before the babe was born. Of course he would. The babe wasn't expected for at least another month.

Sheridan's face rose in Nicholas's mind then, her beautiful eyes staring into his, promising passion and a life that would never be dull.

"You love her that much, hmm?"

Nicholas shook his head, focusing his attention on Jules. A delighted smile tugged at her lips. "To whom are you referring?" As if he didn't know.

"Why, to Sheridan, of course. And please do not try to deny it. Sheridan tried the same thing, and I saw through her as clearly as I see through you. You two love each other, and it is time you both stopped acting like children."

Nicholas cocked a brow. "Acting like children, are we?"

Jules nodded. "I think you should march up those stairs and tell her how much you care before you lose the best thing that has ever happened to you."

Nicholas wanted to march up those stairs and do that very thing, but he was having himself too good a time nudging his cousin to end it just yet.

"And what about Lady Jessica?" he asked, endeavoring to look properly serious.

Jules made a face. "She can go hang, the snooty little—"

Nicholas held up his hand. "I get the point."

"I should hope so. If you had opened your eyes and not behaved so stubbornly, you would have seen Jessica was not right for you a long time ago."

"And I assume you knew all along she wasn't right for me?"

"I did."

"And of course you knew Sheridan *was* right for me?"

"I did. You two complement each other perfectly."

Nicholas shook his head, amused. "William has his work cut out for him."

"As do you. Now, if you would stop procrastinating." She glanced pointedly at the door.

Nicholas knew his cousin was right. He *was* procrastinating about speaking to Sheridan, but suddenly he felt like a green lad with his first crush. What if he did that whole romantic thing Damien claimed women adored, dropped to his knee and proposed to Sheridan, all very gallant, and she said . . . no?

Well, he'd just have to convince her to say yes. That's all. He smiled, thinking about a rather enjoyable method to employ to change her mind, should such means become necessary. Perhaps he'd use it even if it wasn't necessary. His grin broadened.

Nicholas pushed away from the wall and cupped Jules's elbow, leading her out of his office. "I will speak to Danny all in due time, cousin. First I want to show you something."

She eyed him. "Show me what?"

"You are too suspicious, puss." When she continued to bore holes into the side of his head, he said, "I have a gift for the baby."

Her severe mien melted into a smile. "A gift?"

Nicholas chuckled. "You women are all the same. Start mentioning gifts and you become sweet and malleable."

"You men are all the same. Start mentioning commitment and you run the other way."

"Touché, Your Grace."

Jules inclined her head, acknowledging her victory. "Now, about this gift?"

"Ah, yes. The gift. Well, it's something every child should have."

"Oh? And what is that?"

"Why, a pony, of course."

* * *

Sheridan returned to the landing. Nerves had set her to pacing her room until she could no longer stand the oppressive confines, the walls closing in on her, the space seeming to get smaller and smaller with each passing moment.

She reached the top of the stairs in time to see Nicholas and the hint of a woman's skirt as he breezed out the front door. Sheridan's heart plummeted. Had Nicholas resolved the problem with Jessica? Was Sheridan no more than a distant memory? A tumble in the hay?

Sheridan placed a hand on her stomach, trying to hold back the knot of despair forming as she wondered if she had been dismissed yet again.

No! She would not allow Nicholas to treat her like fodder. He would face her and hear what she had to say. He didn't have to want her . . . love her. But she would not be some convenience, his Irish whim. No English aristocrat would ever make her feel worthless again. *No one* would make her feel that way again.

Sheridan started down the stairs. She would await Nicholas's return in his office. Neutral ground. On her terms.

As soon as she entered Nicholas's office, his presence surrounded her in the masculine flavor of the room, the aroma of brandy and cigars, the tidy disarray of the papers on top of his desk.

She moved through the room at an unhurried pace, her fingers smoothing over the top of this teakwood table or that piece of leather furniture, enjoying the subtle textures. She stopped to admire a stunning oil painting, a hunting scene, the man portrayed sitting astride a magnificent stallion—perhaps a forebear of Narcissus or Eclipse.

The man in the picture appeared to be Nicholas's brother, Gray. Intense slate-colored eyes seemed to follow her as she resumed her wandering, as if asking her why she disturbed sacred ground, this bastion of male privilege.

She made her way to the big mahogany desk that was the focal point of the room. Nicholas's desk, the place he spent a good portion of his day. Perhaps at this very spot he had decided Lady Jessica Reardon was the one for him.

Where were he and Jessica right now? They had gone outside. Could Nicholas have taken her to the stables, to the small tack room where he had shown Sheridan heaven such a short while ago?

Was he doing to Jessica what he had done to her?

She pushed the tormenting thought aside. She had other things with which to concern herself, like how she would tell Nicholas about their child. Was it best to be blunt? Or should she lead up to her revelation slowly? She hoped the answer would come to her before he returned.

She sank down into Nicholas's black leather chair. It swallowed her like a bird of prey, clearly revealing that her size did not come near to equaling the size of the chair's usual occupant—a tall man, broad shouldered, solidly built, who, with one glance from his beautiful emerald eyes, could melt her from the toes up.

A piece of correspondence on Nicholas's desk caught Sheridan's eye, one word in particular standing out.

Ireland.

Sheridan told herself the missive was none of her business, that even to lift the paper would constitute a violation of Nicholas's privacy. This was his home, and she was only a guest.

Nevertheless, knowing all that, Sheridan reached for the missive anyway. It was addressed to Nicholas and sent from a place called Mulholland manor.

County Cork, Ireland.

Sheridan's heart chilled with each word she read.

Dear Sir:

Enclosed please find a bank draft for the rents received from your tenants. Except for a few minor incidents, harvesting is going well. You should make a tidy profit this year.

> *Your servant,*
> *Henry Smithers,*
> *Caretaker*

No, Sheridan thought, Nicholas was not a landlord— not one of the hated English aristocrats who lived off the fat of the Irish peasants who toiled for them. He had not lied to her. Yet her mind refuted her disbelief and forced her to look at the compelling evidence against him.

Hadn't he lied to her in the past? Hadn't he made pretty speeches and cleverly charmed her time and again? What more did she need to prove that Nicholas had deceived her? The letter was in front of her . . . and Nicholas's own words rang in her ears.

I don't own any property in Ireland.

Liar!

Sheridan sprang from his chair, a feeling of revulsion singeing her flesh, her heart railing at her for being ten times the fool. Tears flowed down her cheeks, a single drop splashing on the letter.

"Ah, there ye are, Danny girl," a voice boomed.

Startled, Sheridan's head snapped up, her gaze flying to the speaker. Ian McDonough stood in the doorway. His smile dissolved, and a frown immediately creased his brow. Sheridan quickly tried to wipe away her tears, but it was too late. He had seen them.

"What's the matter, lass?" Concern etched his face as he entered the room and hurried toward her. "What's happened?"

Words clogged in Sheridan's throat, and pain slashed

her like a whip. She shook her head, damning the tears that would not stop.

Ian wrapped his large, work-roughened hands around her upper arms. "Has the mon done somethin' tae ye?"

The man had done so much to her that the hurt would follow her all the days of her life. She had confided much to Ian since meeting him. They were more alike than she and Nicholas would ever be. Ian came from a similar background, and he understood her. She had told him about her love for Nicholas, knowing he would take her secret to the grave.

Ian pulled her into his warm embrace, comforting her. "I swear, if Nicholas Sinclair has done anything tae ye, lass, I'll—"

"You'll what?"

Those softly hissed words sent a streak of lightning down Sheridan's spine. Slowly she turned her head and met Nicholas's fierce green eyes. Gone was any tenderness.

It had been replaced by sheer, indomitable rage.

Chapter Twenty-one

Nicholas's gaze riveted to Ian, a tic working in his jaw. He had never wanted to kill a man as much as he wanted to kill the Scottish bastard and he felt volatile enough to fulfill that fatal wish.

"I suggest you run, hide . . . and pray, McDonough," "Nicholas!"

Nicholas's gaze slashed to Sheridan. "Don't say one goddamned word. Not one."

He could barely look at her. Why hadn't he listened to his gut and stayed away from her? Why had he left his heart open for her to rip it from him?

Why had he given a woman an opportunity to bring him to his knees as his mother had done to his father?

He had never intended for McDonough to travel with them to Silver Hills. But Jules had brought him along to "help out"——most likely at Sheridan's request. Nicholas could just imagine what the son of a bitch had been helping with.

How long had Ian and Sheridan been together? Had they been fooling around under Nicholas's very roof? Why had he listened to Jules when she had told him Sheridan and Ian were only friends?

Friends. Christ! Sheridan had a bloody knack for friendship. The kind that poisoned.

Thank God Jules had remained in the stable with Wind Dancer and Hannah. Nicholas didn't want his cousin to witness her friend's downfall, to see Sheridan's true colors.

"Get the hell off my property, McDonough! You're fired."

Ian stepped in front of Sheridan, blocking her from Nicholas's view. "I didna want tae work for ye anyway, Sinclair. Ye are a tyrant and a bully. And I tell ye this, ye've made the lass cry for the last time."

Sheridan clutched Ian's shoulder. "Ian, don't."

"Protecting your lover, my dear?" Nicholas said through gritted teeth.

Her beautiful, treacherous face colored. "Lover? How dare ye imply such a thing!"

Nicholas didn't want to hear denials. "Leave the room," he ordered. "It's time for me and McDonough to talk . . . man to victim."

"Aye, lassie. Go now and close the door after ye. I'll be out shortly."

"Don't bet on it," Nicholas spat. "The only way you'll be leaving this room is in a pine box."

Sheridan stepped in between the two men. "Stop it! Both of ye!"

"Stop what, sweetheart?" Nicholas's tone dripped acid. "I thought this was what you wanted—a bloody battle on your behalf. To see two men pulverize each other. Gives you a certain thrill, doesn't it? Heats your blood. Well, I'm nothing if not obliging."

"Don't be a duffer all yer life! Ye know 'tis you I care for."

Nicholas's jaw clenched, fighting the pull of her words. "And this is the way you show me how you care? I'd hate to see what you do to people you hate."

"Ye're judging me without knowing the facts, and I'll not have it!"

"I know more than I care to." Like the fact that Sheridan had made love to him that first night without any hesitation, given herself up to him like a pagan goddess.

How many other men did she have? How many had tasted the passion he had believed she had given solely to him? The thought twisted like a knife in Nicholas's gut.

"Why are ye so ready to believe the worst? I'm not yer mother."

No, she wasn't his mother. His mother's betrayal had never hurt this bad. A faint dying voice in his head whispered that perhaps he was doing exactly as she accused, ready to jump to a conclusion that might not be the correct one. But just seeing Sheridan in McDonough's arms had brought back that dormant pain and fear—fear of losing someone he cared for.

Fear of losing himself.

"Oh, come now, my dear. What sort of moron do you take me for? If you're going to lie, try something more inventive. Clearly, you excel at trickery and guile. You certainly fooled me. And to think I had considered marrying you."

Sheridan's face paled. "Ye wanted to . . . marry me?"

Disgusted, Nicholas nodded, wondering why had he told her that particular truth, why he had set himself up for another blow. "For one brief, insane moment I had contemplated asking you. But my senses have now returned.''

Nicholas almost mistook the expression on Sheridan's face as despair, as utter ravaging pain. He almost believed she cared for him and that perhaps he had been wrong.

He almost believed tears formed in her eyes. Tears she cried for him.

Almost.

Then that damnably beautiful pride Nicholas loved and hated about Sheridan cloaked her, shielded her from his attack. She tipped her chin up. "Ian is my friend. Nothing more."

Friend. The word made Nicholas see red. "And I, for one, can vouch how *friendly* a friend you are."

"Ye bastard!" Ian exploded, his hands fisting as he stepped toward Nicholas.

Sheridan jumped in front of Ian, yet her words were directed at Nicholas. "I would never hurt ye like that. I—"

"Don't say it! Don't you goddamn say you love me."

Her sad, luminous eyes tore into Nicholas with a force that rammed him against the wall. "I did love ye," she murmured, battling back tears. "But not any more."

"You can't turn it off like that, damn you!"

"I feel sorry for ye. I realize now ye are incapable of loving anyone. Ye can't let go of old pain. Ye're trapped inside a dungeon of yer own making, and it's blinded ye to what could be.

"And I feel sorry for myself for not recognizing that side of ye and for not heeding my own warning. Ye and I are too different. But I continued to hold out hope . . . and that makes me more foolish than ye'll ever be," she finished in a whisper.

Nicholas tried to block out the truth of her words, but they were like bullets, flying at him from all angles.

"What's going on in here?"

Nicholas closed his eyes. Jules. He couldn't face her, couldn't tell her what he'd done with her friend.

Couldn't tell her he had fallen hard and irrevocably for Sheridan Delaney of the goddamned Boston Delaneys.

With a brave mien, Sheridan did what Nicholas could not. She spoke. "I'm sorry, Jules. It seems I've made a terrible mess of things. I never should have come to England."

"What are you talking about? Of course you should have come." Jules stepped forward to stand next to Nicholas. "What is going on here, Nicky?"

Slowly, Nicholas swiveled his gaze to Jules, seeing the worry etched on her face and wishing he hadn't been the cause of it. He opened his mouth, but the words to explain would not come.

"Yer cousin thinks something has been going on between Ian and me," Sheridan answered for him, the pain evident in her voice.

"What? That's ridiculous!"

"Aye, 'tis what I tried to tell him."

"Let it go, Jules," Nicholas said in a hollow voice. "This doesn't concern you."

"Doesn't concern me! Sheridan is my best friend. I know her as well as I know you."

"I caught them together. In my own bloody office, no less. Will that convince you?"

"Caught them together?" Jules eyes swung to Sheridan. "I don't believe that for a moment."

The conviction in Jules's voice shook Sheridan to the core. She almost lost the battle to keep from breaking down. She had to be strong. No matter what had happened to her, she would not leave in shame, nor with lies hanging over her head.

Ian came to Sheridan's defense. "I saw Danny cryin',

so I came in to see why.'' His angry gaze slid to Nicholas. ''She is a sweet lass and isna deservin' such harsh treatment. Open yer foolish eyes, mon, and see what it is ye have before it's too late.''

Jules walked up to Sheridan and took her hands. ''Why were you crying, Danny?''

Sheridan shook her head. It didn't matter any longer what had caused her tears or what she had discovered about Nicholas, his lies, his betrayal—a betrayal more real than hers would ever be.

''Forgive me,'' Sheridan softly beseeched. ''I didn't mean for any of this to happen.''

Jules squeezed her hands. ''There is nothing to forgive. This is all a terrible mistake. If you and Nicholas would just sit down and talk—''

''There's nothing left to talk about.'' Sheridan's eyes lifted and met Nicholas's. ''I don't want anything from ye. Not any more. Marry Jessica. I wish ye both the best. I truly do. I want ye to be with someone who will make ye happy and rid ye of yer demons. But I'll not leave this room until I've spoken my piece. And no matter what ye think of me, I'll know in my heart I did the right thing.''

Sheridan didn't know why, but she waited for Nicholas to say something—hoped he would say something, even as numbness settled over her, a sense of finality.

''Don't say any more, Sheridan,'' Jules begged. ''Not now, when tempers are at the breaking point. We all say things we don't mean when we are upset. In a little while, this situation may look entirely different.''

Sheridan smiled sadly at her friend. ''Things won't be different.'' She only wished they could be. ''Least of all what I have to tell ye.'' A single tear escaped Sheridan's lashes and coursed down her cheek. ''I love ye, Jules.

And I never meant to come to yer home and bring trouble with me. But 'tis a burden I can't seem to shake.''

"You've never been any trouble."

"Ye always were a sweet liar, Jules Thornton. I hope nothing will ever come between us."

"Nothing will, Danny. Not ever."

Sheridan prayed that would still be true after she said what she had to say. She closed her eyes and took a deep breath. "I'm going to have a baby."

"A baby?" Jules gasped.

"A baby?" Nicholas echoed, his voice devoid of any emotion.

Slowly, Sheridan opened her eyes and looked at Nicholas. His usually bronze face had paled. "Aye." She nodded. "A baby."

The flesh over his cheeks seem to sink inward, his eyes narrowing, his jaw clenching. "Jesus, how could I have been so blind?" he said, his voice low and frightening. "I should have known you were a faithless jade."

Jules swung around to face her cousin. "My God, Nicholas! What is the matter with you? Have you lost your mind? Don't you understand what this means?"

Cold, green eyes cut to Jules. "Get her out of here."

"No! Damn you, Nicky! Open your eyes. Sheridan is carrying *your* baby."

"Mine or ten other men."

Nicholas's words sent Sheridan reeling. Dear God, help her, the final blow. Devastating. Fatal. Only now did she see the true depths of Nicholas's loathing for her. He believed her to be a whore, a common trollop. Sheridan could see the whole thing clearly.

She had to remain strong and walk out the door with her head high and never look back. Only then could she give into the torrent of agony washing over her. She wouldn't let his coldness defeat her, bring her to her knees. Her conscience was clean, even if her soul would forever lie in tatters.

Jules stormed over to Nicholas and slapped him hard across the face. "Bastard!"

"Jules, don't!" Sheridan pleaded, but Jules ignored her.

"I always thought you were the sensitive one, the one who would understand love when it found you, not condemn it or order it to your specification, but embrace it and count yourself as one of the lucky. God, how wrong I was. Sheridan didn't disgrace you. You've disgraced yourself. I hope you're happy. I hope you can live with what you've done today."

Chapter Twenty-two

Inebriation.

The salvation of mankind. The mother of invention. The last frontier.

"Here's to me." Nicholas held up his glass, staring through the amber liquor, thinking of the wreck that was his life. Then he downed the entire contents of the glass. "Liquid love," he rasped, a hard edge to his voice. "The best kind of love. It won't hurt you. Or leave you." He clenched his jaw. "Or lie to you."

He threw the glass into the fireplace and watched the blue and orange flames lick at the shards, tasting the residue of alcohol.

The fire hissed, flames warming the cold stone hearth. Logs crackled, spewing wraithlike black wisps of ash bouncing upward and then floating crazily down to earth.

But the heat did not reach Nicholas, though he stood directly in front of the blaze.

An insidious chill pervaded the castle as the sun began to set. The wind keened like the unearthly wail of a soul newly damned, and cold air crept in through the cracks and crevices, speaking Sheridan's name in a haunting whisper.

Sheridan. A completely forgettable woman ... who would stay in his mind forever.

Nicholas had locked himself in his office hours ago after he had acted the madman and thrown everyone out of the room. He could no longer bear the accusing look in his cousin's eyes ... or Sheridan's beautiful, treacherous face.

No amount of alcohol seemed able to assuage the pain or the rage. Nicholas still felt bloodlust, a need to confront McDonough and make his point with a right hook to the man's face.

Why had he allowed the man to walk out of his office unscathed? Given him the chance to breathe another day instead of strangling the bastard with his own tongue? Nicholas had the opportunity to show Sheridan he was very much the fighting man she'd once claimed he wasn't.

So why hadn't he followed through on his threat?

Nicholas shoved a hand through his hair and pushed away from the fireplace, the answer clear. He couldn't hit a man for doing the same thing he had done. Falling for Sheridan. Believing in the sweet innocence in her eyes and the promise of untapped passion.

She radiated vitality, a love of life, captivating the senses, making a man want to seize that essence, possess it, and never let go. She ran as deep as still waters, but could be as elusive as a shooting star, defying anyone to make her change.

Nicholas realized he was no better than McDonough and who knows how many countless other men who had fallen for Sheridan. Not a difficult task.

Nicholas grabbed the scotch off his desk, foregoing the glass and tipping the bottle to his lips, hoping the alcohol's drugging effects would work its way upstream, past memories. Past reckless lavender eyes.

Bottle in hand, he stalked to the French doors. Outside, clouds rolled by like mighty clipper ships. A storm was brewing, but it would never equal the tempest churning inside him.

Nicholas threw the doors wide. A great gust of wind rushed in, shoving him back as if telling him to stay and face whatever came next.

But he couldn't. He had to get out. Merge with the storm.

Perhaps then he could chase away the devil dogging his heels.

Perhaps then he could erase the single question plaguing him.

Why?

"Don't go, Danny."

Sheridan kept her face averted from Jules. If she should turn and see her friend's sadness, the pleading expression, she might break down and lose her resolve to leave, which she couldn't allow to happen.

"I have to." Sheridan tried to put the Delaney strength and fire behind those three words, but she had used up the extra well of strength God had gifted her and all Irish with. Her fire she would leave with Nicholas, for he had taken her spirit as surely as he had taken her heart.

Jules came to stand next to her, snatching away the

blouse Sheridan was folding. "This is ridiculous. You and Nicky are so blind, so utterly pigheaded I want to scream. He loves you and you love him."

Sheridan hesitated and then forced her head up, meeting Jules's gaze. "Sometimes love is not enough. Ye need faith as well." And trust.

But trust was one thing Nicholas didn't know how to give.

He actually believed she carried another man's baby, that she would do something so despicable as to foist someone else's child off on him. Sheridan had not known what to expect from Nicholas, but she had not been prepared for outright denial and accusation.

"Danny." Jules's eyes bored into Sheridan's, beseeching her to rethink her decision. "You are carrying Nicholas's baby. How are you going to just walk out the door?"

" 'Tis for the best."

Jules shook her head. "It isn't the best for this child! Don't let foolish pride make you do something you'll regret."

"Pride? Ye think that's why I'm leaving?" Sheridan glanced down at her small valise, her meager belongings arranged neatly inside, and knew pride was the last reason for her departure.

Unrequited love caused her flight.

"Danny, please. It will be dark soon. Don't go tonight. Wait until tomorrow, after you and Nicholas have had some time to think."

Sheridan moved away from Jules and went to look out the window. Ominous skies mirrored the gloom inside her. A memory tickled her mind as distant thunder rumbled, but it was banished by despair.

She caught a movement out of the corner of her eye. Nicholas. He wove unsteadily down one of the cobblestone pathways that disappeared under a canopy of trees, a bottle clutched in his hand.

Sheridan laid her palm against the windowpane. *Goodbye, my dark angel.* She closed her eyes briefly, willing away the dull ache centered in her stomach. Then she took a deep breath and turned to face her friend.

"I've thought about this, Jules, and I won't change my mind. Please understand."

Tears rimming her eyes, Jules nodded, her expression resigned. She held open her arms. Sheridan didn't hesitate. She flew into her friend's embrace and let Jules comfort her, allowing her despair to spill forth, to let down her guard as she had never done with anyone before.

Except Nicholas.

"Oh, Jules. I'll miss ye so."

"And I'll miss you, Danny," Jules murmured in a choked voice. "I shall never forgive Nicholas for what he's done."

Sheridan pulled back and stared into green eyes so like Nicholas's. "Don't do that, Jules. Don't take yer love from him. He needs ye."

"You need me."

"He needs ye more. His pain goes deeper than mine. His heart has old wounds that have never healed."

"But—"

"Ye told me once about this caring, sensitive boy ye grew up with, who felt things more profoundly than anyone ye knew. He was yer champion, someone who fought for those who couldn't fight for themselves. Well, that caring and sensitive boy is still inside Nicholas, hidden underneath a hard shell. Ye know it as well as I."

A single tear rolled down Jules's cheek. "You've given him so much understanding when he has given you none."

"But he's given me something far greater." Sheridan laid a hand on her still flat stomach.

A knock sounded at the door.

"Come," Jules called out in a hollow voice.

Emery entered and bellowed, "The coach you requested has been brought round, Your Grace!"

"Thank you, Emery."

"You wish to spank me, Your Grace?" Emery's sunken, wrinkled cheeks flushed. "Nobody's spanked me since I was nigh on a lad of twenty-five. I remember the night well." His expression grew reminiscent. "I was at a little tavern in Spitalfields when a robust barmaid came up to me and—"

Chuckling low, Jules crossed over to Emery, hoisted the arm clutching his horn and spoke into it. "Thank you, Emery. That will be all."

Emery bobbed his head. "Yes, Your Grace." He turned to go, but stopped. "Oh, I almost forgot. Miss Delaney's aunt has collapsed on the coach seat. I believe she's ailing again."

Some things never change, Sheridan thought. But at that moment, she was glad to have one constant in her life, something solid to keep the darkness at bay.

Emery frowned and scratched his balding pate. "There was a message she wanted me to relay to the young miss, but it didn't make much sense."

"What was the message?" Jules prompted.

"She said she wants to be carried with her snake girls and her harmony seeds braced in her tight hand."

"*What?*" Jules exclaimed glancing at Sheridan over her shoulder.

Sheridan smiled. How she would miss Emery. "I think

he said that my aunt wants to be buried with her fake pearls and her rosary beads placed in her right hand.''

"Indeed." Emery nodded and shuffled out the door. Knob in hand, he leveled rheumy gray eyes at Sheridan. "You'll be sorely missed," he murmured. "England won't be the same without you. Godspeed, miss . . . Godspeed."

Sheridan's smile faded and she blinked back tears, her emotions having run the gamut in the last few minutes. Emery's words, however, brought everything home with finality.

It was time to go.

Nicholas stumbled into his office the same way he had departed, through the French doors, floating in on a cloud of alcohol fumes, having achieved a state of comfortably numb, where a knife to the heart felt more like an amusing tickle than a deadly blow.

With blurry eyes, he regarded his humble domain, weaving unsteadily on his feet. "The churl has returned to his churldom," he said to the silently mocking room. "Let all bow before his stupidity."

"Okay, boss-man. I bow." A head appeared over the top of a high-backed chair, startling Nicholas, who would have fallen were he not already unbalanced.

Ho-Sing leaped to his feet and bent deeply at the waist. "You big time stupid, Boss-man. Emperor of stupid. High priest of stupid. Number one—"

Nicholas held up a hand to forestall Ho-Sing. "I get the picture."

Nicholas stalked to the chair behind his desk and slid into it, his backbone feeling as if it had been made from rubber. Only the desk kept him from spilling onto the floor.

"Boss-man soused."

Nicholas cracked open one drowsy eyelid. "Y'r power of deduction astounds me, Ho"—he hiccuped—"Sing. What's next, I wonder? Levitation?"

"Boss-man very funny." Ho-Sing bobbed his head, a smile on his lips, while his eyes said, *I question your sanity.*

"Here, have a drink. It'll broaden y'r mind." Nicholas lifted the scotch bottle and shook it. Empty. Not enough left for a thirsty ant.

"Ho-Sing like clear head."

"Suit yourself."

Penetrating black eyes observed Nicholas. "Boss-man drink to douse torch for Missy."

As usual, Ho-Sing's provocative statement spiraled out of the darkness without warning, hitting Nicholas squarely between the eyes.

Nicholas narrowed his gaze, not liking the new direction the conversation had taken. "Everyone needs a pastime, Ho-Sing. Mine's death. This is my chance for an after-life."

Ho-Sing raised an ebony eyebrow, his expression saying he'd like to sit on Nicholas's chest and pummel him with both fists.

Instead Ho-Sing locked his hands behind his back, looking very sage and cerebral. "Ho-Sing mother say women like bread. You leave them alone, you get rise. You leave too long, you get mushy dough."

"How prophetic," Nicholas mumbled, knowing he'd be rolling his eyes if they weren't already spinning. "Now if y' don't mind?" He glanced pointedly at the door. "There's something to be said about solitude."

Ho-Sing ignored him. "Boss-man want to know what else Ho-Sing's mother say?"

"Not particularly."

Clearly, Ho-Sing's question had been rhetorical. "She say a fool's tongue long enough to cut own throat."

Ho-Sing's mother must have been Confucius in disguise. "And do y' know what I say? Brevity is the soul of wit."

"No-no. That's Shakespeare."

A well-read manservant.

"Then let me put it in Sinclair terminology: *Be brief and be gone.* I have to save my energy for my hangover—or for my liver to pickle, whichever comes first." Nicholas's head pounded like a thousand tiny Philistines had pitched camp inside.

Why he drank the entire bottle of scotch when a simple clubbing over the head would have sufficed, he'd never know.

"Ok, Boss-man. Missy gone."

The last two words snapped Nicholas's head up. "What! Gone? What are you talking about? Where'd she go? When? Details, man, details!"

"You say be brief. I brief."

"Not that bloody brief!"

"Ho-Sing not mind reader."

"Ho-Sing not going to be alive much longer if he doesn't start explaining. Now, where did Sheridan go?"

"Home." Ho-Sing shook his head. "Boss-man break her heart. Very bad thing. Should be ashamed."

Nicholas gritted his teeth, wondering why everyone felt inclined to give him opinions he hadn't asked for. "When did she leave?"

"When you gone. Very sad. Ho-Sing's heart weep."

Nicholas cursed under his breath, disgust, anger, and another emotion riding him knowing Sheridan had left him.

Left him. She didn't leave him. He had wanted her to go. She had been trouble from the first moment he'd laid eyes on her, stirring up a maelstrom of emotions better left buried.

"Boss-man's heart weep, too," Ho-Sing added. "He just too much donkey's ass to admit it."

"You don't know what you're talking about."

"Do know. Ho-Sing very wise."

Nicholas rose from his chair and scoffed, "Good riddance to her, I say. Maybe now things will return to normal."

Ho-Sing nodded. "Yes-yes. Normal. Boss-man go back to wandering big empty house with long face, losing card games, and snapping at innocent manservant. Boss-man grow old and wrinkled. Women run from grumpy withered man who try to pinch supple young backsides. Finally, Boss-man drift from room to room talking to himself like Ho-Sing's great uncle Chung Lee, regretting the day he let sweet Missy go. Then he die alone and bards write sad stories about him, minstrals sing about his stupidity—the emperor of stupidity." Ho-Sing bowed.

Nicholas glared at the top of Ho-Sing's head. "Why am I the villain here? I didn't run out on her at Puddlebys. I didn't beat her into the bushes. I didn't throw a shoe at her. I didn't give her poisonous flowers."

"And Boss-man didn't love her."

Nicholas swung on his heel and threw his hand against the mantel, staring down into the cold grate, where only a few dying embers remained. "I loved her more than life."

"Then go get Missy. Bring her back."

"Why should I? She obviously couldn't wait to get out of here with her lover."

Ho-Sing sighed. Loudly. "Boss-man should be skinned and boiled in oil—in Ho-Sing's ever so respectful opinion."

"You're a traitor, Ho-Sing."

"Ho-Sing fly flag of honesty. Boss-man throw hands over eyes and stuff cotton in ears."

Nicholas reeled around. "You weren't here. You didn't see what I saw."

"Ho-Sing no have to see with eyes. Ho-Sing see with heart. Boss-man only see with eyes. Mind closed to possibilities."

"You sound like Jules."

"Round missy makes sense." Ho-Sing pointed to his chest. "She see with heart."

Nicholas didn't want to admit what was in his heart. Even after everything Sheridan had put him through, he still loved her, wanted her back. Would forgive her.

God, what a fool he was! An obsessed, drunken fool.

What if the baby is yours? his bloody inner voice prodded, posing the question Nicholas had been trying to blot out all day. Yet no matter how hard he tried, the thought remained unabated, lurking at the outer edge of his mind, slowly chipping away at him, seeking entrance.

Well, Mr. Sensitive? the voice prodded. *What about your baby?*

That baby is not mine.

How do you know?

I just know.

But what if it is your baby? What then?

Then I'll marry Sheridan.

Oh? You think she'll have you after what you've done? A stubborn, prideful Irish lass like Sheridan? Think again.

She won't have any other choice. She doesn't want our baby to be a bastard.

Who says the baby will be a bastard? Sheridan's beautiful. Another man will want her, pure or not.

Over my dead body.

I'm sure she can arrange that.

Nicholas raked a hand through his mussed hair. What was he supposed to do now?

Go after her. Before it's too late.

But what if it is already too late?

Talk to her. Tell her how you feel.

What if she doesn't feel the same way?

If you don't go after her, how will you ever know?

I'm afraid.

Do you love her?

With all my heart and soul.

Then go.

"Ho-Sing, have Jeremiah saddle Narcissus and have him out front in five minutes."

Nicholas strode toward his office door. Sheridan had a good lead on him, but Narcissus was his fastest horse. Together, they'd find her.

"Boss-man go get Missy?"

Nicholas stopped. Looking over his shoulder, he smiled. "Boss-man go get Missy."

Sheridan peered out into the darkened skies through the coach window, her chest constricting with each passing mile, each stride the horses took carrying her farther away from Silver Hills. From Jules.

From Nicholas.

Sheridan imagined Nicholas toasted his good fortune now at having such trouble out of his life. If only Sheridan felt the same way.

Even after discovering his deception, knowing he was a hated landlord, she couldn't forget the glimpses of the charming little boy, the depth of compassion in his eyes, and the sweet sense of completion she experienced when they made love.

Sheridan glimpsed Ian outside. He rode beside the

coach. He had insisted on seeing her safely back to London. He had not mentioned the fact that he had to return to London to start looking for another job. But she had overheard the coach's driver, Nash, telling Ian of a few gentlemen he could contact.

For long moments, Sheridan watched Ian sitting tall and proud in the saddle, and she wondered if ever a time would come when she wouldn't cause heartache and grief. She had been the reason Ian had lost his job.

Uncle Finny's grunting snort brought Sheridan's head around. He slumped on the seat beside her, his beloved flask still clutched in his hand.

Across from her, Aunt Aggie lay in her favorite position. Supine. She snored as loud as Uncle Finny. Both had had a busy day. Mayhem and madness took a lot out of a person. But Sheridan loved them dearly. They were family. She could only hope they would love her baby as much as they loved her.

The Delaneys had been and always would be devout Catholics, and having a child out of wedlock . . .

Sheridan could hear her mother's voice, her words now seeming prophetic.

For nearly eight hoondred years those blighted English have been steppin' on our necks.

What would her mother say about the English now?

A sharp crack of blazing white lightning brought Sheridan's head up with a jerk. It seemed as if the sky had suddenly blackened from the gray gloom of only moments before. Then the rain began and a powerful wind buffeted the coach.

The lantern posted on the box next to Nash hurled through the enveloping darkness as if a mighty hand had scooped it up.

Sheridan threw back the panel behind the driver's seat. Rain-moistened air whipped in through the opening, driving her back, sending her hair flying about her like a witch's tangle.

She clutched the edge of the opening and pulled herself forward. "Nash!"

Alarmed dark eyes snapped in Sheridan's direction. "Close the panel, miss!" he bellowed over the rising howl of the wind. "You'll catch your death!" Nash tried to shut the panel, but Sheridan pushed it back. "It will be all right! Just stay inside the coach!"

"What's happening?"

Nash shook his head, rain pummeling him in earnest, running in rivulets off his brown felt hat. "The storm . . . it just came out of nowhere. I've never seen anything like it."

Neither had Sheridan. A force, frightening and unseen, howled in the wind and merged with the encompassing darkness, blotting out the hunter's moon that had blazed so brightly the night before. Even the horses whinnied and shied away from the onslaught.

Nash spoke, but Sheridan didn't hear him. A sudden flash of memory held her in thrall.

Something was coming . . .

Something that had begun to take shape on that day long ago.

Rain, hard and battering, pelted down, thundering on the roof like a thousand pebbles . . .

Oh God. Jules!

"Turn the coach around!" Sheridan cried, tugging hard on Nash's coat sleeve in her urgency.

"What?" Nash didn't hear her. His attention was focused on controlling the horses.

"Ye must turn around right now! We have to go back to Silver Hills!"

"Go back?"

"Aye! Now turn around!"

He flashed her a brief look over his shoulder. "We can't go back."

"We must!"

Nash shook his head. "The river under the bridge we crossed a while back floods in the smallest amount of rain. In this downpour it will be impassable. The rising water could sweep us downstream. We can't take the chance."

"But I have to go back!"

Nash didn't hear her. "Whoa, girls!" he called out to the horses who threw their heads up, fighting the bit. "Whoa!" To her, he shouted above the rising clamor of the storm, "We have to find shelter!"

Now Sheridan knew why she hadn't seen herself in the vision she'd had of Jules. She had only gotten a glimpse of that one brief second in time. What would happen to Jules without her help? She had promised Jules she would be there for her.

Sheridan's gaze cut to the window. Outside Ian fought with his spirited mount—a fleet-footed steed on loan from Nicholas's stable. There had been no room in the coach with her, Uncle Finny, Aunt Aggie, and their belongings. Not even the seat on the box next to Nash had been free because Scally's cage was perched there.

A loud squawk pierced the air.

Sheridan flew to the window in time to see Nash lunge for Scally's cage as it rocked against the side of the coach. The rope that secured the cage to the box had worked its way free.

The cage banged one more time and the cage door sprang open. Scally's black form bulleted to freedom. But the little bird was no match for the gale winds.

"*Scally!*" Sheridan cried as the bird was whisked away into the darkness, spiraling upward into the sky.

Sheridan squeezed her eyes shut. If only she'd kept

Scally inside with her, this wouldn't have happened. But she had banished him because she couldn't stand his endless chatter ... or the reminders he chirped about Nicholas.

Nash pulled to a stop underneath a thick canopy of beech trees. Sheridan forced back her heartache over Scally. She couldn't help Scally, but she could help Jules.

She turned to find her aunt's petrified eyes pinned to her. Leaning forward, Sheridan took her aunt's hands in hers and squeezed. " 'Twill be all right," she said, hoping she sounded more confident than she felt. "I have to go back to Silver Hills. Jules needs me. Ye and Uncle Finny stay here. Nash will take care of ye. He is a good man."

Her aunt nodded. "Be careful, lass."

"I will," she vowed and then exited the coach, uncaring of the torrent of rain plastering her hair to her head and soaking her to the bone. "Ian!"

Nash grabbed Sheridan by the shoulder, hauling her back as Ian's horse reared. Its mighty hooves slammed into the ground in the spot where Sheridan had been standing only a moment before.

She shivered, realizing what might have happened should Nash not have intervened. She took a deep breath and glanced over her shoulder, silently thanking him. Then she rushed over to Ian.

"I have to return to Silver Hills! I need yer horse."

Ian hesitated, perhaps thinking to ask her why she would want to return after what had so recently transpired. He must have seen the desperation in her eyes, because he asked no questions.

"All right, lass. I'll take ye."

"It's too dangerous. Ye stay here with Nash."

"Dangerous?" His booming laugh rang out. "For a

Highlander? 'Tis nae much credit ye give me, lass.'' He reached his arm down, his features set in a determined line.

Sheridan had no time to argue. She grasped Ian's arm and swung up in front of him in the saddle. He kicked his mount into action. As the horse's hooves dug into the muddy earth, one thought plagued Sheridan.

Dear God, don't let me be too late.

Nicholas urged Narcissus into a faster stride, rain pouring down over the two of them as they headed along the darkened road.

Memory served Nicholas well this night. Only instinct guided his movements, knowing the twists, turns, and perils that awaited him, made all the worst by the onslaught of the storm.

Had Sheridan found shelter? Or was she somewhere out in this darkness, stranded and afraid? God, if anything happened to her . . .

He had been such a bloody fool. His anger had sent Sheridan flying out into a storm, had caused her to risk herself and their baby in her rush to get away from his condemnation.

Their baby. Nicholas's gut clenched. God, how he wanted to believe Sheridan carried his baby. He wanted children. He wanted the opportunity to love and cherish them as he had never been loved and cherished.

Yet were he honest with himself, he would admit the real reason he wanted to believe the baby was his: to keep Sheridan with him. To make her stay. To find a way to tie her to him and never let her go.

Perhaps if she stayed he could figure out how to mend

the rift between them . . . figure out what he needed to do to make her love him.

A high-pitched scream pierced the darkness.

Nicholas hauled on Narcissus's reins, bringing the horse to a mud-spewing halt. He listened. Nothing but the sound of the wind and the heavy slap of the rain echoed in his ears.

Where had the voice come from? The wind could be deceptive, making voices from great distances sound near or close voices sound distant.

"Ian!"

Nicholas heard the voice clearly that time. Sheridan. His heart slammed into his ribs.

Dear God. The bridge.

"Yah!" Nicholas dug his heels into Narcissus's flanks, and they took off at breakneck speed down the incline heading for the bridge.

Nicholas saw the collapsed wooden bridge and the small drenched figure kneeling by the water's edge. He knew in an instant it was Sheridan. Relief flooded him.

Nicholas jumped off Narcissus's back before the horse had come to a halt. He dropped down next to Sheridan and saw Ian McDonough pinned beneath a heavy length of bridge, the swollen river rushing over his head as he tried to use his one free hand to heave the weight off him.

Nicholas knew the pressure of the water against the broken piece of the bridge added more weight. It wouldn't budge without the use of two good arms.

Wild-eyed, Sheridan glanced in Nicholas's direction. For a moment, he wondered if she recognized him. Then she said two words that tore at his gut.

"Save him."

For the briefest moment, Nicholas thought, *She loves him. Let the bastard drown.* But Nicholas knew he could never leave a man to die.

He jumped to his feet. Briefly, his gaze locked with McDonough's. No pleading for mercy radiated from the man's eyes. He asked for no quarter and was prepared to die if need be.

Nicholas plunged into the icy water, swimming against the fierce current. Coming up beside the collapsed section of the bridge, he sucked in a breath of air and dived under the water. He could barely see, but it didn't matter. He knew what had to be done.

McDonough lay motionless in the water. Time was running out. If the cold water didn't kill the man, drowning would.

Nicholas braced his feet into the shifting sand and mud, trying to find purchase. Then he heaved his back against one of the thick beams of wood. It barely budged. The ends of the bridge had sunk into the mud.

Come on, God damn it! He heaved again and again and again until at last the section gave way. He shot to the surface, gasping for breath.

McDonough didn't move. Nicholas grabbed the man's arm and hoisted him over his shoulder, battling the current and McDonough's weight. He clutched one of the planks jutting out to brace himself, moving slowly but steadily toward the embankment.

"Take my hand!"

Nicholas glanced up and saw Sheridan, one arm looped around the bridge's post, her other arm outstretched. Nicholas ignored her offer, knowing he'd only pull her in.

He made it to the embankment and shoved McDonough onto solid ground. Nicholas crawled up beside him, breath rasping through his lungs.

McDonough twitched, then began coughing up water. Sheridan took Ian's head in her lap, wiping the hair from his face, tears rolling down her cheeks, mingling with the rain as she looked up, her beautiful lavender eyes piercing Nicholas's soul.

"Thank you," she said in a choked voice.

And Nicholas knew he had lost her.

Chapter Twenty-three

The wind flung open the front door as soon as Nicholas turned the knob, sending the heavy oak portal crashing into the wall and startling Emery, who scuttled toward the staircase.

"Oh, thank heavens you're back, sir!" Emery blared, a hand pressed over his heart.

Nicholas took Sheridan by the arm, pulling her nearly frozen form further into the vestibule. Water ran off both of them and puddled at their feet. He went to remove her thin cloak, but she wouldn't let him.

"Jules," she said, her teeth chattering. "I have to go to Jules."

"Get into dry clothes first."

She stared at him, her large violet eyes framed by wet black lashes, luminous in her pale face, peering into his soul as no other woman ever had. God, how he loved her. Her spirit. Her fire.

He wanted to kiss her, to hold her close and thank God for keeping her safe. Yet he imagined she would push him away. Reject what he offered. It would be no less than he deserved after how he had treated her.

Nicholas knew, as he did at the bridge, that Sheridan loved McDonough. The way she had held the man tenderly in her arms, the tears, those actions told their own story.

His gut wrenched as she backed away from him, a hunted expression on her face. She turned sharply and flew toward the stairs, her movements hampered by her sodden clothes.

"Danny!" he called after her.

She ignored him.

Nicholas started forward, but a hand on his arm stopped him.

"Let her go."

He shrugged off the hand and swung around to face Ian McDonough.

Nicholas's fists clenched at his side, the reaction a purely emotional one, the desire to fight for the woman he loved gnawing at him, a burning need to haul McDonough back to the bridge and return the man's body to the raging flood.

"I may have pulled your miserable hide from the water," Nicholas growled between gritted teeth, "but it doesn't mean anything has changed. I only saved you because of Sheridan, because . . . she cares for you."

McDonough returned Nicholas's glare. "Aye, she cares for me, but not in the way ye're thinkin'."

Nicholas and Ian faced each other, nearly identical in build and power, a dangerous undercurrent flowing between them.

Emery's stooped figure stepped in between them. "Sir, I must—"

Nicholas cut him off and said to McDonough, "If it's a fight you want, I'd be more than happy to oblige you."

"And I'd be more than happy to pummel ye intae the floor after what ye've done tae Danny. If I didna have to deal with the girl's wrath for beatin' ye tae within an inch of yer life, I'd do that very thing."

"Don't make excuses, McDonough."

"Sir," Emery tried to interject when Nicholas took a step toward Ian.

" 'Tis nae an excuse, ye thick-skulled whelp!" Ian took a step toward Nicholas.

Emery was jammed between their two hulking forms. "Sir, please!" the butler protested.

"I never touched the lass," McDonough growled, "but I won't say I didna want tae. She is a beautiful and spirited girl. A perfect match for a Highlander. But she would never have me. For some godforsaken reason, 'tis ye she wants." He shook his head. "Never try tae figure out the mind of a female."

Nicholas scowled. "Why should I believe a damned word that comes out of your mouth?"

McDonough cocked a brow. "Why? Because I'd enjoy rubbin' her feelings for me in yer stupid face, that's why. If a lass like Danny loved me, I'd be crowin' it from the rooftop, ye arrogant bastard."

"That bloody well tears it! Come on, you whoreson, take a swing!"

McDonough shook his head. "Ye first."

"Fine!" Nicholas's fist flew out, connecting solidly with the man's face, sending the burly Scotsman reeling backward, sliding across the floor. "Get up!"

McDonough put a hand to his injured face and tested

his jaw. Finding it still attached, he smiled broadly. "Ye do love the lass. 'Tis as much as I suspected."

"Damn you! Get the hell up and fight!"

"I canna fight a man for lovin' a woman and tryin' tae protect her from another man."

"You don't know what you're talking about."

McDonough chuckled. "Aye, lad. I do. 'Tis nae me Danny girl loves . . . but ye."

"No, she doesn't. Now stop changing the subject and fight me!"

"I'll nae be fightin' ye. And ye'll nae be fightin' me."

"Don't count on it."

McDonough sighed as he rose from the floor and dusted himself off. " 'Tis a blind and foolish man ye are. Ye waste yer energies on the wrong things. Ye should be upstairs with the lass mendin' what ye've broken and puttin' this second chance ye've been given tae proper use instead of expendin' valuable time darin' someone tae knock the chip off yer shoulder—which I'll gladly do at some other time."

Nicholas glanced toward the stairs. He wanted to believe Sheridan cared for him even as his inner voice laughed at his ignorance, taunting him that he let Sheridan lead him around by the nose—just as his father had let his mother do.

Yet Jules's words echoed in Nicholas's ears.

I always thought you were the sensitive one, the one who would understand love when it found you, not condemn it or order it to your specification, but embrace it and count yourself as one of the lucky.

Nicholas realized much of what his cousin said was true. He had tried to order a woman to his specifications, controlling every facet, calculating every variable, refusing to allow love to take its natural course.

How could he condemn Sheridan for the child she carried? He hadn't offered her anything, certainly not himself. Now that his eyes were beginning to open, he saw all the times she had taken the chance and given freely of herself, offered her love, and he had turned it aside.

"Go on, man," McDonough urged, humor tingeing his voice.

Nicholas needed no help from the Scottish cur, even if the bastard was right. Nicholas had to talk to Sheridan, and he wouldn't let her leave until he did.

He strode purposefully toward the stairs ... until a piercing cry echoed through the house, stopping Nicholas in his tracks and raising the hair on the back of his neck.

He started as a bony hand settled on his shoulder. His gaze swung around and collided with Emery's. "I tried to tell you, sir."

"Tell me what?" Nicholas demanded.

"Her Grace."

Nicholas gripped Emery's upper arms, not realizing how tightly he held the man. "What about her?"

"She's having her baby."

"Sweet Jesus." Nicholas pushed away from Emery and took the stairs two at a time. He had yet to reach the landing when the front door flew open, cold wind swirling into the circular foyer as a large figure draped in black strode across the threshold. "William?"

"Where is she?" his friend boomed. "Where is my wife?"

Sheridan dropped down beside Jules's bed, clasping her friend's hand to help her through the pain. "Ssh," she soothed. "I'm here now."

Wild eyes flashed Sheridan's way. "Danny?" Jules's voice sounded weak. Her face was pale and sweat beaded her brow.

"Aye. 'Tis me. Ye didn't think I'd leave me best friend in her time of need, did ye now?" Sheridan didn't want to think about the fact that she *had* left, that her stubbornness had taken her away when Jules needed her most.

Tears began rolling down Jules's face. "I was alone. I called for you, but you didn't come. I called for Nicky and . . . and he didn't come. Oh, God." She sobbed brokenly. "I was so afraid."

Sheridan smiled gently. " 'Tis all right. I'm here now. Ye have no more to fear. I'm sorry I ever left ye. I'm goin' to take care of ye now, so ye must try to stay calm for the babe. Will ye do that for me?"

Weakly, Jules nodded.

Sheridan glanced up at Ho-Sing, who stood sentinel at Jules's bedside when no one else had been there, his bearing so rigid one might mistake him for a wax effigy.

Sheridan knew it was not an old Chinese custom that caused him to remain rooted to Jules's side, but something far simpler. Pure, undiluted fear. He looked as scared as Jules.

Sheridan rose and faced him. "Thank ye for stayin' with her."

"Ho-Sing very glad to see Missy." He swallowed and darted a quick glance at Jules. "Round missy in very much pain. Ho-Sing feel weak in head, ten thumbs on hand. Not know what to do. Never deliver baby."

"Ye were here for her. That is the most important thing. Now ye can be my helper."

His eyes widened to saucers. "Ho-Sing . . . help with baby? Ho-Sing very wise Asian man, but go wobbly in knees at women in pain."

Sheridan shook her head. Apparently, men had one malady in common. A pregnant woman felled them. Ask them to go into battle and lop off their enemy's head, this they did with zeal. Ask them to help deliver a baby, and they trip over each other in their attempt to flee.

"Ye can do it, Ho-Sing."

Ho-Sing looked doubtful, but he nodded his head nonetheless.

"Good. Now, did ye send for the doctor?"

Ho-Sing shook his head sadly. "Doctor no come."

Sheridan meant to press Ho-Sing for answers, but noticed Jules staring up at her with frightened eyes. Sheridan didn't want to concern her friend, so she took Ho-Sing out of earshot.

"What do ye mean the doctor's not coming?" she asked in a low voice. "Ye did send for him, didn't ye?"

"Try to send stable master, but the storm send stable master back."

Sheridan closed her eyes. She had never delivered a baby by herself, only helped her mother on a few occasions. Sweet Lord in heaven, what was she going to do?

Sheridan's thought was cut off as the bedroom door flew open. Her heart lodged in her throat at the sight of the huge, black-clad man framed in the threshold, his eyes hard, his expression menacing.

Without thought for her safety, Sheridan hurried across the room and blocked his path, as if her actions might possibly stop this hulking giant should he want to enter.

"I don't know who ye are, ye ill-mannered lummox, but ye had better leave this room at once!"

Piercing, black eyes settled on Sheridan. "Who the hell are you?"

Sheridan tilted her chin up, trying to still her trembling. " 'Tis not important who I am. I want ye out of this room right now, or I'll . . ." What?

"Or she'll clobber you with a wine bottle." Nicholas appeared behind the human brick wall, an amused expression on his face. "Or perhaps a shoe. She's particularly handy with rocks. And a single glare has been known to disembowel a man more effectively than hari-kari. You had best watch out, William. This girl is all action and very little talk.''

Sheridan blinked. William? ''Ye're—''

The man cut her off with a single glance. ''Where is my wife?''

''William?'' Jules called from across the room, her voice weepy.

The hulking giant swept past Sheridan like a black blur, rushing to his wife's side. He kissed her sweetly on the lips and then scooped up her small hand in his huge one and pressed it to his chest.

Sheridan smiled to herself. Her friend would need all the support she could get in the hours to come, and there was no better medicine for a woman in labor than to have the man she loved by her side.

Nicholas stepped up beside Sheridan, the amused grin still riding his face. ''You do realize that man is six-five if he's an inch and more than twice your weight, don't you?''

Sheridan cocked a brow. ''And yer point?''

Nicholas shook his head. ''I've known William for twenty years and I don't recall one female—other than Jules—having the brass to tell William what he could or couldn't do. Most full-grown men wouldn't have the nerve. Yet you felt bold enough to not only do just that, but to call him an ill-mannered lummox in the process. You are something else, my girl.''

Sheridan refused to let the warmth of Nicholas's smile or the charm of his words affect her. She had to be strong.

''The doctor is not coming,'' she told him matter-of-factly.

''What?'' Nicholas frowned. ''Why the hell not?''

''The storm. Jeremiah tried to go for him but failed.''

"Well, the damned fool didn't try hard enough," Nicholas returned ferociously, his concern for Jules evident. "I'll get the bloody doctor myself."

Sheridan knew that if Nicholas loved no other woman, he at least loved his cousin very much. Deep down, Sheridan envied that love even as she told herself it was wrong to be jealous.

" 'Tis a dangerous night."

Nicholas slanted a wry look at her. "Dare I hope that is worry for my welfare in your voice?"

A retort sprang to Sheridan's lips, but she couldn't voice it. Should anything happen to him, she would never forgive herself. He had told her she could not turn her love on and off like a spigot, and he was correct.

Even with all Nicholas had put her through, she still loved him. She probably always would. Over time, she would learn to live with it, to accept her feelings for him as part of her.

She turned away from him and moved to the bed. A moment passed, and she wondered if Nicholas intended to say something. Then she heard the bedroom door open and quietly close. He was gone.

"Thank you, Miss Delaney."

With a start, Sheridan turned to the speaker. William. The menacing looked no longer etched his face. Love and concerned had replaced it.

Sheridan refused to let her own concern show. "The name is Sheridan, and what are ye thankin' me for?"

"Jules told me you came back to help her." Emotion resounded in his voice. "You're a true friend. I can see why my lady wife left me to wallow in despair in the country, leaving me to wander our big lonely house and miss her terribly."

Tears formed in Jules's eyes. "Did you really miss me, William?"

"Night and day, precious girl. When you were gone, I realized how little my life means without you in it."

A tear rolled down each of Jules's cheeks. "Oh, William." She looped her arms around his neck and kissed him passionately.

Sheridan felt like an interloper watching such an intimate scene, even as she wished, as she had so many times before, that she would be blessed with such a love as William and Jules shared.

Sheridan intended to leave them alone for a few minutes, but Jules's groan forestalled her.

"The babe?" William questioned.

Mutely, Jules nodded her head.

William swung worried eyes in Sheridan's direction. "What should I do?"

"The same thing as yer wife. Try to remain calm." Sheridan turned to Ho-Sing, telling herself to take her own advice. Her stomach had twisted into five knots and her palms were sweating. "Ho-Sing, please get me fresh sheets, clean towels, a knife, and warm water."

Looking as pale as Jules, Ho-Sing nodded and hurried from the room.

"Ooh!" Jules moaned, one hand clasping her stomach, the other wrapped so tightly around William's hand his fingers were turning blue.

For a moment, sheer panic rifled through Sheridan. She closed her eyes and thought of her mother's face, how she always remained calm. "Breathe."

Jules's face contorted in pain. "What?"

"I said breathe. Deep breaths, in and slowly out, until the pain recedes."

Jules did as Sheridan asked. The contraction began to ebb, but Sheridan knew the pain would only intensify in time.

Once Jules's body had relaxed, she turned her gaze to

her husband, a frown puckering her brow. "What are you doing here so late, William? And in a storm, no less?"

"I knew you needed me."

"You did?"

He nodded. "It was the strangest thing. I was exhausted by the time I arrived in London, falling into bed as soon as my boots hit the floor. I intended to start out for Silver Hills in the morning, but I was jarred awake by the sound of your voice."

"My voice?"

"Yes, I heard you calling me. So I rode here hell bent for leather."

More tears coursed down Jules's cheek even as she slapped her husband in the chest.

"What was that for?"

Jules sniffled. "For riding so fast. You could have killed yourself!"

"Lady, you amaze me."

Jules blinked, and then threw her hands over her face and sobbed.

William immediately wrapped his arms around her. "Jules, honey, don't cry. Whatever I did, I'm sorry."

Jules wailed louder.

William shot a petrified look in Sheridan's direction. "What did I say?"

Sheridan gave him a reassuring smile. " 'Tis just the way of a pregnant woman. All the changes in her body are making her, well, a wee bit crazy."

Jules went utterly quiet and still. "Ooh, here comes another one!" Her frightened eyes locked with William's. He whispered soothing words as another contraction, more intense than the last, rocked Jules's small form. The effort took its toll. Her face began to pale and glisten with sweat.

Ho-Sing returned with Sheridan's requested items just

as Jules's water broke. Quickly and efficiently, Sheridan and William changed the bedsheets and put Jules into a clean nightdress.

The hours progressed, childbirth weakening Jules, making Sheridan wish she could do more for her friend, take some of Jules's pain onto herself. But this was one battle Sheridan couldn't help her friend with. The best she could do was to be strong for Jules.

With each strike of the hour on the ormulu clock, Sheridan grew more and more concerned about Nicholas. Where was he? What was taking so long? Was he all right?

The storm had grown worse, the cold wind creeping in behind the ancient tapestries hanging on the walls. Tree branches scraped at the window as if demanding entrance. The tempest seemed to be keeping pace with Jules's contractions, escalating with each pant, whimper, and shout.

"I have to push!" Jules cried, her hair plastered to her head, her eyes wide and dazed. "Please, dear God!" A contraction ripped through her. She threw her head back, the veins standing out in her neck.

William turned to Sheridan, his gaze pleading with her to do something.

"Don't push yet, Jules," Sheridan instructed, keeping her voice low and calm. "Keep breathing. Just a few more minutes." Sheridan knew Jules's birth canal had to dilate more than it was if she didn't want the baby ripping her to shreds.

Sheridan breathed with Jules, trying to keep her friend focused. "Do ye remember my story about the wee people?"

Jules nodded weakly.

"Well, picture yourself in the land of Tier na Nog."

Jules rocked her head back and forth on the pillow. "I . . . can't. Must push."

Sheridan sat down on the side of the bed. "Ssh. I know. Just try to concentrate. Think about blue skies and an endless beach of white sand and a beautiful castle that reaches unto the heavens."

Jules gritted her teeth, and Sheridan knew her friend was near to passing out with exhaustion. The babe was large and Jules was very small. Dear Lord, where was Nicholas?

Jules body arched off the bed with the force of the next contraction, and Sheridan knew she could delay no further. She positioned herself at the end of the bed.

"Hold her hand tightly," she instructed William. "And keep her breathing."

He nodded, his face almost as white as his wife's.

"All right, Jules. I want ye to bear down."

Jules squeezed her eyes shut and pushed, holding her breath.

"Breathe, Jules," William ordered.

"One, two, three, four . . . relax."

Jules released her breath in a whoosh. Barely a minute passed before the next contraction.

"Come on now, Jules. Push!"

Jules had to push four more times before the baby's head crested.

"Good girl, Jules. The babe is coming. At the next contraction, I want ye to push as hard as ye can."

"I can't," she whimpered, her eyes closed. "I just can't."

"Ye can and ye will! Do ye hear me, Jules? Ye're almost done. Now, *push!*"

Jules scrunched up her face, a scream ripping from her as she gave a hearty push, sending out the rest of the baby's head and shoulders.

Just then, a limb crashed against the window, shattering the pane and sending glass flying.

Sheridan covered Jules as best as she could as wind and rain came rushing in. William leaped to his feet and ripped one of the pictures off the wall to jam in front of the window.

Jules cried out again. The babe was coming whether Sheridan wanted it to or not.

Alarm rifled through Sheridan as she noted the umbilical cord was wrapped around the baby's neck—and the baby was blue!

Oh, dear God, no. No! Not this baby!

Quickly, Sheridan unwrapped the cord and pulled the baby out the rest of the way, hurriedly cleaning out its mouth.

"Danny?" Jules's voice was weak. "My baby?"

Please, God, Sheridan beseeched. *Don't let this baby die.*

She grabbed a towel and began to vigorously rub the infant, praying all the while. Sheridan felt William beside her. She glanced up and caught the stricken look on his face. She massaged the baby's chest.

Come on! Come on!

Her prayers were answered as a shrill, beautiful cry pierced the air and the baby took its first gulping breath.

Sheridan nearly collapsed with joy. Tears pooled in her eyes as she glanced at her friend. "Ye have a fine and healthy son."

The next moment, the bedroom door banged open. Nicholas stood on the threshold, soaked to the bone but glorious to Sheridan's eyes. Behind him stood the doctor, his spectacles askew and his thin, wet gray hair hanging over his eyes.

The man hustled across the room and took over Sheridan's duties. She thought to protest, but was too drained to utter a sound.

She stepped back, watching the goings-on as if she

stood somewhere outside her body. She flinched at the touch of a hand on her arm.

Her gaze snapped up and connected with Nicholas's. Concern etched his face, but another emotion glinted in his eyes. He tugged her away from the bed and toward the door.

"Where—"

"Ssh."

"I can't leave Jules."

"You can and you are."

"Danny?"

Sheridan stopped in the threshold at the sound of Jules's voice. Sheridan glanced over her shoulder to see the baby wrapped up tightly and cradled in Jules's arms, William wedged next to his family on the bed. Sheridan had never seen her friend look happier.

"Thank you," Jules murmured, tears brimming on her eyelashes. "You truly are the sister of my heart."

Sheridan smiled because no words would come. Emotions choked her throat.

"Your father's name is Joseph, isn't it?" Jules asked. Sheridan nodded.

Jules glanced up at her husband. Then she tilted the baby up in her arms. His small thumb was stuck in his mouth, his cherub cheeks pink and fat and healthy. "I'd like to introduce you to my son, William Joseph Daniel Thornton."

Chapter Twenty-four

"You were wrong, you know."

Sheridan shook herself from the exhaustion that had seeped into her body and discovered she stood in front of her bedroom door with Nicholas.

She steeled herself as she looked up at his face, his jaw covered with a fine layer of whiskers, dirt smudged across one cheek. Even a mess, he was glorious, emanating strength and virility. A man any woman would feel blessed to be loved by—if he knew how to love.

"And what was I wrong about?"

"Jules's baby."

Sheridan frowned. "What about the baby?"

"*She* is a *he*," Nicholas replied, reminding Sheridan of her prediction that Jules's baby would be a girl. "And a fine, healthy boy at that. Thanks to you." Sheridan flinched when he brushed the hair away from her face.

"You did an amazing job. You should be proud of yourself." His voice lowered as he added, "I am."

Sheridan would not be drawn in by his pretty words. "I did no more than anyone else would do in such circumstances."

"But you're not like anyone else. I've finally come to see that."

Sheridan turned away and put her hand on the doorknob. "I don't want to hear this."

Nicholas lay his hand on top of hers. "Do you still believe men don't possess the soul of a lion and the heart of a saint, Danny?"

The way he said her name made Sheridan's throat go dry. "I'm tired." She couldn't face him now, not when her guard was down, not when she was too physically and emotionally drained to ward him off.

Nicholas moved closer to her. "Do you still believe that?" he pressed.

Sheridan laid her head against the hard wood portal. "I don't know what I believe anymore."

"And what about me? Do you believe in me?"

Sheridan shook her head. She would not be so foolish again as to leave her heart open for another devastating blow. She turned the knob and let the door swing open, staring into the room where she'd spent so many nights lying awake, thinking about Nicholas, hoping he would come to her, tell her he loved her. Say anything.

He never had.

Quietly, Sheridan slipped into the room, not looking back as she closed the door, shutting herself in . . . shutting Nicholas out.

She closed her eyes, a single tear slipping between her eyelashes as she leaned heavily against the door. *I still believe in him.*

But it was too late. Too late to change the past. Too

late to recall words already spoken. Too late to believe in girlish dreams.

Sheridan straightened away from the door. Dawn's early light seeped through the curtains. She would rest for an hour, maybe two. Then she would leave and never look back.

Numbly, she began to unbutton her dress, her fingers clumsy, her skin clammy. She'd never removed her wet clothes. They were dry now, but the chill seemed to just reach her. She wanted nothing more than to slip between the cool sheets and seek blessed forgetfulness.

Her dress slipped off her shoulders in a soundless sigh, puddling at her feet, and then the door to her bedroom burst open.

Sheridan whirled around and gasped. Nicholas stood in the threshold, his broad shoulders filling the space.

"What are ye—"

"You wanted me to fight? Well, God damn it, I'm going to fight."

"Get out!"

He shook his head. "You don't scare me."

"I never did scare ye."

"Yes, you did. But not anymore. Now I'm ready for that fight."

"I didn't want ye to fight anyone. That was all in yer head."

"Maybe you didn't want me to fight over you, but you wanted me to fight *for* you, and I didn't. Well, I'm not leaving this room until I've told you how I feel."

"So say what ye've come to say and leave."

"Fine. I love you, Danny."

Sheridan's breath came out in short, angry pants. "Oh, ye love me, do ye? I wonder what tomorrow will bring? Hatred again?

"Listen—"

"Are ye happy now? Does it make ye feel better to have that off yer chest?"

"Not if it doesn't mean anything to you."

Sheridan turned her back on him. "I've given ye a chance to speak yer piece. Now I want ye to leave."

"Damn it, Danny! I'm trying."

"Just leave."

The door slammed and Sheridan jerked. She spun on her heels, the words to call Nicholas back clogging in her throat.

To find him a few feet behind her.

"I told ye to go."

"Do you love McDonough?"

"What?"

"Do you love him, Danny? I have to know."

"Ye lost any right to question me when ye threw me out. Ye do remember that, don't ye?"

His gaze captured hers. "I'll never forget it. But all that proves is that we are human. We make mistakes. You made a mistake."

"And what mistake have I made?"

"You said Jules's baby was going to be a girl."

" 'Tis not the same."

"Maybe not. But you believed it at the time, just like I believed I could choose who I was going to love, predetermine how my life would be, predict every event. I foolishly believed all that until I met you. You blew into my life like a whirlwind, and nothing has been the same since."

"Ye can have yer precious Jessica and yer normal life back. I'll be gone in a few hours."

"But that's not what I want. Don't you see?"

"I don't care what ye want."

Nicholas ignored her. "You made me believe in this magical land where all dreams come true."

" 'Tis a fairy tale.''

"Well, I want the fairy tale.''

"It doesn't exist.''

"It does exist. It exists right here, right now, between you and me.''

"Nothing exists between us.''

"I always knew you were stubborn, and I'm willing to accept that part of you, but you're not giving me a chance. I judged you too quickly. My temper got the better of me—''

"Ye said what ye felt. Don't belittle me now by trying to make me feel better. I lived without ye for eighteen years. I don't need yer pity or regret to help me move forward. In fact, Nicholas Sinclair, I don't need ye at all. Me and this babe will do just fine without ye.''

Nicholas took hold of her upper arms in an unrelenting grip. "But I won't be fine without you. Jesus, can't you see you've changed me? You told me in the stables that you wanted to understand me. I thought you did.''

"I thought so, too.''

"I was too afraid of the unknown, of what could happen should I let myself care too much. Now I'm afraid of what might happen to me should I not let myself care at all, closing myself off to something I may regret for the rest of my life. If you love me, tell me. If you want to make us work, I'll try.'' Nicholas glanced down at her stomach and gently laid his hand on it.

Sheridan's heart lurched at the feel of his hand against her, placed over the spot where their baby grew inside her womb. It moved her when she told herself it shouldn't.

She stepped out of his reach. "There is no us. Perhaps once I had foolish dreams. I don't anymore.''

"You told me we were two souls entwined. I believe that.''

Sheridan felt emotions roiling up inside her, anger and

bitterness, pain. And love. "Aye, ye believe now. Why is that, I wonder? Because ye think ye owe me something? Well, ye don't. And I wouldn't take anything from ye anyway ... ye bloody *landlord!*" His eyes widened for a fraction of a second. "Aye, that's right. I know."

Nicholas smiled, then laughed.

"Ye think this is funny, do ye?"

"Insanely funny."

Sheridan gave him her back again. "Just ... go. Get out. I don't want to see ye."

Nicholas stepped in front of her. "I'm not a landlord. For a short while—"

"Don't ye lie to me!"

"I wanted to tell you. I just didn't know how."

"It no longer matters."

"It matters to me. My brother gave me that property *after* I met you."

"It makes no difference. Ye have Irish laborers, and don't tell me ye don't."

"I don't. I have people who work for me, but they are no longer just laborers."

"I saw the paper from yer caretaker with my own two eyes!"

"But you didn't see the missive I sent back to him. Everyone who now works for me will share in the profits. I guess you could say I've made them my partners. My equals."

Sheridan didn't want to believe him again, because mistaken faith would only chip away another piece of her until there was nothing left—nothing left to give their child, nothing left to give anyone.

Nicholas cupped her cheek. "Was that why you were crying when Ian saw you in my office? Because you saw the missive and thought I had lied to you?"

The exhaustion, the anger, the disappointment all conspired against Sheridan, pushing her over the edge. She pounded her fists against Nicholas chest. "Stop it! Leave me be! I hate ye!"

Nicholas seized her wrists. "You don't hate me," he growled.

"I do!"

"Don't say it, Danny!"

"I do. I hate ye!"

Sheridan realized too late that she had pushed him too far. His eyes turned to a dark, glittering green.

"I won't let McDonough have you. You're mine, Danny."

Sheridan shook her head.

"That baby is mine. I won't let you leave me."

Fear made Sheridan tremble as Nicholas towered before her, reason having left his eyes to be replaced by something harsh and unyielding.

She stumbled away from him. He reached out for her, catching the top of her chemise. Panicked, she tried to flee . . . and her chemise tore down the front. Her knees hit the back of the bed. She tumbled back. He followed her down.

"Nay!" Sheridan's fists flew out trying to ward him off, but her blows were too meager. He wedged his legs between her thighs. "Leave me alone!"

"I'll make you forget him, Danny—by God, if it's the last thing I do." He took hold of her wrists, pinning them above her head as he pressed her down into the mattress.

Fear and excitement warred inside Sheridan. How she wanted him, loved him, needed him. But she wouldn't allow him to take her, to claim her defeat as his right.

She shoved at his chest but could not budge him. His lips came down on hers, searing her to her soul, branding her as nothing else had.

He demanded everything from her. Her traitorous body responded to him, arching up as he took her nipple between his lips, drawing darts of passion, sending heat to the very core of her.

"Nay," she half moaned, half pleaded, even as she writhed beneath him as he laved her other aching peak. His tongue then trailed between her breasts, kissing the underside, her ribs, moving down to her belly button . . . and lower.

Tears trickled down her face. "Nay . . . Nicholas. Please . . ."

"Dear God." He stopped, laying his forehead on her stomach. "I'm sorry, Danny. I . . . damn it! I just feel crazy. I don't know what I'm doing. Forgive me." His eyes searched hers, despair reflected in their depths as he sank to his knees. "I'm so afraid of losing you—of losing the one person who has touched my heart, my soul, who has made me see that it's my time for love."

Sheridan shook her head. "Don't," she begged. "Not now."

"You're beautiful," he murmured, his expression tortured. His gaze slowly moved down her naked form, and Sheridan hated herself for responding to his perusal. He frowned, his gaze stopping at a spot near her waist. "This tattoo . . ." His eyes snapped to hers. "That first night at the inn . . . I remember this tattoo, but I thought I had imagined it." His brows drew further together as he looked between her and the tattoo. "A shamrock."

"Meant to bring good fortune."

"And here you are." Nicholas shot to his feet, staring at her. "Sweet Jesus, you were a virgin." The blood drained from his face. "You let me make love to you, but you'd never been with another man." He stepped further away from the bed, self-condemnation in his eyes. "God, Danny . . . why? Why would you give yourself to me?"

Sheridan's inner voice begged her to protect herself, to lie or say nothing, but her tongue would no longer be stilled. "Because I loved ye. I loved ye from the first moment I saw ye. I loved the way ye came to my rescue."

"I got pummeled."

"I loved the way ye looked at me."

"You slapped me."

"I loved the way ye charmed me with yer smile."

"And got a knee to the groin."

"Ye walked out of my dreams and into my life. It seemed as if I had waited so long to find ye, so I couldn't . . ." Sheridan stopped. Memories threatened to engulf her.

Nicholas moved toward her and took her hand, pulling her to her feet. Gently, he tugged the ripped material of her chemise together. Then he tipped her chin up. "You couldn't what?"

Sheridan squeezed her eyes shut. "I couldn't wait any longer to love ye. I knew . . . I knew ye were the one."

Nicholas pressed his forehead against hers. "Oh, God, Danny," he murmured in a choked voice. "What a blind fool I was. I saw the blood, but I didn't remember anything. The alcohol. The blow to my head. When I woke up and found you had left with another man, I just . . ." He shook his head.

She frowned. "Ye thought I left with another man?"

"That's what the innkeeper said."

"He didn't tell ye it was my uncle?"

Nicholas realized with sudden clarity that his clouded judgment had caused him to think the worst, and that mistake might very well have cost him the one woman he had ever loved. "My pride and fear stepped in," he tried to explain. "I hated the way I felt when I found you gone. It was as if you had taken a piece of me with you. And then when you came here and I saw you with Ian . . ." He glanced away, staring out the window as the sun's rays slanted across their bodies. "I didn't want to end up like my father."

Sheridan raised her hand, cupping his cheek, turning his face to hers. "I would have never hurt ye like that."

"I know that now." Nicholas brushed a kiss against her palm. "Danny, please, give me a second chance to make things right. You said you wanted to heal me. Well, you're healing me. But if you leave, then all that hard work will go to waste. I'll be lost without you. Please . . . marry me. I love you."

"I—"

"Marry him, me girl, or I vow the Almighty will take me up in the palm of His hand this very moment."

Sheridan started at the endearingly familiar voice that had come out of nowhere. Aunt Aggie.

"Aye, lass," her uncle echoed. "Marry him or I'll have to skewer the blighter where he stands."

Quickly, Sheridan snatched up her dress, her fingers flying over the buttons. Then she raced to the bedroom door and flung it open.

Her aunt and uncle stood there, identical smiles on their dear faces, telling her they had shamelessly eavesdropped.

Sheridan wrapped her arms around their necks, hugging them close. "Oh, I'm so happy to see ye."

"Och, now." Her uncle fidgeted. " 'Tis chokin' me ye are, lass."

Sheridan flushed, realizing she held them in a death grip. She loosened her hold and stepped back. Her uncle glanced over her shoulder at Nicholas.

"Did I not tell ye to keep low, lad?"

"You did."

"But ye didn't heed me advice. Ye had to rile the girl, and ye did this knowin' the temper she's possessed of." Uncle Finny shook his head. "Holy Saint Peter, lad, must I teach ye everything? How do ye think I survived all these years?" He brushed passed Sheridan. "Insanity, me boy. Ye got to be a wee touched in the head to be in this family." He tsked tsked. "Ye English always were a dense lot."

Sheridan whirled around. "I knew ye weren't as crazy as ye seemed!"

Uncle Finny pressed a finger to his lips. " 'Tis a secret I'll take with me to the grave, and should ye tell a single soul, niece, then I swear to ye, I'll start bayin' to the moon every night to prove ye wrong."

Sheridan smiled at her uncle and pressed a hand over her heart. " 'Tis a secret between us."

"Good. Now tell the man ye accept his troth, because ye know as well as I, lass, that not every man will take ye and yer family." He slanted a glance at Nicholas. "Ye will take her family now, won't ye, lad?"

Nicholas chuckled. "With open arms."

"There, ye see. He must love ye, girl. 'Tis not every man who will take on the Delaneys."

Sheridan wanted to believe her uncle. But more than that, she wanted to believe Nicholas, and her desire had nothing to do with the babe growing beneath her heart and everything to do with the love she could not shake for this man.

She closed her eyes and prayed—prayed for a sign to tell her she was doing the right thing, that Nicholas truly was her destiny as her heart claimed.

A loud squawk snapped her eyes open, her gaze riveted

to the wildly flapping mynah bird she thought she'd never
see again.

"Scally!"

Scally hovered for a moment and then arrowed past
Sheridan and made a beeline straight for Nicholas, landing
on his shoulder with a great display of feathers.

"Hello, jerk-face."

Sheridan knew then her prayers had been answered.

Epilogue

Four months later . . .

"All right, wife. Open your eyes."

Slowly, Sheridan did as Nicholas bid, staring at the lovely, familiar cottage in front of her.

Nicholas had brought her home. Ireland, the land of her birth, a place Sheridan thought she'd never see again.

Tears pricked her eyes as her gaze roamed over the house she had grown up in, so tiny in comparison to her new home, but one that had been filled with just as much love.

Sheridan looked up at Nicholas's handsome face. "Why have ye brought me here, husband?"

He smiled that smile that never failed to make her weak in the knees. "This is where you said you wanted to raise your children."

"I don't understand."

"I bought your family's cottage from the landlord. This is your house now, Danny, and no one will ever make you leave it again."

"But ye've already given my family Mulholland Manor."

"That is for them. This is for us."

Emotions constricted Sheridan's chest. "What about Silver Hills? And London?"

"What about it?"

"That's yer home."

Nicholas shook his head. "Wherever you are, sweet girl, is home."

A single tear coursed down Sheridan's cheek. Nicholas swept it away and pulled her close. How she loved him.

He pointed to the two rocking chairs blowing gently in the breeze. "I plan to sit right there every night and listen to you tell our children stories."

Sheridan lifted a brow. "Ye do, do ye?"

"Aye, that I do, lady wife," he returned, mimicking her accent. " 'Twill be gazin' at ye with a glint of wickedness in me eye and a hint of a dimple in me cheek, me preenin' rooster ready to crow."

Sheridan slapped him lightly in the arm. "Wretch."

"At your service." He winked. "But you'll have to amend your tale."

"Oh? And what part would that be, husband?"

"Well, you said that it was a mythical land across the water where dreams come true. But it isn't out there, my love. It's here. With you."

ABOUT THE AUTHOR

Melanie George lives in New Jersey with her teenage son and two small dogs. When she is not writing, she is trying to restore her hundred-year-old house. Her award-winning books for Kensington include *DEVIL MAY CARE, LIKE NO OTHER,* and *DANGEROUS TO LOVE.* She looks forward to the release of the next book in the Sinclair series, *THE DEVIL'S DUE,* in November 2001 and to the release of her first two contemporary romances in 2002. Melanie loves hearing from readers. You can visit her at: *www.melaniegeorge.com*

Discover the Romances of
Hannah Howell

__My Valiant Knight   **$5.50US/$7.00CAN**
0-8217-5186-7

__Only for You   **$5.99US/$7.99CAN**
0-8217-5943-4

__Unconquered   **$5.99US/$7.50CAN**
0-8217-5417-3

__Wild Roses   **$5.99US/$7.50CAN**
0-8217-5677-X

__Highland Destiny   **$5.99US/$7.50CAN**
0-8217-5921-3

__Highland Honor   **$5.99US/$7.50CAN**
0-8217-6095-5

__Highland Promise   **$5.99US/$7.50CAN**
0-8217-6254-0

__Highland Vow   **$5.99US/$7.50CAN**
0-8217-6614-7

__A Taste of Fire   **$5.99US/$7.50CAN**
0-8217-5804-7

Call toll free **1-888-345-BOOK** to order by phone or use this coupon to order by mail.

Name_____

Address _____

City_____ State _____ Zip _____

Please send me the books I have checked above.

I am enclosing $_____

Plus postage and handling* $_____

Sales tax (in New York and Tennessee) $_____

Total amount enclosed $_____

*Add $2.50 for the first book and $.50 for each additional book.
Send check or money order (no cash or CODs) to:
Kensington Publishing Corp., 850 Third Avenue, New York, NY 10022
Prices and numbers subject to change without notice.
All orders subject to availability.
Check out our website at **www.kensingtonbooks.com**.

Celebrate Romance with one of Today's Hotest Authors
Meagan McKinney

__**In the Dark** $6.99US/$8.99CAN
  0-8217-6341-5

__**The Fortune Hunter** $6.50US/$8.00CAN
  0-8217-6037-8

__**Gentle From the Night** $5.99US/$7.50CAN
  0-8217-5803-9

__**Merry Widow** $6.50US/$8.50CAN
  0-8217-6707-0

__**My Wicked Enchantress** $5.99US/$7.50CAN
  0-8217-5661-3

__**No Choice But Surrender** $5.99US/$7.50CAN
  0-8217-5859-4

Call toll free **1-888-345-BOOK** to order by phone or use this
coupon to order by mail.
Name_____
Address _____
City_____ State _____ Zip _____
Please send me the books I have checked above.
I am enclosing $_____
Plus postage and handling* $_____
Sales tax (in New York and Tennessee) $_____
Total amount enclosed $_____
*Add $2.50 for the first book and $.50 for each additional book.
Send check or money order (no cash or CODs) to:
Kensington Publishing Corp., 850 Third Avenue, New York, NY 10022
Prices and numbers subject to change without notice.
All orders subject to availability.
Check out our website at **www.kensingtonbooks.com**.

The Queen of Romance
Cassie Edwards

__Desire's Blossom $5.99US/$7.50CAN**
  0-8217-6405-5

__Exclusive Ecstasy $5.99US/$7.99CAN**
  0-8217-6597-3

__Passion's Web $5.99US/$7.50CAN**
  0-8217-5726-1

__Portrait of Desire $5.99US/$7.50CAN**
  0-8217-5862-4

__Savage Obsession $5.99US/$7.50CAN**
  0-8217-5554-4

__Silken Rapture $5.99US/$7.50CAN**
  0-8217-5999-X

__Rapture's Rendezvous $5.99US/$7.50CAN**
  0-8217-6115-3

Call toll free **1-888-345-BOOK** to order by phone or use this coupon to order by mail.
Name_____
Address _____
City_____ State _____ Zip _____
Please send me the books I have checked above.
I am enclosing $_____
Plus postage and handling* $_____
Sales tax (in New York and Tennessee) $_____
Total amount enclosed $_____
*Add $2.50 for the first book and $.50 for each additional book.
Send check or money order (no cash or CODs) to:
Kensington Publishing Corp., 850 Third Avenue, New York, NY 10022
Prices and numbers subject to change without notice.
All orders subject to availability.
Check outt our website at **www.kensingtonbooksbooks.com**.

BOOK YOUR PLACE ON OUR WEBSITE AND MAKE THE READING CONNECTION!

We've created a customized website just for our very special readers, where you can get the inside scoop on everything that's going on with Zebra, Pinnacle and Kensington books.

When you come online, you'll have the exciting opportunity to:

- View covers of upcoming books
- Read sample chapters
- Learn about our future publishing schedule (listed by publication month *and author*)
- Find out when your favorite authors will be visiting a city near you
- Search for and order backlist books from our online catalog
- Check out author bios and background information
- Send e-mail to your favorite authors
- Meet the Kensington staff online
- Join us in weekly chats with authors, readers and other guests
- Get writing guidelines
- AND MUCH MORE!

**Visit our website at
http://www.zebrabooks.com**